Antaram

Antaram

by

Marie Salibian-Best

Paperback ISBN 0 955045 40 1

**Published
by**

Masis Books
34 Julius Hill
Warfield
Berkshire
RG42 3UN

Acknowledgements

I am indebted to my father for handing down family stories in his spellbinding way, and from whom I drew inspiration. A big thank you to my children, Nadia and Garry for their interest and encouragement.

My heartfelt thanks to my dear friend Rosemary for her valuable comments, her wizard editing, the many discussions on the manuscript over the last few years and her belief in me. I would also like to thank the fellow members of my Writers' Groups, each of whom in their unique way have helped me with their observations and suggestions.

Lastly, but most importantly, my gratitude to my husband Clive, for his help, patience, enthusiasm and unwavering support.

To my granddaughters Annabel, Melanie, Clarissa

With Love

Prologue

Adana, Turkey 1921

Zabel was well pleased. The house looked sparklingly clean. Early this morning, while the washer-woman did the family washing, her daughter Mareyam and her three daughters-in-law had cleaned the house from top to bottom. The ironing was done and the washing put away. There would be a special dinner tonight, to celebrate the Name Day of Saint Krikor the Illuminator.

But these thoughts were not uppermost in Siran's mind as she set the table for lunch. She was feeling a lot better today. She had managed to drink a cup of sweet black tea and eat her breakfast of bread and honey without feeling sick.

After their light lunch of lentil soup, bread, cheese and fruit, Siran cleared the table and went upstairs to have a rest. Her mother-in-law had told her that she must take good care of herself now. She took off her dress and looked at herself in the bedroom mirror. Instinctively she laid her hand across the gentle swelling of her belly and she fervently wished her first-born to be a boy. Both her sisters-in-law had already produced two sons each and they often talked about the importance of boys, for they would carry the family name to the next generation.

Siran lay down on the big four-poster bed to rest. She pulled the covers up to her chin and smiled. She was happy. She was so lucky to have married the youngest son of this well known and respected family. Her husband Artin was the tallest and the best looking of the three brothers. Her hand went to her left shoulder and arm, going over the scars softly. He had chosen *her* as his wife even though he could have had the pick of half a dozen other girls. She blushed, unable to hide the intensity of her feelings for him. She closed her eyes and drifted off to sleep.

Zabel was happy too. As she prepared the evening meal her mind roamed. She was proud of her three sons. They were good boys, hard working and obedient to their father's wishes. Except for Artin, who had a mind of his own and could sometimes be as stubborn as a donkey. She shook her head

1

and smiled. Her two elder sons had dutifully married the girls she had chosen for them, but would Artin do the same? He would not! He would only marry the girl of his choice or not marry at all, he had announced in his cheeky way. When she had asked him who this girl might be, he had looked nonchalantly at her and said he had seen her sitting next to her mother in an open carriage, outside the *hammam*. The *hammam* of all places! Zabel laughed, she remembered that episode only too well... Yes, Siran had proved to be a good choice for her son Artin, after all. The girl was quiet, she said little but her eyes – those dark burning eyes - observed all. She had a calming influence on her hot-headed son.

Zabel ran a happy household. As custom dictated, the extended family lived harmoniously under the same roof – ruled by her husband Roupen - the benign patriarch. They carried on the age old tradition of the male bread-winner. She stayed at home and took care of the housekeeping while her husband took care of the business – the apothecary in the centre of the town. He had started it on his own and in time the three boys had joined in and turned it into a thriving business. They had a comfortable life, living in this large house in a most pleasant suburb of Adana. They also had a summerhouse where they spent part of the hot summer months. She sighed. It was time for Mareyam to get married. After all, she was almost seventeen. God willing, it would be soon. Only then, could she and her husband hand over the reigns of responsibility to their sons.

The menfolk came home soon after. The tantalizing aroma of food greeted them as they walked in through the door. As usual they were hungry, so they sat down to dinner almost immediately. The women placed all the prepared dishes for the feast on the table and waited. Roupen said a short prayer of thanksgiving for the food they were about to receive on the nameday of St. Krikor. He helped himself to the food first, then it was the turn of the young men and after that the women. The men drank *Raki* with ice and water. Tonight Zabel also had a glass of the alcoholic drink. It was permissible for a mature woman to drink or smoke a cigarette if she wished. But the young women of the household were not allowed to do so. Instead they drank lemonade.

Zabel watched her family do justice to the food which had taken her hours to prepare. All too soon the huge serving dishes were scraped clean. She smiled, it was reward enough.

The men retired to the living room for coffee and cigarettes. The women cleared the table and washed up before joining them. They listened to the heated discussion Artin was having with his father and brothers, but they said nothing.

Roupen looked at his youngest son and tried not to smile. The boy had flair and imagination, and big ideas. He slowly ground out his cigarette in the crystal ashtray and searched for the right words to tell his son that although his business plan was brilliant, it was too soon to think of expanding again. He had to let him down gently. But the loud, insistent knock on the door prevented him from speaking. Who could be calling at this time of night? Artin rushed out to open the door. A moment later he came back, ushering Father Sahak into the room. Roupen got up from his chair and kissed the priest's hand, welcoming him to his house. But before the others could show the same courtesy, Father Sahak asked them to sit down. He sank down on the nearest armchair and spoke without preamble. He said he heard on good authority that the Turkish government was planning to order all non-Turks to leave Turkey. He advised Roupen to be on the alert for further developments and start planning avenues of escape in case of an emergency.

There was a hush in the room. The priest's words sent shivers of fear down Roupen's back. The expression on Father Sahak's face mirrored his own anxiety. With shaking fingers he took out his handkerchief and wiped his face. He remembered the deportation, persecution and massacre of the Armenians not so long ago. If this was true, then it would be the end. This time they would lose everything. God in heaven, what should he do?

Roupen looked at his large family and saw in their faces the sadness, the hopelessness, the fear that he himself felt in the pit of his own stomach. Then his gaze fell on his youngest daughter-in-law. As always Siran's strange beauty took his breath away. She looked so calm and serene, her huge brown eyes hiding her true emotions. She is brave enough to weather the storm - if it should come, he thought. He prayed that whatever happened, wherever destiny took them, her unborn baby would survive...

PART ONE

Chapter One

Famagusta, Cyprus 1958

The summer months are blisteringly hot in Cyprus. The soles of our feet burned as Eleni and I ran across the hot sand to the cool sanctuary of the giant umbrella. Eleni promptly went to sleep as soon as she lay on her towel, while I settled down to read. The article caught my eye as soon as I opened my film magazine, *Photoplay*. I read it twice, not believing my eyes.

"Wake up Eleni," I said.

"What's up? I was having a lovely dream…"

"Thrilling news! Listen to this. Otto Preminger is coming to Cyprus to make a film called *Exodus!*" I cried out. "And what's more, he will be staying in Famagusta! I can't believe it, can you?" I scanned the page to see if there were any more details about this fantastic event which would take place in our town.

Eleni opened her eyes. "What film? When?" she asked, tonelessly.

"*Exodus*," I repeated. "I don't know exactly when he will start filming, it says in here - sometime next year. And guess what, Paul Newman is the star of the film. He is so handsome …"

"You mean you're in love with Paul Newman now? What about poor old John Derek and James Dean, have you gone off them?" She teased me mercilessly for having 'crushes' on film stars.

"But isn't it exciting? We must watch the filming."

"It might be interesting …"

"Interesting? It will be fascinating. It will be like going to Hollywood!" I almost shouted.

Eleni pretended not to hear me. "Look at us, we look as brown as berries," she said and applied more sun-tan lotion to her face and arms. I was somewhat disappointed at her lack of enthusiasm.

"Do you think they'll stay at the King George or the Constantia when they come?" I persisted.

"Who? What are you talking about now *gori-mou*?" (My girl)

"Preminger and his stars and film crew of course. Where do you think they might stay?"

"How should I know?"

We had a clear view of these two imposing hotels from where we sat, sunbathing. They were a quarter of a mile apart. We had never been in either of these splendid establishments, but we knew all about them. The King George was an old-world type of hotel, luxurious but understated – the kind of hotel where foreign notables, distinguished English writers stayed. The Constantia, on the other hand, was a new hotel, modern and opulent – attracting the rich and famous.

"Probably the Constantia," Eleni said, looking at the luxurious hotel for a long moment.

"I think so too. I read that Preminger has a lavish lifestyle and he and his stars stay at the best hotels when on location," I said with pride, showing off my knowledge of the film world.

"It's very hot. I shall go for a swim to cool off," Eleni said. "Are you coming?" She had hardly finished the sentence when we saw a young man walk towards us and stop. I noticed he had a camera slung over his shoulder.

"Hi ladies! May I join you?" he asked politely.

"Hello …" we answered, somewhat surprised.

"My name is Brad Sinclair. I'm American. Do you mind if I join you?" he repeated.

"We don't mind," Eleni said with panache, gave him a dazzling smile and introduced us. "I'm Eleni, and this is my friend, Reya. Are you on holiday?" There was no trace of shyness or embarrassment in her voice. I put this down to the fact that she had spent a year in London where she had done her secretarial course, and this had given her an air of sophistication which I sorely lacked. As usual, I was too shy to speak. The American sat down on the sand.

"Not exactly a holiday. I'm a photographer working for *Time* magazine. I'm doing a feature on the 'situation' in Cyprus. I would like to take a few pictures of you ladies, if you don't mind."

Eleni and I looked at each other. We couldn't believe our ears. We certainly would *not* mind being photographed by an American for *Time* magazine, or any other magazine for that matter. How fortunate that I was wearing my new swimsuit! It was pale mauve, with tiny, navy blue dots, and had thin straps, which tied behind my neck. Eleni looked glamorous in her black swimsuit which she had bought in London. "We don't mind," we said, trying to hide our excitement.

Brad put us at our ease and started taking pictures of us. After my initial shyness, I relaxed and started to enjoy myself. This was such fun. He made us pose for the camera, walking into the sea, coming out of sea, playing with a huge, multi-coloured ball. "I've hired a boat," he said and invited us aboard. He took more pictures of us on deck, messing about with the ropes, and diving off. A small crowd gathered to watch. We must have made an attractive contrast. Eleni – blonde, petite and curvaceous, and myself – dark, slim and slightly taller.

After the 'shoot', Brad put his camera equipment in the case and said. "I'm staying at the King George." Where else, I thought. "I would be honoured if you would have tea with me on the terrace. Just a small token of my thanks and appreciation."

"Thank you very much Brad, we would love to," Eleni answered.

"I'll see you in a little while then."

In the changing room, we almost shouted for joy. "What a treat!" I breathed. "To be invited to have English tea at the King George …"

"Especially by a handsome young American. This surely is the height of luxury," Eleni pronounced.

We quickly changed into our dresses, combed our hair and checked in the mirror to make sure we looked presentable. A touch of lipstick was called for.

Brad was waiting for us when we emerged from the changing room. He had changed into cream slacks and a blue shirt. He *was* handsome, tall, with crew cut brown hair and brown eyes. He escorted us to the magnificent terrace of the hotel. We sank down on the wicker chairs. The sea looked an azure blue, calm, crystal clear, more inviting, infinitely more beautiful from this perspective.

Our host certainly had *savoir-faire*. No sooner had we sat down than a waiter, immaculately dressed and wearing white gloves, appeared from nowhere and Brad gave the order. The waiter reappeared with a huge silver tray and put it on the coffee table. I watched, mesmerized, as he poured the tea from a silver pot, added milk and offered a cup to each of us. I watched Eleni as she popped two cubes of sugar in her tea and stirred it. I did the same. Finally, the waiter served the dainty sandwiches and various cakes and pastries.

This was my very first taste of English afternoon tea and I relished every moment of it. It was also the first time I had drunk tea with milk – we never added milk to our tea at home. I liked the taste – it was different, but equally refreshing. We took our time over it.

"Do you both live in Famagusta?" Brad asked.

"Yes we do," I answered.

"We are friends, neighbours and we both work in the NAAFI Warehouse – in the office," Eleni quickly added. "Where do *you* live?"

"New York. I would like to have your names and addresses so that I can send you a copy of the magazine with your pictures in it." Brad wrote these down in his dairy. "Oh, I thought you were both Greek, but judging by your surname Reya, you must be Armenian. Almost all Armenian surnames end in *i-a-n*, don't they?" He asked.

"Yes, they do..." I said, surprised that he should know this. "Do you have any Armenian friends in New York?"

"Not friends as such. There is an Armenian community in New York, and a few Armenian restaurants. I go to one in Queens. It's called *Ararat*. It's owned by two brothers, Miran and Movses. They are very friendly and they serve the most wonderful food."

I nodded my head in agreement and smiled, bursting with pride. As far as I was concerned Armenian food was the best in the whole wide world. Just then the waiter came with more tea, more sandwiches and more cakes. We chatted away as though we had known Brad for years. The afternoon sun slid slowly into the sea – an unimaginable distance away. It was time to say good-bye to our American friend.

"If we walk fast we can be home before the seven o'clock curfew starts," I said, as Eleni and I started to walk homeward.

"My God, it is quarter to seven already! We had such a good time that we didn't realize it was getting late."

"It was like stepping into another world wasn't it?" I said. "I don't know how we dared to have tea with a complete stranger. If anyone had seen us..."

"Well, no one we know saw us, so stop worrying, will you?" We quickened our steps. Crowds of people were hurrying to get to their homes. No one wanted to be caught breaking the curfew. "What do you do in the long evenings with this damned curfew?" Eleni asked.

"As you know my Auntie from Beirut is here for a visit. We sit on the back verandah and talk. I mean they – my parents, grandmother and Auntie

– talk far into the night and we, the 'children' listen."

"What do they talk about?"

"They talk about the old days in their country, before they came to Cyprus."

"Oh." She said, unimpressed.

"They, especially my father, tell some really interesting stories about the past. How do *you* pass the time then?"

"Most nights we play cards. Some nights our next door neighbours come over and we have a late supper. It's boring isn't it?" I didn't have time to answer her. We were in front of my house. "See you tomorrow," she called and disappeared round the corner. Her house was only a few minutes' walk away from mine.

"Is that you Reya," I heard Mother call as I closed the front door behind me. "We're going to have something to eat in a moment, so ..."

"I'm not hungry Mother," I said.

"That girl!" I heard Grandmother mutter. "She hardly eats anything. There isn't an ounce of flesh on her."

"I'll have some watermelon later, Grandmother." I called and went to my room. Grandmother would have had a fit if she had seen me eating the delicious sandwiches and cakes. I would have to keep the afternoon's exciting happenings a secret, because if anyone found out about it, I would be in terrible trouble. Nice Armenian girls did not talk to strange men or – God forbid - be photographed by them, in their swimsuits no less! And they definitely did not have tea with them in the best hotel in town, or any place for that matter. I sighed – I wished my parents were not so old-fashioned.

It was time to join the family. I liked my Auntie Mareyam – she was a kind and gentle lady and Father's only sister. They were very close but they hadn't seen each other for years. I remember the day she arrived. "The children have grown up," she said. "I can't tell which is which."

"As you know, Sara, our eldest daughter is married and she lives in Nicosia," Father began the introductions. "This is Lillie, the second daughter, this is Nonnie, the third, and this is little Mareyam – the youngest. The one I named after you." Father said with pride. I don't know why, but everyone, including Father, did not realize that I had grown up too.

"The lucky one, but you don't call her Mareyam, do you, everyone calls her Reya ..." Auntie said, somewhat confused.

"When Marko was little, he couldn't pronounce the name and he started calling her Reya. Somehow the name stuck." Nonnie explained. Thus enlightened, Auntie smiled. "And this must be Marko, I can see the resemblance to our Father, can't you Brother?" She asked, hugging and kissing each of us in turn.

When I went to join the family on the back verandah, supper was over and the table cleared. I went straight over to where Auntie Mareyam was sitting. "How was your trip to Nicosia, Auntie?" I asked.

"It was very nice my sweet," she said. "It was lovely to see Sara again after such a long time. Her children are so beautiful and so well behaved. But what a pity there was no room in the car for you ..."

"That's alright Auntie. I went swimming with my friend," I said and smiled inwardly. I wouldn't have missed my experience of the afternoon for the world.

"You must visit us more often than you do Auntie," piped up Nonnie.

"And what did you do today Reya?" she asked me. She had this irritating (for me) habit of talking to two people at the same time.

"Nothing much," I lied, shrugging my shoulders. "Eleni and I went swimming and then we stopped at *Delice* for a coca-cola and cake." This was a believable lie because *Delice* was a pattisserie type of place, much favoured by young people. Just then Mother emerged from the kitchen with the coffee tray.

Auntie Mareyam's visit was a reunion that brought back memories of the past. The after supper conversation turned to their former lives in Adana, Turkey. "Do you remember ..." started them reminiscing about the past.

"Who would think that we would sit together like this, under the stars eh, just like we used to at our summerhouse," Father said, shaking his head in wonder.

"Do you remember the harsh winters?"

"Do I?" Father said. "It used to be so cold, icicles used to hang from the roofs like white ribbons." I couldn't begin to understand how sad, how traumatic it must have been to leave their country at short notice, and make a new start in another. For them, the past must be like a precious jewel, I thought. They keep it hidden in a box. It comforts them to bring it out once in a while, polish it and put it back again.

Father smoked his last cigarette of the day and went to bed. As soon as we heard his gentle snoring, Lillie turned to Auntie and said: "Will you tell us the story of the *hammam* Auntie? And the first time Father saw Mother?"

"Please, please, will you?" Nonnie pleaded.

"Surely, you have heard this story before?" she said.

"But we want to hear your version of it," we girls chorused.

"Well," she began. "In those days, it was the custom to go to the *hammam* every couple of weeks. The women and children went in the day and the men went in the evenings. It was a fun day, where one met friends and socialized as well as enjoyed the facilities the *hammam* offered. It was a leisurely affair, lasting three of four hours ..."

"What! It took you four hours, just to wash your hair and have a bath!" interrupted Nonnie.

"Yes it did. We arrived at the baths at midday. First to the steam room and after that, the *Tellek* woman would give us a rubdown with a loofah, and then she would wash our hair. After a final wash, she would wrap us in our towels and escort us to the rest rooms. It was tiring wasn't it, Siran?"

"Quite so," said Mother. "You can't imagine how hot it gets in the baths. Your body needs time to cool down."

"The baths were so hot that we would come out looking like boiled lobsters!" said Auntie Mareyam. "While our bodies cooled down, we would have something light to eat, maybe enjoy some fruit and drink a glass of fruit juice to quench our thirst. After a rest and a good gossip with friends, we would get dressed and head for home. It was a real tonic, I can assure you." Grandmother nodded her head in agreement. Many a time she wished she could go to a *hammam*, but there were none in Famagusta.

"In those days, we used to go home in horse-drawn carriages," continued Auntie.

"It sounds really old-fashioned," said Nonnie.

"No," said Lillie. "Victorian." I agreed with Lillie.

"On this particular day, the weather was very warm and your mother was sitting in an open carriage, ready to be driven home. As fate would have it, your father happened to be passing by and he saw her. He was immediately struck by her beauty. She had a lovely heart-shaped face, dark, mysterious, deep set eyes and long, lustrous brown hair, which cascaded down to her waist." Mother kept her head down as Auntie warmed to her subject. I was sure Mother was blushing. I stole a glance at her. She was still beautiful, and her hair was still long and lustrous, even though there were streaks of grey in it now.

Auntie took a sip of water and said. "From time to time, your father was told that it was time he got married and started a family. There were several suitable girls for him to choose from, but he always found an excuse to decline."

"I know how he felt," said Lillie. "You should always wait for the right person." There had been quite a few eligible suitors for Lillie, but she had rejected every offer of marriage. She had a different excuse each time. He was either too short, he was not educated or she didn't like the look of him. Lillie was still waiting for the suitor of her dreams. Nonnie nodded enthusiastically, while Mother and Grandmother exchanged meaningful glances.

"Anyway, the next time the subject came up, your father casually mentioned the girl he had seen in the open carriage outside the *hammam*, a few weeks before."

"You mean Mother!" cried Nonnie.

"That's right. But what he omitted to tell them was that he had passed by the baths several times, in the hope of seeing her again."

"I never realized Father was such a romantic …" said Lillie. But Mother silenced her with a look.

"Of course, I can't tell you all the details, if I thought for a moment that you would upset your mother with such comments." Auntie Mareyam did her best to look stern, and Mother sighed and went into the kitchen to make us a cold drink. Grandmother said she was tired and went to bed. Auntie settled down to continue her story.

"Well, our mother was intrigued that her youngest son was finally showing an interest in a girl. She promptly made enquiries and found out all about your mother's family and background. She decided to find out when this girl and her family would next go to the *hammam*. She would arrange to go the same day and look the girl over."

"Look her over!" Lillie exclaimed. She was furious. "As if she was a piece of furniture …"

"I wish you wouldn't keep on interrupting me my love," Auntie said patiently. "You see it was the custom to do that. The baths were the ideal place to observe a girl discreetly. To find out if she had any physical blemishes, such as unsightly body hair, bow legs and so on." Auntie let out a big sigh and continued. Lillie pursed her lips and remained silent. "Anyway, for some reason, my mother couldn't go that day, and so she sent me instead."

"Is that when you saw Mother's scars?" asked Nonnie, in a whisper. There had been a serious fire, when Mother was fifteen years old, and there were scars all down her back and on her left arm.

"Dai rescued her, didn't he?" I spoke without realizing, and blushed as I felt everyone's eyes on me. Dai was my special name for my Uncle Krikor. Dai was my childhood hero, and not only because he had saved my mother... Auntie Mareyam nodded.

"That's right, my sweet. Our mother was very concerned, when I told her about the scars. She thought her handsome son deserved better. But your father was adamant. If he couldn't have *this* girl, than he would not get married at all. In the end, I managed to persuade her. Your mother is so graceful and serene. She is a good match for Artin. No one else can calm him down when he gets excited." Auntie sighed again. There was a far-away look on her face. "I remember it like it was yesterday ..."

It was past midnight when we eventually went to bed. But I couldn't sleep. I went over the events of the afternoon. I thought about the story of how Father had first seen Mother. He must have fallen in love with her at first sight and he had wanted to marry her, scars and all. What was it like to fall in love? I had a strange dream that night. For some reason, I was standing outside my father's shop. The dress I was wearing was long and it shimmered in the silver light of the moon. A man suddenly appeared from nowhere. 'I have found a short-cut,' he said and pointed to the moon. He took my hand and we started to walk...

I was rudely awakened from my dream by the sound of church bells. The sound of church bells was a part of every day life. They rang at church services, they rang at weddings and they tolled at funerals. But this was different. There was a note of urgency in the way they rang, a warning of danger. They only rang like that when there was a fire somewhere. It was alarming.

I was up like a shot and went into the hall to investigate. "Something is definitely wrong," Father was saying. He opened the window and looked out. Marko opened the front door to find out what the trouble was. The church bells were ringing even louder now.

"Father, come to the front door quickly," Marko shouted. "Crowds of people are shouting and running in all directions." He stopped a man in the street.

"What's going on friend?" he asked. "What's happened?" The man didn't stop to answer.

"Quick! Get inside and shut all the doors and windows. There has been shooting …" he shouted as he ran. There was chaos. Cars and bicycles were whizzing past, as people hurried to reach the safety of their homes as soon as possible. A driver shouted at Marko through the open window of his car.

"In the name of God, man, don't just stand there, get inside and stay there. The Military Police are on their way …"

"Didn't you hear what the man said? Shut that door and everyone stay away from the windows!" Father was shaken. His hands shook as he tried to light a cigarette.

"I've shut all the windows Artin," Mother said. "Come and sit on the verandah. Nonnie will make you a coffee. We'll find out soon enough what the disturbance is, this time." Just as Auntie had said, Mother was good at calming Father down when he felt agitated like this.

Sure enough, before Mother had finished speaking, we heard the roar of the Military Police jeep. I peeped through the shutters. There were four of them and they were armed. One of them was standing and shouting through a megaphone: there was a curfew on and anyone breaking the law would be picked up and taken straight to prison. Within seconds, the streets emptied. Not even a stray dog was to be seen. Everyone was indoors, their windows and doors closed and shuttered. The silence was eerie. The only sound you could hear was the Military Police patrolling the streets, making sure that the curfew was obeyed.

It was strange for the family to be at home at this time of the day. We should all be at work by now. Mother sprang into action.

"I think a hearty breakfast would do us a world of good," she announced.

"What a good idea," Auntie Mareyam said, and they both went into the kitchen. Father had more or less recovered his composure. We sat round the kitchen table and tucked into warmed pitta bread, grilled halloumi cheese, boiled eggs, tomatoes, cucumbers and olives, washed down with coffee and cinnamon tea.

"It must be something extremely serious eh?" Father said.

"No point in speculating," Mother said. "Enjoy your breakfast, Artin. We shall know soon enough what caused the state of emergency."

"You see Father," Lillie said. "If we had a telephone we would ring round and find out what is going on. As it is, we are cut off from the outside world." She had been pestering Father for ages to have a telephone installed.

"Yes, you are right Lillie. We need a telephone in these troubled times. Apply for one tomorrow, will you?" Patience was not one of Father's virtues. He huffed and puffed and sat huddled by the radio, trying to find a news station for information.

"Artin, my son, I'm really worried about this guerilla war for Union with Greece," Grandmother said. There was a tremor in her voice. She took out her black-edged handkerchief and wiped her eyes. "I still remember the first civil disturbance in 1931. We used to hide under our beds when the riots started…"

"Don't worry Mother-in-law," replied Father. "All this will die down. The British will never leave Cyprus. I'm sure of it." He lit a cigarette and took a sip of his coffee. He didn't sound too sure to me.

"I'm old. I can't bear the thought of yet another upheaval in my life. I haven't forgotten the way we left Adana … my Krikor took care of everything then. If he was alive …" Poor Grandmother couldn't go on. She wiped the tears that were rolling down her face.

"What's going on?" Mother called from the kitchen. She hurried over to the little salon, wiping her hands on her apron. "What happened?"

"It's nothing Siran." Grandmother said, trying to hide her emotions.

"I'm telling you Mother-in-law, we are safe here," continued Father. "The British Government has been good to us. Cyprus has been good to us. Cyprus is our home, our country. No one will uproot us from here. I say again: THE BRITISH WILL NEVER LEAVE CYPRUS." This became his mantra.

The morning seemed so long. I went to Lillie's bedroom which she shared with Nonnie and we peeped through the shutters to see if anything was happening in the street. All was quiet, but not for long. We heard the Military jeep approaching. Daringly, Nonnie opened the window and we looked out. The driver saw us and smiled, but the soldier who was standing looked at us angrily. He waved his Sten gun at us and mouthed the words, "Get in."

About two o'clock, we heard an announcement. We rushed to the windows again. From the megaphone came the edict that the curfew would be lifted for two hours – from 2.30 to 4.30. Only women and children under the age of fourteen could leave their homes: to go to the market, to buy food and other necessary items.

This posed a problem, as Mother had never been to the market before. Father did the daily shopping for food, and he always paid a porter to carry the heavy load home. The porter's name was Fano. He was short and stocky, but strong as an ox. He carried the groceries in a *kofina* (a huge basket), tied to his back with a piece of rope. He always deposited the *kofina* in the middle of the kitchen and waited silently for Mother to empty it.

Fano's peculiar smell of sweat and cigarettes permeated the kitchen for several minutes after he left. But if you should happen to see him on a Sunday afternoon, you would see a different person. Washed, shaved and wearing a suit, he strolled to the *kafenion* for a game of backgammon or cards, with an air of confidence quite unlike his working demeanour.

Alas, there would be no Fano to carry the shopping home today. The shopping expedition to the market will be a completely new experience for Mother, I thought.

"Who is coming to the market with me?" asked Mother, undaunted by the prospect.

"I will Mother," Nonnie and I shouted together. The thought of getting out of the house for a couple of hours was a happy prospect.

"I think I would prefer Nonnie to help me," Mother said. "You're not strong enough to carry heavy shopping, Reya." I shrugged my shoulders. I seemed to be permanently on the periphery of things – I was too young to go visiting, too old to play in the street, and now not strong enough to carry shopping! No use complaining, I thought. It was just as well. They came back an hour and a half later, exhausted, carrying five bags of shopping between them. We crammed into the kitchen to see how Mother had fared. Father started emptying the bags, looking closely at every item, nodding his head in approval.

"There wasn't any fresh stuff in the market," Mother said apologetically. "And the crowds … This was the best we could do." Father picked up the honeydew melon and smelled it. "Ripe and ready to eat," he said. "Well done Siran and Nonnie too. We shall have a feast of a meal tonight!" And we did.

Early next morning, Yiannis, our next-door neighbour, told Father the grim news. "The situation is very bad Mr. Artin," he said. "A group of British soldiers were ambushed and three of them were shot dead."

"I knew it was something very serious," Father said, shaking his head.

"Yes. Very serious indeed. I believe nine people were arrested late last night and they were taken in for interrogation."

"When do you think the curfew will be lifted?"

"God alone knows that, Mr. Artin," Yiannis said and went back to his house. The curfew was lifted after forty-eight hours.

Chapter Two

"Thank God it's Saturday!" I said as Eleni and I walked through the NAAFI warehouse and into the office. "I don't know why we had to move from our pleasant offices to this awful place."

Three months before, the Bonded Warehouse and the entire staff had moved to this location. The reason was that it was not only bigger but also more convenient as it was much nearer to the harbour and the Customs offices. Our office was partitioned off in the gloomy nether regions of the vast warehouse. It was small for the eight clerical staff.

"I don't either. It takes us twice as long to get here," said Eleni. "And the noise is unbearable." The labourers had already started opening the hundreds of crates that came in each day. Our first day there had been so awful, Eleni and I had been close to tears. We still hadn't got used to the place.

"Good morning Reya, good morning Eleni," said Mr. Eastman, the chief clerk. Mr. Eastman was always the first to arrive at the office. He was rolling the first cigarette of the day.

"Good morning Mr. Eastman," we replied and uncovered our typewriters. The rest of the staff trooped in. The phones started to ring. The typewriters clicked. The working day had begun.

It was the custom in the office to have a twenty-minute break for coffee. This was anytime between ten and eleven. We started work at seven in the morning, finishing at two in the afternoon. Except on Saturdays, when we finished at one. We all looked forward to this break, as nobody could face breakfast so early in the morning.

At nine o'clock I saw Andreas, the messenger, going round the office taking orders for our breakfast. He also made the coffee and tea for the staff. I was starving hungry and decided to have sesame bread and halloumi cheese as well as a *Tahinopitta* (a sweet pastry with tahini). Like most of the staff, Eleni and I spent our coffee break in the back yard of the warehouse. It was a relief to spend some time out in the open air, away from the dark and gloomy interior of the warehouse.

"That was a very satisfying breakfast," I said and took a sip of my sweet, milky coffee. "How was your *Tiropitta?*" (pastry with cheese) I asked Eleni.

"Melt-in-the-mouth good.   Are you free to go swimming this afternoon?"

"I should think so," I said. "The 'family' is having visitors – half the Armenian community in Famagusta, I suspect. I'll sneak away about three o'clock. No one will miss me. But on the way back I have to go to Agios Nicholaos church and light a candle for my uncle Krikor's soul."

"Can't you skip it for once?"

"No. This is a special errand I do for my grandmother. I can't let her down. She takes such comfort from it."

"O.K I'll go with you ... Look! That English soldier over there is looking at us." I turned my head and saw the soldier smiling at us. He was drinking coffee too. He waved at us and we waved back at him.

"He must be from next-door," Eleni whispered. "I noticed several soldiers going in and out yesterday." The premises next to ours had been taken over by the Army. All week, we had seen trucks delivering office furniture and other stuff. Tin mug in hand, the soldier strolled over to where we were standing and introduced himself.

"Hello. I'm Corporal Paul Ashton."

"Hello," said Eleni. "My name is Eleni and this is Reya." For the second time in as many weeks, I was jealous of Eleni's self-confidence.

"Pleased to meet you," he said and we shook hands.

"Do you both work in the NAAFI next-door?" he asked, addressing me this time. I smiled. "Yes," was all I could find to say. I felt myself going pink. Blushing was the bane of my life.

"I'm doing my National Service."

"How do you like Cyprus?" I managed to ask him.

"It's so different from home. I love the weather - the sun seems to shine every day here."

"And it doesn't rain for months. Have you seen much of the island?"

"No, I haven't had the chance yet."

"We hope you do," said Eleni. "It's got sandy beaches, beautiful mountains and glorious food."

"I shall look forward to exploring all three!" he said, looking at me.

"Do you always come here for your coffee break?"

"Yes, we do," I said. "It's so nice to spend a few minutes out in the open. Our office is dark and noisy."

"We should be getting back," said Eleni. The yard was almost deserted.

"See you again," said the Corporal and smiled, waving his hand in the air before walking towards his workplace.

As we walked back to our respective desks, Eleni whispered in a conspiratorial voice.

"I think the Corporal fancies you. Did you notice the way he was looking at you?"

"Me? You are imagining things," I said, feigning innocence. But I had noticed the way he had looked into my eyes as he talked. And, secretly, I was pleased. "We are getting so daring Eleni. First, tea with an American, and today, coffee with an English soldier! What next?"

"Oh, it's only a bit of fun *gori*, don't take it seriously."

Back in the office, I couldn't concentrate on my work. I was excited that the Corporal seemed to be interested in me, but at the same time, I wondered why it was me and not Eleni, for she wasn't shy like me, and she was prettier too. At one o'clock, just as we were leaving the premises we saw him again. He was getting into a jeep, he saw us and he waved as he drove past. I smiled and waved back. For some reason my heart was beating furiously fast.

We stopped in front of Agios Nicholaos church on the way home after our swim. "Aren't you going in?" I asked Eleni.

"I don't think I will," she said. "I promised my Mother I would do the ironing for her. I hope the seven o'clock curfew will soon be lifted. I miss going to the cinema on a Saturday evening, don't you?"

"I sure do but it can't be helped," I said. "I hope Mother's visitors will have gone by the time I get home. I hate going into a roomful of people, shake their hands and try to make conversation with them. All these old-fashioned customs…"

"I know. We have them too. I better get going. If I should persuade my Father to lend me his car, we can go for a drive tomorrow afternoon can't we?"

"Sure."

"If not, I'll see you on Monday." With that Eleni left.

I entered the church. How sad that the icons in the church had lost their magic, their lustre dimmed, their healing powers diminished, after my beloved uncle Krikor's death. Once, I had visited this church regularly, on my own account, gazing into the soulful eyes of the Madonna in fervent prayer. I had felt a special bond with her, because she was my namesake and her feast day was my Name Day. But now, I hardly even looked at her. I could feel her gaze burning into me, but I refused to be intimidated. She had let me down and I would not forgive her. Nevertheless, I went through the motions of the empty ritual. I lit the candle, kissed the icon of the Madonna and said a prayer for my grandmother's sake. I took a portion of the holy bread to give to her.

My duty done, I walked home slowly. As always, the familiar feelings of anger mingled with guilt, assailed me. Anger that my uncle Krikor had died so young, and guilt that I had lost my belief in divine powers. Mercifully, the visitors had departed by the time I got home.

That evening, after the supper table was cleared and the washing up done, we sat in our usual places on the back verandah to have coffee. The conversation turned to the old days again. I was glad of it. It would rid me of my unwanted thoughts.

"I shall never forget the day you decided to leave Adana – in such a hurry - for Cyprus, Artin," Auntie Mareyam began. "It has been etched in my memory. Do you remember?" Father pulled up a chair and sat down next to his sister.

"Of course I remember, Sister. It was the day our lives changed forever. It was the day the family crumbled …" There was a tremor in Father's voice, a sadness I hadn't heard before. He looked at Mother, as if to say 'why don't *you* continue?' Mother got the message.

"I remember we had prepared a special meal to celebrate the name day of St. Krikor the Illuminator," Mother began. "I even remember what the meal was!" The Name Day of St. Krikor is one of the most important days in the Armenian calendar.

"What did you have to eat?" I wanted to ask, but Nonnie beat me to it. "Surely you can't remember what you ate, after all these years, Mother?" she asked.

"Of course I do," Mother replied. "We had *manti* , stuffed grape leaves and chicken with rice pilav." Even as I listened, my mouth began to water, at the thought of the *manti* – tiny dumplings, filled with minced lamb and served with a garlicky yoghurt sauce. "And for our dessert, we had Paklava with clotted cream. Every time I make these dishes, I think of that fateful day."

"So what happened afterwards?" Lillie was impatient to get to the heart of the story. She wasn't interested in the culinary details.

"After dinner, the men were having a heated discussion about the business, when suddenly, the doorbell rang. It was our priest – I forget his name. Anyway, he came to tell us the bad news." Auntie Mareyam nodded and sighed a great sigh. Mother carried on. "The priest told us that there were reliable reports that the Turkish government was going to order all non-Turks to leave Turkey. There was a hush in the room. St. Krikor was forgotten ..."

"Fear gripped our souls," Father took over the story, now. "We were all thinking the same thing. Surely this could not be true. We would lose *everything* we had worked for. You see, only the year before, we had extended the family business ..."

"The apothecary?" Lillie asked.

"Yes, the apothecary. We made all kinds of powders and potions from herbs and plants, roots and bark. People came from miles around for them."

"They were witch doctors!" Nonnie whispered to me, in English. I put my hand firmly on my mouth, to stop myself from giggling. The story was more interesting now that Father had joined in the telling of it.

"We had expanded into the shop next-door," Father continued. "And turned it into a confectionery. My brothers and I learned the art of the confectioner. It was one of the busiest shops in Adana, I'll have you know!" Father uttered these words with pride. "The next day, all kinds of stories were going round – fears of persecution and exile. There were rumours that travel documents were being issued at the local Council Office. These travel documents gave non-Turks the choice to leave Turkey and go to either America, Greece or Cyprus. I went there, to see for myself." He paused and lit a cigarette, inhaling the smoke deeply into his lungs. "There were huge crowds waiting. There and then, I decided that I had to have the precious documents that would make escape possible. Eventually my turn came. When I saw Yussuf behind the desk, my spirits rose – he was a regular customer of ours – his wife had a delicate stomach. I had no trouble in getting two travel documents, with him there."

"But why only two, Father?" Nonnie wanted to know, a puzzled look on her face. "What about the rest of the family?" Father paused, as he gathered his thoughts.

"Well," he said. "It would be easy enough for us to leave, without uprooting the family. But not so easy for my parents who were no longer young and also for my brothers who had their families and their children to think of. Then there was the business to consider, the house and so many other things. And if the rumours were unfounded, your mother and I could go back and nothing would be lost. But, as it happened, the family *was* uprooted and we did lose everything ..." Father's voice trailed off to a whisper. His hands shook as he took out his handkerchief and wiped his face.

"Don't upset yourself Brother. What happened, happened. There was nothing you or anybody could have done to change the course of destiny."

"You are right of course Sister. I thank God that I was able to come and see you and all the family when you eventually settled in Beirut."

"Yes, so am I. But I have always wondered Brother, what was it that made you decide on Cyprus? Why not Greece, or America?"

"Oh, Father!" I couldn't contain myself. "Why didn't you choose America? We would all have been Americans ..." I stopped short, as I realized what I was saying. How many times had I been told that Armenians remained Armenians no matter which corner of the world they were destined to live in. But Father wasn't angry with me. He just smiled.

"I had to make a decision quickly, my child. America was a shadowy continent on the other side of the world, too far – and don't forget there was a baby on the way."

"Oh, yes!" said Nonnie. "That was Sara!" Her comment went unnoticed.

"So," Auntie Mareyam was not to be denied. "What was wrong with Greece?"

"Greece was a poor country at that time, Sister. Making a living there would have been very difficult. But Cyprus was a British colony and I had heard that there was no discrimination and that British justice was fair. The population of the island was mostly Greek and Turkish. But the Turks were in the minority."

"But you couldn't speak English or Greek." Lillie exclaimed.

"True, but I *could* speak Turkish. Anyway, there was already a small Armenian community settled there. I figured I could get by. And, you see, Cyprus is so near Turkey, I thought – if the rumours did prove to be groundless after all – it would be easy to return home ..." Father leant back in his chair and gazed with moist eyes into the star-filled sky, deep in his memories. After he had gone to bed, Lillie turned to Mother.

"How did *you* feel Mother, when Father suddenly announced you were leaving Turkey?" Mother glanced at Auntie, before turning back to Lillie. Her eyes were misty and sad. "I had no say in the matter, daughter. So I kept my thoughts to myself. My duty was to be by my husband's side. His decision would be my decision also."

"What! Just like that? Nobody asked you what *you* wanted?" Mother indulged her with a smile.

"As I said, daughter, his decision would be my decision also. I would go with him wherever he decided to go, however uncertain the future. We would survive or perish, together."

"Oh Mother! How romantic! You must have been so in love …"

"Shush girl! Love! Love! How dare you use such coarse, unbecoming language?" Grandmother, who had been silent all this time, jumped on Lillie's innocent comment. Grandmother seemed utterly appalled by my sister's words. Love and Romance had sexual connotations and these were not spoken openly. Gripping the arms of her chair, she glared at poor Lillie, who looked as if she had been slapped on the face. There was complete silence. Nonnie and I were open-mouthed. We looked across at Mother and Auntie, but their eyes refused to meet ours. They kept their heads down.

I didn't want the evening to end on a sour note. Fortunately, Auntie managed to smooth it over. She turned to us girls, with a warm smile. "I was looking at the old family photographs," she said. "You must cherish them, girls, as we do." Mother nodded, a far-away look on her face. Grandmother settled back into her chair, returning to her own memories.

"Your mother was so brave. We were all proud of her, the way she coped with the whole thing." Auntie Mareyam's words seemed to open Mother's heart. At last, she told us the real answer to Lillie's question. At last, she told us how she really felt, when Father announced they had to leave Adana.

"I remember sitting on the edge of the bed," she told us. "I was overcome with tiredness, my whole body was cold with fear. After all, not only would I be leaving my home but also my whole family – my own mother, sister and my beloved brother. I wiped away the tears that were rolling down my cheeks. This was no time for weeping, I told myself. I had to be brave – not only for my husband but also for the baby I was carrying…"

My heart went out to Mother. I looked across at Auntie Mareyam. There were tears glistening on her face. Nonnie's next question broke the spell.

"Did you bring a lot of stuff with you, Mother?" Mother smiled at the practicality of Nonnie's question.

"As much as we could carry, my daughter."

"I helped your mother with the packing," said Auntie Mareyam. "We packed the clothes and then some of the bed linen – sheets, pillowcases and the bedcover, which your mother had embroidered herself – part of her lovely trousseau. And then, we put all her jewellery in a big handkerchief. This she would carry on her person - we thought it would be safer that way. And last, but not least, we packed the family photographs – the ones we were looking at this afternoon …"

How sad, I thought, that these few old sepia photographs had come to encapsulate an age and culture which they had left behind forever.

Chapter Three

Eleni and I saw the Corporal again, at coffee-break, on the Monday morning. Coffee mug in hand, he was talking to two other soldiers. As soon as he saw us, he smiled and came over to where we were standing.

"Hello Reya, hello Eleni," he said.

"You remembered our names!" I said, surprised.

"I did, indeed. I was hoping to see you again…"

"Hello Paul," Eleni said. "Did you have a nice week-end?"

"Yes, thanks," he said. "I went swimming with a couple of the boys on Saturday afternoon. And I spent most of Sunday at my Sergeant's house. We had a roast dinner with all the trimmings – a nice change from the usual canteen food! How was your week-end?"

"We went swimming too, didn't we Reya?"

"Yes, we did," I said. "In Cyprus the weekend is a like a national holiday. It starts at one o'clock on Saturday, when the shops close, until they re-open on Monday morning."

"What do people do?"

"Everyone puts on their best clothes and promenades up and down the main street. Or they sit in cafes and watch the world go by," I said, trying to sound cool and sophisticated like Eleni.

"It sounds like a carnival."

"I suppose it is in a way. There are crowds everywhere…"

"We had the biggest scare of our lives, didn't we Reya?" Eleni exclaimed. I nodded my head.

"Oh, what happened?"

"Well, Reya and I passed our driving tests about a month ago, and for the first time my father let me drive his car," Eleni began. "Off we went, for a drive around town. I was driving with such confidence too, resting my elbow on the open window, the way experienced drivers do."

"What went wrong?" asked Paul, sounding amused.

"Suddenly, the car started to stall. We didn't know why. I thought the best thing to do was to drive back home, as soon as possible. As the car laboured, I noticed to my horror that I had left the hand brake on!"

"We half expected the car to blow up." I said, remembering the incident. Eleni had gone deathly pale with worry. I had never seen her in such a state: she was usually quick to react to most situations.

"My father will kill me if I have caused any damage to his new car."

Paul smiled. "I think all new drivers make that mistake. I certainly have."

"Have you really?" we asked.

"Oh yes. It was the very day I passed my driving test. Dad gave me the keys of the van and let me deliver goods to a customer – he has an electrical appliance shop. I sat in the driving seat, pleased as punch, and started the car. Nothing happened. I tried again and again, but the car would still not move. Imagine my embarrassment when Harry, Dad's assistant, rushed out of the shop and said, in a very loud voice, to put the hand brake down! I can assure you I never made that mistake again."

"That makes me feel a lot better," said Eleni.

"And you'll be glad to know that leaving the hand brake on does not actually cause any damage to the engine."

"What a relief! I've been worried sick…" Eleni cried, covering her eyes with her hand. "I can look my Father in the face again." She finished her coffee and started to walk back to the office.

"We've got another ten minutes… " I stammered.

"I know, but I have an urgent report to type for Mr. Eastman. See you later." And with that she was gone.

I took a sip of my coffee, wondering why Eleni had left so abruptly, leaving me alone with Paul. But he didn't seem to be perturbed by this.

"Have *you* driven your father's car?" he asked.

"My father doesn't drive. My brother has a car but I haven't driven it yet," I said.

"Have you and Eleni known each other for long?"

"We started working in the NAAFI at more or less the same time and became friends. We go out together. Although we come from different cultures and nationalities, we have a lot in common…"

"What do you mean by 'different nationalities'? Aren't you both Cypriots?"

"Well yes. But Eleni is Greek Cypriot and I am Armenian Cypriot."

"Armenian?" he asked, somewhat surprised. "I'm afraid I've never heard… I've not met an Armenian before."

"I would have been surprised if you had," I said. "We are a very small nation."

"Where is your country?"

"Armenia - which borders on Russia, Persia and Turkey. It is part of the U.S.S.R."

"I see. But how did you come to be living in Cyprus?" Before I could answer, he went on. "I'm sorry if I sound inquisitive. I hope you don't mind. It's just that... I'm interested."

"I don't mind," I said. "But the history of the Armenians is long, very long. There isn't time... I have to go back to the office now." The yard was deserted. Everybody had gone back except me.

"Yes, of course. I have to get back too. Shall I see you tomorrow?"

I looked up and met his eyes – the bluest eyes I had ever seen. He was looking at me expectantly. "Yes," I said, and rushed back to the office. I smiled – somewhat pleased with myself. I hadn't felt shy with Paul. And what's more, I hadn't blushed - all the while I had been talking to him.

The weeks of Auntie Mareyam's visit had whizzed past. She would be going back to Beirut in a week or so. We would miss the wonderful evenings we spent on the back verandah, listening to the stories that the family remembered and relived with us. These stories of a past age, of a place long left behind, were spellbinding. Even though we had heard some of these stories before, when we were children, we were always ready to hear them again. It was like reading a favourite book over and over again.

"Tell me, dear Brother," said Auntie Mareyam to Father, that evening. "About the time you spent in Larnaca, before you decided to settle in Famagusta. Weren't you happy in Larnaca?" Father pushed his coffee cup further onto the table, and put out his cigarette in the ashtray, before settling back into his chair. All eyes were focused on him. He was such a good raconteur. Every episode of the stories he told us could in turn be moving, exciting, inspiring or adventurous even.

"Well," said Father. "Where shall I begin? As soon as we disembarked, we were put into quarantine..."

"Quarantine?"

"Yes Sister. We were put into quarantine for a period of forty days – it was a rule in Cyprus at that time – I suppose they wanted to prevent disease from entering the island. We were all detained together in some kind of compound – perhaps it was an old military base – I don't know. There was nothing we could do about it, so we got on with it. But we made some very good friends during this time – the kind of friends you never forget."

"I know what you mean. Larnaca must have been so different from the hustle and bustle of Adana."

"It certainly was different. Larnaca was like a village, then…"

"It hasn't improved much since then," interrupted Marko, who had spent four years at a boarding school in Larnaca. He always said that Larnaca had little to offer, compared to Famagusta.

"That maybe so. But it was a safe haven for us. Don't forget, this was 1921 – only seven years since the massacres of 1915. Larnaca may seem like a sleepy little place to you, my boy, but the peace and quiet was just what we needed. I remember… dawn was breaking when the boat docked at Larnaca. We had such a great feeling of calm and relief, as though a huge burden had been lifted from our shoulders. We felt that these welcoming shores would be kind to us and our unborn child." I stole a quick glance at Auntie Mareyam. She was gripped with the story. Father had a way with words. He scratched his head and was silent for a few moments, before gathering up his audience again. "I'll have you know," he said. "Those first six months in Larnaca were the most difficult time of my whole life. It wasn't easy you know, making a new start in a foreign country. It was all very well to feel safe in this haven of peace and tranquility, but I hadn't earned any money yet. It wasn't a question of not liking Larnaca. There were no opportunities… The gold sovereigns in my money-belt weren't going to last much longer. I had to face up to the fact that soon, very soon, I would be obliged to sell one of Siran's gold bracelets, just so we could survive!"

"Oh no! Not one of Mother's gold bracelets!" we girls chorused – as we did every time, without fail, at this juncture in the story. Father was such a good actor too – he looked pained and raised his eyes towards the heavens. "As God is my witness," he said. "I didn't want to. Those bracelets meant home and family to your mother – they were her wedding presents."

"I remember Siran's exquisite, gold jewellery. Did you have to sell any of it, then?" Auntie Mareyam wanted to know.

"God spared me, that time. But I was really worried, Sister. The El Dorado kind of optimism I had started with was fast evaporating. Something had to be done – *now* – without further delay." He paused, as Mother came out onto the verandah, carrying a tray of cold drinks, which she put down on the table. Nonnie jumped out of her seat and handed them round. The ice cubes tinkled in the glasses. Father took a sip of his lemonade and lit a cigarette, apparently deep in thought.

"Well," he began again. "I had heard that there was a nice little seaside town, about twenty five miles North of Larnaca." We girls looked at each other and grinned at Auntie Mareyam. "Famagusta, here we come!" we cried together.

"You are right, my daughters. So, I went to this town to see for myself and I was impressed. There was life and vitality in this place. I was sure there would be opportunities for work here. The Turks lived in the old town. They coexisted with the Greeks amicably and they traded profitably."

"Sara must have been born by then." Auntie Mareyam glanced across to Mother, but it was Father who answered.

"Yes. As soon as the baby was forty days old, we packed our belongings once again and went north."

"Were there many Armenians in Famagusta, then?"

"Not many – just a few families. But I thought being isolated was better than starving. We made the journey to Famagusta in a horse-drawn carriage – a *karotsa* . It seemed as though we were imprisoned in this contraption for an eternity, until at last, we reached our destination. We stopped once during the journey, so that the driver could feed and rest his horses. We stretched our legs and ate our meager meal of bread, cheese and fruit, which our kind neighbours had packed for us. The baby slept most of the way.

"It was nearly afternoon when the driver finally stopped in front of the small house that I had rented. I unlocked the door and started to carry in our few belongings. Siran followed me with the baby in her arms." It was hot and muggy, on the verandah. Father took out his handkerchief and wiped the perspiration from his face and neck, before continuing with his story.

"It's strange, how vividly one remembers certain things and places – our new home was just one large room. We unrolled the mattress and made our bed in one corner of the room, with the baby's little mattress next to ours. Then, we put the cooking utensils and the primus stove in another corner of the room – that was our kitchen. Siran put away the clothes in an old broken wardrobe, which the last tenants must have left behind. I watched her, as she surveyed our new home. It broke my heart." Father sighed, holding out his hands and shaking his head. You couldn't tell if he was really moved, or if it was all part of the performance. We were all spellbound – even Mother nodded her head.

"It was a far cry from the big house she had left behind, only a few short months before. There were no curtains – but at least it was bright and warm, with the sun shining through the windows. There was a lean-to outside, which would have to serve as a washroom, and next to this, was the oldest toilet we had ever seen. But we were surprised at the size of the yard, weren't we Siran?" Father said, turning to Mother – clearly indicating that he needed a break. He lit a cigarette and leaned back in his chair.

"Yes, we were," Mother took up the story. "I remember it well – there were trees in the yard – some of them orange, some of them lemon trees. Good, I thought. We can eat the oranges. I can use the lemons for cooking and also make lemonade. And then, I noticed the grapevine – it was dead now, but it would come back to life, in the spring. I could use its tender leaves to make *Derev* (stuffed vine leaves) - one of our popular dishes."

Father was smiling and nodding his head in agreement. "My spirits rose," he continued. "I prayed to God that maybe, this would be the turning point in our lives – a chance to find peace and security, at last – a chance to erase the nightmares of the past." Father stopped talking and picked up his cigarettes and lighter. This was a sure sign that he had come to the end of this particular part of his story. "It's getting late, it's time we all went to bed," he said.

"It's not that late…" we said, in one voice.

"Look at the sky. The stars are waning…" Father protested.

"If you think I will go to bed before I hear the rest of this story, you are mistaken, Brother." So said, Auntie Mareyam sat back in her chair and waited.

"Oh, all right then," Father said and lit another cigarette. "Well, Sister – God helps those who help themselves! The very next morning, I went to the municipal market – to see if there was any way I could start earning some money. I couldn't waste any time – we needed to buy food and pay the rent – I had to forge ahead. Then, I had some luck. I found out that there were no manufacturers of boiled sweets in the town…" Father smiled to himself, at the memory. "I bought a sack of sugar from the market, but I couldn't find the food colouring or the essences which are absolutely necessary in the production of sweets. Some kind stallholder told me – half in sign language and half in Greek – that I might be able to find these in the old town, where the Turks lived."

"What did you do, Brother?"

"I walked all the way to the old town, Sister, that's what I did. It is about two or three miles to the old town, but it seemed like a hundred miles

33

on that first day. I was dead tired when I walked back, I can tell you. But, as soon as I got home, I rolled up my sleeves, and set to work in the lean-to. By the end of that evening, I had made my first lot of boiled sweets. The next day, I took my wares to market – and before noon – I was sold out! I couldn't believe it!"

Auntie Mareyam clapped her hands together. "Praise the Lord!" she cried. "You were following in our father's footsteps! You must have thanked God a million times, for learning Father's trade."

"I did, Sister – I still do." Father acted out his thanks, raising his hands to the heavens, before turning back to the family. "That's how I became the first confectioner in Famagusta. Soon, I became a familiar figure in the market. I had my own stall. I was known to everyone…" – he paused to give due emphasis to his title, clenching his fists in triumph – "as *'The Confectioner'*. I made friends with the other stallholders – that's when I started to learn Greek." He lit a cigarette and inhaled deeply, enjoying the effect of his performance on his audience.

"So, you never looked back, did you Brother?"

"Well, it wasn't that dramatic a success story, Sister. I made enough money to buy food and pay the rent, but that was all. For years, we lived from hand to mouth. Don't forget, the family was growing. In no time, we had three girls, and another baby was on the way. There were school fees to pay too. It was grim…"

"I suppose you were disappointed that God hadn't given you a son yet."

"Every parent wants a son. It's only natural, isn't it? I wasn't complaining though. But just after our Reya was born, things changed dramatically. It's as if she was chosen to be the herald of good fortune. My luck suddenly changed. I rented a small shop and started the confectionery business - making *Lokum* and *Halva* as well as sweets. It took off spectacularly. I had to move to a much bigger shop. In time, I started to employ people." Father smiled his most gracious smile. "I had this house built for Siran…"

"It's a lovely house too. And, you started helping me and my boys, dear Brother – when we needed it most."

"Oh, that's nothing! Because, only two years after Reya was born, the most unbelievable, the most wonderful thing happened! Marko, the son I had so hoped for, the son I had so wanted, came at last…"

"What a triumph! What an achievement!" enthused Auntie Mareyam.

Marko had listened quietly to the familiar story, but now he made a comment. "It's ironic – isn't it Auntie – that Father got started in Cyprus by trading with the Turks, the very people he had fled from."

"It was not design that brought your parents to Cyprus, or took me and the rest of the family to Beirut, my boy," Auntie Mareyam replied. "But an accident of Fate. And Fate works in mysterious ways." She was wiping her eyes with her handkerchief.

Chapter Four

"We haven't heard from our American photographer yet," said Eleni on the way to work. "It must be more than four weeks since our 'modelling' experience. I thought he would have written to us by now."

"You know what, I had forgotten about him!" I said.

"I know you have, judging by the way you rush out of the office at coffee time, to meet Paul - the 'Corporal', as everyone in the office refers to him!"

"Oh, God! Is the office staff talking about me?"

"No, *gori*, they are just interested, intrigued really, to see how it will develop."

"Develop? We just have a friendly chat, that's all."

"What do you find to talk about, anyway?"

"We talk about anything and everything. We talk about books, films, music and nature even..."

"Oh," commented Eleni with a knowing look.

"Paul is also interested about my culture, language, religion... you know, that sort of thing."

"I don't suppose he had heard of Armenians before."

"No, he hadn't. He was very interested to hear the story of how my parents came to be in Cyprus. He said he looked at his world map and found exactly where Armenia is."

"I see... Did he tell you anything about his family?"

"Yes, he did. He said he has no sisters or brothers. His father has an electrical shop and they live in Surrey. Our backgrounds couldn't be more different..."

"They say opposites attract!"

"Maybe."

"So much to talk about! No wonder you are always the last to get back to the office..."

"I know. I shall get into trouble one of these days."

"Here we are, another day in this gloomy old place," sighed Eleni as we reached the warehouse. My attitude to the office had changed overnight.

The stuffy atmosphere, the noise did not matter to me now. On the contrary, I couldn't wait to go to work, nor could I wait for my coffee break. "I'm amazed that you can speak several languages besides your own," Paul said, when we met during the coffee-break later.

"To me it has always been a necessary requirement, a natural part of my life," I replied. "Did you not learn any foreign languages when you were at school?"

"I did French for a year or so, but found the pronunciation, not to mention the spelling, difficult and gave it up. How long does it take you to switch from one language to another?"

"A few seconds I suppose. I speak in a crisscross of languages. At home I talk to my grandmother in Turkish, my parents in Armenian, my Greek friends in Greek and my sisters and I sometimes talk in English." We both burst out laughing, it sounded so funny.

"Let me explain," I said. "Many Armenians have lived outside Armenia - in Adana and other cities in Turkey - for generations. Grandmother never had the chance to go to an Armenian school, so she didn't learn to speak or read and write in Armenian properly. She finds it a lot easier to speak in Turkish."

"But why do you and your sisters prefer to talk in English?" he wanted to know.

"Because we read in English and we use English at work. Sometimes, we can express ourselves better in English. Mind you, if we can't find the right word in English, we substitute it in Armenian or Turkish!"

"That's very handy!"

"It is indeed."

"I'm beginning to get a picture of your home and family. Does your grandmother live with you?"

"She came to live with us after my uncle Krikor died..." my voice trailed away. The familiar lump came into my throat as it always did at the mention of my uncle.

"What's the matter?" Paul asked.

"It's alright," I said quietly, composed now. "I still get upset when I talk about him... Even after all these years."

"Would you like to tell me about your uncle Kre ... Kregore?" he asked gently – stumbling over the Armenian name.

"Yes," I said without any hesitation. I found to my surprise that I wanted to tell Paul about my uncle, even though I had only known him for a few weeks. "I have always known that my uncle Krikor was a hero: he saved my mother from a terrible fire, many years ago." I began. "But he has been my special hero, since he saved me from a fate worst than death, when I was five years old."

"A fate worse than death!"

"Yes. Uncle Krikor found me hiding in the Little Room, a kind of storeroom in our house, where all the provisions for the winter are kept. I was crouching on the floor, crying my eyes out. *They* were here for a visit again. *They* wanted to take me to *their house*... Everybody wanted me to be *their* daughter. Mother and Father didn't want me any more."

"Who were 'they'?"

"They were an elderly couple, 'Auntie' Teresa and 'Uncle' Josef as they liked to be called. They owned the bakery next to my father's sweet shop. They baked the best bread, cakes and biscuits in town. Every time you walked past the bakery, the wonderful aroma of freshly baked bread enticed you in. At Christmas and Easter, the sweet smell of cinnamon and vanilla cakes and pastries made your mouth water."

"Mm... I can relate to that sensation. I remember as a child going to our local bakery just before closing time on Saturday afternoons. All the bread and cakes were sold off at less than half price. I used to go home laden with goodies..." Paul smiled and shook his head at the distant memory.

"You have a sweet tooth too!"

"I certainly do. But please continue with your story. I can't wait to hear it."

"Well, this couple had no children of their own, so they wanted to adopt me. They were very good friends of the family and every time they came for a visit – which was often – they used to talk about the 'adoption'. On this day, as usual, 'Auntie' Teresa made me sit on her lap and held me so close that I thought she would squeeze me to death. I felt so scared that as soon as she put me down, I fled to the storeroom, closing the door behind me. Hours later my uncle found me. 'I don't want to be *their* daughter' I sobbed. He took me in his arms: 'I promise I will not let *anyone* take you away' he said. From that moment on, Uncle Krikor became my hero."

"I can see why he became your hero. And I'm so glad your uncle saved you. I might not have met you otherwise! You must tell me more about him."

"I'll tell you tomorrow," I said and ran back to the office. The coffee break had been over ten minutes ago.

The next day Paul was not at our meeting place. I waited for a few minutes, expecting to see his athletic figure hurrying towards me, with the familiar coffee mug in his hand. I finished my coffee and walked slowly back to the office. I was so disappointed my heart felt like lead.

Mr. Eastman looked up from his newspaper and raised his eyebrows. No doubt surprised to see me back in the office so soon. "Didn't the Corporal turn up to-day?" he asked.

"No Mr. Eastman," I said, and shrugged my shoulders in an effort to hide my disappointment.

"He is probably on some special duty or other," he said.

"Maybe…"

"Don't look so sad. He'll be back tomorrow," he said, and went back to his newspaper. All kinds of possibilities flashed through my mind. He could be ill. Worse still, he might have been transferred to another unit, in which case I might never see him again. There was no way of knowing. No way of getting in touch with him. I wished Eleni was here. I so wanted to share my anxiety with her. But she was away. She had taken a week's annual leave and was at this moment enjoying herself up in the mountain resort of Troodos with her family. When I didn't see Paul for the rest of that week, I gave up all hope of ever seeing him again.

There was a letter for me when I got home from work on Saturday. I tore open the envelope. The writing was unfamiliar. Then I saw the name at the bottom of the page. The letter was from Paul! My joy had no bounds. I sneaked into my room and closed the door behind me. I heard Mother calling - lunch was ready. I ignored it and quickly read Paul's letter. He was not ill. Thank God, he had not been transferred to another unit. There had been a bomb alert and all army personnel were confined to barracks. He hoped to see me soon!

Mother's second call to lunch came louder. The mouth-watering aroma of the skewers of meat cooking on the charcoal fire had already assailed my nostrils. Today's lunch was going to be special but tinged with sadness too. For tomorrow, Auntie Mareyam would go back home, to Beirut. We would all miss her sweet-tempered nature and her lovely smile. I put Paul's letter under my pillow. I would read it again after lunch.

I went into the kitchen to see if there was anything I could do to help. But as usual, Mother had everything under control. We sat round the dining table to do justice to the *kebab,* the warmed flat bread and the various salads that went with it. Father usually had *raki* while the rest of us had the choice of iced water or *ayran*.

Father raised his glass. "I wish you a safe journey home to-morrow, Sister," he said, and took a sip of his drink.

"Thank you brother," Auntie Mareyam replied.

"I hope it won't be long before we see you again," said Mother.

"Amen to that," said Grandmother. With that we started on the serious business of eating. A cool breeze drifted in through the open window. I took a sip of ice-cold *ayran* and smiled to myself. Paul was safe and I would see him again – soon I hoped.

Chapter Five

On the Monday morning, before I had time to take the cover off my typewriter, Andreas came over to my desk and whispered in my ear: "The Corporal is back!" There was a big grin on his face. He could hardly contain his excitement.

"Is he really back, Andreas?" I asked, and blushed a deep red. He nodded his head vigorously. "I saw him early this morning," he said and rushed off before I could thank him. The dear man. I was touched by his fondness for me; he wanted to be the first to tell me the good news.

My heart missed a beat when I saw Paul waiting for me at coffee-time. "It's so nice to see you again," he said. "Did you get my letter?"

"Yes, I did. I was wondering what had happened to you."

"Were you worried?"

"I was, because there was no way of knowing…"

"I hope your parents didn't mind me writing to you," he said. "I wanted to let you know that I was alright."

"My parents are used to me receiving letters."

"Really? Do you get many?"

"Yes," I said and smiled at the memory. Paul looked at me, surprised.

"Last year I placed an advertisement in *Photoplay*, for pen friends," I explained.

"I see," he said, nodding his head.

"What's more, I promised to answer all letters received."

"Oh dear! Did you get many?"

"Did I! I never thought for a moment that anyone would want to write to someone living on a tiny island like Cyprus. The response was phenomenal. To my own amazement, and to the amazement of our postman, I received over one thousand letters."

"All of them expecting to be answered!"

"Exactly. First they came in bundles, then in bigger bundles. In the end, the postman put them in sacks and delivered them to my father's shop."

"I can't believe it!" Paul said, shaking his head.

"The postman couldn't believe it either. After about a week of this continuing avalanche of letters, he could not contain his curiosity any longer..." I started laughing at the memory.

"What happened?"

"The postman asked my father why one of his daughters was getting so many letters. What was going on? He had never experienced anything like this, in all his years as a postman."

"Your father, I mean your parents must have been curious too."

"I'm sure they were. Surprisingly, my mother never made a comment. As for my father, he was at a loss for words, which is unusual for him. In the end, he admitted to the postman that he didn't know either. His philosophy was not to question things that were beyond his comprehension!"

Paul was silent for a moment. "Where did the letters come from?" he asked.

"Judging by the stamps, they were coming from all over the world."

"Did you manage to read them all?"

"I tried to. I spent hours, opening the letters and reading them. It was fun, but there were far too many. After a few days my sister Nonnie came to my rescue. Quite a few of the letters had photographs in them. We sifted through them and put aside the ones I wanted to respond to."

Paul winked over the rim of his coffee mug. "Did you select the good looking photos to answer to?" he asked.

"Of course," I said and met his eyes. They were crinkling with amusement. "I picked about a dozen to start with, mostly from England, one from San Francisco, and one from an Armenian from Iraq."

"Hm. Interesting mixture," he said. He took out his packet of cigarettes and tapped one out, lit it, and blew out rings of smoke. I watched him, fascinated, I had never seen a smoker do that before.

"Yes, it was. I enjoyed writing to these people and getting to know them. Soon, the number of people I was writing to increased to about thirty-five."

"As many as that?"

"Yes. But I found out pretty quickly that I would not be able to keep this up for long. It was not only the time I was spending writing the letters, but also the cost of the postage!"

"I'm not surprised. Do you like writing letters?"

"I do. But inevitably, my correspondents dwindled to only a few."

"Will you write to me?"

"If you want me to."

"We have so little time to talk here. We'll get to know each other better that way. Tell me more about yourself."

"More about *myself*?"

"Why yes. Write to me about your childhood, your family, your uncle…"

"Will you do the same?"

"Of course."

"O.K. then, I will. I'll write to you this evening," I said. But now, it was time to get back to the office.

And so it was that Paul and I started writing to each other, at least twice a week, sometimes more. Paul was right. The time we spent together seemed to be ruthlessly short. Writing to Paul was so different from writing to my pen friends. Paul's image was with me as I wrote to him, page after page, reliving memories from my childhood years.

My first letter to Paul was very long.

"Dear Paul," I began. "Now that Auntie Mareyam has gone back to Beirut, the summer evenings on the verandah are very short and very quiet. We all miss her. How we all cried the day she left. It was the first time I ever saw Father crying openly.

I'm lucky enough to have a room of my own. It is very small but it has a lovely view of the harbour. I love gazing at the sea. Once, I rose before daybreak, to watch the breathtaking splendour of the sun rising from the waves. It is in this room that I write my letters and read my books.

As I told you, I loved my Uncle Krikor very much. He was not only my Uncle but also my godfather. He gave me a present on my Name Day every year. I gladly ran errands for him. In Cyprus the shops stay open in the winter months. As soon as I ate my lunch, I would take both my father's and uncle's lunch-boxes to their respective shops. I walked really fast so that the food would not get cold.

My first destination was Father's shop. I stayed long enough to help myself to sweets, nuts or whatever else I fancied. Sometimes the pockets of my school uniform would bulge with freshly roasted pistachio nuts, or sugar almonds!

From there I walked to Dai's (my nickname for Uncle Krikor) shop. He was always glad to see me. He worked so hard in his shop. It was one of the best china shops in Famagusta. One could find the most exquisite porcelain, crystal and china which he imported from England, Europe and Japan. Their artful display dazzled you as you entered the shop.

I loved to be in the shop with Dai. It was fascinating to watch him arrange dinner services, crystal glasses, decanters and vases to their best advantage. I can hear the bell-like tinkle as he tapped a crystal wine glass with his thumb and forefinger. 'The clearer the sound, the finer the quality of the crystal' he told me many a time.

Even more beguiling was the array of porcelain clocks on the shelves facing the shop door. I was not allowed to touch anything. I understood this and accepted it without question – they were breakable and very expensive. Sometimes, Dai would let me sweep the entrance to the shop and the pavement outside. I did this with pride because I was helping him and also it made me feel grown up.

It was a big shop but the store-room at the back was even bigger! You should have seen it Paul. It was a magical place, full of crates yet to be opened. I used to watch Dai excitedly as he struggled to open a crate. I used to wait impatiently. What delightful objects would it yield? Would it be a porcelain figurine, a crystal vase, a china doll or a bottle of exotic perfume?

These little bottles of French perfume came in elegant little boxes tied with colourful silk tassels. One New Year's Day, Dai gave each of my elder sisters a bottle of this perfume. Imagine my joy when he gave me one too! I still have it. Unfortunately, soon after that day, Dai became ill and everything changed."

I stopped writing and thought; will Paul get bored reading this letter? I read what I had written so far. It wasn't too bad. I so wanted to tell Paul about Dai's illness and the pilgrimage the family made in the hope of a cure for him. I took up my pen and continued to write.

"My beloved Dai became ill, so the family decided to make a pilgrimage to Apostolos Andreas monastery. We would pray to St. Andreas and ask him to make him well again. We would take with us a huge candle almost as tall as Dai, as a votive offering.

This monastery is on the cape, the far northeastern point of Cyprus. It is set in an idyllic location, high in the hills, surrounded by pine trees and fruit orchards. Four miles beyond the monastery, Cyprus ends. Father says;

from here, on a clear day, one might catch a glimpse of Turkey, Syria or Lebanon.

There are tranquil cloisters and courtyards, and, as in most monasteries in Cyprus, rooms are available for visitors to stay the night. The monks follow the long tradition of farming, making jam, wine and bee keeping. I wish you could see it for yourself Paul. I'm sure you would like it.

People from all over the island go to St. Andreas when they want a special prayer answered. For he is renowned as a great miracle worker, and this place is the Lourdes of Cyprus. Blindness, epilepsy, lameness – the saint heals them all. Pilgrims flock there, bearing gifts and money as well as votive images in wax as offering. We Armenians, like the Greeks, are a religious people, not in any dramatic way, but simply as an everyday part of our lives.

I remember that day so well. I woke up very early, it was barely light outside. My eldest sister Sara came into my room and helped me get dressed. Normally I would have protested, as I felt I was old enough not to need any help, but on this day I said nothing. She combed and plaited my long hair and told me – in no uncertain terms - to have my breakfast, feed the chickens and above all not get in Mother's way. I was so devoted to Sara that I gladly did what I was told. I drank a cup of sweet cinnamon tea but left half of my bread and honey on my plate. I didn't really mind feeding the hens. I liked to watch the dozen or so hens and the cockerel as they scrambled and fought to devour the food. They were insatiable, they ate everything from left-over food to their special feed – the powdery chaff of the wheat – mixed with water. I particularly liked to watch them drink the water - the way they dipped their beaks in the water and then looked up towards the sky. Grandmother told me once that this was their way of thanking God for their daily food and water. I liked the idea but that morning I was too excited and did not linger. I was so impatient to be on our way.

Mother was ready at last. The gigantic basket of food she had prepared was safely packed in the boot of the minibus, which Father had hired for the day. The driver was ready and waiting. The two back seats were arranged to make a makeshift bed for Dai. Every effort was made to make him comfortable for the journey. Grandmother sat near him, so she could see to his needs. Mother sat with my three elder sisters, Father sat next to the driver, and my brother Marko and I behind them. As custom dictated, the driver would be invited to share our food.

At last we were on our way. The driver kissed the cross hanging from the rear-view mirror. This is an old custom that drivers have, to protect them and all who travel with them, from the perils of the road. Mother and Grandmother crossed themselves three times, and then we were off. Do you have similar customs too?

We stopped in front of a *kafenion* (it means coffee shop in Greek) for a break. Father and the driver went into this male sanctuary for a coffee, while the rest of us trooped out to stretch our legs and have a drink of lemonade. Thus refreshed, we continued our journey.

I gazed out of the window, cradling my doll in my arms. This was the doll Dai had given me the year before on my Name Day. She was the most beautiful doll in the world, with blue eyes and rosy cheeks. Her hair was long and golden. She even had socks and shoes on her dainty little feet. I had named her Kalina. I told her about my special prayer to St. Andreas: what I wanted more than anything in the world was for Dai to get well. From time to time I stole a look at him, lying on his makeshift bed. He was sleeping. Grandmother shooed me away, when I tried to change places with her. The journey was beginning to bore me. At last we reached the monastery.

We entered the church of St. Andreas. It was an old church. The hallowed atmosphere was awe-inspiring. The glow of myriad candles and the strange smell of burning wax heightened the emotional impact on me. I sensed the presence of an omniscient God. I felt His all-seeing eyes on me.

I followed the others and walked slowly to the shrine of St. Andreas. I bowed my head, made the sign of the cross and prayed with all my heart and soul my special prayer. I bargained with the Deity. 'Please, please, St. Andreas, make my beloved Dai well, and I promise to light a candle to the Virgin every Saturday afternoon,' I pleaded. 'For as long as I live,' I added quickly. I walked along the Iconostasis. The Pantheon of saints looked down on me, in sympathy. Following the Greek custom, I kissed every one of the many icons.

The light from the candles shone on the icon of the Virgin Mary. This particular icon was legendary for its miracles too. It shone with celestial light. I prayed to her also, just to be on the safe side. I dropped my pennies into the offertory. I took a deep breath. My job was done.

Like many generations before us, I have been brought up to believe in the existence of an Almighty God. To believe that He is everywhere in my life – all knowing, all seeing. He loves the good and punishes the bad. My wonderful Dai was such a good, kind and gentle man, that I thought God will surely love him and make him well.

The rest of that day has a hazy, dreamlike quality. The journey back was uneventful. Dai was so tired he was almost carried to the minibus. He lay down on his bed, exhausted. The rest of us were subdued and silent, for the most part, each wanting to be alone with their thoughts. I sat by the window and went over the events of the day. I ignored Marko, who wanted to talk to me. I wasn't in the mood. I felt strangely calm. I was sure St. Andreas and the Virgin Mary had heard my special prayer. My beloved Dai would be well again. I told Kalina so. All was well with our world."

It was past midnight when I put the light out. I felt good, as if a burden had been lifted from my shoulders. At last I had found someone I could tell my innermost thoughts and feelings to.

Chapter Six

"Thank you so much for your letter," Paul said. "I loved reading about your pilgrimage to the monastery."

"Did you really like it?"

"I did, really."

"But it was a bit long, wasn't it?"

"No, not at all. It was very descriptive."

"I found it easier to write about my feelings in a story."

"You did it very well."

"I hope so. My father is the real story teller in our family. He has a wonderful way of recounting a story."

"I didn't understand what you meant by 'Name Day' though. Is it similar to Saint's day?"

I thought for a moment. "I suppose it is. We don't have the custom of celebrating birthdays…"

"Don't you?" Paul asked, incredulity written all over his face.

"No," I said, apologetically. "We celebrate Name Days instead." He looked even more puzzled now. "Let me try and explain," I said. "If you're lucky enough to be given a saint's name – like I was - then that day is celebrated, and you get presents." I shrugged my shoulders. It was simple enough for me.

"What about those who don't have saints' names? No celebrations, no presents for them?"

I shook my head. "It's unfair, but that's how it is. We have some really strange and old fashioned customs. But I'm glad to say that some things are changing. My eldest sister celebrates her children's birthdays. She even bakes a cake for the occasion."

"I'm happy to hear that!" Paul laughed out loud and lit a cigarette. "Now that we've got to know each other better, is it possible for us to meet, one Saturday afternoon?"

"What did you say?" I blurted out, not believing what I had just heard.

"I said, would you like to meet me at the beach, for a swim and a drink afterwards?"

I had heard correctly. How could I tell Paul that I couldn't go out with him? How could I make him understand that it was not acceptable in Armenian society? I so wished that my parents were not so old fashioned. So steeped in outdated customs and traditions. They would have a fit if they knew that I was friendly with a *man,* let alone a foreign man and a soldier! Paul was waiting.

"I'm sorry Paul…" I stammered. "I don't know how to say this, but I can't go out with you."

"Oh! I'm sorry too. Do you have a boyfriend?"

I was so surprised by the question that I was speechless for a moment. "*Boyfriend!*" I said at last, finding my voice. "No, I don't have a boyfriend. Why do you ask?"

"Because you said you can't come out with me. I presumed that you had a boyfriend…"

I laughed. The very idea was comical to me. "The reason I can't go out with you is because 'nice' Armenian girls do not associate with boys, not even Armenian boys, let alone have boyfriends."

"You mean you've never had a boyfriend?"

"No. It's just not allowed in our culture. I know the rest of the world has moved on from Victorian times, but we haven't."

"How is a girl supposed to meet a man, then, if she's not allowed to go out?"

"She doesn't," I said.

"But… If she doesn't meet a man, how will she ever get married?"

"Well… The age old system of the 'arranged marriage' still goes on," I said. Paul looked at me with raised eyebrows, totally bewildered, as though I was reciting some ancient rite. "I think I told you Paul, that we have some weird customs. The 'arranged marriage' is one of them."

"How does this 'arranged marriage' system work?"

"It's a bit complicated to go into it now, but I can try and explain it to you in my next letter, if you like."

"Please do. I'm curious to find out how it works. Is it the same in the Greek custom?"

"No. Greek girls are allowed to meet boys at parties, picnics and so on… It is considered a good way for young people to meet their future partners."

"How sensible of them."

"But all things considered, compared to most other Armenian parents, mine are almost liberal. I have a friend whose father didn't even allow her to get a job. She could only go out with her parents, never with her girlfriends. They married her off to the first suitor that came along."

"O dear! How awful! Is she happy?"

"I don't know… I think so. I visit her sometimes. She seems contented, with her children and her nice house."

"Hm. Your parents aren't going to marry you off, are they?"

"No! There is no fear of that happening. My elder sister Lillie must get married first. That won't be for ages, because she keeps saying 'no' to every eligible suitor that comes along. After her, my other sister Nonnie is next. Then and only then it will be my turn. So you see, I'm safe for now!"

"Thank God for small mercies. Might you ever consider meeting me for a swim one day?"

"I don't know… maybe." I couldn't tell Paul that if I had the courage I would meet him tomorrow.

"I shall look forward to that day – whenever it might be."

"What about you, Paul, have you got a girlfriend back in England?" I asked, trying to steer the conversation away from me.

"I did have a girlfriend, but when I was called up to do my National Service in Cyprus, she didn't want to see me any more. Two years is a long time to wait."

"I'm so sorry," I said, and thought; I would have waited forever, if I loved someone.

"Please don't be. It was for the best."

I nodded. "It was *kismet*, as my grandmother would say."

"Does she believe in things like that?"

"O yes. She firmly believes that everything is preordained. Things that happen to us – good or bad – have a purpose."

"Do you believe in fate – *kismet* - too?"

"I've never really thought about it; just accepted it…" I looked at my watch. The time had simply flown by again. "I better get back to the office. I'll get into trouble one of these days."

"I'm sure you won't get the sack for being a few minutes late…"

"Get the sack?" I asked, not understanding what he meant. I thought of the dozens of sacks in my father's shop. "What do you mean?"

"I'm sorry… Em… I don't know where or when 'to get the sack' originated from, but it means to be dismissed from one's job," Paul explained, his face creasing into a wide grin.

"I see, but you don't have to wear the 'sack' over your head do you?" Paul shook his head and we burst out laughing. I looked at my watch again.

"See you tomorrow," Paul said, and raised his hand in farewell.

I was thrilled that Paul liked me enough to want to meet me somewhere other than the yard at the warehouse. An unfamiliar feeling swept over me. It was a mixture of joy and caution. It was one thing to see him for twenty minutes at work, but it was a huge risk to meet him in a public place. It could take our friendship to a different level, and that could take me into dangerous territory. I thought long and hard. Should I yield to the temptation, or nip this friendship in the bud? I decided to tell Eleni about it.

Chapter Seven

On Sunday afternoons, it was *de rigueur* for Eleni and me to dress up in our Sunday best and go for a walk along the beach. This Sunday was no exception. On the way back, we stopped at *Delice* , for our usual treat. We sat at a table on the pavement, gave our order to the waiter and watched the world go by.

"Paul asked me to go out with him," I blurted out.

"Did he?"

"He asked me to go swimming with him and then for a drink."

"What was your response?" Eleni looked at me quizzically.

"I said 'maybe', but to be honest, I don't see how I can."

"The question is, do you want to?"

"Of course I do. But is it worth the risk?"

"Let's see now, the little cove where we go swimming is safe enough. You could meet him there."

"I'm petrified that someone I know might see me and tell my father, you can imagine what would happen..."

"Stop being so pessimistic," she interrupted. "We have been going there for months now. Did you ever see anyone you know? Even when we were playing at being 'models', for that American photographer, no one we knew saw us. You can be sure we would have heard about it, if they had."

"No." I had to concede she was right. "But I still feel uneasy about it."

"Look, I can go with you and sit with some of my friends. You've met most of them at Maroula's birthday party. They're alright. That way, I can warn you if I spot any 'danger'.

Just then the waiter came with our order. I had ordered a *charlotte* – a type of custard dessert, and Eleni had ordered a slice of cinnamon and apple cake. We were silent as we enjoyed our treat.

I kept thinking of what Eleni had said. It made sense. Her friends wouldn't tell on me. If I were to be honest with myself, I had enjoyed meeting young people of my own age at the party. I had lied to Mother that time, saying that I was going to the cinema with Eleni. I hated deceiving her, but sometimes it was necessary to do so. Duty and obedience to parental morality were ingrained in my subconscious, but the rebellious side of my nature would sometimes win out.

"What are you thinking about?" Eleni asked, interrupting my thoughts.

"I'll say 'yes' if Paul should ask me again."

"Of course he will. Stop thinking about it. Anyway, it's time we went to the cinema."

We left the café and walked the short distance to the *Pallas,* one of the three open-air cinemas in Famagusta. We were going to see the musical *Meet Me in St. Louis* starring Judy Garland. We went to the cinema every Saturday and Sunday – it was an important part of our weekend activities. On these nights, one was given a free ticket to see a film mid-week. So we were able to see four films a week for the price of two. Not surprisingly, we had seen most of the films made in Hollywood, as well as a good number of British films. But these films were three or four years old, by the time they reached our shores.

After the film, we walked to our respective homes. It had been so hot and humid during the film that our clothes had stuck to our backs. Sitting on the iron chairs in the cinema had made the humidity even worse. We walked at a leisurely pace, enjoying the cool breeze that had suddenly appeared. Stopping in front of my house, we chatted for a few minutes more.

"See you tomorrow," Eleni called out, as she walked on to her own house.

Ordinarily, I would have had something to eat before going to bed – some bread and cheese and maybe some cold watermelon – but on this night I went straight to my room. I could not shake off my sense of unease, about meeting Paul in a public place.

I wanted to write to Paul and tell him about the custom of the 'arranged marriage'. But how should I do it? Then I had a thought.

"Dear Paul," I began.

"The other day, you asked me to explain to you the system of the 'arranged marriage'. I will tell you about the day my eldest sister Sara received her first proposal of marriage – exactly as it happened. So, here goes.

The custom of the 'arranged marriage' is still the norm in Armenian culture. Girls are not allowed to choose their own husbands. This is how it happened with my sister Sara.

One Friday afternoon, my brother Marko and I came home from school to find that our Auntie Roza (Mother's only sister) had come from Nicosia to pay us a visit. As soon as we opened the front door, we heard her infectious laughter.

'Wait a minute,' I said to Marko. 'Why has Auntie come to visit us on a Friday?' Why indeed. Auntie Roza knew that Friday was Mother's washday and that she would be tired and not in a very receptive mood. Marko and I exchanged glances. Something must be up!

We all adored Auntie Roza; her energy, her vitality and her endless capacity for entertaining gossip. She was like a cool breeze on a hot and sultry day. Grandmother, Mother and Sara were sitting in the 'little salon' – our informal sitting room – having coffee and listening intently to Auntie. She was sitting in our most comfortable armchair, her feet resting on a stool, a coffee cup in one hand and a cigarette in the other. (I hope you get the picture.) Auntie Roza was a modern lady. Not only did she smoke, she even had a drink of ouzo or brandy now and again – for medicinal purpose of course – whereas Mother always stuck to coffee.

How could two sisters be so different? They were opposites in every way. While Mother was quiet, thoughtful and serious, Auntie was cheerful, vivacious and always optimistic. They were different in appearance too. Mother was dark, with dark brown melancholy eyes and she wore her long, silky brown hair plaited in a severe chignon. As a child I loved to watch her plaiting it, her short, work-worn fingers working with practiced skill, without even looking in the mirror. Auntie was fair with hazel eyes dancing with mischief. Her hair was light brown, with hints of red in it and she wore it short, in a soft bun with little tendrils curling around her face.

Auntie Roza could also 'read' coffee cups. Even though she always said the same things – good fortune, a letter of great significance, a long journey, an offer of marriage or the mysterious visitor from abroad – we listened open-mouthed to each and every prediction.

At this point, I must tell you Paul, that in order to have one's fortune told by the coffee cup, it is necessary to follow a procedure. When you finish drinking the coffee, you must swirl the cup three times, making a secret wish. Then you turn the cup over onto the saucer and leave it to dry for a few minutes. Only then, the 'reader of the cup' begins the fortune telling.

I hope you got that!

On this day, Auntie Roza began to read Sara's cup with more interest than usual. Taking the cup in her hand, she looked for the hidden patterns within.

'Yes! Today, there is definitely the sign of a betrothal in this cup,' she said importantly.

'About time too,' came from Grandmother.

'Heh!' and raised eyebrows came from Mother, who did not believe in coffee cups or fortune-tellers of any kind, and dismissed them as a waste of time. Auntie was unperturbed by her sister's disapproval.

'Sister, if you don't hurry up and marry your daughters off soon, you will end up with spinsters on your hands.'

'It is true that I have three girls of marriageable age, but you can't hurry these things,' explained Mother patiently, and not for the first time.

'But don't you think it is time Sara got married? Unless she gets married first, the others don't stand a chance.'

'You know my views about marriage, Sister. Every girl's destiny is preordained. When the time comes – God willing – my Sara will get married.' But this time, the conversation did not end there. Auntie Roza made a show of looking even deeper into Sara's cup, before replacing it, with its saucer, on the table.

'Well!' she paused for dramatic effect before continuing. 'My dear Sister, providence has knocked on your door. There is a proposal of marriage for Sara. That is why I am here today.' Everyone was quiet, transfixed by this announcement. Grandmother was the first to recover.

'Who is this suitor, Roza? Do we know the family?'

'Oh yes, Mama,' Auntie Roza answered. 'We know these people from way back. We were in quarantine with them, when we escaped from Adana. Don't you remember Victoria and Mikael?'

'You mean the suitor is Victoria's son?'

'That's right, they are my neighbours. They are asking for Sara's hand in marriage for their son Vahram.'

'God be praised!' Grandmother said and wiped her eyes with her black-edged handkerchief, which she held in her hand at all times. 'He was about four years old when we were in quarantine. I can't believe he is old enough to get married...'

'I know Mama. All the children of that time are adults now. Where have the years gone, eh?' I stole a look at Sara. They were talking about her as though she was not in the room. Yet it was her future they were discussing! Sara was listening to what was being said. Her eyes were misty and her face flushed. I wondered what she was thinking.

'But the family is not well off,' Grandmother said, her memory restored. 'As far as I know, Mikael has no gumption, no ambition to do well. And the house they live in…"' Her words drifted in the air.

'I know the family is not rich, Mama, but the boy is educated. He went to the English School on a scholarship, so he must be clever. He is good looking and he has a good job. Victoria said his salary is not much at the moment, but he has good prospects of promotion.' Auntie Roza stopped and waited for some kind of reaction from Mother.

'We'll think about it,' said Mother at last, in a matter of fact voice. 'Artin will make some inquiries. After all, the decision lies with him.' With this brief announcement, Mother left the room and went into the kitchen. By the time Father, Lillie and Nonnie came home, the table was set and the meal ready. It was one of Mother's 'light' suppers. There was a mountain of toasted bread, a selection of olives, a huge plate of sliced tomatoes and cucumbers, a plate of thinly sliced *Basderma* (which is similar to pastrami), a plate of the spicy beef sausages called *Yershig* and of course, a giant pot of sweet cinnamon and clove tea.

After our satisfying feast of a meal, Marko and I reluctantly left the dining room and busied ourselves with homework. We could hardly contain our curiosity. Would there really be an engagement soon? What would Father's decision be?

'But if Sara gets married, she will leave us, won't she?' Marko worshipped Sara. He would miss her very much. So would I for that matter. She was like a second mother to us both - especially on Fridays which was Mother's washday.

On Fridays, Mother would get up very early and take herself to the washroom to do the weekly washing. Father's offers to buy a washing machine fell on deaf ears. Consequently, she would not emerge from the washroom until the early afternoon. As a result of this Friday regime, our orderly and pleasant existence would have turned into chaos, if Sara hadn't taken over as 'mother'. She prepared our breakfast and made sure that we went off to school properly dressed and on time. When we came home for lunch, Sara would have prepared a meal for us. Admittedly, it wasn't much. We either had leftovers, haricot bean salad or lentil soup, but we were grateful for it nevertheless. Yes, we would definitely miss Sara if she got married. We tried to be very quiet, so we could hear what was being discussed in the dining room. Suddenly we heard raised voices.

'What! The boy earns five pounds a month? Ridiculous, I spend more than that on my cigarettes. No. This proposal of marriage is unacceptable. My Sara deserves better.' Father had spoken. That was the end of it. The subject was not mentioned again. But neither did it go away. Because, the coffee cup triumphed!

The betrothal, which Auntie Roza had 'seen' so clearly in Sara's cup some months before, came to pass. I never found out exactly how it happened, but Father was persuaded to give his consent to the proposal. No doubt, it was Auntie Roza's constant reminders that Lillie and then Nonnie could not even hope to be married until Sara was settled, that finally clinched the deal. Grandmother declared that it was *Kismet* (that word again) and no one should go against it."

That does it, I thought, and wondered how Paul would react to my letter. I won't be surprised, nor will I blame him, if he changes his mind about asking me out, I told myself. I wouldn't be upset; I was happy just to see him during my coffee break and talk to him. Tomorrow was Monday. My spirits lifted. I would see Paul again, after the long weekend.

Chapter Eight

My rendezvous with Paul took place on a Wednesday afternoon. It was a boiling hot day. A light, salty breeze wafted in off the sea, but it did nothing to relieve the heat. I sat on the sand, under the shade of an umbrella, waiting for Paul. I gave up pretending to read my film magazine. I felt nervous at the prospect of meeting Paul in such a public place. As Eleni had pointed out, we had never seen any one I knew on our regular outings here, but nevertheless, I was taking a big risk.

I looked around me. Eleni and her friends were walking towards the sea. There were hardly any waves. A little further out to sea, there was a floating raft. Boys were diving from it, showing off their physiques and diving skills to the girls sitting on the shore.

A shadow fell across my vision and I looked up to see Paul standing in front of me, two bottles of Coca Cola in his hand.

"Hello Reya."

"Hello…" I said. I almost didn't recognize him without his uniform. He looked different in his swimming trunks. He sat down beside me and handed me one of the ice-cold bottles. We were shy at first. This was our first 'date'. Then, all at once, we started talking.

"What a lovely spot," said Paul. "I'm so glad you decided to meet me somewhere other than the work place. I've been so looking forward to it."

"I'm surprised that you wanted to meet me at all… after reading my last letter."

"I understand that we come from different cultures, but that doesn't stop me from wanting to get to know you better," he took a sip of his drink. As we talked, I looked at him properly. He was so handsome. His eyes were the blue colour of sapphire, warm and friendly. The Cyprus sun had given him a healthy tan and it suited him. His hair had glints of gold in it now. When he smiled, which he did often, his eyes crinkled at the corners. I was looking at the real Paul and I liked what I saw.

"We have such old-fashioned customs…"

"I like them all! Your Auntie Roza is a real character isn't she? I would love to meet her. Maybe one day, she will 'read' my coffee cup too."

"That is not possible," I said, shaking my head from side to side.

"If you believe in *kismet,* then you must also believe that everything is possible under the sun," he challenged.

"I wish that it was ..." I whispered, and gazed at the endless expanse of the sea. We were silent for a moment, reflecting on things.

We finished our drink. "Shall we go for a swim now?" Paul asked. "The water looks so inviting."

"Alright. But I better warn you, Paul, that I'm not a strong swimmer," I said. "I don't like to leave the safety of the shallows to swim in the deep waters." Paul looked at me with concern and let me continue. "I get a shiver down my spine, every time I look at the dark, sinister green depths." Paul nodded. He seemed to understand my fear.

"I'll look after you," he said. Standing up in one fluid movement, he took my hand and we walked into the sea.

"See that rock over there?" I said, pointing my finger in the direction of a group of rocks.

"Yes, it seems a very long way away. Why?"

"It is named the *gamila* – the camel. The two smaller rocks look like the humps of a camel!"

"Yes, I see what you mean."

"Many years ago, my father and his friend used to swim up to that rock and back. They were both strong swimmers. One day, when they were swimming back to the shore, the weather suddenly changed. The calm sea turned into a ferocious whirlpool. The waves were sky-high. It was getting dark. They struggled for hours, just to stay afloat. Just when they thought they would drown, they were saved by a huge wave that literally lifted them out of the water and threw them onto the shore." I took a deep breath. "It was nothing short of a miracle."

"What a dramatic escape. Do you believe in miracles?"

"Of course I do... Anyway, Father has not been anywhere near the sea since."

"Never?"

"Never. He said he acknowledged the superiority of the sea, preferring to gaze at its beauty and its power from a distance. We are very superstitious about the sea. When we were children, we were not allowed to swim in it after the 15th of August."

"Why on earth not?"

"I don't know exactly, but I think it is because the 15th of August is the

Feast Day of the Madonna. Mythology has it that the sea forbade it and anyone who disobeys will drown."

"That's a bit drastic!"

"It is, but every year after that date, a person somewhere in the island drowns in the sea. The sea must be avenged."

"Mmm. I'll keep that warning in mind."

"You had better," I said. "If you value your life."

"I won't let you drown," he said, teasing me. "We don't have to swim that far out. But we could swim to that little boat there, and then on to the next one further down. What do you say?" I agreed. I trusted him. We swam for a while in the warm shallows. The sea was crystal clear, little fish and sea shells of many sizes and shapes could be seen at the bottom of the sea. Then we walked along the seashore, the wavelets lapping at our feet. The sun was still hot and we returned to the welcome shade of our umbrella and sank down gratefully on the sand. We watched the pleasure boats drifting in the calm shallows.

"Is this where the American photographer took pictures of you and Eleni?"

"Yes. And over there, by the raft."

"Did he send you a copy of the magazine?"

"No, we never heard from him. Eleni and I talked of nothing else but our 'modelling experience', for days on end. It is rather disappointing."

"That's a shame. I would have liked to see the magazine with your pictures in it. He might still send them to you."

"He might. And that's the hotel where he took us to tea."

"Shall we have a drink there?" I nodded, happy to have spent a few hours with him. Happier still, at the prospect of spending more time with him again. But the afternoon was waning. I couldn't see Eleni or her friends anywhere. They had gone home.

"Maybe some other time, Paul. It's getting late, we should be thinking of going…" I couldn't finish the sentence. The look in his eyes mirrored my thoughts. We were both reluctant to end the afternoon.

"Please stay a bit longer," he pleaded. "We'll have a cold drink and then head for home." We quickly got dressed and walked to the nearest café. I had a glass of lemonade and Paul drank a bottle of ice-cold *Keo* beer.

The sun was setting when we said our good-byes. "Thank you for a lovely afternoon," Paul said. He took my hand and held it in both of his.

"I enjoyed it too," I replied. Then, reluctantly, he let go of my hand. I watched him walk away before I turned left and started to walk home.

As soon as I opened the front door, I heard a babble of voices coming from the 'formal' sitting room. This room was only used when visitors came. I heard Father's voice among them. He must have been summoned from the coffee shop. I wondered if there was a proposal of marriage for Lillie. Something was definitely up. Father did not interrupt his game of cards or backgammon for nothing. Should I go in and find out? I still did not like entering a room full of people. Suddenly, the sitting room door opened and Nonnie came out, with our best silver tray in her hands. Her eyes were dancing with excitement.

"Guess what?" she breathed. "We are going to inherit three and a half million dollars!"

"Three and a half million dollars," I repeated, stupidly.

"Yes, yes and yes again!" She sang the words. "A cousin from Beirut is here to try and trace relatives of an old man who died in America recently. I can't stop now. I'm going to make some more coffee." The words came out fast and furious. I could hardly keep up with her. I followed her into the kitchen and absent-mindedly put my beach bag on the table. I watched Nonnie make the coffee.

"I don't want to miss any of the conversation," she said and carried the tray back to the living room. To my surprise, I didn't feel excited about the prospect of inheriting a fortune, but then I didn't really know much about it. I had other things on my mind. I put my swimming costume and towel out to dry, and went to my room. I lay on my bed and relived every moment that Paul and I had spent together, and every word that we had exchanged this afternoon.

I got the story out later. Nonnie told me that the doorbell had rung in the middle of their afternoon siesta. She had answered the door to find this divine creature standing on the doorstep.

"He is the most devastatingly handsome man I have even seen," she said.

"Really?" I said, open-mouthed.

"Yes, really. Tall and blond, with lovely green eyes!" I considered Nonnie's words for a moment, I was sure she was exaggerating as usual. Tall, good-looking Armenian boys were few and far between. I had never seen one, anyway. They were usually short, dark and hairy! Apart from Marko, of course, who was fairly tall, and looked a bit like Glen Ford – we girls thought so anyway. This heavenly creature had introduced himself as our second cousin once removed. He and his family lived in Beirut.

"Apparently we are related on Grandmother's side," Nonnie enthused.

"What's his name?" I asked.

"His name is Dickran. You should have seen him…"

"Who is the rich old man who died, then?"

"He is a relative of Grandmother's, a cousin or something. I don't yet know the exact relationship."

"Oh, I see."

"Anyway, this rich old man left Adana just before the 1915 massacres and went to Chicago, where he made his fabulous fortune. No one had heard from him for years and years. His lawyers are now searching for his relatives, who will inherit his vast fortune."

"And Grandmother is one of them!"

"Precisely. Strangely enough, Grandmother remembered this 'cousin' after all these years. I know her physical health is deteriorating, but her mental agility and long-term memory is unbelievably good."

"She often talks nostalgically about her old life, doesn't she?"

"You should have seen her. She was remembering everything! And Dickran was taking down everything she said in his notebook – names, dates and places of long ago."

"Why did he leave so soon? Didn't Mother ask him to stay to supper?"

"Of course she did. He couldn't stay, because he is going to Athens early tomorrow morning, to talk to one more person on his list."

There was pandemonium as soon as our cousin took his leave. Everybody started talking at once. "Imagine inheriting millions of dollars!" Lillie said. "It's an incredibly vast sum of money."

"But the question is, how many are to share this great fortune?" asked Marko to no one in particular.

"Grandmother, do you know?" came from Nonnie. Grandmother shook her head. She had been asked too many questions in a short space of time. She seemed confused. In the end she refused to talk about it. She wasn't in the least bit interested in fortunes – large or small. To relive the past was enough for her.

"I should think there is enough money for an army!" Father said. He always saw the funny side of things. "I think we should decide how to spend our share of this fortune." This suggestion instantly fired everyone's imagination.

"I know," Father began. "We shall build the most beautiful house in Cyprus – right by the sea. It will have acres of garden and I shall grow all kinds of exotic fruits, not to mention the grape vine which will in time cover the whole house!"

"I think we should build the house up in the hills, Father," suggested Nonnie. "We can spend the long summers there."

"We could build it on a pine-clad hill…"

"With a breathtaking view of the valley and the village below…"

"The house must have a name. Why not *Tara* or *Manderley*?"

"No, something more original. How about *Lemonia*?"

It was unclear to know who was saying what. In the end we agreed on *Lemonia*. After all we all loved the taste of lemons. We used them a lot in our cooking. Yes, the house would be surrounded by hundreds of lemon trees. We could almost smell the lemon blossom. Mother, who had been listening quietly to our conversation, spoke up. "You are a selfish lot," she said. "Not one of you suggested we should build a church and a school for the Armenian community in Famagusta." We were shocked into silence. Mother was right. Her suggestion was perfect. We did not have a church of our own. Father realized his mistake but he recovered quickly. "Of course we shall build a church and a school, that goes without saying," he replied. "What's more, Siran, we shall have a resident priest!"

Chapter Nine

To say that I was feeling euphoric was an understatement. Paul and I had such a wonderful time on the beach that we decided to meet again. Everything had gone so smoothly. I had seen no one I knew. Thus emboldened, I felt quite confident to continue seeing Paul. And here I was, on the same beach for the second time in as many weeks, sitting under an umbrella, waiting for Paul. Just then I saw him and waved my arms. He walked over and sank down on the sand beside me.

"I'm sorry I'm late, I was detained at the last moment," he said, breathlessly. "Unfortunately, I have to get back to camp earlier than I had planned." I saw the disappointment in his face.

"That's alright, I'm glad you could come at all," I said, hiding my own disappointment. "I'm sorry I haven't answered your letter yet. But in answer to your question, yes, I would love to visit England one day."

"I'm sure you would like Surrey..."

"My sisters have been to England, you know. They somehow persuaded my parents to let them go to London for the coronation of the Queen."

"Surrey is not like London at all. Did your sisters have a good time?"

"They did. They said it was the experience of a lifetime, but they couldn't live there, as it was raining all the time. It was so cold that they had to have hot water bottles every night, and this was in June!"

"Yes, the English summer can be wet and cold, but the countryside is always green and lush. England in springtime is the most beautiful place in the world. The forget-me-nots, the daffodils, the tulips are a sight to see."

"I like the spring too, but most of all I love the spring flowers that grow abundantly in the fields. They are called *Antaram* in Armenian."

"I've never heard of those. What kind of flowers are they?"

"They come in white, pink, blue, yellow and other colours. They keep their colour even when they are dried. They are called *Antaram* because they never fade or die, in the same way that memories never fade or die. When I was a child, I used to pick handfuls of them from the fields and put them all over my room."

"*Antaram*," said Paul slowly. "It has a lovely sound to it. Something that doesn't fade or die, what a beautiful word. Will you teach me a few Armenian words?"

"If you really want to…" I couldn't help smiling. "Armenian is a difficult language to learn. Not least the pronunciation… but if you want to have a go at it."

"I do. Let's start with an easy word, shall we?"

"An easy word… Let's see. What about *parev* – which means 'good afternoon'."

"That *is* easy. *Parev, Parev* Reya!" Paul said, well pleased with himself. "Give me another."

"*Avaz* – sand, and *arev* – sun."

"*Avaz, arev* ," Paul repeated after me. This time he was jubilant. "More, more…"

"I think three words are enough for today," I said, in my best 'teacher's' voice. "I'll test you tomorrow, to see if you will remember them."

"I promise you, I will. But this is thirsty work. I'll walk over to that café we went to the other day, and get us some cold drinks."

While I was waiting for Paul, I realized just how much I liked him, how much I enjoyed his company. I shook my head in wonder. Apart from my beloved Dai, Paul was the only person I was completely at ease with. My reverie was interrupted. I heard a voice and looking up, I saw, to my utter dismay – Marko, standing silhouetted against the sky.

My breathing stopped in my chest. What was he doing here? He always went to the Alasia beach, never to this part of the bay. I took off my sunglasses, in an effort to cover my rising sense of panic.

"What are you doing here, on your own?" he asked suspiciously.

"I'm waiting for Eleni," I lied. I closed my eyes, invoking the Madonna and all the saints to come to my rescue. "She said she would be late," I added for emphasis. I looked around to see if Paul was anywhere near, but mercifully he was nowhere to be seen. The saints must have heard me.

Marko said nothing more and, with a wave of his hand, he hurried off to catch up with his friends. The moment of danger had passed, but I was so shaken by the incident that I felt frozen inside. If Marko had walked by a few minutes before, he would have caught me with Paul, and the consequences of that would have been unthinkable. I was upset for another reason too. Marko and I had been so close, when we were children. We were still close, but no longer on an equal footing. He was a man and he could do more or less what he liked, whereas I - a mere female - had to live within the restrictions of Armenian social convention. How sad that I could not confide in him.

I don't know why, but I started to put my things in my beach-bag. Just then Paul appeared. I told him what had just happened. "Drink this," he said calmly, handing me a bottle of ice-cold lemonade. He listened to what I had to say, with a look of resignation on his face. "I'm so sorry. Do you think he might come back?"

I shrugged my shoulders. "I don't know," I said. All I knew was that our afternoon was ruined. "I should go home now."

"Finish your drink first. It's strange. A few short months ago, I would have thought it weird and incredibly funny that Armenian girls were not allowed to be seen talking to boys. But now, I understand and accept the huge differences between our cultures – our worlds."

"Do you?"

"Yes. I understand that something as innocent as our meeting on the beach is taboo in your society, whereas it is perfectly acceptable in England."

"Maybe we should not see each other again…"

"No! Don't say that!" I was surprised by the intensity in his voice. "Why don't we walk towards the Constantia beach?" He saw the reluctance on my face. "Please – I have something important to tell you." With that, we walked towards the Constantia beach. Paul stopped when the magnificent hotel came into view, with its huge, multi-coloured umbrellas swaying in the sea breeze. I thought he had stopped to admire the stunning setting of the hotel overlooking a group of huge rocks and the sapphire blue sea beyond. Instead, he dropped my beach-bag onto the soft sand and took me in his arms. I felt something like an electric shock the moment he touched me. "I love you," he whispered and held me for what seemed a second and yet an eternity.

To my surprise, I didn't pull away from him. "I love you too," I murmured. The words came out of my mouth independently. They echoed joyously in my mind. Paul tightened his arms around me. "I love you," he repeated. "Will you marry me?"

After what seemed like an interminable silence, I looked at Paul with sorrowful eyes. "How can I? My parents…"

"I will find a way. I shall work my special magic on your parents. They won't be able to resist me!"

"You will have to use sign-language!" I said, and pictured the scene: Mother and Father, not forgetting Grandmother, sitting in the 'little salon' with Paul facing them. The tableau I envisaged was so comical that I burst out laughing.

"I think I'll manage perfectly well with sign-language, and the three Armenian words I already know," he said and laughed - catching my mood. We did not swim, but talked and talked. Paul, making plans for the future; and I, willing them to be true. At last, we stopped talking and watched the huge red sun disappearing into the sea, like Apollo's chariot.

It was here, on this tranquil shore of the bay, that Paul gave me my first kiss.

Chapter Ten

I seemed to be living a double life. One was the day-to-day routine of work and home, and the other, my friendship with Paul, which had been conducted in secrecy, except for Eleni. But when this friendship blossomed into love, I felt that I had to confide in someone within the family. Nonnie was the only sister I could talk to. The gap between our ages didn't seem so big now.

Nonnie worked in a shipping company as a clerk. There was a newly opened coffee bar just around the corner from where she worked, and that's where we agreed to meet. This coffee bar was the only one of its kind in Famagusta. It was called *The Milk Bar* and was owned by a Greek man called Chris, who had lived in England for some years. The running of the bar was more of a hobby than a business for Chris. He was a very friendly man and it soon became a popular place for young people to meet.

Nonnie and I sat at a table by the window, and sipped our milk shakes. This was the first serious conversation I had ever had with her. When I told her about my friendship with Paul, her reaction was surprise and then disbelief. She had been so preoccupied with her own life that she had not realized that I had grown up and was no longer invisible.

I looked at Nonnie across the table. She was so much like our Auntie Roza. Pretty, charming, with deep-set hazel eyes and short dark hair. Boys were attracted to her like the proverbial moths to the flame.

"It's alright to talk and flirt with boys, to go out on harmless 'dates' with them," she began. "As long as nobody finds out. But anything more serious than that is asking for trouble."

"Like what?" I wanted to know.

"Well, like falling in love or allowing any kind of physical contact. It would be utterly wrong, Reya. You haven't fallen in love with this Corporal, have you?" Before I could say anything, she went on; "I'm just telling you to be careful – that's all. Can you imagine what would happen, if Mother ever found out that you were seen out with a boy – and not just any boy – an English soldier, for heaven's sake?"

"But you talk to boys…"

"Yes, I talk to boys. In my work, I have the opportunity to meet them. I might go out with them a couple of times, but I don't fall in love with them. It's just a bit of fun, some excitement, that's all."

"The other day, you said your latest conquest was a Canadian naval officer…"

"I met him here - twice - for a coffee, that's all. Falling in love is all very well in the movies – but it's not for us Reya. It's difficult, I know, when your head is full of romantic stories, but there's no place for those ideas in our culture." Nonnie was clever and outgoing. She wanted to try everything, and usually found a way to do it. She even broke a few of the taboos and got away with it – smoking (secretly of course) being one of them. I had been so sure that she would be sympathetic. Now I didn't know what to think.

"I know you, Reya, you're not like me. You're much more serious." I had to admit it. I was not like her. I admired her, but never wanted to emulate her.

"It's true, Nonnie – I am in love with Paul – and he wants to marry me."

"Reya - listen to yourself! I understand you - of course I do. But this kind of love is an English notion - an American… belief. What would Mother - or Father - think, if you told them you were 'in love', eh? 'In love' with an English soldier, eh? Do I have to spell it out for you - they would think you were having an illicit relationship with this soldier. As far as they are concerned, marriage is something that is arranged between families - it's not a question of romantic proposals."

"But things are changing. One day…"

"Nothing will change. Take it from me, say goodbye to your soldier and forget about him."

"So, when your turn comes, you will follow Sara's example and marry the man our parents have chosen for you."

"You know, as well as I do, that girls of our generation have a pattern to follow in life, like the generations before."

"Yes, to marry a nice Armenian man - preferably rich - get married, have children and live happily ever after, in a comfortable house, of course," I said with a touch of sarcasm. "Is that what you want to do?"

"Yes, that is exactly what I will do, when the time comes. In the meantime, I want to enjoy myself." I had often wondered what falling in love would really be like - and now I was beginning to find out.

"But I love Paul. I'm so happy I could fly…" I stopped, unable to finish the sentence. The look on her face told me I had said too much.

Nonnie shook her head, disappointed that I did not share her views. She said: "Come down to earth, little sister, before you burn your wings."

There was no time to dwell on what Nonnie had said to me. Right after supper, our cousin Dickran appeared on our door-step again. I had a good look at him this time. Nonnie had not been exaggerating, for once. He was Adonis personified. He was charming too. The way he talked made you feel that he was the only one who could make this 'inheritance' happen. Grandmother was ill in bed with a bad cold and cough. Dickran spent an hour by her bedside, taking down more information in his notebook.

"I think I have all the information I need," he said. "I've seen every one on my list. God willing it won't be too long before I hear from the lawyers in Chicago."

"How many people did you have on your list?" asked Marko. This had been the burning question that every one of us had been asking.

"I have seen eighteen people I could trace," he answered with a smile. "But of course, I can't be sure that they are all eligible for a share of the 'inheritance'."

"Time will tell," said Father. "You are doing a good job, my boy. I hope you will be well rewarded for it."

"I'm doing my best," he said graciously. "You must come to see me and the family, next time any of you visit Beirut. Our house is not far from where your sister Mareyam lives."

"Thank you, we certainly will, by boy." With that, he finished his coffee, and he was gone.

"I was beginning to think of this whole 'inheritance' thing as a joke," said Father. "But now, after this second visit, I've begun to think that there might be something in it for us, after all." Our imagination was fired anew. Pen and paper was called for: serious accounting was needed. It wasn't easy to divide millions of dollars into eighteen. "Whichever way you look at it, children, it's not a fortune to joke about," Father said finally.

I don't think any of us slept well that night.

When four weeks passed and there was no word from our cousin Dickran, Marko came up with a brilliant idea. "Why don't I go to Beirut, Father, visit Auntie Mareyam and also look up Dickran…"

"I can go with Marko, and together, we can find out about the 'inheritance'!" squeaked Nonnie. She couldn't fool me. I knew why she wanted to go — it was to see 'Adonis' again! Father scratched his head absentmindedly, which meant he was thinking. "I suppose you could go: visit with your Auntie Mareyam and get acquainted with your cousins," he said.

Nonnie clapped her hands happily. But her joy was short-lived. Mother, who had been silent all this time, spoke up. "You've been abroad, Nonnie, but Reya hasn't. I think she should go with Marko, this time." I couldn't believe my ears. "Oh, I would love to go Mother," I cried, too excited to say anything else. "It's settled then, I'll make all the arrangements," said Marko.

On the way to work the next morning, I told Eleni about the prospect of my going to Beirut. "That will be an experience for you. You've never been abroad, have you?"

"No, I haven't," I said. It seemed everybody in Cyprus had been abroad, except me. "But there is a problem. We are so busy at the office… I doubt if Mr. Eastman will let me take four days of my annual leave."

"I'm sure he will. He likes you, *gori*. Use your charm, for heaven's sake!" But even with Eleni's encouragement, it took me some time to gather enough courage to broach the subject with Mr. Eastman. The other thing was that I wouldn't see Paul for four whole days.

"You know how busy we are, Reya," Mr. Eastman said, taking off his glasses and raising his eyebrows, quizzically. "We might have to work overtime."

"I know Mr. Eastman, but this is a trip abroad! My very first trip abroad," I pleaded.

"Hmm… It's a bit awkward, my dear. Supposing everyone else in the office did the same. Where would we be then, eh?" He began to shuffle through the pile of papers on his desk. I shifted from one foot to the other, watching him intently — at last, he looked up.

"Where are you planning to go, anyway?"

"Beirut! I have an aunt there and two cousins. I've never seen my cousins before. Please say yes, Mr. Eastman."

"Alright then, Reya. I'll let you off this time. But don't make a habit of it, will you?"

"Thanks a million, Mr. Eastman," I said, unable to hide my relief. "I shall bring you *Paklava* from Beirut. It's a delicious, sweet pastry." He grinned and went back to his papers. I rushed out to tell Paul my news. I wondered how he would take it.

"I'm happy for you, *sirelis,*" Paul said, with the perfect pronunciation of the Armenian word – 'my loved one'. I had taught him about a dozen words and he could remember every one of them. "Four days, eh? I shall miss you terribly."

"I shall miss you too..."

"You can write and tell me all about it. I have something to ask you. I had a letter from Mum. She would like to have a photo of you..."

"What! Have you written to your parents about me?"

"Of course I have. They want to see the beautiful girl I'm going to marry," he whispered in my ear.

"I'll see what I can do," I blurted out, blushing a deep red. I was silent for a moment, staring into space. Nobody had called me 'beautiful' before. I thought I was the ugly duckling, forever waiting to turn into a swan.

"Are you flying to Beirut, or going by boat?"

"Flying. It will be my first time."

"You'll enjoy it. I shall write you long letters while you're away. I shall also help my Sergeant in his garden, it's in a terrible mess. So you see, I shall be very busy." I smiled my thanks. He really did want me to enjoy my first ever trip abroad.

It was so wonderful to see Auntie Mareyam again and meet our two cousins – Toros and Vartan. Toros was the older of the two brothers, and he undertook to show us the sights of Beirut, while Vartan minded their shoe shop. They lived in Bourdj-Hamoud – a suburb of Beirut.

"Bourdj-Hamoud is like a little Armenia," Toros explained. "Many Armenians who survived the Turkish massacres fled here, and over the years they formed a big Armenian community. Many of these people were destitute, but they worked hard and in time it became the bustling town it is today. It thrives with commerce – attracting people from all over Beirut." We were surprised to hear Armenian being spoken in the streets. We were more surprised to see the streets named after the names of towns where they had once lived.

"Look! Adana Street," said Marko. "The place where our parents came from!" It was unbelievable. There were more surprises. In the Armenian neighbourhoods, the shop signs were written in Armenian, with Arabic translations, in smaller letters, underneath. What's more, there were Armenian doctors, dentists, butchers and tailors. We went into several bookshops where Armenian newspapers, magazines and books stood side by side with Arabic and French publications.

"You both look so overwhelmed with the presence of so many Armenian industries," beamed Toros. "We even have a football team. Come on, I'll take you to a coffee shop: both the owner and the waiters are Armenian!" The coffee shop was exactly like a Greek coffee shop – smoke filled, noisy and a male domain. "Hello Garo, my friend," Toros said to the owner.

"Hello Toros. Your cousins from Cyprus have arrived then."

"Yes, they arrived yesterday. Three coffees to take: one with sugar, two without." While we waited for the coffees, the men talked. "Here we are, three coffees – on the house," said the owner, with a flourish . One could feel the camaraderie that existed between the shopkeepers. We thanked him and Toros picked up the tray and we started to walk the short distance to his shoe shop. The shop sign read: *Fashion Shoes by Toros*. It was very much like the dozens of other shoe shops in the vicinity. The smell of leather hit my nostrils, as soon as we entered the shop.

"Do you like the shoes?" Toros asked. "These are the latest fashion."

"Very much so," I said, surveying the hundreds of pairs of shoes that came in many different designs and colours.

"Please try the ones you like, you too Marko. It will give me so much pleasure if you would accept them as a small gift from us." I felt shy and embarrassed, but both brothers insisted. In the end, Marko opted for a pair of sandals, and I chose a pair of bright red 'ballet' shoes. "What about a matching hand bag?" Vartan said and showed me the matching shoulder bag. I refused but he insisted. "I think you liked this black belt," he said, and put it in a big paper carrier bag, together with the rest of the stuff.

The next day, Toros took us to the gold market. "Here also, most of the goldsmiths are Armenian," he said with pride. Whole streets were taken up with jewellery shops. I had never seen so much gold in my life. Every shop displayed an unimaginable array of gold, silver, diamonds and other precious stones. Some were so ostentatious, that I wondered who would possibly wear them, while others were so expensive, that I would not dare enter the shop. Toros took us to a small shop in one of the side streets. The goldsmith was a friend of his.

"He will give you a good price, if you want to buy anything," he said to me. I certainly wanted to buy something, but what? I was spoilt for choice. We entered the shop and Toros introduced us to the goldsmith.

"My cousins from Cyprus – look after them, Levon." It was like entering a golden cave. I was dazzled by all the gold and diamonds. Everything glittered and sparkled like the rays of the sun. After much deliberation, I bought a tiny but exquisite gold cross and heart on a thin chain, all in twenty-two carat gold, of course. "Good choice," the goldsmith said as he put it round my neck.

On our last day, Toros took us and Auntie Mareyam to Wadi, a resort up on the hills. We had lunch at a restaurant, perched on a hill overlooking the town below. It was our first real taste of Lebanese food. We had *meze*. The waiter brought more than twenty-five varieties of food in small dishes. Marko and I looked at each other. "Cyprus is renowned for *meze*, but this is something else," he said. "We shall not forget this magnificent feast in a hurry."

"Well, how did you like Lebanon?" Toros asked, when we were having coffee. "How does it compare with Cyprus?"

"Cyprus is so quiet, so 'tame', compared to the colour, the noise, the vibrant hustle and bustle of Beirut," Marko said. "I feel so proud that the Armenians in Beirut have not only integrated with the existing community, but they have also built a reputation as sound business people."

"And we are well respected for it. We also live in harmony with the Lebanese.

"And what did you most like about our city, my sweet?" Auntie asked me.

"I liked the shops and the markets, Auntie. But most of all I loved the food and the sweet pastries. Such a variety…"

"You have such a sweet tooth, just like your father," she said, her face creasing into a smile.

"It's strange, how are lives turned out to be so different. You had to learn Greek and English in order to survive, while we had to learn Arabic and French," Toros said.

"I've said this before and I'll say it again – Fate has mysterious ways of shaping our lives," said Auntie.

"I'm sorry, Marko, that we couldn't get hold of Dickran," Toros said. "It seems that he is still in Chicago. That boy is trying very hard to sort out the old gentleman's will. I do hope you get a share of the fortune."

"We shall all benefit from it, if we do," Marko said.

Fortunes were not uppermost in my mind. I was more interested to know how Fate was planning to shape my life. I missed Paul. I couldn't wait to see him. There was so much to tell him.

Chapter Eleven

The weather was changing. The heat of the summer had faded; autumn was here. The swimming season was over for another year. For some reason I was feeling pleased with myself. Maybe because I was wearing my red 'ballet' shoes for the first time, with the matching handbag hanging over my shoulder. Or, maybe because Mr. Eastman had the day off, and I could spend a few extra minutes with Paul.

"I couldn't sleep last night," Eleni said suddenly. We stopped walking.

"What is it?" I asked. She looked flushed. "Do you feel ill?"

"No, *gori*. My uncle, you know – the one who works in the Justice Department in Nicosia – he telephoned my father last night, to say that there will be a vacancy for an experienced secretary for one of the lawyers there!" she declared breathlessly.

I had a sense of foreboding, but I dismissed it and forced myself to look pleased and excited. "Really? Tell me more. Are you going to apply for the job?"

"Oh yes. It's an opportunity I cannot miss. My uncle is posting me the application form. The present secretary is having a baby and she is leaving at the end of January."

"Isn't it a bit early to apply now?"

"Not really. It's less than three months away. My uncle said to apply as soon as possible."

"Good luck. I'm sure you'll get the job." I would be happy if Eleni got the job. But that would mean that she would have to leave Famagusta, and me.

The morning dragged. At last it was time for my break. I took a last sip of my coffee and went out to the yard to meet Paul.

I was early. If Eleni got the job in Nicosia, I would lose my only good friend. I got on with Anastasia – the other girl in the office – but I didn't communicate with her after office hours. I was so deep in thought that I didn't see Paul walking towards me.

"Penny for them?" he asked.

"Eleni is applying for a job in Nicosia…"

"Oh. You'll miss her, won't you?"

I nodded. I noticed that Paul didn't look his usual happy self somehow.

"What's wrong?" I asked. He lit a cigarette and inhaled it deeply, before he answered.

"I received my Demob. papers yesterday."

"Oh no! When…?"

"In six weeks' time." His voice sounded like a sort of strangulated croak.

Even though I knew he would be leaving Cyprus at the end of the year, it was still a shock to hear that it would be so soon. Six weeks. A million disconnected thoughts ran through my mind. Was this the end of our romance? The sense of well-being I had woken up with evaporated. First Eleni, and now Paul. A feeling of desolation swept over me.

"What are we going to do?" I asked. The words sounded so hollow and hopeless.

"I can't tell you how sad I am at the thought of parting from you, but I know one thing. My feelings towards you will never change. I will find a way."

"But how?" I couldn't see a way for us to be together.

"I don't know how. But as long as we love each other, I *will* find a way." He paused to light another cigarette, his hand shaking slightly. "I promise you I will come back for you." I was silent. "If you will wait for me."

"I will," I said. That was one thing I could promise him. I would wait for years, if need be. I wasn't going anywhere. There was no one else. "Of course I'll wait for you," I repeated.

"I knew you would!" he said, and his face brightened perceptively. He was the optimist: forward thinking and positive. "I must see you before I leave – somewhere other than here. Somewhere private, so we can talk."

"Where?"

"I'll ask my Sergeant if we can meet in his house."

"He might not agree…"

"Will you come?"

"I'll come."

I woke up to the tinkling sounds coming from the kitchen. It was a typical Sunday morning. Mother didn't cook on Sundays – it was a 'holiday' from the kitchen for her. She only prepared the lamb and the potatoes in the oven tray, which Marko took to the baker's oven to be roasted. Sunday was a 'free day' for the rest of us. We got up when we liked, had breakfast when we liked. If I go back to sleep for a couple of hours, it will make the morning go faster, I thought. I turned over and closed my eyes, but sleep would not come. I was too worked up. I was meeting Paul this afternoon – our last meeting before he went home.

Paul's Company Sergeant had kindly let us meet in his house. The living quarters of the Army Personnel were situated about four miles outside Famagusta. It was an estate of two-storey brick built houses with pleasant gardens. How was I to get there? Too far to walk – too risky to even consider a taxi.

Eleni had come to my rescue. "I'll take you *gori*," she had said in her breezy way. "I'll borrow Father's car like I usually do on a Sunday. What time are you meeting him?"

"About half past two. I told Paul I would leave about five. Will it be alright?"

"Of course it will. I'll drop you off, and then I'll pick you up at five. We can go to *Delice* afterwards, and then to the cinema, as usual."

Here I was now, in a strange state of mind. Happy to be seeing Paul for a whole afternoon, yet sad and miserable, because God only knew when I would see him again. The last six weeks had whizzed by. But now time passed very slowly. It seemed ages before it was time for Marko to bring the roast from the bakery. The meal itself was interminable. I normally loved Sundays, when the whole family sat down to a leisurely lunch, but not on this day. I hardly tasted the tender lamb and the potatoes cooked in the meat juices. At last the meal was over, the washing-up done, the kitchen tidied. Father went to the coffee-shop, Marko to a football match and the women sat on the sunny verandah with their coffee, to enjoy the rest of the afternoon.

I looked in the mirror one last time, pleased with my outfit: pleated black skirt, pink knitted blouse and matching cardigan, black patent shoes and handbag. I wore my gold chain with the cross and heart, and my gold earrings – a christening gift from Dai. My newly washed hair shone. A touch of lipstick completed the picture. I so wanted to look nice for Paul.

At last it was time to go. "I'm going over to Eleni's house," I said over my shoulder. "We're going for a drive…"

"Let's have a look at you," piped up Nonnie. "Is that your new skirt?"

"You're looking very nice," came from Mother. "That rose colour suits you. But why are you in such a hurry to go out?"

"Eleni is waiting for me," I said, my heart racing. Lies came so easily to my lips now. I caught Nonnie looking at me strangely. Did she suspect anything? I rushed out of the door, not caring. After today, I wouldn't be sneaking out, or telling lies.

Eleni was waiting for me. We were silent all the way to the Sergeant's house. "See you at five. Don't worry if you're a bit late," she said through the open window, and drove off.

I walked up to the front door, took a deep breath and rang the bell. Paul opened the door and smiled his wonderful smile.

"I'm so glad you came," he said and took my hand. He introduced me to the Sergeant and his wife. They had two lovely children – a boy of about five or six and a girl who looked about three. We chatted for a few minutes and then the family discreetly left us on our own. We sat in the living room, overlooking the garden. The weather was still warm. The fragrance of the sweet-scented jasmine wafted through the open window. The playful chatter of the children lapped gently around us.

"You look lovely," Paul said, sitting down beside me on the sofa. I tried to smile but blushed instead. I felt tongue tied. My stomach was churning. What could I say or do to make this meeting bearable? I said nothing.

"As soon as I'm demobbed, I'll get a job," Paul said. "I shall save every penny I earn. I reckon I can earn twenty pounds a week, if not more."

"You said your parents wanted you to go to college."

"I can go to evening school. When the conflict here ends – it is bound to be resolved one way or the other – I shall come for you." He made it sound so simple, so easy: a fairy tale with a happy ending. I nodded my head, not trusting my voice. I looked at Paul. There was a subtle change in him. A new self-assurance, a determination to bridge the chasm that separated us. "I shall write to you – long, very long letters – so you will know my thoughts, my day to day activities, my plans and the progress I shall be making."

"I will write to you too."

"When I've saved enough money – it won't be long – I shall come to Cyprus and we shall get married."

"But how will you persuade my parents to let me marry you?" I had to ask Paul this question. I wanted to remind him that the obstacles in our path were too great to overcome. I knew beyond any doubt that my parents would never entertain the notion of one of their daughters marrying a 'foreigner'. They would surely disown me. But he had it all worked out.

"I shall tell them the simple truth, of course. I shall tell them that we love each other and that we want to get married." He paused for a moment and then went on. "I shall also tell them that we could live here in Cyprus, if they want us to. It makes no difference to me where I live, as long as we are together." He was so optimistic, that for a pulse-beat, I let myself believe that there might be a glimmer of hope. That somehow, he might be able to find a way for us to be together.

We fell silent, lost in our thoughts. I noticed the beautiful crystal ashtray on the coffee table. Facets of the glass caught a ray of sunlight and split it into a rainbow of colours. I gazed at it, mesmerized. A gentle knock on the door broke the spell. The Sergeant's wife came into the room, carrying a tray. She put it down on the coffee table. On the tray were two cups of tea and a plate of chocolate biscuits.

"Please help yourselves," she said with a smile. She was about to leave, when the little boy charged in with his toy car. He wanted Paul to play with him. The boy looked at me curiously, but said nothing. Only after Paul promised to play with him later, was he persuaded to leave the room. I could see Paul loved children and how good he was with them.

We were on our own again. We sipped our tea and Paul absent-mindedly reached for a biscuit. I looked at the clock on the mantelpiece. It said a quarter to four. The time was speeding by. The ticking of the clock was the only sound in the room, each tick advancing the moment when we would have to say goodbye.

"Wouldn't it be lovely, if we could open the curtains of time and glimpse the future?" I said. Paul took my hand and pretended to read my palm.

"I can see our future, right here," he smiled. "I can see a long life together, a cottage in the country, two or maybe even three children! See, there are no obstacles in our path," he concluded with a flourish.

"You paint a pretty picture," I said, blushing at the mention of children. "But, sometimes palm readings, coffee-cup readings and premonitions do come true."

"If you say so, *sirelis*."

"I know you tease me about these things…"

"I don't really. Not everything is black or white, so I think of your 'Armenian superstitions' as grey."

"I'm glad you don't dismiss them outright. Because there is one thing that will sustain me when you've gone…"

"What is that sweetheart?"

"Promise me you won't laugh?"

"I promise."

"Two days ago, I had my fortune told by Tia Despina - a wizard coffee-cup reader!"

"You don't say!" Paul tried to hide his amusement, but failed. I carried on regardless.

"Tia Despina is a close friend of the family. She is a very charming Greek lady who came to Cyprus at the same time as my parents and under similar circumstances," I began. "She was a constant visitor to our house after my uncle died. She was a great comfort to my Grandmother." Paul was listening intently.

"You still haven't told me about your uncle's sad end," he said.

"I know. I will tell you about it in a letter."

"Good. So what happened?"

"Tia Despina has a mesmerizing voice. My sisters were always glad to see her because of her famous skill at 'reading' the coffee cup. Well, when she came the other day, she said - right out of the blue - that it was time she read my coffee cup too. I watched her, almost hypnotized, as she looked into the muddy grinds at the bottom of the cup and saw my future."

"What did she say?"

"She said: 'Sometime in your life, maybe in two or three years' time, you will cross the sea with the man you will marry. And, you will live in a strange country for the rest of your life. You will have one or two upheavals in your life, but it will turn out alright in the end'. Isn't it amazing?"

"It's uncanny!" Paul said, quite seriously. "You see, *sirelis,* it' written in the cup as well as the stars, that we should be together."

I glanced at the clock again. Paul followed my eyes. "How quickly the time has gone," he whispered. He pulled me close to him and held me tight. We stopped talking. There was no need to say anything more.

I said goodbye to the Sergeant and his wife and thanked them for their kind hospitality. The children waved, as Paul walked with me to the front gate. He took my hand one last time and my fingers curled into his. Resolutely, yet gently, he took me in his arms and we kissed one last time. "Remember that I love you," he whispered before he let me go. I don't know how we managed to say goodbye without breaking down, but we did. I walked round the corner to where Eleni was waiting for me, with Paul's last words echoing through my head. She took one look at my tear-stained face, and drove off without saying a word.

Chapter Twelve

I could think of nothing but Paul, and the scene of our parting, for the next days and weeks. My first day at work after he left was unbearable. I worked through the solitary morning as though my life depended on it. Head down, not wanting to talk to anyone. The office assumed its former dreary state. Suddenly, there was a void in my life. I didn't go out during coffee break. There was no point, there was no Paul waiting for me. I missed him already, couldn't wait for his letter to arrive.

I didn't bother about breakfast either. But Andreas appeared at my desk with a steaming cup of coffee and a *Tiropitta*. "Still hot," he whispered and walked away before I could thank him.

Eleni came over and sat on the edge of my desk. "Are you alright?" she asked. I nodded. It was all I could do, to stop myself from bursting into tears. We were alone in the office, except for Mr. Eastman.

"Are you looking forward to going to England for Christmas?" Eleni asked.

"Yes my dear, I am. And so is my wife. Even though we love living in Cyprus, we miss England at Christmas. We shall spend the festive season with our niece and her family."

"How long will you be away?" I asked, just to be sociable. I had been so preoccupied with Paul that I hadn't been interested in anybody else.

"We shall be away for three weeks, my dear," he said.

"You'll miss the office party, Mr. Eastman," Eleni said. "We had a lovely party last Christmas, didn't we?" Last Christmas seemed centuries ago. So much had happened. I had grown up. I had fallen in love. Life would never be the same again.

"We did, indeed. You enjoyed it too, didn't you Reya?" he asked, looking at me in a fatherly way. I nodded and smiled. "That's better! Your Corporal wouldn't want you to be miserable now, would he?"

"I suppose not."

"You will write to each other, won't you?"

"It's the only thing we can do, for now…"

"That's the spirit! One never knows what tomorrow may bring."

The next day was not much better. My sense of humour deserted me completely. I couldn't bear the harmless remarks and jokes my colleagues made. They were meant to allay my melancholy, not to make fun of me. To make matters worse, Eleni had taken the day off and was this very moment having a second interview for the secretary's job. I was sure she would get it. She was well qualified for it. But this meant that I would lose her.

It was only when Paul's letter arrived, that I came out of my unhappy mood. It was a long letter. A day to day, detailed account of his journey home. From the moment he left Cyprus, to his reunion with his parents, and the days after that. I read the letter three times, kissed his signature and then put it under my pillow for future readings. I felt so close to him, seeing him in my mind's eye, like a film, everything he had described in his letter. I even saw his mother's tears when she hugged her son and told him how much she had missed him. The last sentence in Paul's letter said - 'I miss you terribly, *sirelis,* Christmas will not be the same without you, but remember that I love you'. These words would continue to sustain me in his absence.

Suddenly the festive season was here. It was the custom in our office to finish work at twelve o'clock on the day before Christmas. Soon after the coffee break, we more or less gave up on work and started getting into the festive spirit. A few of the boys smuggled in several bottles of drink such as *Anglias* (Cyprus brandy) and made Brandy Sours, while others brought in soft drinks, crisps and nuts. When Andreas came with our breakfast orders, we were ready to begin. Soon, the desks were cleared and the party was in full swing. I liked Brandy Sour - a delicious concoction combining equal quantities of brandy and fresh lemon juice with a dash of Angostura bitters, and topped with ice and soda. This was my favourite drink, which I had first tasted on my first and only visit to *Acteon*, the only nightclub in Famagusta. The office version of this drink was a bit uninspiring, though, due to the unavailability of ice and soda, but it was welcome, nevertheless. Eleni and I were not drinkers, so after our second drink, we wished everyone a happy Christmas and left to do some last minute shopping.

Eleni chatted all the way to the shops. She was bursting with vitality and enthusiasm. She had got the secretary's job and she would hand in her resignation on the first day of the New Year.

"I'm so happy, I could fly," she said and then stopped, covering her mouth with the back of her hand in that funny way of hers. "Oh *gorimou*, how insensitive of me to go on about my good fortune, when you are missing Paul..." She trailed off not really knowing what to say.

"It's alright. I feel so much better for having received his letter. I'm as thrilled as you are about your new job. You are wasted here. Come on, let's go to the *Fashion House* and choose an elegant dress for your party."

Eleni smiled her thanks. "Have you answered Paul's letter yet?" she asked.

"Yes, our postal romance continues," I said.

"I don't suppose he has started looking for a job yet."

"No. His parents want him to take it easy, before going into 'civvy street' as he calls it. He says he goes to his father's shop and helps out, some days."

"His parents seem to be very nice..."

"I know! They even suggested that Paul and I could live with them, until we could afford our own place... I'm surprised how easily, how quickly, they have accepted their son's choice of marriage partner – without even seeing me! I wish my parents were so trusting."

"Well, I suppose they want to make their only son happy..." Eleni didn't have time to finish the sentence, as we had reached our destination. The *Fashion House* was aptly named. It was the most exclusive ladies' dress shop in Famagusta. The latest fashions arrived from London, at regular intervals. We both gazed at the tastefully displayed dresses and fashion accessories. My eyes fell on a lovely sea-blue cocktail dress. I fell in love with it instantly. No chance. I wasn't going to any parties or dances. The owner of the shop knew Eleni and her mother. Eleni's mother was a favoured client. After trying on half a dozen dresses, Eleni settled on a black, three quarter length, taffeta evening dress. It fitted her perfectly. The full skirt accentuated her slim waist and the colour complemented her blonde hair.

"You'll definitely turn heads in that dress," I said, as we left the shop. She was going to a twenty-first birthday party on New Year's Eve.

"I hope I meet a nice young man there. My brother said that his best friend, Panayotis, is coming home for Christmas. I haven't seen him for ages."

"Where is he coming from?"

"Athens. He is studying law at Athens University. I think he graduates in June. I'm sure he'll be at the party." The streets and the shops were crowded with last minute Christmas shoppers. The jostling and pushing through the crowds had tired us out. We decided to go to the *Milk Bar* for some peace and quiet. The place was almost empty. Thirsty from our shopping expedition, we sipped our milk shakes gratefully.

"When do you start your new job, then?" I asked Eleni, with a sinking heart.

"The first of February. My aunt is preparing one of her spare rooms for me. I shall come home at weekends, though. Nothing will change, you know."

"I shall miss you."

"I shall miss you too. But we can still go out on Saturdays. We shall have so much to talk about, so much to catch up with." Deep down, I knew that things would not be the same. I would be sad, if I were to lose my only true friend. I remembered how close I had been with Arpi, my best friend at school. We had vowed to stay friends forever, but now I hardly heard from her.

"Have a nice Christmas and enjoy the New Year's Eve party," I said.

"I'm sure I will. Are you doing anything special?"

"No. As you know, we don't have a church of our own yet, so there are no religious celebrations to look forward to. But it will be a welcome break from work."

"What about that little church you told me about, the one in the old town?" Eleni asked. For so long, the Armenian community had dearly wanted a church that they could call their own, where proper Armenian services could be held. The Church Commissioners and the elders of our community petitioned the Antiquities Department that a church in the old town be leased to us. After lengthy meetings and negotiations it was given to us. "Have they started renovations yet?"

"I think they'll start early in the New Year. Father said it will probably be ready by the spring. The Archbishop will consecrate it."

New Year's Eve always made me think of Dai. When we were children, we would put on our new clothes and new shoes, these being our New Year presents, and kiss Grandmother's hand first, then Father's, Mother's and Uncle's, wishing them *'Shad Darinerou'* , which, in Armenian, means 'Many years of life'. Dai would give each of us a gold sovereign. We looked forward to this treat. Between us, we accumulated quite a pile of gold coins!

In our family, we always celebrate the New Year in style. After our splendid traditional New Year Eve supper of *Harissa,* (chicken and wheat puree), *Topig,* (chick pea *Kofte*) followed by *Khorshaf* (dried fruit compote), we sat in the main salon and played card games.

At one minute to midnight, Father switched off the electric light and we were plunged into darkness. We waited with bated breath as the last seconds ticked away. Finally, Father put the lights back on, and another New Year was ushered in.

Then came the moment we were all waiting for - the cutting of the *Vasilopita* (New Year Bread). This bread is traditionally cut at midnight on New Year's Eve. After baking, a coin is inserted through a slit in the base. The person who finds the coin will have plenty of luck in the New Year. Many years ago, the coin used to be a gold one, but later a silver coin was used. This bread tastes like no other bread. It is slightly sweet and the cinnamon and *mahleb* (the kernel of the black cherry stone) give the bread a subtle flavour, which lingers in the mouth for some time afterwards.

Father cut the *Vasilopita* carefully, into equal portions. When everyone had their portion, we began to eat, wondering who would get the lucky coin. We relished every mouthful of this bread, which is washed down with cups of sweet cinnamon and clove tea. Suddenly, I felt the coin against my teeth.

"I've found the lucky coin!" I cried and took it out of my mouth.

"Typical!" lamented Lillie. "You find it more times than anyone else."

"I can't help it if I'm lucky," I retorted.

All too soon, it was over for another year. Reluctantly, we dragged ourselves to bed. I put the lucky coin next to Paul's letter under my pillow and made my wish. I had grown up knowing that I was the 'lucky one', that I had brought prosperity to our family. I wondered now, if I could ever be lucky enough to make my dream life with Paul come true. That night, I dreamt that Paul was back in Cyprus. Miracle of miracles: my parents had consented and I was engaged to Paul! My eyelids fluttered. I knew I was in the middle of a dream. I closed my eyes tight – I wanted the dream to continue.

Chapter Thirteen

We were in the grip of an unusually long spell of cold weather. It was the second week in March and it was still cold - unheard of really. I had caught a nasty cold the week before and could not get rid of it. I was still taking all the remedies for colds, but to no avail. If anything, it was getting worse. I had a sore throat and a nasty cough too. The cold weather was supposed to kill germs, but it had not succeeded in my case.

Mother's kitchen cupboard contained all the home remedies ever to be needed by the family. Mint tea, with a slice of lemon and a teaspoon of honey was the panacea for most ailments, but it didn't always work. Yoghurt worked every time. It was the only effective cure for food poisoning, indigestion and stomach upsets. Pure alcohol was a reliable stand-by. It eased headaches and muscle pains when rubbed on the affected parts. It was also effective, if rubbed on the chest and back, for shivers and colds. If one of us had diarrhoea, Mother boiled rice and added plenty of lemon juice to it and you had to eat it unsalted. It tasted awful, but I must say it worked!

As children we suffered frequently from toothaches and earaches. A known cure for toothache was to rub Raki to the infected gums. It numbed the pain. Gargling with warm salt water was another alternative. Father was the expert in dealing with earache. I remember him vividly, drawing on his cigarette, cupping my ear in his hand and exhaling the cigarette smoke right into my ear. He would repeat this about a dozen times and then he covered my ear with his hand so that the smoke would stay there. I know it is hard to believe, but it worked every time. I suppose the mildly narcotic properties of the tobacco deadened the pain and eventually nature did the rest.

But on this day, I had something more important to worry about than my own ills. Grandmother's health had been failing for some time. Her health had deteriorated to such an extent that she was now confined to bed. She had taken no food these past ten days. She only asked for water and even that had stopped now. She was gradually slipping away.

Word had been sent to Auntie Roza. She had arrived three days before and had hardly moved from Grandmother's bedside. I went to Grandmother's room every morning before going off to work, to see how she was. This morning, I had seen Mother and Auntie sitting on either side of her bed. They both knew that the end was near.

By mid-morning, I was feeling so rotten that Mr. Eastman ordered me to go home. He waited until I got over a bout of coughing.

"I don't want you back in the office before you are fully recovered, do you hear?" He was unable to hide his frustration. He couldn't understand why I had not gone to the doctor yet. "Do something about that nasty cough. It could turn into pneumonia, you know. Go to the doctor now, he will give you something for it." How could I tell the dear man that I had never been to a doctor in my whole life?

With Mr. Eastman's words still echoing in my ears, I left the office and started to walk home. It was bitterly cold and then it started to rain. By the time I got home, I was soaked to the skin. I caught sight of my face in the hall mirror - I looked dreadful. My hair was sodden and dangled like black ropes down my back. All I wanted was to get something hot inside me and go to bed. But there was no aroma of food coming from the kitchen. The house looked deserted. Then, I heard Father's key in the door. One look at him and I knew instantly that Grandmother had died, but I asked Father just the same: "Is Grandmother...?"

"Yes, she has gone," he said. "You don't look very well, daughter. Why don't you go and see your Grandmother and then go to bed?" He had already made the funeral arrangement. He was home now, having shut his shop for the rest of the day, as a gesture of respect for Grandmother.

I stood there in the hall in my wet clothes. I refused to enter Grandmother's room to pay my last respects, to kiss her marble cold hand. I couldn't bear to see her dead. I wanted to remember her as she had been - alive. Somehow, I forced myself to get out of my wet clothes and into bed. I was chilled to the bone, my teeth chattering uncontrollably. I lay in bed: cold, hungry and miserable, silent tears falling softly down my cheeks. I did not feel sad that Grandmother had died. In a strange way, I was relieved that she had gone. At long last, she had thrown away her mantle of sorrow and joined her beloved son. They were united in death, and at peace.

I must have slept, for the sounds of noisy chatter woke me. Then my bedroom door opened and in walked my young nephew, Seto. He was a lovely little boy of four - my favourite out of Sara's three children. Seto promptly jumped on my bed. "Why are you still in bed, Rori?" he wanted to know, using the special name he had coined for me. I felt so ill that I could barely raise a smile.

When Sara was told that Grandmother had died, she had come with the youngest child so she could be near Mother and help her with the million things that had to be done in times like this. By mid-afternoon, the house was full to overflowing. Friends and neighbours came to pay their last respects to Grandmother and express their sympathy to the family. Mother and Auntie Roza sat in the big salon, dressed in black - and received the guests. On these sombre occasions, only black coffee was served, anything more would have been inappropriate. All three elder sisters - also in black - took turns to make the countless cups of coffee.

There was a constant stream of people coming to the house until very late at night. I was oblivious to all this, as I was in and out of consciousness throughout. Sometime during the evening, Nonnie came into my room with a bowl of chicken noodle soup.

"Mrs. Varvara brought the soup and also chicken with rice," she informed me, sitting down on the edge of my bed. "Mrs. Ayda brought stuffed cabbage and macaroni cheese." At times like this, friends and neighbours brought food to the bereaved family. They would set the table and eat with the family and afterwards wash up and tidy the kitchen. This usually went on for three days or even a whole week, sometimes.

"What a feast," I murmured. I was famished. I hadn't eaten anything since the morning. Somebody had brought me a cup of mint tea at some point, but I must have been asleep, for the cup was still on my bedside table, cold and untouched. I sat up and tucked into the soup. It was hot and soothing to my sore throat.

"I have to go," said Nonnie. "We are about to sit down to dinner. Is there anything you want?" she asked. I shook my head and, with that, she left the room.

Grandmother's funeral took place the next day, which was a Saturday. All the preparations had been made. Grandmother would be buried in my uncle's grave in the Armenian cemetery in Larnaca. The family would go in Marko's car. Father had hired a van for the coffin and three taxis to take the rest of the family and close friends.

Just before she left, Mother came to see me. She was shocked at my appearance. She put her hand on my forehead in her habitual way and was satisfied that I had no fever. Her hand was warm on my cold skin. Just then, Sara came into the room and I heard Mother talking to her in a low voice.

"Everybody is waiting, Siran. We'll be late if we don't start right now." We heard Father's impatient tone of voice. He hated waiting around for people who lingered.

"I'm coming," Mother answered, equally impatiently. One last look at me and she was gone. Suddenly, the house went very quiet. Everybody had gone except Sara and Seto. He came into my room to tell me that all five vehicles had driven off. He kept talking to me until I dozed off again.

Sara took one look at me and decided that something must be done. I remembered Mr. Eastman's advice about seeing a doctor. Neither I, nor any of the family had ever gone to the doctor - the necessity had never arisen. Only Dai had ever needed to go to doctors and they hadn't been able to cure him. Not surprisingly therefore, a doctor was not called in - even though I was clearly not well. Once more we resorted to home remedies.

"I'm going to give you the 'hot glass treatment'," announced Sara.

"Oh no!" I groaned. *"Not the hot glass treatment!"* But Sara took no notice of me. Having made the decision, she set about the preparations for this age-old remedy, which supposedly cured ailments such as colds, and chills, and even pleurisy and pneumonia. Being the eldest daughter, Sara had learnt the procedure from Mother. She had applied it to her own children many times, when they had been ill with colds or flu. I was resigned to my fate. I felt so miserable that I didn't care if it worked or not.

Sara disappeared from the room, but came back with 'The Box' a moment later. She knew exactly where it was kept. This cardboard box contained all the vital implements - twelve small, thick glasses in the shape of light bulbs. She made a torch by wrapping layers of cotton wool around the tip of an old kitchen fork and securing it with cotton thread. By this time, Seto had crept into my bedroom and was watching his mother intently. Sara took out a small bowl from the box and poured pure alcohol into it. Then she dipped the torch into the bowl, letting it soak up the alcohol, and lit it with a match. Taking up one of the glasses, she inserted the burning torch inside, warming it thoroughly. Finally, she placed the hot glass directly onto my bare back. Sara proceeded to do this with the remaining eleven glasses. She had to work fast.

When the first glass started to cool, she pulled it off my back and it came off with a plop. She continued until the whole of my back had had the treatment. As the flesh on my back got warmer, it swelled and became painful as Sara pulled the glasses off. Then she rubbed the remaining alcohol on my back and chest. Eventually, she pulled my pyjama top down and tucked me in with extra blankets. Only then was it over.

The whole thing lasted no more than ten minutes, but it seemed like a never-ending assault on my poor back. Seto was wide-eyed with disbelief. His mother had been playing with fire! Sara started putting everything back into the box.

"That wasn't too bad was it? You will soon feel better for it. Come on, my boy. Let's go into the kitchen and make Auntie Rori a nice cup of mint tea."

"Is Rori going to die, Mama?" I heard Seto ask, as the two of them trooped out of my room. My back seemed to be on fire! The fumes of the alcohol and the smell of the charred cotton permeated my bedroom. But soon, the heat spread to my body and I felt deliciously warm and drowsy. I shut my eyes and drifted into a dream-like sleep, safely enveloped in a cocoon of warmth.

I woke up to the sound of Seto playing. I felt different, somehow. Better than I had felt in the morning. Then I remembered the 'treatment'. It must be working. My skin was no longer painful to the touch. That awful chill had gone out of my body. I saw the cup of mint tea by my bedside. It had gone cold. Just then, the door opened and Sara came in with a tray. She had made lentil soup. The aroma of it made me realise how hungry I was. She looked at me and smiled with relief.

"See, it worked. You look better already. There's some colour in your cheeks. Get this soup down and you'll feel as right as rain." I had already started on the soup. It was delicious. I felt even better when I finished it, together with a slice of bread and cheese. I wanted to get up and get dressed; the family would be coming home soon. But Sara would not hear of it. I was to stay in bed and concentrate on getting my strength back. When Seto was reassured that I would not die, he jumped on my bed and wanted me to play with him. After a few minutes, I began to feel weary and went off to sleep again.

It was late afternoon, when the family came back from Larnaca. Everyone was tired and emotionally drained. Our friends and neighbours went back to their own homes. Most of them would be back later in the evening. Two different ladies would bring the food for our supper tonight. This period of 'comforting' would probably continue until the end of the coming week.

Mother came to see me as soon as she could. She looked pale and tired. But her expression changed visibly when she saw me sitting up in bed.

"You look so much better," she said. When I told her about the 'treatment', she nodded her head. "It works every time," she said. Her faith in age-old remedies had been renewed.

Grandmother's funeral marked the end of an era. The two sisters seemed to be comforted by the idea that their Mother and their beloved brother Krikor were at last reunited. The mourning period went on for forty days and during this time Mother never left the house. She welcomed the friends and neighbours who came to keep her company. Tia Despina was one of them. I could hear her mesmeric voice from by bed. At the end of the forty days, a memorial service was held. Relatives and friends were invited to go first to the church, then to the cemetery for a short service at the graveside and afterwards to the house, for the customary lunch. This lunch was in memory of the soul of the newly departed.

Chapter Fourteen

It was a week before I was fully recovered and able to go back to work. While I was convalescing, I wrote to Paul. I described my illness and the ordeal of the Hot Glass Treatment. I told him the sad news about my Grandmother, and my thoughts went back to the day that my beloved Uncle Krikor had died. I decided it was the right time to tell Paul the end of my uncle's story.

"Dear Paul," I began. "It was the third year of the Second World War. Even though we were comparatively safe and far enough from German invasion, there had been several false alarms. The air-raid siren was so loud and scary, when it went off to warn the population of impending attacks. It pierced the night with its unsettling wail, seeming to go on and on. During these times of danger, Marko and I hid under the kitchen table, too scared to utter a word. Father put out the lights and paced up and down, clearly anxious. Only after the all clear, did people venture out of their hiding places to find out what had happened. We were told later that it was the German planes flying over Cyprus on their way to Greece.

Father felt he had to do something. He rented a house in Pedoulas, up in the mountains, and insisted that we move. Mother was not impressed with the idea of uprooting the family, but changed her mind when Father reassured her that Grandmother and Dai would come with us. We knew how worried Mother was about her brother. His illness had taken a turn for the worse. He was not well enough to run his shop, even with Grandmother's help. He should have been in the prime of his life. His business had been so successful. But now it was closed. Father would have to stay behind, to look after his own shop, but he would join us for the odd weekend, whenever he could.

If Mother was disappointed with the house that Father had chosen, she did not complain. It stood high up on a hill, with spectacular views of the village. The rooms were all right, but the kitchen was awful. It was dark and very small. I don't know how Mother managed to cook for all of us, in there. The washroom was hardly adequate for our weekly baths, either, as there was only a coldwater tap. But the terrace compensated for all the inconveniences. It ran the whole width of the house. We practically lived on the terrace, it was so cool and pleasant. The garden was full of trees – cherry, peach, apple and, of course, a grapevine. Jasmine covered the kitchen wall: its fragrant perfume would fill the night air.

Our landlords were a young couple, Christos and Ellie. They lived in the small extension at the side of the house. Christos hardly did any work and spent most of his time at the *kafenion* in the village. But his wife worked very hard – she left early in the morning to work in their cherry orchard and didn't come home till late at night.

We loved Pedoulas. It was a popular summer resort. We found a small Armenian community already there, and we made new friends. Released from the shackles of the classroom, Marko and I felt as free as birds. Together with our new friends, we had the run of the village. We played under the blazing sun, climbed trees, stole apples from orchards, grapes from the vineyards. Somehow, they tasted so much better, when we got them that way.

We were fascinated by the big *kafenion* in the village, and we lingered in front of it. It was the focal point for the men of the village. The floor was covered with cigarette stubs and the air thick with cigarette smoke. They talked, drank coffee and played backgammon while the women worked. We saw them picking fruit in the orchards, loading them on their donkeys, ready to take to market. Women were never seen in a *kafenion*: it was strictly a male domain.

But it was not all play for me. I was still the 'errand girl'. Every afternoon, I walked down to the concrete freshwater fountain in the village to fill a flask with the pure spring water for Dai. I ran down the hill fast but walking up the steep hill took more time. My second errand was more important. Every Saturday afternoon I went to the Greek Orthodox Church in the village, put a few pennies in the offertory and lit a candle. I then kissed the icon of the Panayia and prayed to her to make Dai well. In time, the icon's face became so familiar that I talked to her as if she were real.

After the liturgy, bread and *kollifa* were offered to the congregation. The bread was unleavened and thickly sliced. The *kollifa* is boiled wheat, mixed with raisins, sesame seeds, blanched almonds and the seeds of the pomegranate. It was piled high in huge, flat, woven baskets ready to be blessed by the priest. Two church wardens stood outside the church and handed pieces of the bread and cupfuls of the *Kollifa* to the congregation as they came out. This is an old religious custom. It is an offering for the souls of the dead. I quickly ate the *Kollifa,* but saved the bread for Dai.

By midsummer Dai's health deteriorated. It seemed that my prayers to the Panayia and the spring water I fetched for him were not helping him. He looked even paler than usual and more tired. His legs were swollen and painful. He could barely walk the few steps from his room to the veranda. After breakfast, he sat in his usual chair by the jasmine, his feet resting on a stool. The garden looked beautiful. The trees were heavy with fruit. It was cool and peaceful, and Dai either read or gazed wistfully at the breathtaking view of the valley below.

Mother lovingly administered to his needs. With infinite gentleness, she changed the dressings on his legs.

'Is it too painful, Brother?' she would ask.

'Not too bad, Sister,' Dai would whisper, even though the pain must have been excruciating. After the dreadful ordeal was over, he drank the cool water. I sat by his side and talked to him. He smiled and ruffled my hair.

'Thank you for fetching the water for me. God bless you, my little gazelle.'

The doctor came twice a week. He was a friend, and they drank coffee and chatted for a while. One day, I saw the doctor talking to Grandmother in a low voice. The anxiety in her eyes was plain to see.

Then came August and the most celebrated Saint's Day of all. It was the Name Day of the Panayia and therefore my Name Day too! My father had come to Pedoulas to spend the holiday weekend with us. He had given me two shillings, which I had already spent at the fair the day before. Dai had not forgotten either. He had given me the little porcelain figure of a shepherdess, which I had seen and admired in his shop, months before. I couldn't believe my eyes when he took it out of the tissue paper and handed it to me.

'Thank you so much, Dai,' I said, and kissed his hand, as children were taught to do, then.

'Go with God, little gazelle, and enjoy your Name Day.'

'I wish you could come with us, Dai. We are going to Prodromos for our picnic.'

'I know. Maybe next year, eh?'

'Alright, next year then.' I kissed his hand again and ran to Mother to show her my Name Day gift. Most unusually, Mother had been persuaded to come with us on this occasion. Father planned to go to the *kafenion* later in the day to meet a few of his friends and discuss the war. Grandmother stayed behind, of course, to look after Dai. We said our goodbyes and set off. Mother took only a few steps, before she stopped and looked back at Dai who was sitting in his usual chair. A strange look passed between them – as though a message was sent and understood. It was a curious thing to witness. The moment passed. Mother raised her hand in farewell. He returned the gesture and finally we set off.

It was a glorious summer day. We soon turned off the main road and climbed the twisting road into the hills. We caught up with Auntie Roza and my two cousins, who had started off before us. We were all in a joyous mood, laughing and singing all the way. It took us most of the morning to walk the few miles to Prodromos, a nearby village renowned for its pine forests. We stopped several times to rest and have a drink of water. We could hear the sound of bells in the distance, and see goat farms dotted around the hillside. At last we reached our destination.

The picnic area was a flat plateau, dotted with pine trees. We picked a shady spot under the trees, where we could admire the magnificent view of the town below. Marko and I dumped our rucksacks, picked up the empty water flasks and promptly went in search of the fresh water fountain. Using our cupped hands we drank the cool, sweet, crystal-clear water.

"We must not forget to fill the flasks before we go back, for Dai," I said to Marko.

"I expect Mother will remind us," he said. We drank greedily, for we were very thirsty after our long walk. We filled the flasks and went back to where Mother, Auntie Roza and Sara were busy setting out the picnic lunch. After lunch, the siesta hour was observed. Some stretched out on blankets and promptly went to sleep. Others read or gossiped. I had never seen Mother so happy and relaxed. Soon, it was time to start back. The return walk was a lot easier, as we didn't have anything heavy to carry, and also because it was downhill all the way.

When we were about half a mile from Pedoulas, we saw a car coming towards us. The car stopped, and to our amazement we saw Father get out and walk to where Mother was standing. There was something wrong. We could see it in his expression. He said something to Mother. She stood there, rooted to the spot. She opened her mouth to say something, but no words came. Then she made hysterical, gasping sounds. After a second, the tears came, unchecked and in floods. Probably for the first time in her life, her composure and dignified calm in moments of crisis had deserted her. She was so grief stricken, that she did not care who saw her pain.

Nobody moved. The rest of us looked at each other in bewilderment. What was wrong? Something froze inside me. *Had something happened to Dai?* At that moment, Auntie Roza, who was in the group behind, caught up with us. She surveyed the scene, but before she could grasp the seriousness of the situation, she and Mother were whisked away in the car.

All this took no more than a few minutes, but it seemed like an eternity to us. In a daze, the rest of us somehow managed to walk the final half-mile home. No one said a word. We wanted to get home as soon as we could, even though we dreaded facing whatever it was that had so unexpectedly and so cruelly spoiled our day.

In the glorious light of a Cyprus afternoon, a heartbreaking scene was being played out on the terrace. There were about a dozen friends and neighbours, who had come to comfort Grandmother as soon as they heard of Dai's death.

There, I have said it Paul: *my beloved Dai was dead!* I did not believe it. I ran over to where his chair was. It was empty. A huge pain rose in my chest. He could not be dead. I loved him. Did I not go to church every Saturday afternoon? Did I not light a candle for him and pray to the Panayia? Did I not fetch the pure spring water for him to drink? Rage joined the pain in my chest. God had not kept his end of the bargain. I would never forgive Him for taking Dai away from me.

Then I saw Grandmother, with Mother and Auntie, huddled in a corner. They were clasping each other in an effort to comfort one another. They had let their grief overtake them. They were weeping uncontrollably. Incoherent words escaped from their mouths and floated in the air. I made a move to go to Dai's room, but strange hands held me back. Mrs. Arsha who was our nearest neighbour, took Marko and me to her house, where we would spend the night.

I could not sleep that night. I lay awake thinking about Dai. Never to see him again. Never to help him in his shop again. It was inconceivable. So many questions were going round and round in my head. They demanded answers, but none came. Death was something unknown in my young life. What did it really mean? I knew about heaven and hell. I also knew that the good went to heaven and the bad went to hell. They burned in hell for all eternity. We had been told about it enough times at school. I knew for sure that Dai would go to heaven, but how would he get there? Who would take him?

Fear gripped my whole being. I shivered. I was in a strange house, lying on a strange mattress on the floor. My brother was sound asleep beside me, oblivious to my anguish. There was no one I could turn to, no one to tell me why Dai had died, no one to hold me and comfort me. Before sleep finally dragged me down to blissful oblivion, I somehow knew that this was a moment in my life when nothing else could ever be so intense or so agonizing.

When Marko and I were taken home the next morning, the funeral arrangements had already been made. Grandmother, Mother and Auntie wore black. Black scarves covered their heads. They looked so strange, with their red swollen eyes and deathly pale faces. The nearest Armenian cemetery was in Larnaca. Dai would be buried there. The women were not in a fit state to travel, so it was decided that my father and my eldest cousin Matheos would take Dai to his final resting place. He lay in the open coffin, his arms crossed as though in prayer. His skin had a strange grey pallor. We all lined up, to kiss his hand and whisper our goodbyes. It was hard to believe that this cold and lifeless form had been a living person – my darling Dai – only a few short hours before.

Years later, I learnt the nature of Dai's illness. The doctors in Cyprus had not been able to diagnose what was wrong. He had gone to Beirut to be seen by a renowned American doctor, who worked in a private hospital there. His first visit to the eminent doctor had been optimistic. But on his second visit, six months later, the doctor told him that he had an enlarged liver, possibly cancer. This was an incurable illness at the time. Only then, did I truly understand the pilgrimage to Apostolos Andreas. It was a last resort. There was nothing more any doctor could do, nowhere else Dai could have gone. So the family turned to miracle workers, saints and icons. I suppose, when all real hope was gone, they had to put their faith into something intangible, something beyond normal explanation."

As I put down my pen, the tears were rolling down my face. I had held my grief for Dai inside for so long, and now my feelings were out. I had told them at last, and to the man I loved. Dai had been my protector, and after his death, I had felt so abandoned and alone. But now that I had written down his story for my new beloved, I felt strangely at peace. Dai was safely in the past now. I had a new hero to protect me.

Chapter Fifteen

During my convalescence, I had plenty of time to think about the problems Paul and I faced. Our long-distance romance was continuing and, if anything, it was flourishing. We wrote to each other at least twice a week. In our letters, we said all the things we hadn't had time to say when he was in Cyprus. Paul always asked the same question: "Have you had the chance to tell your parents about us?"

His parents supported him and offered him help. They were so happy for him. But the mere thought of a confrontation with my parents brought me out in a cold sweat. It was better to let things drift for the time being. I was happy with things as they were. Nevertheless, I couldn't help thinking about the Day of Reckoning. I could picture the scene: the family sitting in the 'little salon' after supper, the shock on everybody's face - except Nonnie's. Maybe I could ask her to be my spokeswoman. She could start in her usual way: "Guess what, everybody," and then the bombshell: "Reya wants to marry an Englishman..."

No. Even she couldn't get away with it. I imagined the disbelief and the eruption that would follow the shocking announcement, my father's embarrassment and his attempts to escape. I could picture Mother, and the look on her face that would surely turn me into stone. How could one of her daughters do such a disgraceful thing? To fall in love! To choose your own husband! And a man who was not even Armenian! How unspeakably shameful! My mother would never get over it, and my father would support her, whatever his own feelings. It was all simply unthinkable. At least I was feeling better, and looking forward to going back to work.

My first day at work was very strange. I felt as though I had been away for ages. The boss and the staff were very good. They let me take things easy. Mr. Eastman was genuinely glad to see me back in the office.

"Are you fully recovered, my dear?" he asked kindly. "I've missed our chats at coffee-break."

"I feel alright Mr. Eastman, thank you." I didn't tell him that I had recovered by means of home remedies. The only concession to conventional medicine had been to get some cough mixture from the pharmacy.

I gradually got back into the old routine of work and home. I missed Eleni terribly. The days dragged. I could hardly wait for the weekend. The last time she had come home, I had hardly seen her. But we met on the Saturday.

We spent the afternoon and evening together. We sat in *Delice* and talked for hours, catching up with each other's news. Eleni wanted to know how things were going in my romance. She wasn't impressed by the lack of progress.

"I am beginning to think that you are quite happy to have a long-distance love affair with Paul."

"I have no choice, have I?"

"And how long do you intend to keep him waiting?"

"I don't know…"

"You don't really want your secret romance to develop into anything more permanent, do you, *gori*?"

"What do you mean?"

"I think you are content just to correspond with Paul, because with him being away, your romance is safe from discovery, isn't it?" I was taken aback by her shrewd observation. I thought how different Eleni and I were. She made things happen, while I retreated to the safe walls of my fairy castle and made wishes.

"Are you happy with your new job?" I asked, wanting to change the subject.

"I love my new job, and I love living with my Aunt and Uncle. They spoil me. I didn't realise they had such a large circle of friends. As a new face on the social scene, I'm being asked to outings and parties all the time."

"Have you met any nice young men yet?"

"I have met a few, but no one special. I'm having such a good time."

"I'm so glad for you Eleni."

"I've kept the best news for last – I'm going to buy a car!"

"A car! Really?"

"Isn't it wonderful? No more taxis for me. I shall come home in style, driving my own car."

"When will you get it?"

"At the end of the month. I'm so excited, I must have another slice of this delicious sponge cake. What about you?" She did look so happy. Her big brown eyes sparkled with exuberance. She looked the epitome of chic in a new dress.

"I'm thirsty, I'll have another coke," I said, determined not to sound downhearted.

"How is work, *gori?*"

"It's alright. Mr. Eastman and I have got into the habit of chatting during the coffee break. His dry sense of humour lifts my spirits."

"Does he still tell funny jokes?"

"Yes. He makes me laugh."

"How do you get on with Anastasia?"

"Alright. We walk into town sometimes… Look at the time, we better start walking to the cinema. We don't want to miss the film."

At last, the Armenian community in Famagusta was to have its own church. The small church stood some distance away from the centre of the old town. It was a beautiful church, probably dating back to the 14th century. Extensive renovations had brought it back to its former splendour. It was to be named St. Krikor, and the great event of its consecration would take place next Sunday.

The morning of this auspicious day dawned bright and warm. The sun beamed down from a cloudless sky. The family was up and ready. We three girls all had new outfits. Lillie looked very chic in her green spring suit. She was the tallest and the best dressed of the girls. She only bought expensive clothes and took good care of them. Green was her favourite colour, as it matched the colour of her eyes. Nonnie and I didn't look too bad either. Nonnie wore a melon coloured dress, which accentuated her small waist. I was wearing a short-sleeved suit, the colour of a sun-ripened peach. Like Lillie, I had long legs and felt more comfortable in suits rather than dresses.

The church was almost full when we got there. We made a grand entrance. All heads turned to look at us, as we walked in. Father and Mother led the way and we three girls followed them, with Marko bringing up the rear. We sat down and, as custom dictated, we nodded and smiled to the people nearest to us. After a quick and discreet look at the congregation, Nonnie turned to me and confirmed what I was thinking - we three were the best-dressed girls there.

Soon afterwards, the service started. The Archbishop, Father Serop and the choir had come from Nicosia for the consecration. The church was full by now. In his sermon, the Archbishop stressed the importance of the church in any Armenian community. "The church and the school are the twin foundation stones that hold the people together, for without them the Armenians would have perished a long time ago," he said. The Archbishop spoke with such eloquence, such feeling, that he moved the congregation to tears. The choir sang beautifully. The whole thing was a moving experience for everyone.

After that memorable first service at the Church of St Krikor, Father Serop would come to officiate in the new church, once a month. And also, at Christmas, Easter, on the Feast day of St. Krikor the Illuminator in June and on the Feast day of Mary the Mother of Christ in August - thus providing an opportunity for the whole community to come together.

I thoroughly enjoyed describing the occasion for Paul in my letter that night, blissfully unaware that my appearance at the consecration ceremony had set into motion a train of events, which would threaten all our dreams.

Chapter Sixteen

On a Wednesday evening, some weeks later, we were all sitting in the 'little salon'. Mother was darning. Her sewing basket lay open, the spools of thread, her scissors and her darning egg lay on top. She was wearing her new round glasses – for close work – her eyes lowered, her hands busy. We girls were reading and Father was drinking his second cup of coffee. Marko had gone out. Suddenly, Nonnie closed her book and announced that she had something important to say. I put down my *Photoplay* magazine and waited expectantly for her to continue. The only sound in the room was Mother snapping the thread with her teeth.

Nonnie had everyone's attention. I am quite sure that we were all thinking the same thing - the *Inheritance*! Some new evidence had come to light. Maybe our cousin from Beirut had come - this time with the money. No one spoke. We let Nonnie have her moment of drama. After a moment of suspense, she went on.

"I saw Agnes this afternoon," she began. I was disappointed that she hadn't used her usual opening gambit of 'Guess what?' Perhaps, this omission should have alerted me, but I simply wondered what juicy bit of gossip she was going to regale us with, this time.

"And she told me – in strictest confidence - that her brother Stepan wants to marry our Reya!" I couldn't believe my ears, but Nonnie went on. "His parents want to come for a 'visit' to confirm it with an official proposal according to the traditional custom. But before that his father will go to Father's shop to talk about it." She uttered these apocalyptic words in a very casual way, as if this kind of thing happened to me every day of the week. There was complete silence. Mother stopped darning and looked up to make sure that she had heard correctly. I stared at Nonnie in disbelief for several long seconds. Was this some kind of joke or had she gone mad?

Suddenly, there was pandemonium. Everybody spoke at once, but nobody listened. Father put his unfinished cup of coffee down on the table and looked at his watch.

"I want to catch the nine o'clock news on the radio," he announced. "I shall go to my bedroom, where I can listen to the news in peace and quiet."

His expression said clearly, "Not another proposal, please!"

"Don't you want to know more about this?" demanded Mother.

"What is there to know? There will now be hours of futile discussions and arguments. I want none of it. I've told you many times before that I prefer to leave these matters to you and the girls."

"But in this case we know the family. It is Rafael's son we are talking about. I would like to know your thoughts about it." Father sighed and picked up his coffee cup.

"I know… I shall go along with whatever you decide." And with that, he promptly left the room. I, on my part, had a fit of uncontrollable laughter. I couldn't help myself. It was so absurd. I knew beyond a shadow of a doubt that I would not be expected to respond to this proposal. There was no way that Mother would agree to my being married before my elder sisters.

"You must be joking," I managed to say - to no one in particular - between bursts of laughter. Mother looked at me in exasperation. Lillie had already lost interest in the matter and gone back to her book. She was most probably relieved that this time the proposal of marriage was not for her. Undeterred, Nonnie carried on:

"It seems that Stepan saw Reya in church on the day of the consecration. One look at her, and he was smitten! It must have been her peach coloured outfit! Anyway, that very evening, he told his parents that he had found the girl he wanted to marry. His parents were delighted, as they had been telling him for ages that it was time he settled down." She stopped for breath. "His parents were even more delighted, when they found out that the girl their son had chosen was none other than the daughter of their old friends, Artin and Siran! They said they didn't remember seeing Reya before."

I bet they hadn't seen me before. Nobody had seen me. After all, I'd been invisible until now, hadn't I? I knew of this Stepan person, of course, as the families had been friends for years. I wouldn't be surprised if they had become friends during the days of quarantine. I'd even seen him a few times. He was the only son and, from all accounts, the spoilt son of a rich father. His mother worshipped him and even his younger sister Agnes – Nonnie's best friend - pampered him. He worked with his father in their jewellery shop in the high street. He often went to Beirut on business, but it was rumoured that he had 'women' friends there! I knew all this through Nonnie. I had never set foot in their shop - there was never a need for me to do so.

Mother was silent, deep in thought. There was a serious problem. And we all knew what it was. I could contain myself no longer.

"This is so ridiculous! I'm not interested in getting married. And in any case, it's not possible. There are two older girls in the family who should get married first. As far as I'm concerned, the matter is closed. If you don't change the subject, I shall go to my room." Mother ignored my outburst. With a stab of her index finger, she pinned me to my seat. Then she turned to Lillie:

"Lillie, would you object, if one of your younger sisters got married before you do? Sometimes, I fear that none of you girls will ever get married."

"I don't mind at all Mother, if they want to get married. They are free to do what they like. I should not be held responsible for them."

"In that case, maybe it is time we took a fresh look at old customs and traditions. If a few of these traditions must be discarded, then so be it. Kismet has knocked on our door, we must not send it away." Mother sounded just like Auntie Roza, voicing sentiments she had always refused to allow before. Nonnie, for once, was lost for words. She did not have to say anything, really. I'm quite sure she never dreamt that her announcement would be taken seriously. I began to feel uncertain at the way things were escalating. I found myself being pushed onto centre stage, wholly unprepared for the role.

"I shall discuss this matter with your father, before we take it any further," Mother concluded. I felt as if a balloon of anger was lodged in the pit of my stomach, ready to explode at any moment. I was suddenly possessed with rage at Nonnie for throwing this bombshell. Why hadn't she told me about it first? She knew perfectly well that if I wanted to marry anyone, it would be Paul. I was angry with Lillie too. How dare she announce so casually, with a shrug of her shoulders, that she didn't care who did what and when. And Mother – she was the worst. I simply could not comprehend the astounding readiness with which she was prepared to abandon inviolable customs and traditions, which had been so close to her heart – until this moment.

The balloon in my stomach burst. "It's not fair!" The words tumbled out, angrily. "I don't want to marry Stepan - or anybody else!" I pointed to Lillie and Nonnie: "Why should *I* get married before they do? As far as I'm concerned, the matter is closed." And with that, I picked up my magazine and stalked away, with as much dignity as I could muster. I reached the sanctuary of my room and locked the door. I was bristling with anger. I looked at my reflection in the mirror, and spoke my thoughts aloud: "If Lillie can reject her proposals of marriage with a simple 'no', then so can I."

The next morning, everyone went about their business as usual. Nothing was mentioned about my angry outburst. It was as if the incident had never taken place. Two weeks passed, and not another word was spoken about it. I assumed that Mother had discussed the proposal with Father and they had decided not to go against my wishes. I felt a lightening of my spirits. In his last letter, Paul had written that he had found a job in London. He would be moving at the end of the month. He was going to stay with a friend until he found his own place. I wondered if I should write and tell Paul about the 'proposal' episode. I could write it in such a way that it would sound funny, even absurd. I wanted to reassure him that I loved him and I would never want to marry anyone but him. I missed him more than I thought possible. But in the end, I decided not to mention it at all.

Instead, I wrote to him in detail about something entirely different. Otto Preminger was in Cyprus! He was making part of the film *Exodus* in Famagusta. He, and his entire cast and crew were staying in the Constantia hotel. I told him how Eleni and I, together with crowds of young locals had invaded the hotel grounds to catch a glimpse of Paul Newman and Eva Marie Saint, the stars of the film. The next day we had watched the filming. It took the director hours to shoot a brief scene where Paul Newman came out of a taxi office, looked left and right and got into a car! It had been exciting to watch it at first, but after several 'takes' it became boring. On the Sunday we had gone to the beach and watched them as they sunbathed and frolicked in the sea. The newspapers were full of the stars' glamorous pictures and there were so many stories written about them. Famagusta was buzzing with activity: they had brought so much excitement with them. They would be staying for another week, giving the 'film fans' more opportunities to follow them around and take pictures of them.

Sadly, the day of their departure came.

"We both thought they would stay at the Constantia, didn't we?" said Eleni. She had taken a few days off work and was spending it at home with her parents.

"Yes. But it looks deserted now. The beach looks so desolate without them," I said. "They have taken all the excitement and glamour with them."

"Have they gone back to Hollywood?"

"No. They went to Israel first, to shoot more of the film. I'm so glad we spent these few days together. You did enjoy watching the filming, didn't you?"

"Yes, *gori* , I did. But what do you think of Paul Newman now, having seen him at close range?" she asked.

"He is as handsome as his pictures, but my Paul is far more…"

"Ah! You must love your Paul very much. Have you told him about your proposal of marriage?"

"No, there's no need to. It won't come to anything. Anyway, you said you had something to tell me. What is it Eleni? Have you had a promotion?"

"No, not promotion, something much better. I have met someone special," she said excitedly. Her face was glowing with happiness.

"Go on, tell me all about it." I took a sip of my coca-cola and waited.

"His name is Chris, and he is a lawyer. We met at a party and liked each other immediately. We went out a few times and then, last week, he proposed and I accepted!"

"So, *gori,* you're engaged. How exciting!"

"It's not official yet. He is coming on Saturday with his parents. It will be announced then."

"When will the wedding be?"

"I think it will be a long engagement. We want to save, so we can buy a house. Will you be one of my *koumera?"* (Bridesmaids)

"Of course I will. I've never been a *koumera* before. I'm so happy for you Eleni. At least one of us will marry their Prince Charming."

"Don't say that. You don't know what fate has in store for you. Anyway, who is this man who wants to marry you?"

"I don't think you would know him. He works with his father. They've got a jewellery shop in Hermou street…"

"I know the one! It's a lovely shop. I don't know him of course. What does he look like?"

"I haven't seen him for years. From what I remember, he looks a bit like my old Armenian pen-friend from Iraq, without the moustache. You've seen the picture haven't you?"

"Yes, I remember you showing it to me. He's not bad looking then."

"I don't know and I don't really care…"

"The family must be well off, judging by their shop."

"I suppose so. Nonnie said he has recently bought an expensive car," I agreed, without much enthusiasm and shrugged my shoulders.

"My goodness Reya, what a catch. If only you didn't…" she stopped, covering her face with her hands.

"I know what you are thinking. But it's not only Paul. I don't want to be pushed into marriage. I want to have the choice – same as everybody else."

I was in a happy mood, the fiasco of the 'proposal' completely forgotten. Tonight, Marko was taking us to dinner at the newly opened restaurant in Alasia and then to *Acteon* - the nightclub. And *I* was to be included in the party. Two outings in one evening! I couldn't believe my luck. One last look in the hall mirror, and I was ready. I was pleased with my new dress. It was one of three, which Florentia had made for me. This one was the colour of dark rose, sleeveless with a square neckline and a flouncy skirt.

Dinner was excellent. We had *meze*, a selection of dishes - dips and vegetables and a variety of fish and meats. We had about twenty plates of food, so everyone had plenty to choose from. A *meze* is meant to be lingered over, so we took it slowly and savoured the flavours of each dish. No meal is complete without a drink. Beer or ouzo were the preferred drinks to accompany this feast. After coffee, we headed for the nightclub. We sat at a table near the dance floor. With a brandy sour in my hand, I settled down to watch the floor show. And then, ten minutes into the show, I saw Nonnie nudge Lillie and point to the table opposite us. They looked at each other and smiled. It was difficult to see what they were looking at in the dim lights, but after a few minutes I realized what had caught their attention. There, sitting with a group of people I did not know, were Agnes and – to my utter embarrassment – her brother, Stepan. I looked at my sisters with a growing resentment: it was surely a set up.

I said nothing and continued watching the floorshow. The evening was spoiled for me, but worse was to come. When the floorshow was over, Stepan and Agnes came over to our table. Introductions were made and Stepan ordered a round of drinks for everyone. I thought that was the end of it, but no, he asked me if I would like to dance with him! I was in such a state by then that I just sat there mutely, but someone must have nudged me, because I found myself on the dance floor and in his arms. I was glad that the lights had dimmed again. At least he couldn't see my beetroot coloured face. Guiding me expertly across the dance floor, Stepan seemed completely unaware of my embarrassment.

"Did you like the floor show?" he asked.

"Yes, I did."

"I thought the 'magician' was good. It was quite believable wasn't it?" At that moment I wished for *him* to disappear like magic.

"It was quite good." Would this dance never end?

"Don't you just love the tango? I could dance to the music of *Jealousy* all night. Do you like dancing?" I said nothing. Would he never stop asking questions? I looked up. I had never seen him at such close range before. He seemed delighted to be with me. His dark eyes sparkled with pleasure. He looked at me and smiled, a teasing smile, coaxing me to smile back at him.

"I'm waiting."

"Waiting for what?"

"First, to see if you can smile, and second, to hear if you like dancing." I blushed again. This time, it was a pink flush that covered my face. His grin was so cheeky, that I couldn't help but smile. I realised he was trying to ease my discomfort. The tango came to an end.

"I hope I have many more opportunities to dance with you again, Miss Reya," he said, as he escorted me back to my table. I sat down gratefully, to recover from my ordeal. Nobody said anything. Later that night, Nonnie came to my room and sat down on the edge of my bed. "I swear I had no idea that Agnes and Stepan would be at the *Acteon* tonight," she said. "It was just a coincidence."

"I believe you," I said. We were silent for a moment. "It doesn't matter anyway, because my answer is still 'no'. So I can safely say that the matter is closed."

Chapter Seventeen

But this Stepan person was not so easily put off. The matter was not closed. Two weeks later, it came up again. This time, Nonnie did have the consideration to put me in the picture first. I was still angry with her - she had let me down. But I listened to what she had to say, nevertheless, and prepared myself for a showdown. It transpired that Stepan's father had had a word with our father, expressing his wish for the union. Nonnie warned me that Mother wanted to talk to me, privately.

That very evening, the second act of the drama unfolded. Mother said she would like to talk to me. After supper, I helped her with the washing up and sat down at the kitchen table facing her. I felt a sense of dread in the pit of my stomach. This would be the *real* confrontation - not the imagined one.

"Your father and I have discussed the marriage proposal of the young man," she began. "We have known the family for years and we think that Stepan is a suitable candidate for a husband. He will give you a very comfortable life." I felt my throat tighten. I wanted to speak out. Worse still, I felt like being childish and stamping my feet and shouting, 'It's not fair, it's not fair'. If only I could tell Mother everything, every single emotion I was feeling. But I did not, of course. I prayed instead - for a thunderbolt, an earthquake, anything that would free me from this emotional torture. I looked at Mother. The electric lamp with its pink shade cast a soft glow over her face. I studied the pattern of tiny white flowers on her navy blue dress, with its pretty white collar. With an enormous effort of will, I began to speak.

"I'm sorry Mother. I feel that I cannot get married before my elder sisters do. I'm not ready to take up the responsibilities of marriage…" My words subsided into an embarrassed silence. We stared at one another. It was the first time we had ever had a serious talk. Mother's face softened, her eyes went slightly misty.

"You are our lucky daughter. I am sure that if you say 'yes' to this proposal, then your two elder sisters will follow your example. Their luck will change also." Her face had taken on an almost religious fervour. "On the day you were born, our luck changed - your father's business took off, Marko came. Please, think about it very seriously and make the right decision." I was helpless.

"Alright, Mother, I will think about it." What else could I say? The words sounded flat and lifeless to my ears.

Over the days that followed, I lived with my dilemma. The devil was on one side of the abyss and on the other, the deep blue sea. I was going to hurt people either way. This was the most important decision of my life: the only decision I had ever been asked to make. There was no one I could turn to. No one I could confide in. Paul, who was the other protagonist in this drama, was far away. I hadn't heard from him for two weeks. I had been so emotionally worked up that I hadn't worried about it. But now I was worried. Had something happened?

I knew what Nonnie would say: "Grow up, Reya. Forget about your dreams of the Englishman. Come down to the real world - for once in your life." I knew how hurt and shocked my parents would be, if I threw caution to the wind and raced off to the other side of the world - they would surely disown me. To abandon my family would be folly of the first order. But was my life to be entirely subordinate to other people's wishes? To abandon happiness with Paul and embark on a loveless marriage would be equally foolish, wouldn't it?

Questions and yet more questions bombarded my brain. I had enjoyed an easy Mediterranean childhood. I had often felt like the pampered daughter of an indulgent father. I relived the happiness of my short romance, clinging desperately to the image of the dream world I had created. But reality was catching up with me, shattering the fragile walls of my fairyland.

Two weeks had passed since my 'talk' with Mother. She was still waiting for my answer. A strange atmosphere pervaded the house. I felt as though everybody in the family was tiptoeing around me. Even Nonnie was quiet, showing none of her usual exuberance. She avoided me, in case I had another outburst. But my revolt was silent now and it was not likely to find a voice. I desperately wanted to say 'No', but I didn't know how to say it. Every night, as I lay in bed unable to sleep, I rehearsed my refusal speech. Lillie had dealt with this kind of situation so many times, just by saying a simple and determined 'No'. But when morning came, I got cold feet and remained silent, hoping that the whole thing would just go away. Why was I finding it so difficult? Why was I such a coward?

Mother did not bring up the subject again, but the gentle persuasion continued. On Sunday, Sara and her family arrived, unexpectedly. It was almost lunchtime. Marko had just gone to pick Father up from the *kafenion* and collect the roast lamb and potatoes from the *fourno*.

"I brought *lahmajoun,* still warm from the Baker's oven," Sara announced. This was my favourite dish. We call it Armenian Pizza. The difference is that you have to prepare the topping yourself - ground beef mixed with chopped tomatoes, onions, parsley and spices. You take it to the baker, who makes the dough, shapes it into rounds, puts on the topping you have given him and cooks it in his oven. Since it is an Armenian dish, the Greek bakers don't know how to make it.

"I'm sorry we are late," said Sara. "We planned to come much earlier, but Mr. Vartan's bakery was very busy. It seems that everybody wants to eat *lahmajoun* today. We thought we would surprise you." Our Sunday lunch turned into a feast. For the duration of the meal, I forgot my problems. We fell on *the lahmajouns* like hungry wolves. They were still warm. The proper way to eat them is to squeeze lemon juice on them, roll them and eat them with your fingers - a delicious treat. We sat on the veranda to have our coffee. After a while, I went to my room to read, while the others continued their conversation. I wasn't in the mood to hear the latest gossip.

I had hardly opened my book, when I heard a knock on my door and in walked Sara. She saw the quizzical look on my face and quickly sat down at the foot of my bed.

"Before you say anything, Mother didn't ask me to come here today. I came of my own free will. I thought you might feel more inclined to discuss the matter of the 'proposal' with me rather than with Mother."

"Oh."

"Have you thought about it? What is your answer?"

I remained silent. I was so weary of the subject. I just wanted to shut my eyes and forget about it. But I knew that Sara cared for me. I loved her too. She was like a second mother to me.

"I have thought about it, Sara, and the answer is 'No'." The words came out so easily that I was taken by surprise. I felt a great weight lifting from my shoulders. I sat up, my weariness gone.

"I see. You want to waste your youth, just like your elder sisters are doing. Let me give you some advice..."

"I don't want an arranged marriage."

"*I* had an arranged marriage, and I'm happy. Despite the fact that we are always short of money, we are happy and I'm raising a happy family."

"You are very lucky then."

"Luck has nothing to do with it. It's how you go *into* a marriage. What are your objections anyway? Stepan is a presentable young man. His family is well off. Not like my lot, poorer than church mice. And most important of all, the two families have known each other for years and they are the best of friends. From what I hear, his parents can't wait to see you and welcome you into their family. This is a match ordained in heaven. What more could you possibly want?" We fell silent. What more, indeed?

"I want to wait until Lillie and Nonnie are married. It's not right that I should marry before them."

"You might have to wait forever. That Lillie... she could have had the pick of suitable young men. If she hadn't been so stubborn, Nonnie would have been married by now, too."

"I'm not going to marry someone I don't know and don't like."

"How can you say you don't like him, when you've only seen him once. You will like him when you get to know him. And love him, even - in time."

"He is a lot older than me, for a start."

"Only eight or nine years. That's nothing. Anyway, you need someone older who can keep your feet firmly on the ground. Someone who has experience of life and will know how to treat you and care for you."

"But I don't..."

"No, listen. I've got a good idea. Why don't we tell Mother that you are willing to let Stepan and his parents come to see you? If all goes well, we can drink the *Sherbet* to observe the custom of *Hosgap* and then set the date for the engagement." The *Hosgap* is like a betrothal ceremony; it literally means 'to tie with words'.

"Wait a minute! You talk as though it has all been planned."

"No, no. There is always two or three weeks between the *Hosgap* and the engagement ceremony. During this time, you will get to know Stepan, as he will be taking you out - with a chaperone, of course. If, after this time, you still find him unacceptable, then you let *me* know and I promise you that the engagement will not take place."

"As if..."

"I mean it. *Parole d'honneur.*" Sara uttered these last words with such sincerity, such conviction that all I could do was to stare at her in amazement. We looked at one another for a long, silent moment. She was pleading with me to take her advice and say 'Yes'. And I was pleading with her not to make me go through with what she was suggesting.

I don't know what it was. Maybe the moment had come, when I could no longer hold back the tidal wave that had been threatening to engulf me these past weeks. I surrendered.

That night, I experienced my own private epiphany. Maybe, I could use the *Hosgap* to my advantage. It would give me two or three weeks to do everything I could to make sure that Stepan realised that he and I were incompatible. He would call off the engagement and I would be free! To break the *Hosgap* was not considered to be socially and morally unacceptable. It could be hushed up swiftly, without either party losing face. The reason given was normally 'unsuitability' between the couple or between the two families. Mother would be devastated, of course, when the whole thing collapsed, but she would get over it.

A great weight lifted from my shoulders. I would go along with Sara's plan. After all, it was only for a few weeks. My only worry now was that I still hadn't heard from Paul.

Chapter Eighteen

The day of the *Hosgap* arrived. The big formal salon was full. Stepan and his parents had arrived. Sara had come, without the children, for moral support. And Auntie Roza 'happened' to be visiting us. Mother and Father had welcomed the guests and they were talking and smoking as they waited for me to make my entrance. I could hear their muted voices from my room. I looked at my reflection in the mirror and shrugged my shoulders. I was simply dressed, in a skirt and blouse, no make-up, not even a trace of lipstick, my shoulder-length hair tied back and flat-heeled shoes on my feet.

There was no point in delaying the moment any longer - I might as well get it over with. I took a deep breath and walked in. The conversation stopped and I felt everyone's gaze on me - taking in every detail, from my clothes and hair down to my shoes. I shook the visitors' hands dutifully and sat down. I saw Auntie Roza looking at me with surprise. I knew what she was thinking: "Why, in heaven's name, have you not made an effort with your appearance?" I didn't look at Mother, because I didn't want to see her disapproval. Instead, I made polite conversation by answering questions with monosyllables, and stared out of the window, letting their conversation lap around me. The formal ritual of 'Proposal' and 'Acceptance' began. Stepan's father was the first to speak.

"Well Artin, the time has come to talk about why we are here today," he said. "Now that we have seen your daughter - and like what we see - we would like to ask her hand in marriage to our son Stepan. Have you any objections to our proposal?"

"No Rafael. We have no objections at all. We are honoured to accept your son's proposal of marriage to our daughter, Reya."

"Thank you Artin. We are privileged to welcome your daughter, Reya, to our humble home. Let us then seal the *Hosgap* with the *Sherbet* and congratulate the young couple."

"Yes, we will do that." Even though the two families were good friends, they still had to go through with the prescribed formula.

"The ladies can set the date for the engagement ceremony," said Father.

"We have to notify Father Serop in Nicosia to perform it."

"Would three weeks on Saturday be suitable?" asked Stepan's mother.

"Yes, that would be fine," answered Mother, with no hesitation whatsoever. No sooner had these words been exchanged, than Lillie and Nonnie left the room to get the *Sherbet*. They were back within minutes, with a tray of our best chrystal glasses filled with the sweet, rose-coloured drink. They all raised their glasses.

"To the young couple," they chorused and started to sip their drinks. I sat there watching a ritual that seemed to be totally unconnected to me. Surely, this was not happening. I would wake up and realise that it was just one of my bizarre dreams. For it *was* bizarre. In a very short space of time, they had sealed my fate, or so they thought. Apart from our handshake and a brief 'hello', Stepan and I had not spoken. I hadn't even looked at him. I wondered what he was feeling at this moment. Stepan's mother took something from her handbag and came over to me.

"Welcome to our family, my daughter. Please accept this small token of our affection for you. I am sure you and Stepan will be very happy together." It was a delicate gold bracelet she held in her hand. "It suits your slender wrist perfectly," she said as she slipped it on. I got up and thanked her. She gave me a hug and went back to her seat.

Not long afterwards, they left, but not before hearty congratulations and good wishes were exchanged, one more time. Stepan was the last to say his goodbyes. He shook my hand and then turned to my father.

"Mr. Artin, can I have your permission to take Reya, Lillie and Nonnie to the cinema on Saturday and then to dinner afterwards?" he asked. "I shall ask my sister Agnes to come, too."

"Yes, of course my boy!" Father beamed. So, I thought. With a few words of exchange between the two men, Father's responsibility for his daughter had shifted effortlessly to her suitor.

We all went out to the front door to see them off. They got into Stepan's car - a convertible - and he drove off. The family was in a celebratory mood after the visitors left. Everybody started to talk at once, going over the 'event'. They 'ah'd' and 'ooh'd' over the gold bracelet. Over coffee, the conversation turned to the forthcoming engagement ceremony. There was tremendous amount of work to be done in the following three weeks.

"I can come with you to help you choose the engagement dress," volunteered Nonnie. "The *Fashion House* is the only place to go for a formal dress, isn't it?"

"I suppose so," I said absent-mindedly, for I had other things on my mind. I had only three weeks to prove to Sara that I was not compatible with Stepan.

Saturday night arrived. Nonnie and I were ready. Lillie had promised to go out with one of her colleagues, so she couldn't come with us. Nonnie was to be my 'chaperone'. Stepan came to pick us up about six. Nonnie and Agnes sat at the back, while I sat in front. I felt strange sitting next to him. Girls always sat at the back. There weren't any exciting films showing in the three cinemas that weekend. We ended up watching a mediocre musical starring Jane Powell.

Afterwards, Stepan took us to a *taverna* in Paralimni, a village on the outskirts of Famagusta. I had never been there before. It was a typical village *taverna*, with bright bougainvillaea blazing against its white walls and Greek folk music playing in the background.

"They make the best *souvlakia* here," he said, as we walked under the vine pergola into the bar and restaurant area. "It's really nice and cool here in the summer." The owner of the *taverna* came to greet us.

"*Yiassou*, Mr. Stepan. Good evening, ladies." He beamed at us and led us to a table by the window overlooking the garden. We had a wonderful meal. The pork was charcoal-grilled to perfection. The accompanying salads were crisp and colourful and the beer was ice-cold.

"Almost as good as the *souvlakia* I make at home," Stepan joked, when we finished eating. He ordered coffee and lit a cigarette with his gold Dunhill lighter. He did not ask any of us girls if we would like to smoke - he knew the rules of female social etiquette - respectable girls did not smoke in public. He was a charming host throughout the evening. There was nothing remotely shy about him. He was no Clark Gable, but he kept us entertained with an easy repartee. His voice was deep and musical and held a hint of laughter.

It was past midnight when we got home. We shook hands again, and before he drove off, he spoke to me.

"I'm going to Beirut on Tuesday, on business. I'll see you when I get back."

Chapter Nineteen

We were very busy at work. So busy that we were working overtime. We had an hour's break for lunch and then carried on working until five in the afternoon. I was glad of it, because it took my mind off the recent activities, in which I was unwillingly taking part. In the morning, the postman had delivered four long-awaited letters from Paul. The postal strike in England was over at last.

During the lunch break, I started reading my letters. Each one harped on the same, familiar question. His parents accepted me, he argued, why couldn't my parents accept him? Why was I finding it so difficult to tell my parents about us? For the first time, I felt frustration towards him. I had hoped that his letters would cheer me up, but instead they made me realise that the gulf that separated us was wider than I had envisaged.

I was reading the last letter when Mr. Eastman came over to my desk.

"I see you've heard from your Corporal," he said, with a big grin on his face.

"Yes, at long last. What is a 'bed-sit', Mr. Eastman?"

"It's a rented furnished room in a house, where one can live and sleep. Why do you ask?"

"Paul writes that he has a bed-sit in a house in Barnes, S.W. l3. Is that a nice place?"

"I should say so. It is a suburb - a lovely little village - of London by the River Thames. What is he doing these days?"

"Well, he is now settled in his new job. He is very busy, as he has started evening school. He wants to be an aeronautical engineer."

"Aeronautical engineer, eh? Very enterprising of him, indeed."

"How long will it take him?"

"Oh, at least four or five years."

"As long as that?"

"Well yes, as it's a part-time course. It will be difficult for him, because he will be working in the day and attending classes and studying in the evenings. Are you alright, my dear?" I was silent, taking in what Mr. Eastman had told me. "You look so preoccupied these days. You hardly talk to me. Is everything alright on the home front?"

"Oh, Mr. Eastman!" I blurted it out. "I have to make an important decision, and it is far more difficult than I thought possible."

"My dear girl! How sad! Is it about your Corporal?" I nodded. There was no mistaking the concern in his eyes. We were silent for a moment. Then he put his hand on my shoulder.

"If there's anything I can do…"

"I'll be O.K. I'll tell you about it, when I can see things more clearly. How long are we to work overtime?"

"Oh, I should think it'll be another two weeks at least. Still, a few extra pennies won't hurt our pockets, will it?" he said, attempting to sound cheerful. Extra money was the last thing on my mind. I tried to imagine living in a bed-sit with Paul in Barnes, both of us working hard to make ends meet. Waiting for four or five years, before Paul achieved his goal. My feelings were so confused.

It had been a long day. At five o'clock, tired and with a slight headache, I left the office. The walk home would do me good. I had hardly walked for a few yards when I noticed a car pass by, slow down and stop. My heart gave a lurch. I recognised the car immediately. It was its unusual colour - pistachio green. Stepan got out and came towards me.

"Hello! Nonnie told me you were working overtime."

"Oh… Hello! I didn't know you were back."

"I came back early this morning. I thought we might go to the *Milk Bar* for a coffee." I hesitated, not knowing how to respond. "I know we are not supposed to go out without a 'chaperone', but I wanted to talk to you in private." Stepan mistook the reason for my uncertainty. "It's all right, don't look so scared. Nonnie and Agnes will cover for us."

The *Milk Bar* was crowded when we got there. There was a strong aroma of coffee, mingled with cigarette smoke. We sat down at a table by the window, facing each other. It felt so strange and awkward, being alone with him. Stepan ordered coffee for us both, and when it came, he lit a cigarette and inhaled deeply. He must have felt awkward too, because he started to fiddle with his lighter. I waited for him to speak.

"I came back a day early, as I finished my business quicker than I thought. Look what I brought you." He took out a small box from his pocket, opened it and passed it to me across the table. "Do you like it?" I was so surprised, I didn't know what to say. A large solitaire diamond ring nestled on the velvet cushion. It was a beautiful ring. Despite myself, I was impressed, not to say overwhelmed, by his action. He took the ring out of its box and put it on my finger. "Perfect fit. I remembered you had slender hands. I know it is not our tradition to give engagement rings, but I thought it was time we adopted this custom. Do you like it?" he repeated. I found my voice, at last.

"Oh! It is... beautiful... but we are not engaged yet..." I stammered, blushing a deep red.

"We will be, in about two weeks or so. My mother is so taken with you. During lunch today, she said, 'I can't wait for the day when Reya will come to live with us.' She is planning on redecorating the big room at the back of the house for us."

"You mean to live in the same house with your family?" I blurted out, alarmed. There was a flicker of something in his eyes - surprise perhaps - but it was gone instantly.

"No, no. I told my parents that it would be better if we started our married life on our own. Father agreed. He owns a plot of land at the back of Alasia beach and he said he would build a house for us." He put the box back into his pocket. "I see you're not wearing your bracelet," he said, looking directly into my eyes.

"No. Not yet…"

"Have you not told your colleagues at work?" He looked puzzled.

"No."

"I see. Mother has told all the family and our close friends." He looked at me inquiringly. "This afternoon, when I told Stelios that I was getting engaged to a girl who works in the NAAFI, he said he knows you."

"Who is Stelios?"

"He is a friend of mine. He works at the Customs & Excise. Don't you know him?" I looked at him blankly and shook my head. "He also said that he used to see you some mornings, talking to a soldier. Is it true?"

I was startled by his words. I now remembered the man, Stelios. He was a Customs Officer. He brought Bills of Lading and other documents to our office. He had meetings with Mr. Eastman. I hardly knew the man, apart from exchanging a 'hello' or 'good-morning'. Realisation of what he was saying began to dawn on me. I understood perfectly what he was hinting at. My plan might work after all.

"What if it is?" I looked at him somewhat challengingly, shrugging my shoulders. Was he trying to call off the engagement? And if he was, why had he just given me an engagement ring? Whatever his intentions, this was my chance to make him realise that I wasn't the right girl for him.

"It is true, then."

"Yes it is. I was friendly with a soldier. We talked during our coffee breaks. We used to write to each other - we still do. We went swimming together, a couple of times. He went back to England last November, after doing his National Service." I stopped and blushed. My words sounded like a confession.

"Hmm... I see," he said, smiling and nodding his head.

"And *I* can see that you find this unacceptable. You can have your ring back. It's not too late you know, you can call the whole thing off." Stepan started laughing. I looked at him coldly. "I don't find this funny at all. You don't have to mock me." I took the ring off my finger. The light from the window caught it and the diamond exploded into a thousand fiery stars.

"Hey, take it easy! Don't be so quick to..."

"I don't like to be ridiculed, or to be cross-examined."

"I wasn't trying to do that. I merely wanted to know if Stelios was talking about you or some other girl."

"It sounded like a criminal record."

"I'm sorry." He put the ring back on my finger and held my hand for a moment. "Please don't take it off again - ever. I'm not interested in your past - it belongs to you, just as my past belongs to me. Not that either of us has got a 'past' to speak of." He took a sip of his coffee and fidgeted with his lighter. He was thoughtful for a moment and then he continued. "But I would like you to know that this *Hosgap* business is something beyond my experience, too. I cannot understand why our culture does not allow young people to go out together and get to know each other. I can't understand why we can't have parties where young people can meet. Do you think I like the idea of getting engaged to a girl I hardly know?"

"Why are you doing it, then? You are a man. You can do what you like. You can refuse to marry someone you don't know. Whereas a girl cannot continue to go against the wishes of her parents, forever."

"It's not so different for a man, you know. I was saying 'no' to girls my parents were choosing for me. But when I saw you in church that Sunday, something happened here, in my heart. I didn't even know who you were, but I said to myself, 'I'll marry that girl, if she'll have me' and that's how it started. And later, when I saw you in the nightclub and danced with you, I was more than sure that you were the one for me."

"And Nonnie said it was probably my peach-coloured outfit you were attracted to!"

Stepan grinned. "So you do have a sense of humour! That's the first time I've seen you smile! You always seem either preoccupied, or somewhere far away. Look, we can't talk here. We'll go for a drive and then I'll take you to the *Alasia* for dinner. They make the best *kleftiko* in town. Do you like lamb?"

"Yes, I do, especially the potatoes that come with it."

"Let's go, then," he said.

He picked up his cigarettes and lighter, took my arm and propelled me out of the *Milk Bar* and into his car, before I could utter a word.

An hour later, we were sitting on the terrace of the restaurant. It was a beautiful evening. The stars shone. A million shimmering lights reflected on the surface of the sea. In the distance, pleasure boats rocked gently at anchor. A yacht was preparing to set sail.

"Is the *kleftiko* alright?" Stepan asked.

"It's delicious," I said, and took another mouthful of the tender lamb.

"Would you like another *ouzo*?" I shook my head. He ordered one for himself. He had once again proved to be a charming host, never at a loss to find a topic of conversation. Instead of disliking him, I was being drawn to him against my wishes. He was not the ogre I had imagined him to be.

With Paul, it had been the fascination with each other's differences that had first drawn us together, but now those differences were proving to be obstacles in the path of our love. With Stepan, the culture that we shared was fast becoming the main attraction. There was harmony between us. I no longer felt so acutely shy in his company. The *ouzo* helped of course.

"I almost forgot. I have a box of *Paklava* in the car for you..."

"Lebanese *Paklava*! I love it, and so does the family."

"I know. Everybody loves it. You can't go to Beirut and not bring home a box of *Paklava* with you. You could not be forgiven for it!" We both laughed at the often-used phrase. It was true, though. Lebanese *Paklava* was the best in the whole of the Middle East.

"As I was saying earlier," he said. "This out-dated *Hosgap* business is just as difficult for a man."

"But you have a choice, and I do not."

"I'll tell you something that might surprise you. There was a rebel in me once. I never wanted to go into my father's business. I never wanted to be a jeweller."

"What did you want to do, then?"

"I wanted to become a singer. I have a good, strong voice, even if I say so myself. I might have become another Aznavour, if I'd had the chance. On the other hand, I might have failed miserably. Who knows? But I was never given the opportunity to find out. I wanted to go to Beirut to study music and singing. Father would not even consider it. Instead, as soon as I graduated from the American Academy in Larnaca, I went into his jewellery business."

"Didn't you try to persuade your father?"

"Of course I did. I begged him to give me a chance. He refused even to discuss it."

"Oh."

"Being the only son did not help either. I resented working in the shop, but it didn't make any difference. I learnt then that duty is a cruel master. I dutifully went into the family business. After a couple of years working in the shop, Father sent me to Beirut, but not to study music - to learn about gold, gems and so on, for heaven's sake."

"How long for?"

"I lived in Beirut for a year. I stayed with my Uncle Noubar and his family in their big house on the outskirts of Bourdj-Hamoud. Uncle took me under his wing and taught me everything about the jewellery business - from designing, to cutting, to selling. He has two jewellery shops in the centre of Beirut." I thought of my morning in the gold district of Beirut, with my cousin Toros. It seemed like a whole lifetime ago.

"I've been to Beirut…"

"Have you, when?"

"Last year. I went with Marko, we only stayed for a few days."

"Did you like it?"

"Yes, I did."

"Did you go to the gold and jewellery section?"

"My cousin took us. It was an unbelievable experience. We liked the food and everything, but I wouldn't want to live in a country where the police carry guns."

"That's the way I feel too. I wouldn't change Cyprus with any place in the world."

"Your father must be very proud of you."

"Yes, he is. But do you know what he told me, when he took me to the airport, that day? He said, 'If you decide to abandon my plans for you, then you are on your own - don't expect any help from me'."

"My God! That must have been terribly painful for you."

"It was, at the time. But later, I realised that he was being cruel to be kind. I don't agree with his way of thinking, but I do understand it. It was the same when I got my first motorbike. Father used to stomp about and shout when I was late coming home, but that was only because he was worried sick about me."

"I know, my father behaves in the same way when Marko is late coming home on his motorbike. He rants and he raves, 'I'll break that bike in two, when that boy gets in', but as soon as he hears the roar of the engine, he says, 'Thank God he's alright' and goes to bed, and never says a word to Marko the next morning!"

"We 'boys' are also trapped by the boundaries of our culture. We are given a twentieth century education, but we are expected to live in the nineteenth century!"

"But I still say that you have a much better deal than us girls. You can smoke, drink, go to nightclubs and stay out till the early hours of the morning."

"Do you smoke?" He opened his packet and offered me one. I shook my head.

"I tried it once and I nearly choked. But that doesn't mean that I might not want to smoke in the future." Stepan tried hard to disguise his amusement, and despite myself, I had to smile back.

"I don't mind if you smoke," he said. "Do you think I don't know that Agnes and Nonnie smoke in secret?"

"I remember the day Mother caught them smoking," I told him. "The shock and disapproval on her face is something I shall never forget."

"I can imagine. My mother is not so strict. She will have a cigarette with her coffee. I also know what Nonnie and Agnes get up to when they go swimming - talking and flirting with boys, when they get the chance. I'm not an 'old-head', you know - as you will discover, in time."

"Do you get on with your father, now?"

"Yes, we work well together. He let me modernise the shop, the way I wanted to. So you see, little one, it hasn't been easy for me either, but thankfully it turned out alright in the end."

"Your mother must be proud of you, too."

"Yes. I've made my parents happy by being a Dutiful Son. I shall make them even happier by marrying a Nice Armenian Girl!" I looked at him, as he lit another cigarette. His eyes were full of mischief. I felt a surge of realisation sweep over me. This man, Stepan Manoukian, was real, not a figment of my imagination. The marriage he offered me was the reality. I thought of Paul – all our dreams. I felt him slipping into the past. I tried to conjure up his face. But it refused to come into focus. All I could see was Stepan's smile.

PART TWO

Chapter Twenty

The date of the engagement loomed like a nemesis. Three days more, then the die would be cast. Mother was panicking, because I hadn't yet bought my engagement dress. I had looked - half-heartedly – in the *Fashion House*, on my way home from work a couple of days before, but I'd seen nothing that I liked. Unfortunately, Florentia, our dressmaker, was too busy to make the dress for me.

"Why don't we go to Nicosia to find your dress?" Nonnie asked me. I'm sure Mother had prompted her, as time was really running short. "I've got Thursday off," she said. "We can go to *Maison Louise* first. I'm sure you'll find a dress there. Failing that we can go to *Moderna*. What do you think?" These two dress shops were the most fashionable and prestigious establishments in Nicosia. If you didn't find what you wanted there, then there was something wrong with you! I was resigned to my fate.

"I'm sure I can get Thursday off," I said.

The taxi dropped us at the main shopping area. We went to *Maison Louise* first. I tried on three cocktail dresses, but none of them looked right on me. As soon as I put on the fourth dress, we both knew that this was the one. It was a lovely, peacock blue taffeta cocktail dress, with a scooped neckline. It fitted me perfectly except for the length. It was too long. The assistant assured us it wouldn't take long to have it shortened for me. While the alteration was being done, we went to several shoe shops to look for a suitable pair. In the end, I settled for a pair of sling back evening shoes in black satin, with a two-inch heel.

After we had finished shopping, we collected my dress and walked over to Sara's house for lunch. I was desperate to see her before the engagement party. I longed for her to reassure me that I was doing the right thing in going through with the betrothal, and to confirm again that if it didn't work out, she would support me.

We were late. The family had already had their lunch and the children had gone back to school. Sara was waiting for us.

"It's chicken and rice *pilav* with onion and tomato salad," she said, piling our dishes high with the rice and succulent chicken. "I saved the chicken liver for you, Reya. I know you like it."

"Shopping makes you hungry," said Nonnie, as we both tucked in. Sara was delighted with my dress and shoes.

"The colour really suits you," she said. "I know you'll look very pretty in it." Then she showed us the dress she had made for herself and the half-finished one she was making for her daughter. "See you on Sunday," she beamed. "We'll come early, so I can give Mother a hand with the last minute preparations." She was so happy for me, so utterly convinced that I was happy too, that I didn't have the heart to ask her anything. I just hugged her and got into the taxi next to Nonnie. We waved to her, as it pulled away.

Mother was relieved that our shopping trip had been successful.

That evening, I saw Stepan. He came to the house to pick me up. We were going out to dinner without a chaperone. This time he took me to a fish restaurant, by the sea. Stepan seemed to know so many places to eat. He ordered a cold beer for himself and a coke for me.

"How was your day in Nicosia?" he asked. "Did you find the dress you wanted?"

"I did," I said.

"I won't ask you what colour it is. I want it to be a surprise!" He flashed his mischievous grin. I smiled, aware of the dreaded blush that was spreading on my face. The waiter appeared with our drinks. Stepan ordered for both of us: red mullet grilled on charcoal, with a mixed salad and crusty bread.

"I'm assuming that you like fish," he said.

"I do like fish, but I have to be so careful with the fish bones that it puts me off…"

"Why? What happened?"

"When I was a child, a fish bone got stuck in my throat and it just wouldn't budge. It was so painful. It hurt every time I tried to swallow. Grandmother made me eat slice after slice of bread - without the crusts. She said it was the only way to dislodge the bone. I wouldn't eat fish for years after that!"

"I'm not surprised. But don't worry, little one. I'll take out all the bones, before you take a single mouthful." We were silent for a moment, sipping our drinks and listening to the music coming from the radio. We watched the boats, skimming across the water. The moon was up and it lent a shimmer to the calm sea.

I watched Stepan as he lit a cigarette and inhaled deeply. I felt sure any number of mothers would have gladly given their daughters to him. But he had wanted to marry me. I wondered why. Why hadn't he gone for Nonnie or Lillie? They were beautiful and charming, not shy and self-conscious like me. Before I met Paul, I had assumed that I would get married some time, but only in the distant future. I was completely taken by surprise by Stepan's proposal. I had certainly not expected it to happen so soon or in quite the way it did, before Lillie and Nonnie were married. I wasn't ready for this, and I wasn't sure I ever would be. My romance with Paul had made me question my destiny – why should I not be free to choose my own husband?

"Penny for them?" Stepan whispered. I didn't dare voice my thoughts. Fortunately the waiter came with our food and I didn't have to answer him. True to his word, Stepan carefully picked the bones from my fish, before handing the plate to me with a flourish. "Happy eating," he said and started to pick the bones from his.

"Thanks," I said, and looked at my plate to see if there were any little bones which had escaped.

"You can see I have a fondness for food," he said. "My mother is a very good cook. Do you like cooking?"

"I like food too, but I can't say I like cooking – especially not fish! I enjoy baking, though."

"Baking? What kind of baking?"

I shrugged my shoulders. "Cakes, biscuits, Easter cookies, that sort of thing."

"Oh! That's good to know. When you don't feel like cooking, we can eat cake!" The now familiar cheeky grin lit his face and he burst out laughing. His laugh was so infectious that I started to laugh too. When the coffee came, he lit a cigarette and then offered me one. I declined.

"You can smoke if you want to, I don't mind at all."

"No thanks," I said, shaking my head.

"I am so looking forward to Sunday," he said. "It will all be official then and we can start getting to know each other better. Mum and Dad don't mind you wanting a small engagement party, just family and very close friends. After all, it is your choice."

"I remember Sara's engagement party. Preparations went on for days. There was music and dancing that went on till the early hours of the morning. I didn't want all that."

"That's absolutely fine with me. A small engagement party, but a big wedding, eh?"

"Only if you want it," I told him. He took my hand, holding it in both of his, as he looked directly at me.

"Yes, I do. I want a big wedding and a big party afterward," he said. "Just like the big Name Day parties our parents used to give. I remember the preparations that went into these parties. The food, not to mention the *raki* they consumed!"

"I remember those parties too! We children were allowed to stay up late and listen to the music. My father played the *duduk* and some one else – I don't remember who – played the mandolin. They played so beautifully together."

"They played records on their old-fashioned gramophones and they sang too, all the old songs from the old country. These parties went on till morning sometimes. Or so my father used to tell us."

"I can almost hear them singing the song *Adanali,* or something like that, can't you?"

"I sure can. My favourite song was *Iskudar* ," Stepan said and promptly started to sing the first stanza of the old Turkish song in a low voice.

"They must have felt so nostalgic…" We were silent for a while, each remembering those parties.

"You know what?" Stepan asked, jolting me back to the present. "I believe, no, not believe, I *know* we shall be happy together. There are no obstacles in our way, are there?" The question was so unexpected, it took me by surprise. What was I doing here? I couldn't bring myself to look at him, nor answer him, even though I could feel his eyes burning into mine. Paul's handsome face swam before me: his fair hair, his determined jaw and the love in his sapphire blue eyes. With an enormous effort, I drove the image from my mind, forcing Stepan's face into its place. Stepan with his cheeky grin, his dark searching eyes, fringed with long lashes and his thick black hair.

"*Are* there any obstacles?" he repeated. Here was the moment I was waiting for, a last opportunity to draw a halt to the engagement, but I found I couldn't take it. I met his gaze and answered him.

"There are no obstacles."

Later that evening, I lay on my bed and tried to think straight. I had become quite an expert in hiding my true feelings. I had pretended to enjoy my day off from work, shopping for my engagement dress, and sharing a meal with my fiancé to be. But now, in the privacy of my bedroom, the turmoil deep down inside me surfaced again. I had not written to Paul yet. I had been telling myself that was because I hadn't yet decided what to tell him. But I wasn't being truthful – to myself, or Paul. With trembling fingers, I picked up my pen for the umpteenth time. Again, I hesitated. How on earth was I going to write this letter? I remembered the first time I had written to Paul. It had been the start of our romance. I reached into my handbag and took out Paul's last letter. I didn't have to read it again. I knew the contents by heart.

Conflicting emotions ran through my mind. Again and again, I had tried to visualize the scene where I announced the engagement was off. Over and over, I tried to hear myself telling Mother and Father about Paul. They were expecting me to perform the role they had set out for me. My announcement would dash all their hopes and bring disgrace and separation. I couldn't do it to them. It was unthinkable. I felt guilty. My last letter would hurt Paul - deeply. I shouldn't have gone along with his dreams. I should have made him understand that the cultural differences between us were just too great. What a fool I had been. And now he would hate me forever. Because he would never understand that my future was mapped out for me. There was nothing I could do to change it.

Tears of anger and frustration sprang to my eyes. I was angry with Stepan. If he hadn't come along when he did, my life would have gone on as before. I would have been happy to continue my long distance romance with Paul, hoping that one day we could be together. But now my life had changed forever. The dream was no more. I went over the options again. But there weren't any options, not really. There never had been, if I was honest with myself.

If writing this letter was proving to be painful, breaking the news of my forthcoming engagement to my colleagues at work had been just as difficult. On Monday morning, Mr. Eastman had come over to my desk and asked me if I had a nice weekend.

"I've got something to tell you Mr. Eastman," I'd said. I think he knew what I was about to say.

"Yes my dear?"

"I am getting engaged next Sunday. Can I have Thursday off? I need to buy a new dress…" I had blurted it our, glad to have it off my chest.

"Of course you can have Thursday off, my dear. Congratulations. Who is the lucky chap?" The dear man, he hadn't batted an eyelid. Instead, he had tried to make it easier for me.

"He is Armenian. The families have known each other for years. I… I couldn't go against my parents' wishes…"

"Of course you couldn't. Sometimes decisions are taken out of our hands. I wish you every happiness." I had been so relieved at his reaction. Would Paul be so understanding? Within a few minutes, everyone in the office had known about my forthcoming engagement. They were all so kind, nobody even mentioned Paul, or 'the Corporal', as they fondly called him. When Andreas came to take my empty coffee cup, he bent to whisper, "You cannot go against your destiny, so be happy." But his misty eyes had belied his words.

It was past midnight, when, at last, I picked up my pen and started writing. I stopped railing against my destiny.

Chapter Twenty One

If my parents were disappointed that I didn't want a big engagement party, they did not show it. The party was nothing like Sara's, and I was glad of it. In all, there were about twenty-five people. Eleni couldn't come, because she was on holiday in Athens.

It was a delightful May morning. The sky was a perfect bright blue. The promise of a glorious summer was everywhere. When everyone was seated, Father Serop performed the ceremony. Stepan and I stood by the window. On the coffee table, resting on a small satin cushion, lay the two gold engagement rings. My ring was engraved with Stepan's name, and his ring with mine. Father Serop started with a prayer, and then blessed the rings, before placing them on our fingers. He said a few words to the 'congregation' and then another prayer, and it was over.

Once again, Mother did us proud. There was a sumptuous buffet lunch with plenty to drink, followed by a variety of desserts and coffee. By five o'clock, the party was over.

"It was a wonderful engagement party, wasn't it? You looked lovely in your blue dress," said Stepan.

I felt relieved that it was over. I must say, though, I was pleased with my dress, not only because of its unusual colour but also because it was my first party dress. "Thank you," I managed to smile at him. "You didn't look so bad yourself." In fact, he looked almost dashing in his new cream coloured summer suit. It suited his swarthy complexion.

When we said goodnight, he put his arms around me. Tilting my face up to his, he kissed me softly on the lips. I had crossed the Rubicon.

During the weeks that followed, I dreaded the postman. I was so sure that Paul would reply to my letter. What would he say? How would he respond to my change of heart? Would he suffer rejection with good grace? Would he ever forgive me? Probably not. Worse still, would he think that my love for him had been just a selfish whim? But Paul did not reply. The summer wore on, and still no letter came. Gradually, I stopped being anxious. But the guilt was still there. I had to put the whole sorry 'episode' of my romance behind me - I realized - if I was to continue my new life with any measure of success.

If anyone had asked me if I was happy, I would have answered that I didn't know. I was in limbo. But nobody did ask me. For her part, Mother was delighted that I had taken her advice and was behaving like any obedient daughter should. There was always a big smile on her face when she greeted Stepan. When he came to dinner, she treated him like a long lost son. As the days went on, I allowed myself to be seduced away from my old dreams. It was not difficult. Stepan played the role of seducer so well. He was charming, sophisticated and attentive, always cheerful, as though he didn't have a care in the world. He showered me with gifts, and made me feel that I was the centre of his universe. What more could a girl possibly want?

Every evening after work, he came to the house, smartly dressed and ready to enjoy the evening with me. If there was a good film on, we would go to the cinema, or otherwise out to dinner at one of the many Tavernas by the sea. On Saturday afternoons, we would go swimming and on Sundays, we had lunch together, either at his house or mine.

A couple of weeks after the engagement party, Stepan said he wanted me to meet his friends.

"There won't be many people, I only have a few really close friends. I thought we might have a Kebab party at my house. We could go out, but I think it would be more informal at home. What do you think?"

"It sounds good. I should like to meet your friends."

"Next Sunday, then? You'll like them, they're a good crowd."

"I hope they'll like me too."

"Of course they will! There's Bedros and his wife Araxi – Roxi for short. They have two children, a boy and a girl."

"I know of him. Marko takes his car to Bedros's garage to be serviced – it's on Elephtheria Street."

"Yes, that's the one. Then there's Kevork and Sona. They have a daughter."

"Yes. I know of them too. I've seen Sona at our house several times, even spoken to her, but I can't say that I know her very well."

"Oh! Why is that?"

"Because I'm the youngest daughter. After showing my face and saying a few words of welcome, I'm banished to the kitchen to make the coffee and tea – not to be seen again until the next time!" Stepan shook his head in disbelief.

"All these old-fashioned customs! It's time our grandparents and parents accepted the fact that we no longer live in the past century."

"I know. The world has changed, but they have not."

"And yet, you didn't object... I mean your parents didn't object to your getting married before your elder sisters did!" That mischievous gleam came into his eyes again. "And of course I'm grateful for that. Otherwise I might have had to wait for years, before I could marry you!" I didn't comment on this remark. It was one custom I would gladly have abided by.

"Where was I? Oh yes," continued Stepan. "I don't think you know my Greek friends – Nico and his wife Anna. They got married a couple of years ago, but they have no children yet. I was one of the *koumbaro* (best man) at their wedding."

"No. I don't know your Greek friends at all."

"Nico and his brother George own the shop next-door but one to ours."

"Oh, the fabric shop."

"That's the one. Father and I get all our suit fabric from them. So do Mother and Agnes. I'll take you there one afternoon, and you can choose as much dress fabric as you like. Nico and I have been friends for years, more like brothers really. There is nothing we wouldn't do for each other."

"I know what you mean, Eleni and I were very close. But now she lives in Nicosia, and we hardly see one another. Our lives have gone on different directions."

"Don't feel sad. Next time we are in Nicosia, we'll pay her a visit."

Stepan's party took place the next Sunday evening. He picked me up about five. His parents had already left. They wanted Stepan to have the freedom to entertain his friends, without having his parents around.

"Where have your parents gone?"

"They've gone to visit friends. They won't be home till late. By the way, mum and dad are so pleased that you call them *Mayrik* (Mother) and *Hayrik* (Father). It's wonderful."

"I don't find it difficult at all. It seemed quite natural. What about you?"

"I have no problem with it either. It is a measure of respect isn't it"?

"Yes, and tradition."

"It makes our parents happy. I'm beginning to value the old ways, after all!" I returned his smile. I looked around the kitchen. It was spotless.

"Shall we start preparing the food?" I asked.

"Yes. I've cut the meat in cubes and marinated it. All I have to do is put them on the skewers. Do you know how to make the salads?"

"I'm rather good at that. We used to have Kebab every Saturday, for lunch. We girls took turns to make the salads, light the charcoal fire and cook the meat. Everything had to be ready by one o'clock. The moment that Father walked through the door, we sat down to eat! Saturdays and Sundays were the only days when the family sat down to dinner together."

"I know. It's the same in our family, too." Stepan started to put the meat on the skewers, while I started to the make the onion salad. I sliced the onions as thinly as I could, added salt and left them to wilt. In the meantime, I made the yoghurt and cucumber relish, and after that the mixed salad with lemon and olive oil dressing. "We work well together, don't we?" said Stepan. "I've finished with the skewering, is there anything I can help you with?"

"Maybe you can set the table, while I finish the onion salad." I squeezed the sliced onions, to get rid of the bitter juices and sprinkled a liberal amount of *sumac* onto it, which turned the onions to a lovely shade of pink. Then, I chopped a big bunch of parsley and mixed it with the onions. "*Voila!* The pink salad is ready!" I said, displaying the bowl.

"Excellent! What would you like to drink? I'm having a beer."

"Coca-cola, please." Stepan took my hand and we went into the garden. "You do have a big garden, don't you?" I said.

"Very big. Father is a keen gardener and he's made a good job of it." The terrace ran the whole length of the house. The vine-covered pergola overhead created a cool and shady oasis, protecting against the ferocious heat of the sun. The late afternoon sunlight filtered through the thick vine leaves, and there were already dozens of bunches of grapes hanging from the branches. There would be an abundant harvest of grapes, later on in the summer.

"You've got quite a few trees too. I've just spotted the mulberry tree. When I was a child, I used to keep silk worms and I fed them on mulberry leaves. I like its fruit as well."

"They're sweet as honey. We have lots of trees - orange, lemon, apple and *mesbilla* (cumquats) and even a banana tree."

"*Mesbilla!* I like those too." The tree was groaning under the weight of the ripe golden fruit.

"We'll pick some, now," he said. We filled a big dish. I couldn't resist washing a few under the garden tap and eating the wonderful lush fruit there and then, relishing the sweet taste. "What else did you do, as a child, apart from keeping silk worms?" Stepan asked.

"Nothing much, really. One favourite place was the woods behind the Municipal Park. I used to go there with Marko and Arpi – my best school friend. The main attraction was the carob trees. Marko would climb up to the top of the tree, pick the carobs, and throw them down to us. We filled our pockets with them, and ate them on our way home. The sugary pods are sweet, but very hard. It's a wonder I didn't break my teeth!"

"I myself prefer to eat the syrup made from carobs. Mixed with tahini and spread on bread - mouth-watering!"

"Nectar! What did you get up to when you were a boy?"

"Oh, I'm passionate about football and swimming. The beach was my destination in the summer holidays. A group of us used to go swimming every day. I've always been fascinated by the sea. I'll take you swimming to my favourite, secluded cove, you can see for yourself how spectacular it is."

"The only time Marko and I went swimming, was when Mother had the time to take us, which wasn't often. The best part was when we came out of the water, so hungry that we demolished the picnic food in no time. We would sit on the sand, wrapped in our towels, watching the sun disappear behind the horizon." Stepan and I were quiet for a moment, with our childhood memories, and then we walked over to the far corner of the garden.

"This is the coolest spot in the garden. We sit here, by the jasmine, early in the morning and have our coffee, and then again in the evening." There was an old wooden bench, two chairs and a small table. Apart from the jasmine, there were rambling roses and dozens of flowerpots, displaying a mass of colour. I could smell the heady perfume of the jasmine.

"It's like a secret garden! You could hide here and nobody would find you!" I cried out, delighted.

"I can just picture you here, engrossed in your book, oblivious to the world."

"Yes, I can, too…" My words were lost, as Stepan swept me up into his arms. Surprised by his unexpected ardour, I tried to back out from his embrace, but he held me closer.

"Don't move away. I want to share this perfect moment with you." He held me like that, for what seemed an age. Then, as though embarrassed by his rush of emotion, he let go of me. He lit a cigarette and looked at me.

"I know you're still shy with me, and I'm hoping that maybe that's the reason why you are so cool…"

"I'm sorry."

"I'm sorry too, but don't worry. I can wait. In time you'll get used to me and my ways. For now, I'm happy just to be here and share a cool drink with you – before the gang arrives. O.K?" I nodded.

Not long afterwards, his friends came. Nico and Anna were the first to arrive. Anna was friendly and lively, almost flirty. She was as tall as her husband - attractive, with green eyes and long dark hair, which she frequently tossed from side to side.

"I made *Daktila* for our dessert, as we all like it so much!" she said, with a flourish.

"*Daktila!* One of my favourite desserts," I said, my mouth watering at the sight of the dainty pastries dripping with honey.

"Stepan, did you hear that? Your fiancée has got a sweet tooth - just like you." Stepan was talking to Nico, but when he heard his name mentioned, he came over to where Anna and I were standing.

"Don't I know it!" he said with mock incredulity. "I shall have to hide the *Paklava* from her, in future!" He put his arm around my shoulder, instantly putting me at my ease.

Just then, the others arrived. After more introductions, the men went over to where the barbecue stood, all four of them concentrating on the task at hand – the cooking and enjoyment of food. There was an easy camaraderie between them. They seemed so happy and relaxed in each other's company. The women, in the meantime, had taken the salads from the fridge and put them on the table, set under the vine. Roxi had brought her speciality, which was houmous. It must have been another favourite with Stepan and his friends, as she had made a large quantity of it.

"I had no time to make anything for tonight, I've been so busy with my visitors," bemoaned Sona. "It was nice having them, but I was glad when they went! So we got some *Gadayifi* , from that new patisserie. I thought we might give them a try." She put the plate of dessert on the kitchen table, next to the *Daktila*. All three girls were friendly towards me. They seemed happy to accept me as Stepan's future wife, and welcome me into their happy little group. I liked them instantly. They were very different individuals, but together, they were in perfect harmony.

"What will you have to drink, Reya?" asked Anna. "I'm in charge of the drinks, tonight." I looked at the array of bottles on the kitchen table. There was ouzo, raki, brandy and whisky.

"I think I'll have an ouzo with ice and water, Anna. It goes with kebab, doesn't it?"

"It certainly does, I'm having one too." I could see she was good at this. She was quick too. She measured the ouzo, added the ice and water, and handed it to me with a flourish. Anna knew what the other two girls drank. She made a brandy and coke for Sona, a glass of ice-cold beer for Roxi and then she made another ouzo drink for herself. The girls knew their way around the kitchen. They obviously felt at home in Stepan's house.

"Come on girls! Stop chattering. The kebabs are ready," Bedros called, taking the cooked skewers of meat to the table. He didn't have to tell us. The tantalizing aroma of the meat cooking on the charcoal fire was like no other. It had drifted into the kitchen and was making our mouths water.

"Alright, alright, we're coming," answered Roxi, in the same teasing way as her husband, her dark eyes dancing with merriment.

"Don't let the girls talk to you till your ears drop off!" Bedros said to me, in a loud whisper. "It's a ploy, so they can eat more than you!" I took a sip of my drink and felt bold enough to say to him, "Watch me!" as I tucked into my kebab.

There was silence for a few minutes, as we munched our way through the perfectly cooked meat, the salads, the *houmous* and the mountain of *pitta* bread, warmed on the barbecue. The silence was an appreciation of the food. The men took turns, to keep an eye on the rest of the meat cooking, making sure that it did not overcook or burn.

"Compliments to the chef!" said Bedros, picking up his glass.

"Correction," said Stepan. "It's 'chefs' from now on. I'll have you know, that my lovely fiancée made the salads!"

"I thought as much," said Sona. "You never slice your onions as thin as this, Stepan. Well done, Reya." I turned as pink as my salad and smiled.

"Let's drink to the newly engaged couple. May their partnership in the kitchen be as happy and exciting as their partnership in their married life!" Many more toasts followed, during the evening.

We did justice to the food. Then we started on the dessert. There wasn't a morsel left, by the time we finished. The boys kept on drinking, while we girls cleared the table.

"I'll wash up," I said. The second ouzo had been a mistake. Stepan had gently persuaded me to have it and I hadn't been able to refuse. I wanted to clear my head.

"No you won't!" The girls chorused.

"You talk to us, while we quickly wash up and make the coffee," said Sona. She was small, with soft brown hair and surprisingly blue eyes. "We were intrigued, when Stepan told us that he had seen you in church, and decided then and there that you were the one for him…"

"We know why, now! Love at first sight! I felt the same way, when I saw my Nico for the first time. I said to myself, if I don't marry this boy I shall die!"

"Don't listen to Anna. She likes to dramatise everything. How are you two getting on? We know Stepan very well. He is a good man. I'm sure you'll be happy together," said Sona. She was the eldest and the others seemed to look up to her.

"I think being engaged is the best time in a girl's life," said Roxi, who had been silent up to now. "All the attention you get, all the new clothes and the gifts… I had a lovely time being engaged, but once you get married and the babies come …"

"I don't agree. Life is what you make it," said Sona. "Come on, girls. The coffee is made, let's join the men."

Stepan offered cigarettes to the girls and - to my surprise - they accepted. He turned to me then, and offered one to me. I blushed and shook my head. I remembered the last, and only time, I had attempted to smoke. I didn't want to make a fool of myself.

"Come on my sweet, try one. You don't have to inhale the smoke." Without thinking, I took a cigarette from the packet in his outstretched hand and put it between my lips. He took out his lighter and lit it for me. Just like in the movies, I thought, as I took a puff and blew it out. I realized to my embarrassment that they were all watching me! But I continued, regardless. I was determined to learn all the modern social graces, and smoking was definitely one of them!

The party broke up soon after. The next day was a busy working day for all of us. As I said goodbye to them, I knew, instinctively, that this 'gang' - as Stepan liked to call them - and I were going to be good friends.

It was past midnight, when he took me home. The house was in darkness. Nobody, least of all my parents, minded my staying out so late. When a girl got engaged, she was free to go wherever her fiancé took her and she could stay out as late as her fiancé wanted her to. Stepan switched the engine off.

"See, I told you. The 'gang', without exception, adores you. Did you enjoy the party?"

"I enjoyed it more than I thought I would. I think I drank more than I should, as well!" I giggled, wondering how he and the boys could stay sober after the amount of alcohol they had consumed.

"I'm glad you did, because it put you in a relaxed and happy mood. It helped to bring out your true self."

"Which is?"

"A lovely, graceful little girl, hiding beneath her cloak of shyness." Before I could answer him, he wrapped his arms around me and kissed me.

"I'd better say good night now and get you inside, before I forget my manners!" he whispered in my ear. We walked to the front door and he took my key and opened the door.

"Goodnight, little one," he said.

"Goodnight," I whispered and waited till he got in his car. He raised his hand in farewell, and drove off.

It was a blisteringly hot summer. There was no respite from the heat. Not even a summer storm to quench the parched earth. One Saturday afternoon, Stepan and I were sitting in the 'secret garden', making plans for our future. It was here that we had our first tiff.

We had agreed on most things. The date for the wedding was set for the first Sunday in October. We were to live with his parents until our new house was built, which would take at least six months. As promised, Stepan had taken me to Nico's shop and Anna had helped me choose the material for my wedding dress, and also several lengths of pretty material to be made into dresses. Florentia had already started on them. We had even agreed on the honeymoon. The mountain resort of Platres seemed the ideal place in October. The weather would be cooler, and the days long enough to make day trips to the pretty villages nearby. Everything changed, however, when the matter of my resignation from work came up.

"Have you given in your notice yet, at the office," he wanted to know.

"No, I wanted to carry on working, at least for a while."

"What! I can't have you working, after we are married!" he said. There was a look of utter disbelief on his face. His reaction was totally unexpected. It unnerved me. I paused for a moment.

"I thought I would continue working, until we moved into our own house. You said yourself, it might be nearer a year before it is built…"

"No, I cannot agree with you on this. There is no reason for you to work at all. I can provide everything you want." It was the first time I had seen him annoyed, if not angry. He lit a cigarette, fumbling a little with his lighter, and threw the packet on the table.

"It's not a matter of need." I was determined to remain calm. "What will I do all day in the house? I shall probably be in your mother's way."

"Is that the only reason"? I shook my head.

"What then?"

"I shall lose my independence, my financial independence," I blurted out.

"Independence? But you will be my wife!" The astonishment on his face was plainly visible. I blushed a deep red and the tears welled in my eyes. It was unthinkable that I should have to ask him for money.

"Other women work, after they are married…"

"I don't care what other women do. I won't have MY wife working!" An awkward silence followed. Then Stepan's anger evaporated, as suddenly as it had come.

"Don't you see?" He pleaded, in an almost tender voice. "People might think that I can't provide for you. You won't lose your 'independence', as you call it. I shall see to that. You won't be bored either. You can help Mother in the running of the house, and with the cooking if you like. You can visit your new friends, and I know they'll come to see you. I'll take you to the shop, some afternoons, if you like. You can watch me charm the customers with my selling skills! I'm sorry, if I have upset you." He looked deep into my eyes, waiting for my answer. I shrugged my shoulders.

"It's alright. I understand. I won't hurt your pride. I shall give my notice at the end of the month."

That night, as I lay in bed, I went over every detail of our conversation. I remembered Sara saying that compromise was the key to a harmonious relationship. I hoped that I would not always have to be the one to compromise, every time there was a decision to be made. I had seen a different side of Stepan's character, today. Were there any other sides of him not yet revealed? On the other hand, how did he see me?

Chapter Twenty Two

I woke with a start. It was not yet morning. I turned over and prepared to go back to sleep, when suddenly, my heart leapt and I remembered what day this was - my wedding day! I got out of bed and walked over to the window. The sun was rising over the calm surface of the sea. It cast a strange loveliness over the small boats. I was filled with melancholy. I looked around the little room, which had been my haven, my own little world – a place where I had reluctantly and painfully shed the cocoon of childhood. I had felt joy as well as sadness here. I had lain in my virginal bed and dreamed of love and romance; of Paul and the life we would share in England. And now I was to be married, to a man I didn't love.

The room looked quite bare now. The wardrobe was empty. The drawers were empty. Every one of Paul's letters had been disposed of. In one corner, stood two suitcases. One was packed with clothes for my honeymoon. The other, bigger one contained all my other clothes and personal items. A box full of my books, photographs and records stood at the end of my bed. These would be taken to my new home later. The only things I would leave behind were the faded pictures of my celluloid heroes: from Clark Gable to Paul Newman. I looked at them one last time...

My courage and confidence began to falter. Was I ready for marriage? How had Sara felt, when she was in this position? How had Mother felt? The subject of marriage, like many other important issues, was never included in our after dinner conversations and discussions. It remained firmly on the 'taboo' list. I looked around my room once more. The next time I came here, I would be a woman, a married woman with responsibilities.

During the summer, I had come to know the 'gang' quite well. I had learned so much from Sona, Roxi and Anna. All three were happy and content with their lives. At first I had felt sorry for myself and envied their uncomplicated lives. But gradually, as I came to know them better, I realized that I could be like them if I tried.

The summer had been a time for reappraisal. I shed my childish and fanciful notions, like a butterfly sheds its chrysalis. Sara was right. I had come to like Stepan and his enthusiasm for life. Maybe, one day, I might even come to love him. He had paved the way to this unknown place called marriage, guided me towards it slowly and patiently. And as long as he stayed by my side, unchanging and reassuring, I would try to be a good wife and carry out my wifely duties.

A knock on the door interrupted my reverie. I was still standing at the window, gazing at the azure blue sea. I turned round to see who it was. It was Nonnie. She came in with two cups of tea and stood at the end of my bed.

"Good morning," she said, brightly. "What a perfectly lovely day for a wedding. Here, drink this." She handed me a cup of hot, sweet cinnamon tea. "How do you feel?" I smiled and shrugged my shoulders. How did she think I would feel?

"If I survive this day, then I can survive anything!" I said, wryly, sipping my tea. "I hope it won't be long before you and Lillie go through the same 'performance'. I want my revenge, and I shall have it! I haven't forgiven you and Lillie for what you've done to me!" Nonnie opened her arms, and I walked into them. We hugged and stood like that for a long moment, each knowing what the other was thinking.

"Please don't think like that. This was meant to happen. It didn't happen in the right order, but does it really matter?"

"I don't know…"

"You are happy, aren't you? Everybody can see how much Stepan adores you. Am I forgiven for being the herald?"

"Oh, alright then, I forgive you," I said, in the same wry tone.

When Nonnie left, I sat down on my bed to drink my tea and contemplate on the day that lay ahead. It would be a long day, probably the longest day of my life. I hoped, for Mother's sake, that everything would be alright. I had refused a big engagement party. I had also refused to allow my trousseau to be displayed. It seemed such an outdated custom! Sara hadn't minded, because at that time it was not only the custom but also a matter of pride to display a girl's trousseau.

Father had wanted Sara to have the best trousseau a girl could wish for. Even though the war had ended, there was still rationing. But Father somehow managed – no doubt through the black market – to get the yards and yards of cotton, silk and linen, needed. All that summer Mother, Sara,

Lillie and Nonnie had worked diligently to produce a trousseau to be proud of. They embroidered tablecloths, napkins, pillowcases, bedspreads, while Florentia made Sara's wedding dress as well as suits, dresses, skirts and blouses for her. By the end of that summer we were all sick of seeing the house turned into an *atelier*.

As custom dictated, Mother had invited her friends and neighbours to come and view Sara's trousseau. It had been 'open house'. The visitors came early in the afternoon. They were offered tea, coffee and lemonade, with a variety of home-made cakes and biscuits. Everyone was impressed with the display. They took their time to 'inspect' and admire each and every garment, especially Sara's wedding dress which hung on a rail together with her other dresses and suits. It had been a proud moment for Mother.

So, when Mother suggested – almost pleaded with me - that I should observe the custom of inviting the matron of honour and a few close relatives to the house, while I was getting dressed for the ceremony, I couldn't very well refuse her. Here I was now, surrounded with well-wishers, trying to get dressed, and trying even harder to stay calm. Soft drinks, dainty little cakes and sugared almonds were being offered. There was an air of festivity, mingled with noise, anxiety and nervous tension.

Kevork was to be Stepan's best man, and therefore his wife, Sona, was to be my matron of honour, with their eight-year-old daughter, Sevan, as my only bridesmaid. Sevan was very pretty with huge brown eyes and long curly hair cascading down to her shoulders. On this day, she looked like Shirley Temple. Only Sona and Nonnie were allowed to help me with the dress and with my veil and make-up.

"Stepan is going through the same 'ritual' as you are," said Sona, as she expertly pinned the veil to my headdress. "All of the groom's side are at his house. But their 'do' is a little more relaxed. They have brandy and whisky to give them Dutch courage."

"I hope they don't drink too much, and be unsteady on their feet..." piped Nonnie.

"I've never seen them drunk or even tipsy. Believe me, I've watched them drink gallons," said Sona, anxious to reassure me. But I wasn't really listening. I was staring at the image in the mirror. Surely, the face that was staring back at me was not my own! It could not be. My skin, which was normally pale, was positively glowing. I didn't know that my almond shaped eyes were that deep or that dark. They looked so calm and yet so mysterious, as if they were guarding a secret. I kept looking at my face, in utter disbelief. Then I smiled, showing off my new soft pink lipstick. 'Thank you Mr. Max Factor, you've done a good job!' I whispered to myself.

I hadn't wanted to go through this added ordeal, but in the end it was worth it, if only to see Mother's eyes shining with happiness. She firmly believed that Lillie and Nonnie would soon follow in my 'lucky' footsteps to the alter. Who was I to contradict her?

Well, I survived the day. Stepan and I were married in the little Church of St. Krikor in the old town of Famagusta. This was the same church where he had first seen me – on the day of the consecration.

The little Church was full to overflowing. A sea of faces turned to look at us, as our little procession came in - little Sevan, walking serenely in front, and Father and I following close behind. I held on to Father's arm for sheer life. Stay calm, stay calm, I repeated to myself. Then, I saw Stepan's eyes on me. Never before had I seen such an expression on his face - it was a mixture of love and pride, and reassurance.

The Armenian wedding ceremony is not long – about half an hour. Father Serop looked an impressive figure, in his ceremonial robes. He started with a prayer. Then he placed a 'crown' on Stepan's head and another one on mine, blessing them. We stood, facing each other. At a particular point in the ceremony, Father Serop asked Stepan to drink from the cup of the 'wedding wine'. Then he turned to me, and I sipped the wine too. Throughout this time, poor Kevork stood very still, holding the silver Holy Cross over our heads. Sona stood nearby, so she could hand me back my bouquet, when the service was over.

Then, came the blessing of the wedding rings. Stepan slipped my ring onto my finger and I slipped his ring onto his. After that, Father Serop removed the 'crowns' from our heads, and said the Lord's Prayer, with the congregation joining in. Finally, he made the sign of the cross, and pronounced us man and wife. It was over.

From then on, everything took on an air of unreality. Leaving the Church, being photographed outside, driving to the *Golden Sands Hotel* by the sea, for the wedding reception, and being kissed, hugged and congratulated by a crowd of people. Stepan and I stood by the door of the big reception room, and received the wedding guests. As they shook our hands and wished us happiness, we offered them sugared almonds, wrapped in a square of white tulle tied with white ribbon. Sugared almonds have always been a symbol of good fortune in our culture, of new beginnings and happiness.

Another old tradition is for members of the family to give the bride an item of jewellery. As custom dictated, my new mother-in-law was the first to do so. She gave me a hug and then she slipped a thick gold bracelet on my right wrist. Next, it was my mother's turn. She kissed me and held me tight for a moment, before she slipped one of her own bracelets onto my arm – the one with the snake's head on the clasp - next to the one from my mother-in-law. Then, it was the turn of the Aunts. Before long, my right hand was heavy with the weight of all that gold. I also had a thick gold chain round my neck, and two rings on my fingers. The bracelets and bangles jingled, as I shook hands with the guests!

Stepan had wanted a big wedding, and his father had obliged. After all, he only had one son. There were about hundred people. Family, friends, neighbours and colleagues were all invited. It turned out to be a lively and informal gathering. There was music and dancing, a lavish buffet and plenty to drink. I was so happy, that Eleni and her fiancé had come. We hadn't seen each other for some time, so we chatted for quite a while, catching up with all the latest news. It was good to see old friends, and be introduced to new ones.

Suddenly someone shouted, "Speech from the bridegroom!" And then came the best man's voice, equally loud: "Not a speech – a *song* from the bridegroom!" The 'gang' was up to something - they didn't stop chanting, "Song! Song!" until Stepan had put his hands up, in mock surrender. Taking hold of the microphone, he started to sing. I had only heard him sing snatches of songs before. There was complete silence, as he sang *Only You*, looking directly into my eyes, and thunderous applause when he finished. He *was* good. With proper training, he could surely have become a professional singer. The party was in full swing when Stepan whispered in my ear. "Shall we make our escape, now?" I nodded. I had enjoyed myself more than I had thought possible, but it was time to leave.

Chapter Twenty Three

When we came back from our honeymoon, we found that both our families were waiting to greet us. It was a nice gesture - to welcome us home. I felt strange, when it was time for my family to leave. It was as though they were officially handing me over to my new family.

It was even stranger when I woke up the next morning, in an unfamiliar bedroom. It was a large room, overlooking the terrace. The walls had been given a coat of paint and there were new voile curtains at the windows. The sun filtered through the shutters. I looked at the little clock on my bedside table - eight o'clock! I'm late for work, I thought, in panic. A second later I remembered. I had resigned from my job - I was a lady of leisure now, a married lady of leisure!

I was alone in the big bed. The house was silent. Where was Stepan? I must have been very tired, for I had slept like a log, not even hearing him get out of bed. I felt like a guest in a strange house. I didn't know what to do. Should I get up? Why had Stepan left home, without a word? Surely, he didn't have to go to work so early, on my first day here. Just then, I heard the front door open. A minute later, Stepan entered our bedroom.

"She's awake! The little one is awake!" he crooned. "You were sleeping like a baby, so I didn't wake you."

"Where were you?" I asked.

"I went for my early morning swim first, and then to the market for the food shopping."

"Swimming? The water must be freezing cold…"

"Not at all. I find it invigorating. Breakfast in five minutes, in the secret garden – our very first breakfast at home." As he talked, he pulled back the bed-covers, lifted me out of the bed and gave me a big hug.

"Give me a chance to get dressed…"

"No… Just put your dressing gown on. I shall make the coffee." I felt a bit flustered when he left the room. I didn't want my mother-in-law to think that I was a late riser, or that I would spend the morning in my dressing gown. Nevertheless, I could smell the aroma of the freshly made coffee, so I made my way to the terrace.

"I see you've been busy," I said, surveying the little table. There was freshly baked sesame bread, cheese and figs – the perfect seasonal breakfast.

"I thought we might have breakfast together, before I go to work. Mother is putting the groceries away." Just then, she came to join us, with a cup of coffee in her hand.

"Good morning, my dear," she said.

"Good morning, *Mayrik*," I said, hoping I didn't look too dishevelled.

"Did you sleep well?" she asked. "It takes time to get used to sleeping in a strange bed, and in strange surroundings. But I'm sure you'll get used to it, in no time."

"I'm sure I will," I agreed. This breakfast on the terrace became our morning routine.

I spent my first morning in my new home, unpacking our suitcases and putting away clothes in the drawers and wardrobes. As I worked, I reviewed the week of our honeymoon. It had been a wise decision to spend it up in the mountains. It was so dramatically different from the beach.

The approach to our hotel was everything it should be. Wrought iron gates, a winding drive overhung with huge bougainvilleas. Built in the style of the l930s, the *Pine Forest Hotel* had an air of old-world dignity. Perched on top of a pine-covered hill, the building looked as though it had been kissed by the sun. I shall never forget the spectacular view from our hotel balcony on that first morning, where I breathed the cool, pine-scented mountain air.

We had our breakfast on the dining room terrace, gazing out over the surrounding countryside. We lingered over breakfast, enjoying the local bread and cheese, figs, grapes and watermelon washed down with cups of coffee. When we could drag ourselves away from the enchanting views, we went for long walks, discovering unfamiliar plants and flowers. We had picnics by waterfalls. We bought dried cherries, dried figs and jars of bottled preserves – apricot, cherry and walnut, as well as watermelon and aubergines from roadside vendors. One day, we went to a fair in the next village and walked hand in hand among the crowds of people. We bought more goodies from the fair, to take home to the families.

Sometimes, we walked on old donkey tracks, chatting easily with elderly women working on their land.

"Look at that baby donkey," I cried. "It can't be more than a few days old." The baby donkey stood on wobbly legs in the shade of an olive tree with its parents, head down. "He looks so happy and contented, munching away."

We had our evening meals at different *tavernas*, sampling the local delicacies and drinking the local wines. As night descended, the only twinkling lights came from the stars and the only music came from the cicadas. They cast a seductive spell – a romantic prelude to nights of love.

"Would you like to go anywhere special, today?" Stepan asked me, one morning. I thought for a moment. Should I tell him? I so wanted to return to Pedoulas. It still haunted me in my dreams.

"Well?"

I smiled at him, shyly. "I would love to spend a day in Pedoulas. Visit some of my childhood haunts. We spent a whole summer there, towards the end of the war. Father thought it was not safe to stay in Famagusta. Did your family go away too?"

"No. Mother was adamant. She refused to leave Father, to face the bombs on his own!" Stepan got up from his chair and hugged me. "So, you want to go to Pedoulas do you, little one?"

I nodded and smiled up at him. "It would be so good to see the house again."

"Do you remember where the house is?"

"I most certainly do." How could I forget.

"We'll have a picnic lunch, if you like."

We reached Pedoulas around noon. The roads were no safer to drive than they had been in the past. The hairpin bends seemed as dangerous and scary as I remembered. The village hadn't changed much, either. We left the car at the top of the hill and walked down the narrow pathway, which led to the house.

"The place is deserted. Are you sure this is the house?"

"I'm quite sure. Let's ring the bell." We waited but nobody answered. I looked at the house. It looked so old and neglected. Where had the terrace gone, that huge terrace that was bigger than the house itself? It had shrunk to a tiny square. I ran to the edge of the terrace, to see if my peach tree was still there. It had disappeared too. There were a few cherry trees left. The vine was still there – preparing to shed its leaves, which had already started to turn purple and gold.

"There's nobody here," I said, unable to hide my disappointment. We were about to leave, when a young girl appeared. I told her who I was and the reason for this unannounced visit. She smiled.

"My grandfather used to tell us about the Armenian family who rented the house."

"Are your grandparents still alive?" I asked.

"My grandfather is – he is at the *kafenion* – but my grandmother died a few years ago. She fell from a cherry tree and broke her back. She was bedridden for years." Her eyes filled with tears. I was misty eyed too. Ghosts were emerging from every part of the house. We said goodbye to the young girl and walked into the village. I stopped by the concrete freshwater fountain, next to the *kafenion*.

"I used to come here every afternoon, to fill a flask with the pure spring water for Dai," I said. Using my cupped hands, I drank the cool, sweet water, thirstily. Stepan did the same.

"Where to next?" he asked, drying my hands with his handkerchief, before wiping his own.

"I want to take you to the church, over there. It's a beautiful little church. I used to go there every Saturday afternoon, and light a candle for Dai."

"You *were* a dutiful little girl weren't you?"

"I was the 'errand girl', until Marko took over from me. But I didn't mind running errands for Dai, he was my hero." We entered the church. Without thinking about it, I went directly to the offertory box, put in a shilling and lit a candle. The church hadn't changed at all. I glanced at the icon of the Virgin and remembered how fervently I used to pray to her, to make my uncle well again. My prayers had not been answered in the way I expected, but I had forgotten my childish resentment. My religious fervour may have dimmed over the years, but nevertheless, I had to acknowledge her strange influence over me.

I felt happy, almost elated, for having visited these childhood places. I was happier still for having taken Stepan with me. I took his hand, as we came out into the warm sunshine.

"I'm starving, shall we have lunch now?" he asked.

"It must be the mountain air," I said. "I feel hungry all the time!"

"We'll forget the picnic then, and go to a restaurant." We found a small *taverna*, in the centre of the village. The waiter found us a table, overlooking the church. The smell of meat cooking on charcoal drifted enticingly towards us. We looked at each other, and nodded our heads. "*Sheftalia*," we chorused. These tasty sausages, cooked over glowing charcoal, came with fried potatoes, village salad and warm crusty bread, all washed down with beer.

Replete with delicious food and drink, we proceeded to climb up the hill, where the car was parked. Suddenly, the weather changed dramatically. The sun disappeared and black clouds filled the sky.

"We'd better hurry, there's a storm coming," said Stepan. Even as he spoke, I felt huge drops of rain falling on my head. We ran the last few steps and got into the car, before the heavens opened and a deluge burst forth. We hoped that the rain would exhaust itself. Instead, it turned into a cataclysm, falling out of a steel grey sky. Safe and sheltered from the rain, sitting close together, we watched the fury of the elements at war. The rain came down relentlessly, in great sheets. Forked lightning lit up the sky and the roar of thunder sounded, loud and threatening. The roads turned into rivulets – making them impassable, until the storm had passed.

"What a spectacular sight!" we said, over and over again. The storm lasted half an hour and then, having spent its fury, it went out meekly. The sun returned and, within minutes, the sky was blue again.

"Thank you for today," I said. "I had a wonderful time. I hope you didn't mind me revisiting my childhood. It seemed the right time..." Stepan smiled into my eyes.

"Mind? I felt proud and privileged, to share glimpses of your life with you. Every day this week, I've been discovering different sides to your character and I like what I see, little one. Shall we drive back to the hotel now?" He opened the car windows to let the fresh air in. A few drops of rain found their way into the car, falling softly onto my face and hands. I felt refreshed. I was so happy, that these hillside villages had not changed since my childhood days. I wished that we could have stayed longer in these mountains, with their mystery and silent beauty.

Chapter Twenty Four

The first two weeks, after we came back from honeymoon, were very busy. Every afternoon, we had a string of visitors. Virtually every member of the Armenian community in Famagusta, not to mention Greek friends, came to the house to see the happy couple. It was the custom to visit the bride in her new home, and view the wedding presents. They were all displayed on the dining room table. We had our fair share of glassware, crockery, cutlery and linen. We would take them to our own house, once it was built.

Something else the visitors would expect to see, was the jewellery the bride had been given. To my dismay, I was gently but firmly reminded, both by *Mayrik* and my new husband, that I should wear *all* my jewellery when the visitors came. It was a matter of prestige. And so, every afternoon, I had to show off my gold bracelets, chains and rings. As soon as the visitors left, I took them off and put them in a box in the drawer. The only thing I wore all the time was the exquisite bracelet, made of gold chain, which Stepan had given me on my wedding night. He himself had carved my new initials onto the clasp.

The transition from my father's house to my husband's was seamless. The rhythm of life continued in the same way. The mornings were busy. I helped *Mayrik* with the housework and then, while she prepared the lunch, I sat in the garden to read. When one of our neighbours dropped in, I would make the coffee and we would sit at the kitchen table, chatting.

I didn't help with the cooking, but I would watch *Mayrik*. She could do several things at once, all with expert precision, and still manage to drink her coffee and chat at the same time. She was a good cook, like my mother. I had never bothered to learn to cook before, but gradually, I developed an interest in it. I watched how she skilfully divided a leg of lamb. She used the bones to make hearty soups, made the fatty meat into mince, and used the tender part for kebabs or stews. Like most households, lunch was our main meal of the day. Everything would be ready, and as soon as Agnes and the men came home from work, we sat down to eat.

After my initial shyness, I came to relax in *Mayrik's* company. I learned a lot from her. Her washdays – also on Fridays - were not chaotic like Mother's used to be. But then hers was a small family. By the time I had got out of bed, she would have the first load on the line. I did the ironing, though - I didn't mind taking on this chore. If anything, I found it relaxing, as well as a good excuse for daydreaming. In time, I found out that it was so much easier to iron clothes – especially shirts - when they were still damp.

I also came to know Agnes. Before I was married, I had only known her as Nonnie's best friend, and she had known me only as Nonnie's shy little sister. But now she saw me as someone in her own right, as well as her sister-in-law. We came to like and respect one another very well.

The day started like any other in our household. The morning routine was always the same. We had a coffee break only after the housework was done. It was the middle of December, but the weather was still mild. The week before, the house had its annual 'thorough' clean in preparation for the New Year and Christmas festivities. There was also the feast day of St. Stepan, the Protomartyr, to think of - on the 24th of December. It was a special tradition in the Manoukian family to celebrate this particular date in the Armenian calendar. Stepan was named after the saint, so it was his Name Day. The fact that it was also Stepan's birthday was secondary. Name Days were more important than birthdays, in our culture.

I had helped *Mayrik* as much as I could, but I found I got tired very quickly. To make matters worse, I felt sick most mornings and didn't want anything to eat. This morning, even the smell of coffee – which I had always loved – had been sickening. All I wanted to do was sleep. It must be the brandy that I've been drinking every night, these past few days, that's making me feel this way, I thought. I shall be very firm with Stepan and refuse to drink any alcohol until his name day party, I promised myself. I continued with the ironing. There were only four more shirts on the washing line to iron, and then I could have a rest. As I went out to the garden to fetch the shirts in, I heard *Mayrik's* voice calling to me from the kitchen.

"Don't stretch your arms like that Reya," she cried.

"Why ever not?" I asked. She rushed out and took the shirts from the line.

"Well… I might be wrong, but I suspect you are probably pregnant. Stretching your arms like that might bring on a miscarriage. One must be very careful for the first three months." I blushed a deep red. I didn't know if I was embarrassed for being pregnant or for not knowing the signs.

"Don't be shy, my dear girl. Every married woman goes through this process and only an older woman can detect the signs. Come, let's go in and have our coffee. Forget the ironing. Forget the housework for a time. I always say it's the only time in a woman's life when a big fuss is made of her. Enjoy it while you can…"

I felt so confused. I felt emotions I could not explain. *Me* to have a baby! I was dizzy with shock and disbelief. It was *not* true. It *could not* be true. I had only been married for less than three months, for heaven's sake!

Just then the doorbell rang. It was Sona.

"Am I in time for coffee?" she asked. I was still reeling from the shock of my possible 'condition'. I looked at Sona, unable to utter a word.

"What's the matter, Reya, are you not well? You look so pale…"

"Oh! Do I?"

"Come in Sona. You're just in time for coffee. We have something to tell you," said *Mayrik*.

"Really? I have something really exciting to tell you!" We sat round the kitchen table, drinking our coffee. I willed my stomach not to let me down in front of Sona. I waited till my coffee was cold, and drank it in one gulp.

"Well, what's your news then? Tell me. I can't bear the suspense any longer," said Sona. I remained silent, but I was annoyed that my 'condition' was to be discussed so casually, as part of the day's gossip.

"Reya hasn't been feeling too good lately…"

"Don't tell me she is pregnant! It's a bit soon isn't it? But these things happen, sometimes… Have you been to the doctor yet?" she asked, turning her head to face me. I blushed again.

"No," I said.

"You're the first to know. We'll tell Stepan at lunch time," said *Mayrik*. Sona then went into a detailed account of her own pregnancy and – God save me - childbirth. But I was not listening. I was thinking that this was all wrong. I should have been allowed to find out for myself, if I was pregnant or not. I should have been the one to tell Stepan the news. That's how it was in the novels I'd read. That's how it was in the films I'd watched. The conversation swirled around me like waves, until suddenly I heard Sona say, "Are you ready to hear my news?"

"Yes, of course we are," said *Mayrik*.

"As you know, my cousin, Aram, is here to spend the New Year and Christmas with the family. He wants to get married, and his mother and I thought of Agnes. We think it would be a good match." My curiosity was aroused. It took the conversation away from me, for a start. I listened with interest.

"How long has Aram lived in London? I can't remember the last time I saw him," said *Mayrik*. I could tell she was excited. I was sure she was thinking 'It is time for Agnes to get married'.

"It must be nearly ten years. He seldom comes back to Cyprus for a visit. Usually, his parents go there once a year to see him. He has worked very hard these past years, and now he is quite well off. He can give Agnes a good life, a very good life, indeed."

"Really?"

"Yes. The only thing is that he would like to get married and take his bride with him, when he goes back to London, soon after Christmas. So you see, it has to be arranged quickly."

"I must say, this has come as a complete surprise to me, Sona. What does he do for a living?"

"He's in the grocery business. Two years ago he bought a run down grocery store and built it up into a very profitable 'supermarket'. He's got a very nice house, newly redecorated and furnished, which he has recently moved into. And now, he is in the process of buying another property, for letting. He says renting is very profitable these days. You can't go wrong with property, can you?" She paused for breath. She couldn't hide the pride she felt for her cousin. She had done her homework well.

It took a few minutes for *Mayrik* to recover from this unexpected piece of good fortune, which had come to her door.

"It's very good of you to think of our Agnes, my dear Sona," she said. "How and when do you think we should meet the young man? What's his name again?"

"His name is Aram. You must remember him, surely. Anyway, I thought we might bring him to Stepan's name day party on Saturday night. It won't be so obvious that way. If they like each other, then things can go ahead officially. But if they don't, then the matter can be dropped, without anyone losing face."

"I think that's the best way, dear."

"Look at the time! I'd better be off, or else there won't be any lunch..."

"That won't do will it? Feed your man and the rest will take care of itself! That's what my poor old mother used to say."

I liked and admired Sona - except when she talked about me as though

I wasn't in the room. I was closer to her than Roxi. She had embraced the yoke of domesticity, just like our mothers had done, and their mothers before them. Sona enjoyed her role of matriarch and used it to her advantage. She had a humorous way of giving me tips on 'how to keep your husband happy' or 'how to get your own way, without your husband knowing'. On one occasion, she told me that her husband gave her his wages every month, so that she took care of the household bills herself, and even saved a little each month, for a rainy day. She held the domestic reins firmly in her hands.

"Men don't have a clue about money. They have to be controlled – in a subtle way of course. If it were left to Kevork, he would spend his wages halfway through the month! He doesn't even know that I save a little each month. You never know when the rainy day will come." The phrase 'You never know' became her mantra.

I listened to Sona, just to humour her. The saving of money was part of our culture. So was learning the value of money and spending it wisely. But somehow, this important attribute had been poorly neglected among the women in our family. My sisters and I spent our salaries as we pleased. Only if there was anything left at the end of the month, did we put anything aside for saving. We, Mother included, did not really concern ourselves with any household finances. It was Father who took care of it all.

It was the same in my new home. Stepan and his father took care of all financial matters. True to his word, Stepan made sure there was enough money in my dressing table drawer for my personal needs, books and magazines. If I needed to buy dress material, all I had to do was go to Nico's shop and get what I wanted. He would settle it with Stepan later. If I wanted to buy anything else, or pay the dressmaker, all I had to do was mention it to him and he would give me the money. It was not the ideal way, but, unfortunately, it was the only way.

Maybe the pattern was changing. Maybe modern young wives wanted to be like Sona. I hoped so. But I couldn't see how it could ever change in our household. If only Stepan had let me carry on working, I would not have been dependent on him for everything. It riled me to have to ask him. I had carefully 'saved' the money in the little drawer and unbeknown to him, had bought him a pale blue Van Heusen shirt and a silk tie for his name day!

Very wisely, *Mayrik* did not bring up the matter of Agnes's possible marriage proposal, until after lunch. I watched Agnes, to see how she took the news. I remembered my reaction, when Stepan's proposal was first mentioned. I had been hysterical with laughter! But Agnes took the idea quite seriously.

"I don't mind meeting him at your party, Stepan. Maybe I could go out with him a few times, and see if I like him."

"Why, yes. But not on your own. First, we go out in a group, and if you like him then we can talk about the engagement."

"What about living in London, my dear?" asked *Hayrik*. Usually, he left these matters to Stepan.

"I don't mind, Father," Agnes replied. "I've always wanted to see London. You can all come and visit me! Mother, did Sona say anything about his looks? I hope he is good looking, not short, fat and ugly!"

"Be serious, Agnes! No man is ever considered ugly. It is a man's character and his standing in society that counts, not his looks. And don't you ever forget it!" Her mother had spoken. I was amazed at Agnes's reaction. I never dreamed that she would agree so readily to meet this man from London, let alone contemplate marrying him, in such a short space of time. She didn't seem to have any qualms about living so far away from her family and friends. Still, it was not for me to voice an opinion.

I was so relieved that the excitement of the impending 'proposal', together with the final plans for the name day party pushed the possibility of my pregnancy into the background. I had been so anxious about it, that I hardly touched my food. I just sat there, listening to the conversation around me. It was only when I got up to clear the dishes, that Stepan really noticed me, and my untouched plate.

"You haven't eaten anything, little one. You look so pale. Are you not well?" I almost always enjoyed my food. It must have surprised him to see me not eating. He turned to his mother. His mother looked at him and raised her eyebrows, then she nodded her head and glanced towards the kitchen. He understood and kept quiet. She would tell him later.

Soon after coffee, Stepan left to go back to work and so did Agnes. His father stayed behind, to work in the garden. We didn't go out that evening, but had an early night instead. We were in bed. I was reading, or pretending to read, and Stepan was listening to the news, when suddenly, he switched off the radio. Gently, he took the book from my hands, and put in on the bedside table. Taking both of my hands in his, he looked at me, with a puzzled expression on his face, as though he wasn't sure of what he wanted to say. I waited, tense and nervous. I could guess what he wanted to talk about but I wasn't at all sure what his attitude would be.

"Mother told me the news."

"Did she?"

"I was as surprised as you must have been. I was thrilled, of course."

"Yes."

"Believe me, little one, I didn't want to start a family so soon after getting married, but 'accidents' happen…"

"Yes, so I'm told."

"But Mother said, we can't be sure until the Doctor examines you."

"Yes."

"Don't keep on saying 'Yes'. Say something different! How do you feel about it? Are you glad? Are you sorry?"

"I don't know."

"What do you mean, you don't know?"

"I don't know what I mean." I shut my eyes. This conversation was getting out of hand.

"Anyway, I've made an appointment for you to see Dr. Makrides at his clinic tomorrow morning. The sooner we know one way or the other, the better." I looked at him, panic rising.

"Didn't you hear me? I said I made an appointment to see…"

"I heard you. But why? What's the rush?"

"Don't you want to know if you are pregnant?" I shook my head. "What's the matter with you? What's wrong?" I could tell by his voice that he was getting impatient with me. He let go of my hands. He reached for his packet of cigarettes, decided against it and threw the packet on the floor. I didn't care. I was upset and angry at the way he was behaving.

"If you really want to know what's wrong, I'll tell you," I said, blushing to the roots of my hair, my voice trembling with emotion. "I am so stupid and naive that I didn't even realise I might be pregnant. Your mother had to tell me. She told Sona, she told you, she has probably told the whole world by now."

"Does it matter who…"

"It does matter. I should be the one to tell you. I should have been left to find out for myself first. To get used to the idea…"

"Surely, you're exaggerating…" All day long, I had been struggling to keep my fears and frustrations, my uncertainties under control. Why couldn't he understand that maybe, just maybe, I might not yet be ready to face up to motherhood? Something snapped inside. All these emotions rushed to the surface. There was no holding them back. I felt trapped.

The helpless tears stormed out of me, in torrents.

"Leave me alone! Why don't you all leave me alone? I want to go home…" I wanted to lash out at everybody, especially at him. But his strong arms held me tight. So tight, I couldn't breathe. Then his arms relaxed and he held me tenderly, comfortingly. He let me cry. And I cried, until I could cry no more. He found a handkerchief and dried my eyes. He wiped my nose. He held me for a long time, saying nothing.

"I'm so sorry *hokis* (my soul)," he whispered. "I'm sorry for being so insensitive. I should have known… Don't worry, everything will be alright. Go to sleep now. We'll sort things out in the morning." He stroked my hair and kissed my forehead. "Sleep *hokis*, sleep the sleep of angels."

With infinite tenderness, he eased my head onto the pillow and covered me with the blanket, tucking me in. Exhausted, I fell asleep instantly.

Hours later, I woke with a start. It was barely light. Stepan was lying on his back with his arms above his head. I watched his face, the gentle rise and fall of his breathing. I wanted to reach out and touch him but I didn't. I felt a strange emotion stir within me and surge forth, unbidden. I shivered, and realised with a shock that I was falling in love with my husband.

Chapter Twenty Five

Stepan's Name Day party was an unqualified success. The hours of preparation were worthwhile. Agnes and I spent the whole afternoon in the kitchen, helping *Mayrik* with the party food, while Stepan and his father rearranged the furniture in the living room. They pushed the dining room table against the wall, to make more room for people to move in. I ironed the snow-white embroidered tablecloth and smoothed it onto the dining table. It was going to be a cold buffet. We arranged huge platters of bite-sized *borek*, *kofte*, slices of roast pork, stuffed vine leaves, macaroni baked in the oven. There were numerous relishes, several different salads, olives and cheeses and crisp fresh bread.

On another table, stood the bottles of drink. Whisky, brandy, wines, ouzo, beer and liqueurs. On a smaller table, we arranged the cutlery, crockery and the napkins. Everything was ready. We were ready. Stepan looked smart in his favourite cream suit. He was wearing the shirt and tie I had given him. He had been delighted, impressed by my choice. Agnes looked very pretty in a jade cocktail dress. Her long, dark brown hair hung on her shoulders in soft curls. Her dark eyes, so like Stepan's, shone with excitement.

I wore one of three cocktail dresses that Florentia had made for me, as part of my 'trousseau'. It was silk, the colour of soft apricots. It had a scooped neckline, pinched waist and a full, gathered skirt. I had never worn it before. Black patent shoes completed the picture. I looked at myself in the wardrobe mirror. A touch of rouge and lipstick put some colour into my cheeks. I wondered if Stepan would like my dress. He always noticed what I wore and if he liked what he saw, he gave me a nod of approval. "Don't wear that dress again," he would say, if he didn't like it. He was making drinks, as I entered the living room. His mother and father were sitting on the sofa and Agnes was standing by the window, looking out. Stepan saw me, put his glass down and came over to where I was standing.

"You look good enough to eat, little one," he whispered, putting his arms around me.

"Happy Name Day and happy birthday," I whispered back. Then I turned to his parents and spoke aloud. "Your new dress looks very elegant,

Mayrik," I said.

"Thank you, my dear. I always have a new dress to wear on Stepan's name day. And so does Agnes. It has become a tradition, I suppose."

"You mean it's a good excuse to want a new dress!" said *Hayrik* in a good-natured way.

"Well!" said Agnes. "Neither Mother nor I have a Name Day of our own, so I reckon we deserve new dresses to celebrate Stepan's. Come to think of it, we should have new dresses for Reya's Name Day, too." We all laughed at that. It was nice to enjoy a few moments of light-hearted banter, before the visitors arrived. I sipped the brandy sour Stepan made for me, and started to relax.

"I have a few words to say, before our friends arrive," said *Hayrik*. "Mother and I have had a Name Day party for Stepan, since he was a baby. It has become a tradition. We welcome our new daughter to this tradition, and we hope that she will continue with it after we've gone…" His voice trembled as he spoke. I was touched by his words. Without thinking, I went straight over to where he was standing and hugged him.

"And so we will, *Hayrik*. I promise." Just then, the doorbell rang. Kevork and Sona were the first to arrive, with her cousin Aram. They had come early, so that the introductions could be made before the others arrived. Agnes and Aram hit it off immediately. They started chatting and laughing, as if they had known each other for years. He was a little taller than Agnes, with open features and dark hair, already receding at the temples. His skin was pale, he had been away from the Cyprus sun for too long.

Soon, the other guests arrived. Marko came with the family. I was so happy to see them. I hadn't seen much of them lately, just flying visits from Nonnie when she came to see Agnes. Bedros and Roxi came with Nico and Anna. There were a few more Greek friends of Stepan's, who I hadn't met before. Before long, the party was in full swing. Everybody did justice to the food, which was mouth-wateringly good. Surprisingly, I managed to eat a little. I hoped I wouldn't pay for it later. I was on my second glass of brandy-sour, and enjoying it too.

Later, Nonnie helped me clear the table and bring the sweets and dessert out. There was *Paklava*, *Gadeifi* and *Shamali*.

"Who is that man talking to Agnes?" she said. "I was introduced to him, but I forget his name."

"Oh, his name is Aram, and he is from London."

"London! They have been talking and laughing all evening, and now they are dancing, oblivious to anyone around them."

"Yes. They do seem to like each other. He has come back to Cyprus to look for a wife. I think he will ask Agnes to marry him. But keep this to yourself, won't you?"

"Yes, of course I will. Agnes will put me in the picture no doubt. I'm happy for her, but I shall lose my best friend."

"I know. I was devastated when Eleni went to Nicosia. But you will get over it in time, you have to."

"Happy now, little one?" Stepan whispered in my ear as we joined the other dancers in the hall.

"Yes," I said and I meant it. Everything had been sorted out, as he had promised. He must have talked to his mother, because the word 'pregnancy' was not mentioned again. We would see the doctor, sometime in the New Year. "It's a wonderful party," I reassured him. "I think everybody is having a good time."

"Not as good a time as I'm having. I feel my life is complete now, with my little love by my side."

December 24th is Greek Christmas Eve, so our Greek neighbours and friends left by twelve o'clock. They wanted to be up early for Christmas Day.

"We should be leaving too, but we are having such a good time, that I think we'll stay another half an hour," said Anna. In fact, they stayed until the party broke up. Nico had to drag her away!

Three days after the party, Aram proposed to Agnes and she accepted. The next day, his parents were invited to dinner, so that the families would get acquainted and make plans for the wedding. We saw Aram every day, and got to know him. He had become Anglicised, using 'thank you' and 'pardon' much more frequently than we did. Stepan liked him and they got on very well together. They found they had a lot in common. They talked about business, life in London, the political situation in Cyprus and a lot more besides. Aram was very quickly treated like a member of the family.

On Christmas day we went to church. It seemed like only yesterday when I had stood nervously at the altar, on my wedding day. So much had changed. More change was on the way. I was sure that I was pregnant, my morning sickness was proof of that.

The little church looked beautiful this morning. The Armenian community in Famagusta was grateful to have a church to call their own, at long last. St. Krikor was a far cry from the schoolroom rearranged to look like a place of worship. I remembered how it had been, then. A table would be set up at one end of the schoolroom and on it the priest would arrange the holy book, the communion cup, the jewel encrusted cross wrapped in a lace handkerchief, the tray of paper thin unleavened bread torn into small pieces and of course the icon of the Mother and Child. Two vases of fresh flowers would complete the makeshift altar.

The church was full to overflowing. The choir was ready and waiting. Father Serop began the liturgy. He had a good voice and he used it to good advantage in his sermon. Every member of the congregation listened to him intently. What with the burning incense in the censer and the rousing voice of the choir, we came out of the church spiritually uplifted.

The day after Christmas, Father Serop performed the ritual of the 'blessing of the house'. With the help of one of the choir boys, he visited every home of our community to 'bless' it. Stepan and his Father had come home early for the occasion. It was late afternoon when he came to our house. *Mayrik* had prepared for the ritual. On the coffee table stood a tray on which there was a loaf of bread, a glass of water and a small dish of salt. After a refreshing cup of tea and a chat we stood round the coffee table and Father Serop began the 'blessing'. He burned the incense and blessed each of the items on the tray with a special prayer. Then he put the traditional *neshkar* (holy bread) on the tray. This bread is unleavened, moulded into thin, round shapes with the sign of the cross on it. With the Lord's Prayer, the ceremony was over. *Hayrik* was the first to kiss Father Serop's hand and receive the blessing. The rest of us followed suit.

During dinner the date of Agnes and Aram's wedding was decided. "I'll see you in three weeks time," said Father Serop as he prepared to leave. *Hayrik* discreetly gave him an envelope – the customary contribution to boost a priest's wages - and walked with him to the car.

After he had gone, we each took a sip of the blessed water, and ate a piece of the bread. *Mayrik* put the *neshkar* in the big bag of bulgur, just like my mother used to do.

We were sitting round the kitchen table one evening, having coffee. The architect's drawings for our house were spread on the table, and we were looking to see if there were any major changes to be made. I was very excited about the house, soon to be built on a prime site overlooking the sea. I couldn't wait to have my own home.

"I know it is early days, but how do you see the future of Cyprus now?" asked Aram.

"To be honest, after Cyprus became a republic, we were not sure how we would fare in the new scheme of things," said Stepan. "But I am glad to say that nothing has really changed. If anything it has been good for business. Tourism will transform Cyprus, in a very short space of time."

"It has already changed the island, Stepan, judging from all the building that's going up. But the important question is, does the Armenian population feel safe here?" Stepan did not answer for a moment. Then he looked up from the drawings.

"To be honest, Aram, I think we feel quite safe…"

"But, what if something unexpected happens. It worries me that so many Armenians are leaving for England. There is a growing Armenian community in West London, where I live. When I first moved there, I was the only Armenian. Now there are more than a dozen families."

"Yes, I'm aware of that. But it is mostly people who work in government offices or in the British bases. They are either resigning or being made redundant. They leave their jobs with a lump sum and they want to start a new life in England. Some of them have relatives established there already. I can't blame them for wanting to start again, somewhere other than Cyprus."

"I know it is not so easy for people who have their own business. I was only thinking… Maybe, it would be prudent not to put all your eggs in one basket."

"I suppose you could be right. What do you suggest we do?"

"Well, sometime in the future, you might consider buying a property in London."

"What do you mean? What kind of property?"

"A property you could let out. I'm in the process of buying a three-storey house, now. I'm going to convert it into three self-contained flats and let them out."

"How much is a house like that worth?"

"I paid just over five thousand pounds for mine. I don't know what the renovations and conversion to flats will cost me yet, but I reckon the rent I'll be getting from it will eventually pay for the property."

"That certainly sounds like a good business proposition."

"Once Agnes and I have settled in, you and Reya must come to visit us.

Anytime from May to August is a good time to visit England. The days are so long – it's still light at ten o'clock in the evening!"

"How wonderful. Yes, we shall definitely take a trip to London." I could see that Stepan was excited by all the things that Aram had told him. Then he caught my eye. We both knew that a trip anywhere in the near future was out of the question. Only this morning, Dr. Makrides had confirmed that I was, indeed, pregnant.

Chapter Twenty Six

The routine of our household changed only slightly, after Agnes left home to live in London. After the hectic preparations for her wedding, the wedding itself and the hasty departure of the newlyweds, the quiet that followed was an anti-climax. We went to Nicosia airport, to see them off. We would miss Agnes of course, especially her girlish giggle. How would she fare in a strange country, so far away from home? One great consolation to *Mayrik*, was that Agnes was so happy with Aram. She had made the right choice in choosing him for her husband.

"Promise me that you will all come and visit us soon. And I promise to telephone you, once a week." Agnes hugged us all in turn, before boarding the plane with Aram. We were all happy for her, but it was still a silent journey back home to Famagusta.

Stepan decided that we should move into Agnes's room. It was much bigger than ours, and it overlooked the garden.

"There's plenty of space for another wardrobe and a cot for the baby," he said, pointing to the corner by the window. "He can have light and fresh air, sleeping in his little cot here."

"He!" I said, surprised. "What makes you think it will be a boy?"

"Of course, it will be a boy. I heard Mother say that when a mother-to-be gets spots and blotches on her skin, she usually has a girl. But if her skin doesn't have such blemishes, then she has a boy. Your skin is positively glowing. In fact, I've never seen you look so well. So you see little one, it is a forgone conclusion that it will be a boy."

"Oh! I see. I suppose you have already chosen a name for 'him'!"

"But, of course. We'll name him Rafael, after Father. But we'll call him Rafi, for short. You have no objections, have you?" he asked as an afterthought, smiling his mischievous smile.

"Your question defies an answer," I said with mock scorn. "I won't pay any attention to myths and old-wives tales. Whatever will be, will be." That being said, I had noticed that my skin was entirely without any blemishes, and I did feel well and happy. What I didn't tell him was that I did not want to tempt fate. Of course, I would be happy for him, if it was a boy. Didn't

I know that men wanted their first born to be a boy? Hadn't my own father longed for a boy? Superstition forbade me to guess the gender of an unborn baby. Whatever will be, will be, became my way of thinking.

The days seemed so long now. I had little to do. *Mayrik* would not let me do any housework at all. Even with friends and neighbours dropping in for coffee, there were long, empty hours. Knitting became the order of the day. It seemed that everybody I knew was knitting something for the baby. White, yellow and blue being the predominant colours. *Mayrik* was never seen without a crochet needle in her hand. All her spare time was spent in crocheting every conceivable item that a baby could ever want or need. As if all this was not enough, Agnes had promised to post baby clothes from London. She assured me, on one of her weekly telephone calls, that these items were not to be found in the shops in Famagusta. As for me, apart from accepting these gifts gracefully, there was nothing for me to do. Fortunately, reading anything I could lay my hands on saved me from absolute boredom. Only when Stepan came home, did the house come alive. His presence filled the whole house. I so enjoyed his banter. We started going for leisurely walks in the evening. 'Good for you and Rafi,' he joked.

One lunchtime he came home with a huge box. His father had to help him carry it into the house. It was a television!

"We won't be able to go out much when Rafi comes," he said. "It will be nice to stay in and watch television." The television soon became an accepted part of our family routine. The programmes started at seven o'clock in the evening. Friday evening was the best night to watch television. There was always a good film on – either Greek or Turkish. Pretty soon, the 'gang' got into the habit of coming over on Friday evenings. We would have a light '*meze*' before settling down to watch the film.

The following months were a period of peace and contentment. The one disappointment in my life was not having my own home. With a baby on the way, it was decided to postpone the building of the house. There was time enough for that.

It was the first Sunday in May. I opened our bedroom window, to let in the glorious sun. The sky was a pure blue. Springtime in Cyprus is short and sweet. Therefore, we make the most of it. We enjoy the exquisite wild flowers that burst into life in the fields and on the roadside. We breathe in the intoxicating perfume of the orange blossom. The golden beaches beckon - soon we shall be wading in their warm waters. We must do all these things before spring gallops into the long, ferociously hot summer.

During our leisurely breakfast on the patio, I had a sudden urge to spend the day outdoors. Stepan was engrossed in the Sunday newspapers. I handed him his second cup of coffee. He lit a cigarette and continued to read.

"Shall we go on a picnic to-day?" I said. He looked up from his newspaper, with a surprised look on his face. It was unusual for me to suggest going on outings.

"Of course we can, *hokis,* where would you like to go?"

"Somewhere by the sea. I feel restless. I would love to sit and gaze at the sea, and maybe go for a walk by the sea-shore."

"Is everything alright? Why do you feel restless?"

"I don't really know. I had such strange dreams… I was tossing and turning all night, unable to sleep."

"Why didn't you wake me up?"

"I didn't want to. You were sleeping so peacefully…"

"I would have tossed and turned with you! Seriously though, you must wake me up if you feel unwell. I've told you that before, haven't I?"

"Yes, yes. I will."

"O.K. Now then, where can we go? Somewhere quiet and yet not too far away." He thought for a moment. "I know, we can go to the Old Town. We can look at the ships in the harbour first, and then find a deserted cove and have our picnic there! Would you like that?"

"That would be lovely! I haven't been to the Old Town since I was a child. Father used to take us children on Sunday afternoons - in an open, horse-drawn carriage. We used to love it, playing in the ruins of the churches, while the grown-ups sat in the coffee shop enjoying a drink or two. I remember one time, we were so late getting back to the coffee shop that my uncle came to look for us." My beloved Dai…Tears welled in my eyes. I was sure he was in my dream. Rising from his chair, Stepan came round and put his hands on my shoulders. "What's wrong little one?" he asked.

"It's nothing," I said. "I didn't have a very good night, that's all."

"Are you sure?" I nodded.

"Shall I phone round, and see if any of the 'gang' is free to join us?" I nodded again. The girls will help me get out of the melancholy that has suddenly come over me, I thought, as I went indoors to get ready.

It was dusk, when we started for home. It had proved to be a glorious day. As it happened, none of the 'gang' was free to join us. I was secretly glad that they couldn't come. I had wanted us to spend a day entirely on our own. It was wonderful, revisiting the harbour and the tower of Othello.

I had my wish. We found our deserted cove and had our picnic lunch of bread, cheese, olives, tomatoes and fruit washed down with beer. Afterwards, we lay on the soft, golden sands. Pretty soon, Stepan was fast asleep. I sat in my deckchair and gazed at the azure blue sea stretching to the horizon, watching the gentle wavelets caressing the golden shore.

I sat like that for a long time, thinking of the past. How dramatically my life had changed. It was less than two years since my meeting with Paul at his Sergeant's house. Where was that carefree young girl, so in love with a dashing soldier? And where was my Corporal? I hadn't thought of Paul in a long while, but I did now. I wondered if he had found a new love. And what of the future? I knew that the moment the baby came, my life would never be the same again. I sighed. Let the future take care of itself, I said to myself.

"That was a deep sigh," said Stepan. I was startled out of my thoughts. I hadn't realized that he had woken up.

"I've been watching you, for the last five minutes. You looked so anxious, as though you were carrying all the troubles of the world on your shoulders."

"Did I? I was only thinking of all the changes that have taken place this year."

"And yet more changes, when the baby comes." He got up and knelt by the side of my deckchair. "I haven't felt Rafi kick, today," he said, putting his hand on my stomach. He waited for a moment. "There he goes," he cried, happy as a sand boy.

Later, we walked barefoot along the shore, hand in hand, with the waves coming up to our knees.

"Happy now?" he whispered.

"Very happy. It's been a wonderful day."

On the way home, it started to rain. It was unusual to have rain in May, but very welcome. It washed away the dust and watered the gardens. I watched the windscreen wipers, swishing rhythmically. It was mesmerising, inducing in me a languorous feeling. I hadn't felt so calm and relaxed for a long time. Pleasantly tired from my day, I went to bed early and slept soundly.

It was the pain that woke me. Instinctively, I lay my hand across the mound of my stomach. Something was wrong. Surely it was not time… Waves of panic rose up within me. I must keep calm, I told myself. It was dark. The small porcelain clock on my bedside table told me it was two o'clock. I waited, not knowing what to do. The pain subsided, but after a few minutes it came back with such ferocity that I screamed.

My scream not only woke Stepan, but the entire household. Stepan was awake immediately, while his parents knocked on our bedroom door wanting to know what was happening. Events moved swiftly. One look at me, and *Mayrik* knew exactly what was happening. Her grave and ashen face mirrored my fears.

"Quick Stepan. The baby is on the way. Hurry, hurry!"

"But he is not due…"

"I know my son. He's early. Don't waste time asking questions! You must take Reya to the clinic, now!" Next thing I knew, Stepan wrapped me in a blanket and carried me to his car. He made me lie on the back seat, and as soon as his mother was seated, he drove at breakneck speed to Dr. Makrides's clinic.

The next few hours passed in a fog of pain, and more unrelenting pain. Every time I thought I was coming out of the fog, more pain assaulted my body. I struggled to remember where I was, what I was doing, in this hellish place. White clad, faceless figures drifted in and out of my consciousness. They peered at me, from a great height. They seemed to be creatures from another planet, another time.

The night was almost gone, when I gradually drifted out of the mist of pain that had enveloped me for so long. I opened my eyes. I was alone and in bed, in a darkened room. My hand went to my stomach. The mound was not there. The baby had come. It was over! Relief swept over me in waves for the ending of such a painful ordeal. But where was the baby?

I craned my neck, to see if there was a cot by my bed. Suddenly a light came on. I wasn't alone, as I had thought. A face was staring at me. The face came closer and closer and I realized with a start that it was Stepan. The soft light spread a gentle glow over his features, he looked different somehow. I tried to smile, but my lips stuck to my teeth. I tried to speak, but my throat was so very dry. I must either be dreaming, or I am in the land of the dead, I thought. Just then, Stepan's hands found mine, and I saw that he was weeping. The tears gleamed like jewels, in his long dark lashes.

"What's the matter?" I croaked, not recognizing my own voice. The door opened and Dr. Makrides walked in, followed by a nurse. Their sombre faces made my heart jump with fear. With devastating frankness, the doctor told me that he and his team had done everything possible to save the baby, but unfortunately, it was already too late, when I was brought to the clinic. Another two weeks, and the baby boy might have stood a chance... The baby boy...

I stared at the doctor in disbelief. His words hung heavy in the silent room. I started shaking my head from side to side, my confused gaze going from Stepan to the doctor, and back again.

"Is it true?" I asked my husband.

"Yes." He, too, had been stunned by the news. His voice cracked with emotion, relaying all the pain he felt. Leaning forward, he took my hands in his. "Try and rest now." I refused to believe it. "It's not true, it's not true!" I shouted. "Where is he? Where is my baby? Please Doctor, take me to him..."

"I'm so sorry. The baby was still-born." The doctor's words went round and round in my head. He could not save our baby boy... I had never felt so devastated in all my life, except when my beloved Dai had died. This is how my grandmother must have felt when her son died, I thought. The tears came then, unchecked, unstoppable.

"Let her cry, Stepan," said the doctor. "It's only natural, for her to sob after such a painful ordeal. She will feel better for it. I'll be in my office, if you need me. I'll talk to you later." The doctor left. The nurse gave me something to drink. She tidied my bed, and left also. We were alone again.

This was our darkest moment. We stayed frozen in this darkness, for a long time - each of us wrapped in our own grief. I looked at him – it seemed, from a great distance. There were deep shadows beneath his eyes. He looked haggard. His boyish enthusiasm had gone. I closed my eyes. I felt incredibly tired.

At the end of that week, I was well enough to go home. I felt empty inside, drained of all emotions, except for grief. Soon, grief gave way to guilt. Should I have been more careful on that fateful day, I asked myself time and time again. Had the long walk by the seashore brought on the premature labour? Worse still, I hadn't exactly been overjoyed when my pregnancy was confirmed. I hadn't felt ready for motherhood, only just getting used to being married. I was sure God was punishing me for it.

The burden was too heavy to bear. I couldn't share it with anyone. I withdrew into my shell, shutting Stepan and everybody else out. Mother, the family, friends and neighbours expressed their sorrow, tried to comfort me with words and deeds, but I could not respond to them. Stony faced and silent, I listened to them but didn't take anything in. When help finally came, it was from an unexpected source.

On Monday mornings, *Mayrik* would go to Ayios Nicolaos church and light a candle. She followed this religious custom most Mondays. On this day, she had left before I got out of bed. Stepan and his father had long gone to work. We no longer had breakfast together on the terrace.

The doorbell rang. Still in my dressing gown, I reluctantly went to open the door.

"Auntie Despina," I said, astonished to find her there. I hadn't seen her for ages. She looked old now, leaning heavily on her walking stick. "Come in, it's so nice to see you."

"My old bones need to rest. Are you alone in the house?"

"Yes Auntie." I became conscious of my appearance. "I'm sorry... I was still in bed. Come and sit on the veranda. I'll make the coffee." But she followed me into the kitchen, and sat down. I made the coffee, and wondered why she was here.

"I won't read your coffee cup today *agabimou* (my love), I know what's in it," she said. "Don't you think you have tortured yourself enough?"

"I feel so guilty."

"Why do you feel guilty, my child."

"If only I hadn't gone out that day. The night before I saw Uncle Krikor in my dream. Maybe he was warning me... It's my fault."

"Your fault? There was nothing you could have done. It was the will of God. It was written, here..." she touched her forehead "...that it should be so."

"But, if I had only been more careful..."

"No buts, my lovely. It was meant to be. You are young. You might not think so, now, but you will get over this trauma. But only, if you help yourself."

"How...?" Somehow, I found myself kneeling at her side, my head buried in her lap. She stroked my hair and remained silent. I found my voice at last. I poured out my heart to her, shedding the tears that would cleanse the dark places of my soul.

"Don't push your husband away," she told me. "He is suffering, just as much as you are."

"But he didn't let me see the baby - the doctor - none of them did. Why didn't they...?"

"The doctor knows best, doesn't he? What would be the point, if you did see the little angel? He is at peace now, with your uncle and your grandmother, in the arms of God." I lifted my head and looked at her, helplessly. "Don't let this tragedy come between you and your husband, like a sword. Open up to him and share your pain." With difficulty, she gathered herself up to go.

"Stay a bit longer, Auntie," I pleaded.

"No dear. I want to go to church and light a candle for both of you. Why don't you do the same, when you are ready."

"I will." I felt a rush of gratitude for this wise old lady, whom I had known since childhood. I took her hand and kissed it. She gave me her bright, well-remembered smile, and left. For the first time in weeks, the burden of guilt began to lift from my heart.

Over the following weeks, my recovery continued. None commented, but all took note that I had come back from the brink. The shadows under my eyes gradually disappeared. I felt refreshed, renewed and strong even. Losing a baby was a terrible thing, but I now accepted it, without remorse. The wonderful thing was that Stepan was there, waiting for me when I came out of the darkness. This crisis did not become a barrier between us. On the contrary, it brought us closer together. We had no secrets from one another. All things were shared.

During this time, Agnes and Aram were in touch with Stepan almost daily. When the news of my recovery reached them, they invited us to visit them.

"The change will be good for us both," said Stepan. "Father and Chris, my new salesman, will manage the shop perfectly well, without me. We've not been to England before, and Agnes will be only too pleased to show us the sights of London."

"Yes, it will be a wonderful holiday for you both, my dears," said *Mayrik*. "Spend some time together, away from it all."

"And find out what the attraction of London is, that so many people we know are deciding to sell up and go there," said *Hayrik*. "It can't be the weather, can it?"

"I doubt it, Father," smiled Stepan. "Although, the last time Agnes phoned, she said the weather was very warm – all of 75 degrees – a heat wave for them!" We all laughed, at that. We were in the middle of a real heat wave, here. This weekend, we were going to drive to the mountains, to escape the blisteringly hot weather. The nights were the worst, they were hot and humid. The sheets clung to our bodies, making sleep impossible.

"What do you say, little one? Shall we embark on our first grand tour?" Stepan asked. His face crinkled into a smile. His ebullient spirit had returned. He had started to call me 'little one' again. For some unexplained reason, this filled me with a deep tenderness for him.

"Yes, let's," I said, with equal enthusiasm. "It will be lovely, to see all the places in London we've only read about, or seen in films. And to enjoy cool weather will be an added bonus."

"I can go to Hatton Garden, to see how their designs compare with Lebanese and European designs. Maybe, I could even 'copy' some of their designs, if I like them. What do you think Father?"

"No harm in looking and learning, my son." There was no mistaking the happiness in both Stepan's and his father's voice, the relief that everything was all right again.

"That's settled, then. First thing tomorrow morning, I shall go to the travel agent and book our flights to London."

Chapter Twenty Seven

I held onto Stepan's hand as the "No Smoking" and "Fasten Seatbelts" signs flashed, and the plane prepared to land. We looked out of the window, to see the unfamiliar London skyline. We were both nervous and excited, at the prospect of our first visit to England. The plane made a perfect landing. We collected our hand luggage and followed the crowd, through endless corridors to the luggage carousel, and then on to Customs.

At first we didn't see Agnes and Aram, in the sea of people in the Arrival lounge. Then, we spotted them, frantically waving their arms and walking towards us. After what seemed an age, we were finally driving away in Aram's car, to Ealing in West London, where they lived. Everybody talked at once, there was so much to tell, so many questions to ask. London was so big, so bewildering. I looked out of the car window, at the traffic coming from all directions. So many roundabouts, so many traffic lights. How on earth had Agnes adjusted so quickly to living in a big city? For she had adjusted, pointing out places and names to us, as if she had lived here all her life.

It was four o'clock, before we finally reached Ealing. We drew up in front of No. 32, Acacia Crescent, a detached house in a quiet, leafy suburb. It was identical to the rest of the houses in the road. It was well set back from the road, with a sizeable front garden with a cherry tree. Agnes took out her key, opened the front door and we entered the large, oak-panelled hall. The boys followed us, carrying in our suitcases.

"What a lovely house, Agnes," I said, unable to hide my surprise. I had thought houses in London were old, dark and dingy. Agnes smiled. She was clearly proud of her home.

"Let's have a cup of tea, first, and then you can have a guided tour of the house!" she said. Taking off her jacket, she walked into the kitchen, to make the tea. "Feel at home," she called, over her shoulder. I followed her into the kitchen. It was big, light and airy and spotlessly clean, like her mother's. The golden afternoon sunshine shimmered in, through the window. I watched Agnes make the tea. First, she poured some boiling water in the teapot, swirled it round and emptied it. Then, she put four teaspoons of tea leaves into the teapot, filled it with the boiling water and stirred.

"Here we are," she said, with a flourish, putting the teapot on the table, next to the milk jug, the sugar bowl and a plate of biscuits. "Aram showed me how to make proper English tea. We drink it at breakfast, and in the afternoons. I love it. I hardly drink coffee, now." I remembered the sumptuous English tea Eleni and I had at the King George, courtesy of the American photographer. I decided then that I would adopt this custom, when I had my own home.

"This is wonderful," I said, drinking my refreshing cup of tea. I reached for a biscuit and bit into it. "Did you make these Agnes?"

"I did. Do you like them?"

"They melt in the mouth," I said and passed the plate around.

"Wait till you see our bedroom," said Stepan. "It's a huge room, overlooking the back garden – which, incidentally, looks as if it needs Father's 'green fingers' to bring it up to scratch."

"I know. It looks like a jungle doesn't it? I don't know anything about gardens, and even if I did, I don't have the time to do it," said Aram.

"The garden can wait, Stepan," said Agnes. "The house is more important. Come, I'll show you the rest of the house. See for yourself what your clever sister has achieved."

"You have every right to feel proud of your handiwork," I told her, upstairs. Every room was tastefully decorated with wallpaper – something not yet available in Cyprus. It was very effective, as it matched the curtains.

"These two rooms haven't been done, yet. They are used as store-rooms, at the moment," said Aram. "Most people redecorate a couple of rooms at a time, here. Do you like the house, Reya?"

"I do. It's a lovely house." I answered, genuinely happy for them both. "We'd better unpack the suitcases, Stepan." The bigger of the suitcases was full of 'goodies'. There was halloumi cheese, green and black olives, pistachio nuts, as well as two bottles of Cyprus brandy, two bottles of whisky and duty free cigarettes. Agnes shrieked with delight, at the sight of them.

"This is for your house, from your parents," I said, handing Agnes a parcel. She opened it. There was a tablecloth with six matching napkins, and four doilies, of various sizes and shapes.

"*Lefkaritika!*" exclaimed Agnes. This was the unique embroidery that is only made in Lefkara. It takes weeks and months, for the women of that village to embroider a medium size tablecloth. This remarkable craft is handed down, from one generation to the next.

"And this is from Stepan and me," I said, handing her yet another parcel. "I hope it has survived the journey." Agnes opened this parcel also. It was a large fruit bowl, of the finest Bohemian crystal, just like the ones I used to admire in Dai's shop.

"It's beautiful. It will look lovely on the sideboard," she said, happily. She was very pleased with all her gifts.

"No wonder the suitcases were so heavy!" teased Aram. "Nevertheless, I shall enjoy my glass of brandy all the more, after dinner."

I followed Agnes into the kitchen, to help her with the evening meal. We left the boys to their talk, while Agnes made the sauce for the spaghetti. I made the salad and set the table.

"Do you miss Cyprus?" I asked her.

"Of course, I do. But not the unbearable heat of summer. I miss my family and my friends, and Mother's cooking. I do regret that I didn't learn how to cook. I'm learning though, with trial and error. But I have adapted remarkably easily, to my new life here."

"Yes, I can see that. Like you, I avoided the kitchen if I could. I must learn to cook though, before we move to our house. By the way, I brought the recipes you asked for. Your mother wrote them out carefully for you, with step-by-step instructions and measures."

"Good. Maybe we can try a couple of recipes together, and see what we come up with!"

"You seem to have mastered the art of making spaghetti, anyway. Are those mushrooms you are slicing?" I knew what mushrooms looked like, but I had never tasted them. In Cyprus, we had to be extremely careful to make sure that they were not poisonous. I think you had to put a gold ring in the pan, as you fried them, and - if the gold didn't go green - then they were not poisonous, and safe to eat! Mother had decided that it wasn't worth all that trouble, and so she never used mushrooms in her cooking.

"Yes. But don't worry, mushrooms are not poisonous here. They are cultivated. I like them, and use them a lot in soups and casseroles." Agnes's spaghetti turned out to be very good. Aram opened a bottle of red Italian wine, and it was like a celebratory dinner.

"Tomorrow is Saturday, the busiest day of the week, in my business," said Aram, after his second brandy. "You two are tired after your long day, so we should all have an early night. If you are up by eight o'clock, Stepan,

I'll take you to the shop. Would you like that, or would you prefer to have a relaxing day at home?"

"That's a good idea," said Agnes, before Stepan could answer. "I can take Reya to the local shops, and then we can come by the shop afterwards." It was agreed. I quickly unpacked our few clothes – we hadn't brought much, as we intended to buy lots of clothes in London – and we got into bed. The cool sheets were welcoming, after the heat and humidity of Cyprus. Stepan went to sleep as soon as his head touched the pillow. Even though I too was tired from our long exciting day, I couldn't go to sleep.

For some reason I thought of Paul. I wondered if he was still living in Barnes. Barnes couldn't be that far from Ealing. What if I meet him in the street one day, I asked myself. How would I feel, what would I do? More to the point, how would Paul feel? At that moment, Paul rose up in my mind like a physical presence. He would still be unforgiving of me, and would surely walk away from me, without saying a word. And what about Stepan? I had to stop this nonsense. It was late, and I was being silly. The possibility of meeting Paul in a big place like London was virtually none. I tossed and turned, and eventually drifted into a dreamless sleep.

Chapter Twenty Eight

The following morning, I woke to another bright and sunny day. The house was silent. I put on my dressing gown and went downstairs, to investigate. Agnes was alone in the kitchen, making tea.

"The boys must have left early, because I didn't hear them," she said. "Let's have some breakfast. What would you like? I usually have cereal, toast and marmalade." She put packets of cereal on the table, and set the table as she talked.

"I'll try the cornflakes," I said. Cereal was another thing we didn't have at home. "Toast and marmalade sounds good, too." I felt pleasantly hungry. What a nice way to start the day, I thought, as I poured myself a cup of tea.

"It must be the weather here," said Agnes. "I need to have breakfast before I start doing anything, whereas in Cyprus I never even thought about food, before the eleven o'clock coffee-break." I smiled inwardly, remembering my coffee breaks at the office.

"The boys will have something to eat at the shop," she said. Just then, the telephone rang and Agnes rushed to the hall to get it. She came back after a moment, to tell me that Stepan wanted to talk to me. He sounded happy and excited. He was helping Aram in the shop, as they were very busy.

"It's amazing," he said, "People are queuing to be served. I've never seen anything like it. There are four assistants besides Aram, and they can hardly keep up!"

"Really? I can't imagine it."

"It's nothing like the Municipal Market, in Famagusta! I made coffee for them, but they haven't had time to drink it. By the way, tell Agnes not to cook dinner tonight, as we are going out."

"Alright," I said. "When are you coming home?"

"I thought you girls were coming to the shop…"

"Yes, of course we are. I'd forgotten about it."

"I'm needed! I'd better go. See you later."

"I'm glad he found the shop interesting," said Agnes, as we continued with our breakfast. "I was afraid he might find a green-grocery shop boring. It's a far cry from a jewellery shop isn't it?"

"I don't think Stepan will be bored. I wouldn't be surprised if he rolled up his sleeves and started weighing potatoes," I said, smiling.

"I'm going to take you to the shopping centre. We can go to *Branden's* – it's a department store – and spend some time there. And afterwards, we can take the bus and go to the shop. You can see for yourself how Stepan is getting on."

I helped Agnes with the washing up and tidying. It was almost midday, when we were ready to venture out. There was no real hurry, as there was no cooking to be done this evening. I was looking forward to see anything and everything. Agnes picked up two umbrellas from the stand and handed one to me.

"What do we need umbrellas for?" I asked in surprise. "It's not raining." She smiled.

"You never know when it might start raining here," she said. "Sometimes, we get several seasons in one day! So, we are always prepared."

Wide-eyed with excitement, I kept looking left and right, in order not to miss anything. There were crowds of people on the pavements, a succession of cars speeding by, but everything seemed to be going in an orderly manner. It was a far cry from the jostling crowds on the roads of Cyprus, and the cars, with their ear-splitting horns, warning pedestrians to get out of their way, their car radios blaring. Not to mention the hundreds of cyclists, ringing their bells to claim the right of way, adding to the noise and confusion.

"Different here, isn't it?" said Agnes, guessing my thoughts. "No pushing or shoving - everyone crossing the road safely and sensibly, at zebra crossings."

"The cars are so quiet, I haven't even heard the sound of a horn, yet."

"You won't. Everything is orderly and civilized here. There's *Branden's*. We'll have a coffee first, and then we'll look around. I'll take you to all the floors – all four of them!"

I couldn't wait to see it all. We did go to all the floors - on the escalators, no less. When we came to the baby and children section, Agnes took my hand and tried to lead me away to another floor, but I resisted. "It's alright, Agnes," I said. A stab of pain shot through me, as I silently looked at all the beautiful little baby clothes, the cots, prams, milk bottles, and sterilizers… I remembered the big parcel of baby clothes that had arrived from Agnes, on the day I had come home from the clinic. She must have bought them from this store. The parcel was hidden somewhere in the house – unopened. Agnes looked at me enquiringly, not wanting to upset me. I smiled at her. "It's alright," I repeated. And it was. Looking at the baby things had brought back the pain of loss, but as I watched the expectant mothers, browsing in the store, I began to see them as the symbol of the future. My turn would come. The scene had a cathartic effect on me.

Sure enough, it was raining when we came out of the department store. We joined the sea of umbrellas at the bus stop. People were queuing patiently for the bus. It came after about ten minutes or so. Again, I noticed how the passengers boarded the bus quietly, without pushing or shoving. We settled in our seats, grateful to be out of the rain. I sat by the window, looking out. Unaccountably, I missed Stepan. It seemed such a long time, since I last saw him. I wonder what kind of day he's had, I thought to myself.

"We get off at the next stop," whispered Agnes. The queue at the bus stop waited till we got off, before they tried to get on. Agnes and I smiled at one another. After a short walk, we reached Aram's shop. The big sign above the shop read "ARAM" and under it, "High Class Greengrocers and Fruiterers." The shopping day was all but over. There were a few late shoppers, buying their fruit and vegetables for the weekend. A young man was serving them. "Hello Simon," smiled Agnes, as she led the way to the back room. This was a big room, which served as kitchen, staff room and office. Aram was sitting at the desk, smoking and writing, while Stepan was washing cups at the sink.

"Meet the new cook and bottle-washer," he grinned, drying his hands, as he came to greet us. He ruffled my hair, and asked me if I had a good time. I smiled and nodded my head.

"You should have seen her, Stepan," said Agnes. "She was like a little girl at the *Panayiri* (fair), not knowing where to look and where to go!" She grinned at me. "I was like that, when I first came…"

"Oh! That's nice. I, on the other hand, have not stopped working for a moment. Isn't that so, Aram?"

"That is absolutely true," Aram said, putting his pen away. "This 'boy' has worked hard all day, carrying sacks of potatoes, making tea and coffee for us, getting lunch and actually getting his hands dirty!"

"I don't believe that!" cried Agnes. "I've never seen my brother's hands dirty." Stepan spread his hands out for all to see. I had never seen them dirty either.

"Would you like to see Covent Garden Market, Stepan?" asked Aram. "I go every Monday, for fresh supplies. It's a wonderful experience."

"I'd love to," said Stepan.

"It's very early in the morning, though – at about four o'clock."

"That's alright. I'll be up."

"Right. I'll give Simon his pay packet, and then we'll be off."

That first weekend was the beginning of a wonderful two and a half weeks in England. That night Aram took us to a Greek restaurant in Goodge Street, in the very heart of London. It wasn't a very smart place, but the food was mouth-wateringly good. The proprietor's wife – a very stout woman – cooked the kebabs herself. We drank Cyprus Ouzo as we waited. For a moment, we forgot we were in London. We could hear Greek being spoken not only in the restaurant but also in the street outside.

After our wonderfully satisfying meal, Aram took us to Soho. We had heard of Soho as being a den of iniquity, but we didn't witness anything bad happening. The place was buzzing with people, mostly tourists. The strip-tease joints looked seedy, to say the least. The door of one such place opened, and loud music filled the air. We stopped, to gaze at the scantily clad girl seen clearly in the light. The door shut abruptly and we moved on.

On Sunday morning, we woke up to the tantalizing aroma of cooking emanating from the kitchen. Aram was going to treat us to a genuine 'English Breakfast'. What a feast, what a culinary experience! We had bacon, sausages, mushrooms, fried bread, fried eggs, grilled tomatoes and baked beans, followed by toast and marmalade, and a big pot of tea to wash it down with! The surprising thing was that we could enjoy such a big meal in the morning. It would be unthinkable to do this in Cyprus. Some bread and cheese with a slice of cold watermelon would be more than enough for breakfast.

Three days before we were due to go back home to Cyprus, Aram telephoned to say that the local Estate Agent he dealt with, who was also his friend, had told him that a very nice house had just come onto the market. Would Stepan like to go and see it? This house was in the next road to his – No. 12, Bedford Lane.

We had discussed the possibility of buying a property in London, but as far as we were concerned, it was just an idea. This phone call took us by surprise. We were sitting at the kitchen table, having our mid-morning coffee. We had decided to take a day off. The last ten days had been taken up entirely with sightseeing. We left the house in the morning and didn't return till the evening. I think we walked the length and breadth of London, twice over. There was so much to see and marvel over. Stepan had a good sense of direction, and soon became expert in finding his way around the city. We both loved the red London buses and the 'tube'.

Stepan looked at me, questioningly. He knew that what I wanted more than anything else in the world was to have our own home in Famagusta, not a house in London. What to do? Aram was waiting for an answer at the other end of the phone.

"Aram says this property will be snapped up..."

"In that case, we'd better go and see it," I said, surprised that I had made this decision all by myself. I was even more surprised that Stepan had asked for my opinion on the subject, in the first place. "We don't lose anything by viewing it," I added, emboldened by the confidence this had given me.

The estate agent – Mr. Cunningham – was waiting for us at the house, an hour later. No. 12, Bedford Lane was much like Aram's house – a 1930's four bedroom detached house with a big garden at the back. It was in good decorative condition throughout. The curtains and carpets were included in the asking price, which was seven and half thousand pounds.

"I told Mr. Aram that a firm offer will be considered, if it leads to a quick sale," said the estate agent, as we took our leave. Stepan looked at his watch. It was almost lunchtime.

"You'll have my answer before five o'clock, Mr. Cunningham," he said, and shook the estate agent's hand. Stepan lit a cigarette and we started to walk the short distance home. I could see he was taken with the house. I think he was attracted by the idea of owning a fine house in London. But the question was, could he afford it? I had no idea about our financial position, of course. I was given to understand that we could afford to build a nice house, on the plot of land that his father had bought, years ago. Could we afford both? We reached home in silence. Agnes was back from the hairdresser's.

"Aram told me about the house in Bedford Lane. He wants you to phone him straightaway. Did you like it?"

"We liked it very much, Agnes," said Stepan. "Didn't we, little one? It would certainly be a good investment." He turned to me. I nodded. That's all I could do. He had to make the decision.

The clock on the mantelpiece told me it was almost six thirty. Stepan had gone to Aram's shop hours ago, and was still not back. I put the magazine I was reading on the table, unable to concentrate. I was anxious to find out what was happening. I suddenly had a thought. Maybe it was a good idea to buy this house, if we could afford it. We could convert it into two separate flats, the way Aram had done with his second house. Why not let one flat and get some income from it, and keep the other for the family's use? My imagination took wings. After all, with Agnes living in London, we were bound to visit her again. So would her mother and father. One thought loomed in my mind, though – if Stepan decided to buy this house, would it mean the postponement of the building of my dream home, or worse still, would it mean the abandonment of the idea altogether?

I jumped out of my chair, when I heard Aram's key in the door, and went to the hall to meet them. Stepan ruffled my hair absent-mindedly and flopped on the sofa. He made room for me, and put his arm around me, as I sat down next to him. I wondered if he had made a decision on the house, but I remained silent and waited for him to speak.

"We've got a deal," he said, smiling broadly. "I went back to the house with Aram and had another look at it. He persuaded me that it was a bargain, not to be missed. Then I sat down and worked out the finances. I shall telephone my father and ask his opinion first, of course, but I think I can afford it with a little help from my bank manager!"

"Good," I said. "But, surely there isn't enough time…"

"Buying and selling property is very different here," said Stepan. "It takes almost three months to complete a sale. Solicitors are involved and all sorts of other things need doing, before you can take possession of it. Isn't that so, Aram?"

"That's right," Aram confirmed, as he and Agnes came to join us. "I know - in Cyprus you can buy or sell a house in one day, but things are different here. It will give you time to sort out the financial side, while I take care of everything else here."

"I'm so excited and happy for you both," said Agnes. "I won't feel home-sick, knowing you will have a house close to ours. Aren't you excited, Reya?"

"Of course, if that's what Stepan wants," I stammered. Now that the decision to buy the house had been made, I was unsure of my feelings. All I knew was that I would be very disappointed, if I didn't have my own home, as he had promised.

"Don't worry, little one. You shall have your dream house by the sea - even if I have to build it myself, with my own hands!" said Stepan, pulling me closer to him and planting a kiss on my forehead.

Nine months after coming home from London, our son was born.

Chapter Twenty Nine

My second pregnancy was very different from my first one. For one thing, I didn't suffer from morning sickness or tiredness, and secondly, I was four months pregnant before we told anyone. Surprisingly, no one, not even *Mayrik* guessed my 'condition'. This time, I was glad I was going to have a baby. I felt I was ready for motherhood and all the responsibilities that came with it. I didn't even mind not having my own home, as I had hoped. The bank loan, which had enabled Stepan to buy the house in Ealing, had to be paid off first, before other projects could be undertaken – I understood this and accepted it. My energy was boundless, I did a lot of the housework, but I also made sure that I had rest periods and, every evening, Stepan took me for a walk.

I went for regular checks at the clinic. Dr. Makrides advised me to have the baby by Caesarean section. He said he didn't want to take any unnecessary risks with a natural birth. Stepan agreed with him. I certainly didn't want to go through the pain and anguish a second time. Neither did we want to tempt fate. There was to be no guessing the sex of the baby, or choosing names. Perhaps I went too far, when I forbade anyone from knitting or making baby clothes. Nevertheless, I had a sneaking suspicion that both the Mothers were busily making things, anyway, whatever I said.

Nurse Christina put the baby in my outstretched arms. "Here is your baby son, don't you think he looks like an angel?" I looked down at the soft bundle of new life I was holding, and promptly fell in love with him. He was the most beautiful baby I had ever seen. His skin was soft and smooth, not puckered like other babies I had seen. I couldn't see the colour of his eyes, as he had them firmly shut, but he had a mop of dark brown hair on his head.

I gazed down, with wonder and amazement, on this miracle that Stepan and I had created. I knew that our lives would never be the same again. I didn't hear Stepan come into the room. I looked up and saw the same expression of wonder on his face, as he looked at his newborn son. He put his arms around the baby and me, relieved that everything was alright this time. We stayed like that for a long moment, until Stepan stepped back and grinned at me.

"And baby makes three," he said. He sat down in the chair at my bedside, having regained his usual bright and breezy self. After a few minutes, the nurse came in.

"Your wife needs to rest now, Mr. Stepan, but you can come back this evening and stay for as long as you like."

"Alright, Nurse," said Stepan, trying to hide his disappointment. She took pity on him.

"Why don't you hold your son, for a minute, before you go?" she suggested. I offered the precious bundle, and, so gently, Stepan took the baby from me and held him close. Just then, the little one opened his eyes and, at last, I could tell that they were like his fathers - dark eyes, fringed with long black lashes.

That evening, I had a string of visitors. After my rest and a light supper, I felt refreshed. The baby had been bathed and fed, and slept peacefully in the cot next to me. Both sets of parents arrived at the same time. There were big grins on their faces. They all looked at their precious grandson with pride, and nodded their approval. Each of them, in turn, patted me on the shoulder, as if to say 'well done' for producing a boy!

"We are going to name our son, Nathaniel, after my grandfather," announced Stepan. It was understood by the family that Stepan wouldn't want to call this baby Raphael, after his father. That name had been chosen for the first boy, it would forever be associated with him.

"Thank you, my son," he said, the tremor in his voice reflecting his joy and pride. "Your grandfather was a wise man and he lived to a ripe old age."

"Yes, I remember how wise and witty he was, Father. The stories he used to tell me, when I was a child…" replied Stepan. "We'll call him Nathan for short." Everyone was happy with the choice of name for the baby, and they all voiced their approval. If the baby had been a girl, it wouldn't have mattered so much, what name was chosen for her. I wondered what name I would have chosen if the baby had been a girl. I smiled inwardly. Maybe, I would have called her Scarlett or Lara, or even Amber!

After ten days in the clinic, I went home with Nathan, to a wonderful welcome. Both families were waiting for us. The 'mothers' had cleaned the house, done all the washing and cooked my favourite dish – stuffed aubergines, tomato and onion salad and home made thick yoghurt – with crusty bread. Stepan had been pretty busy too. He had been to *Panayoti's Baby Shop*. He had got the cot, the baby bath and a chest of drawers to store all the baby's things. I opened the drawers. One drawer was full of the knitted items, which the 'mothers' had been knitting away secretly. The next one was full of terry towels, and the last two drawers contained every other item of clothing a baby could ever need.

Although we had a nursery for Nathan, I wanted him to be with me, in our bedroom. Stepan wasn't keen on the idea at first, but I insisted. If he was in another room, we might not hear him crying in the night, I argued. Stepan gave in gracefully, and now he had placed the cot on my side of the bed, within touching distance. I didn't tell him that I had hardly had an uninterrupted night in the clinic. I would get anxious, and tiptoe to the cot to make sure that the baby was breathing. One night, Nurse Christina found me, listening to his heartbeat.

"All new mothers do that," she smiled. "But don't make a habit of it. Babies are tough you know, tougher than you think. You won't do him or yourself any good by being over protective." She took my hand and led me to my bed. I knew it was good advice, but it was hard to follow.

The 'mothers' decreed that I should not be allowed to do any housework or cooking, for the first forty days after the birth. It was customary for the older women in the family to take over all the household tasks and look after the new mother and baby for this period. *Forty days* was a kind of magical threshold. It had echoed all through my life. The first time I was aware of it had been the 'forty days' in quarantine my parents had lived through. Then there was the memorial service 'forty days' after the death of my beloved Dai and later for my grandmother. And now, I was to have 'forty days' of complete rest after motherhood.

"But I want to look after my baby..." I argued more than once, fancying myself a capable and modern young mother. My protests fell on deaf ears however. Predictably, Stepan supported the 'mothers' in this respect. I was still anxious, wanting to get up several times in the night, to make sure that Nathan was breathing. But Stepan forbade this, and when Nathan woke up crying, he would jump up himself to prepare his bottle and even change his nappy. I was amazed at how quickly he had taken to being a father, and how efficient he was.

I was feeling so tired with lack of sleep, that I gave in and enjoyed a few weeks of being pampered and spoilt. The 'mothers' took turns in looking after Nathan and spoiling him too. There was a stream of visitors, wanting to see the new baby. They came with good wishes and pretty gifts. Nathan was admired, cooed over and passed on from one pair of loving arms to another. During this period of 'convalescence' I had the time to plan Nathan's christening. He would be baptized in the church of St. Krikor and afterwards there would be a big christening party at the house.

At the end of the 'forty days' I was pronounced fit to take up my new role as mother. Nathan was a good baby, happy and contented. After a short while, the family got into a new daily routine. The mornings were busy. *Mayrik* was occupied in the kitchen with the preparation of food, while I bathed and fed Nathan and washed his clothes, by hand of course, never in the washing machine. I tackled the housework when the baby was having his mid-morning nap. We were free in the afternoons, to receive visitors or go visiting ourselves.

"Do you realize just how lucky we are to have your kind and loving mother, who cares so much for us and the baby?" I asked Stepan one evening. He turned away from the television and looked at me enquiringly.

"What do you mean, little one?"

"She is always there for us, especially in a crisis. I have learned so much from her. When Nathan has a tummy upset, she tells me to cut out the sugar from his feed. When he has a fever, she rubs his forehead with pure alcohol. I guess I'm still learning…"

"Of course you are, *hokis*. Like all mothers, she has experience of these things, and she is passing them on to you. I saw you rubbing *raki* on Nathan's gums, and dip his dummy in it."

"It numbs the pain, so he goes off to sleep straight away. I do appreciate all the help I get."

"I know you do. We both do. I suppose we are doubly lucky really, because we can leave Nathan with his grandparents anytime. They are only too pleased to look after him."

"I know. Roxi was telling me the other day that she had no one to help her when she had her two children. She had to ask her neighbour to baby sit for her. She said your mother often came to her rescue."

"That's true. But then, Mother is like that. She likes helping people and she loves children."

"I sometimes doubt if I could have managed on my own…"

"Of course you could. Anyway, you'll have your chance to prove it to yourself, when Mum and Dad go to England next week. Stop worrying, little one, and come and sit by me. The news will be on in a minute."

For the first time since we got married, Stepan and I were on our own in the house with baby Nathan. Stepan's parents were in England, visiting Agnes, who had just had a baby boy. They were planning to stay there for two months, to help their daughter, as they had helped me.

During their absence, I grasped the reins of domesticity with both hands. I continued with the usual daily routine, and before long, I realised how like the 'mothers' I was becoming. So many of their traits and habits had rubbed off on me. Like them, I hated clutter and did things in an orderly way. Even though looking after Nathan and doing the housework took most of my time, I resolved that I would learn to cook and be good at it, too. I was cautious at first, experimenting with quick and easy recipes, only gradually trying more elaborate and time consuming dishes. Before starting to cook, I would gather all the ingredients, together with the pots and pans that I would need. This not only saved time, but also made sure I did not leave anything out! There were no cookery books I could rely on, as neither of the 'mothers' possessed any. Nor did they use kitchen scales. Like their mothers before them, they used what we call in Armenian *'the measure of the eye'*, meaning that they could assess, by eye, exactly how much of each ingredient to use in any given dish. The only 'measure' they used was a cup when they made rice or bulgur *pilav*.

I made a list of the dishes I wanted to try, and every time I saw Mother, I asked her for the recipes. She could only give me approximate measures and cooking times, of course, so last-minute dramas in the kitchen became commonplace. My determination surprised even myself, as I persevered with heroic determination to master the art. During my 'apprenticeship', as Stepan called it, he endured quite a few burnt offerings, not to mention the ones that were undercooked. He never told me which was the lesser of the two evils! I was grateful that he accepted my 'trial and error' efforts with such good grace. But his eyes would shine with undisguised pleasure, whenever Mother invited us for lunch (which was, luckily, quite often). I also noticed that he would suggest that we eat out at a *taverna* more often, and we definitely visited the 'gang' much more often than they visited us.

I had my triumphant debut as chef and hostess, on the day Stepan's parents came back from England. I planned a 'welcome home' dinner for them. I woke up early and worked the whole day, cleaning the house from top to bottom, before preparing the food. When Stepan brought them home from the airport, everything was ready and waiting for them. The table was set. The salad was in the fridge, the chicken was boiled just right, the rice *pilav* and the stuffed cabbage leaves cooked to perfection and 'resting' nicely on the cooker – covered with kitchen towels to keep them warm.

My only disappointment was that I hadn't had the time to make a dessert – the *daktila* that I had learnt to make from Anna.

"Never mind, *hokis*," Stepan had said in sympathy, before setting off for the airport. "You've done enough already. Fruit and cheese will do very well."

"My goodness, hasn't Nathan grown!" Stepan's parents chorused as soon as they came into the house. "He has changed so much in the two months we've been away." They took turns hugging and kissing him. They were tired after their long journey so we decided to have our meal straight away.

I was nervous as a kitten, as we started to eat. Would they like what I had cooked? Would anyone comment? I needn't have worried.

"Well done, daughter," *Mayrik* said. "You've done us proud. That was an excellent meal."

"See, little one, I told you everything would turn out alright," said Stepan, and winked. "So, Mother, did you enjoy your first visit to England?"

"I did. I liked Ealing, especially the shopping centre at Ealing Broadway. I was impressed with Aram's house, and the new furniture."

"We had a look at your house, my son – only from the outside, of course – and your mother and I liked it," said *Hayrik*.

"It's a solid house, isn't it Father?"

"Yes. And it is in a very nice neighbourhood, with the park only five minutes away."

"Touch wood, we've been lucky with tenants so far. According to my last bank statement, there is a tidy sum in the bank. Interest rates are quite high at the moment."

"The house has proved to be a very wise investment. I thanked Aram for his good advice. Without a doubt, our Agnes has done very well for herself. Very well indeed."

"They are good for each other. How is Aram doing these days?"

"There's no stopping him. Everything he touches turns into gold. He is in the process of buying yet another property."

"Really?"

"Yes. This time it is a freehold shop with living accommodation above."

"Holy angels! Whereabouts is it?"

"It's actually just off Ealing Broadway."

"Did you have a chance to see it?"

"Aram took me. It's in a busy parade of shops. There's a hairdresser's, a hardware shop, a tobacconist and, if I'm not mistaken, a launderette."

"A launderette?" Stepan asked.

"Yes. It's a shop really, where there are commercial, coin-operated washing machines and driers. Your mother was interested…"

"I was very interested. People bring their washing – from sheets to socks – in big plastic bags, they wash and dry them in these machines. And if you're too busy to do it yourself, you pay a bit extra and the manager of the launderette does it for you!"

"How convenient!"

"It is very convenient for busy people. And also not everybody has a washing machine. Agnes sometimes dries the baby's nappies in there. It does rain a lot in England as you know."

"And how is the baby?" I asked, when there was a pause in the conversation. "Who does he look like?"

"He is a lovely little boy!" exclaimed the proud grandmother. "He is the spitting image of Aram and as you know, they have named him Mickael, after his father, but they'll call him Mike for short. They're hoping to come to Cyprus for a visit when the baby is a bit older."

That night, in the seconds before sleep overcame me, I felt a great sense of achievement. My first attempt as hostess had turned out better than I had expected. All my hard work had been worthwhile. The family was pleased. I would try to be more adventurous with the menu, next time. A whole way of life had passed on from one generation to another, unnoticed and unheralded.

Chapter Thirty

We moved into our new house, a week after Nathan's fourth birthday. It was one of the happiest days of my life. Stepan and I had watched the house 'grow'. We had celebrated the day the foundations were laid, and thereafter, we had visited the site at least twice a week, to make sure that everything was going according to plan. When the roof went up, it was time to celebrate again.

I loved every inch of my house, every piece of furniture. It was a double-fronted house with three bedrooms, a huge living room, dining room, and a very modern kitchen with a breakfast area. It had a wide veranda at the front, and a terrace at the back. From the bedroom windows, I could gaze at the sea, in all its fascinating moods and its changing colours - from emerald, to sapphire, to pale blue and grey. We had chosen the furniture, the two Persian rugs and various Kilims that graced the floors, with great care. The pictures that hung on the walls were painted by local artists. The living room was warm and informal, with bookcases and a radiogram.

"Happy now, little one?" asked Stepan. We were sitting on the terrace, enjoying one last cigarette before going to bed. It was late and we were both tired but pleasantly so, as our house warming party had been a great success. I looked up and watched the millions of stars winking in the sky. "Happy now?" he repeated.

"Yes, very happy. I'm so glad everybody enjoyed themselves. I should start clearing up…"

"We'll do that tomorrow. Let's enjoy the cool breeze for a moment longer. You know what, I believe you *were* born under a lucky star. You brought luck to your father and you brought luck to me too."

"Oh, no! Not you too, please."

"It's true though. We were well off before, but look at us now. The house in Ealing is paid for and you have your long awaited 'dream' house, all in the space of a few years. I know the Cyprus economy flourished when we joined the Commonwealth, but…"

"What about tourism?" I asked, thinking of the hotels, apartment blocks, supermarkets, souvenir shops and *tavernas* springing up like magic, to accommodate the tourists that were flocking to Aphrodite's golden isle.

"Tourism is the key to the expansion of the economy of Cyprus, of course. But at the moment, only Famagusta is profiting from it. Because of the harbour, it has always attracted visitors, as we know, but the 'experts' believe that this new wave of tourism is surpassing all expectations. But, on the other hand, not everybody is benefiting from tourism. So, little one, I'll say it again, it was *you*, who brought me luck."

Tempting though it was to take the credit for Stepan's good fortunes, it was tourism that was bringing untold wealth to Cyprus. And, sadly, the Famagusta I knew and loved was changing fast, too fast. The golden beaches of my childhood were taken over with crowds of sun-worshippers, intent on turning brown under the fiercely hot sun. I looked up at the sky again. My so called 'lucky' star was there somewhere. It had been my companion for as long as I could remember.

"If you say so. But surely this myth has grown out of all proportion?"

"Not at all. Anyway, I'm going to take you to Nicosia for a shopping spree next week."

"Why? I never thought I would say this, but I don't need anything…"

"You will. I'm taking you on a tour of Beirut, Syria and Egypt…"

"What brought this on? I thought we were going to England next year."

"We are. It's time we went abroad more. I want to see the pyramids, don't you?" I nodded, not yet over the surprise.

"So, I want you to have more dresses like the one you're wearing. I like it very much."

"I like it too. Anna said it was the last word in chic and elegance. I agreed with her!"

Stepan reached over and took my hand. "I pray to God, our good fortune will continue. I know we shall be happy here," he whispered.

"We will," I said, with passion, looking at his misty eyes. "I shall never want to live anywhere, but here, in our beautiful house, for as long as I live."

It wasn't easy for me to go out on my own, because the house was a long way away from the town and therefore a long way from either of the families and our friends. Unless Stepan took us to visit friends or family, on his way back to the shop after lunch, I was stuck at home. Of my friends, only Anna had a car and she was a frequent visitor. I looked forward to her visits. She had a boy of her own – Takis - who was six months older than

Nathan, and the two boys played happily together for hours. She sometimes brought Roxi and Sona with her, and we spent the afternoon chatting and gossiping like old times. On these occasions, I served my, by now renowned, English afternoon tea on the terrace, in my bone-china tea-set, with home-made cakes and biscuits.

"You are a bit isolated here, aren't you Reya?" said Anna on one of her visits. "Why don't you ask Stepan to buy you a small car? You would be independent like me. You can visit your family and friends, without relying on anyone. You can drive, can't you?"

"Yes I can drive. I passed my test years ago, but I haven't driven since. To be honest with you Anna, I have never driven on my own. I would be scared stiff. It's a good idea, but…"

"Nonsense! Of course you can drive. All you need is a bit of practice. Shall I put the idea into his Stepan's head?"

"No! Don't do that please," I pleaded and changed the subject. But I should have known better. Anna, being Anna, did mention the matter to Stepan, the very next time she went to the shop.

"I don't know why I didn't think of buying a car for you?" wondered Stepan, one evening. "Anna is right. You should have your own car. You should be independent like her. Anyway, Nathan starts school in September. You will have to take him there and back, twice a day. I can't really spare the time to do the school run. Did you say you passed your test on a Morris Minor?"

"Yes, but I haven't driven…"

"No buts. I shall find you a lovely little Morris Minor."

"But, I'm scared."

"You won't be scared, because I myself will see to it. And what's more, once you've gained enough confidence, you will be able to drive my car, too."

"Never!" I cried. He had recently bought a new car, a Mercedes - his pride and joy.

A few weeks later, Stepan came home in a leaf green Morris Minor. My heart jumped, not with excitement but with alarm. Could I trust myself to drive it?

"I found the car I wanted for you, little one. It's perfect for you, only a year old. I'll take you for a spin first, and afterwards you will have your first 'advanced' driving lesson - from the master himself, no less!"

"Where is your car?"

"I left it in Father's drive. I'll use your car for now. You do like it, don't you?"

"Of course, I do. It's almost new, and it has two doors…"

"Yes. It's safer for children sitting at the back."

That evening and the following five evenings, I drove 'my' car with Stepan in the passenger seat and Nathan at the back. I wasn't doing too badly, if a little too cautiously, with the cars whizzing past me. On the sixth evening, Stepan asked me to drive to his parents for a short visit. When it was time for us to drive home, he got into his own car and started the engine.

"Off you go," he said. "Follow me if you want, but you know the way." And to my astonishment, he drove off. I sat in the car, frozen. How could he do this to me? I was not ready to drive on my own yet. His parents were watching me. What should I do? Why hadn't he taken Nathan with him?

"He wouldn't have driven off like that, if he didn't have enough confidence in you, my dear," *Hayrik* said. "You'll be alright, just drive carefully, like you always do." To this day, I do not know where I got the courage from, to start the car even. Nor do I remember how I drove home. But I did it! Relief swept over me in waves, as I turned the corner into Salamis Road, and pulled up in front of the house. I sat there, shaking like a leaf.

Stepan was waiting for me, on the veranda. He ran down the stairs, two at a time and opened the car door.

"Bravo! You've done it, my brave one. It was easy, wasn't it?" Then he turned to Nathan, gathering him up into his arms. "Your mama is a very clever little girl, isn't she?" As we went into the house, I glared at him, but I couldn't be angry for long. If he hadn't done what he did, I don't know how long it would have taken me to gain any confidence in myself. As it was, I never looked back, after my baptism of fire.

Chapter Thirty One

I was very nervous, the day Nathan started school. I hoped and prayed that his school days would be happier than mine. I thanked God that he was not shy like me, but had inherited his father's confidence. He looked so smart, in his school uniform. Nathan himself had decided what pencils and copybooks to take to school and had packed them in his brand new satchel. He was a friendly little boy, who loved sports, especially football. Stepan took Nathan with him to football matches now, and they were both fanatical about the game – talking endlessly about the match they had seen, and even demonstrating to me how the players had scored the goals.

I pulled up in front of the schoolhouse. It was the same one I had attended, so many years ago. The Armenian community in Famagusta was still very small, and therefore we still didn't merit a proper school. The schoolhouse may have been the same, but the teacher was not. She was a young and pretty girl of twenty-two or so, with a bright and breezy manner and a wonderful smile. Her name was Alice.

Miss Alice greeted all the new students and ushered them into the one big classroom. Nothing had changed since I was there. The same benches were still there, as well as the gigantic blackboard that covered an entire wall. I shuddered inwardly, as my eyes wandered to the far end of the room, and the bench where I used to sit. I could still see my teacher – Miss Anna – sitting behind her huge desk. She had ruled her charges like a dictator, never smiling. She had a high-pitched voice and when she got angry – which was often – her nostrils flared and her face turned a dangerous shade of red.

In my day, the teacher's word was law and any insubordination was swiftly and severely dealt with. A few of the boys were unruly, and had to be disciplined. The cane was used often. It was no use complaining to your parents, because they *always* sided with the teacher. It wasn't just that I disliked my teacher – I was frightened of her. Being painfully shy didn't help, of course.

One day, the teacher decided that every child in the classroom would either recite a poem or sing a song. To say that I was petrified at the prospect was an understatement. To sing solo in front of the whole class was a fate worse than death. I prayed that by some miracle, I would be spared this dreadful ordeal. As the other children stood up to perform, one by one, I decided to recite a very short poem, which I knew by heart. I rehearsed it silently, over and over. But when my turn came, I froze.

"Come on, stand up and *recite*!" bellowed the teacher. At last, I stood up. Summoning all my courage, I took a huge breath and opened my mouth to speak, but nothing came out. I couldn't utter a single word. It seemed an eternity before the teacher gave up on me.

"Sit down! You are a stubborn, disobedient little girl. You shall *not* go unpunished for this." The whole class witnessed my humiliation. The teacher never forgave me, for my 'act of defiance', and neither did I forgive her, for being so insensitive to my predicament. Nor did I ever forget the look of pure rage on her face.

Miss Alice was talking to me. I came out of my trance. "I'm sure Nathan will be happy here, Mrs. Reya," she was saying. I managed to smile and thank her. I sighed a great sigh of relief as I came out into the September sunshine - Nathan was in safe hands.

I was in the middle of preparing the mid-day meal, when the telephone rang. It was Marko. He often phoned or dropped in, to see Nathan or to take him swimming. Marko doted on his nephew, and Nathan adored him. His eyes would light up, when he saw his uncle, for he knew that there was something wonderful in store for him. Sometimes, Marko came on his motorcycle, and as soon as he heard the roar of the powerful machine Nathan would run to the veranda and wait for him. But this time, Marko was phoning for a very different reason.

"Mother was taken ill yesterday..." he said. The tremor in his voice warned me that this was something serious.

"What's wrong with her? What happened?"

"Father said she had felt unwell all day yesterday, vomiting and so on. He was alarmed and he called Dr. Michailides. He examined her and found a lump..."

"Oh, Marko, what are you saying!"

"The doctor came again this morning, and he brought a colleague with him for a second opinion. They had a consultation and decided that she must be operated on, the sooner the better."

"I shall go and see her, now. I'll phone Stepan and..."

"I've already done that. He said he would pick Nathan up from school and give him his lunch. You're not to panic, alright?"

"Yes Marko." I put the phone down. I felt numb with shock. I sank down on a chair wearily. It took a moment or two, before the implications of what I had just heard sank in. Mother ill? I had never seen Mother ill, never heard her complain of a headache even. The telephone rang again. I must be brave, I thought, as I picked it up. This time it was Stepan.

"I'm so sorry, *hokis*. Don't worry about anything. I'll stop by at your Mother's, before I take Nathan back to school."

"I'll see you later then," was all I could bring myself to say.

Mother was lying in bed, with her eyes closed. I noticed that her skin had a yellow tinge. She's got jaundice! I thought, with alarm. I'd heard or read somewhere that jaundice in newborn babies was quite common, but jaundice in adults was always serious. I prayed to God that I was mistaken. She opened her eyes and when she saw me, she smiled. I sat on the edge of her bed, took her hands in mine and kissed them.

"Can I get you anything, Mother?" I asked, forcing a smile to my lips. She shook her head and closed her eyes. I had always been shy and distant with my mother. I found it difficult to talk to her about anything, whether it was serious or not, whereas Nonnie could chat to her for hours and did, with great humour or theatrics, as the topic of conversation demanded. The old saying - that a daughter never really bonds with her mother until she is a mother herself - was true in my case. It was only after I had my baby that I was able to share my feelings with her in an easy and friendly way.

It was almost time for lunch. Father and Marko would be coming home. I went to the kitchen and opened the fridge door. There was half a watermelon, salad stuff, cheese and olives. There was half a loaf of bread in the bread bin. Father must have been very worried about Mother because he hadn't gone to the market this morning. I decided to wait for them - I could make a salad quickly enough, if need be.

Instead, I went to my old room. It was the only place in the house, where I could shut out the world and think. The room was hot. I opened the window and looked out. The sight of the brilliant, shimmering sea quietened my uneasy spirit. Then, I went to the room that Lillie and Nonnie had shared. The room seemed to echo with their voices. Their perfume still lingered in the air. What adventures had been relived, what dramas had unfolded, what secrets had been shared – all in this room. I could see my younger self, sitting on the edge of Nonnie's bed and listening with awe – privileged to be *allowed* to listen to their exciting tales - as clearly as if I were looking at a black and white photograph.

The house seemed too big now, too silent - the actors had left the theatre. My thoughts went back to Mother. It was so unfair. This was the most wonderful and peaceful time of her life. All her girls were married now and had their own families. My status as the 'bringer of luck' had held. First Lillie, and then Nonnie had married their respective suitors. Lillie had married the tall, dark and handsome Armenian man (one of very few) of her dreams. There was a collective sigh of relief, when she said, 'Yes, I'll marry him'. The date of the engagement was set swiftly, before she had time to change her mind!

And, lo and behold, only two months after Lillie's grand wedding, Nonnie had a proposal of marriage, too. He was a classmate of hers, in the Armenian elementary school. They hadn't seen each other since their school days. He had spent the last twenty years in South Africa, but he was back for good now (having made his fortune) and looking for a wife. He must have liked Nonnie when they were children and when he found out that she was unmarried, she was his first choice.

So, I did have my revenge, after a fashion. I sat back and watched my two older sisters go through the same rituals as I had, but there was one difference – both my sisters enjoyed every minute of the old-fashioned customs and rituals! So be it - the important thing was that all three of us were happy, in our own way. But, I was the only daughter living in Famagusta. They both lived in Limassol, some distance away.

Marko was the only one not married yet. But Mother did not worry about that. It was alright for her son to wait till he was older. It was fine for a man to sow his oats and enjoy his freedom – there would be time enough for marriage and children, later.

"When are *you* going to get married?" I asked Marko, one day. He was sitting on the floor, playing with Nathan. He would make a wonderful father. Marko looked up at me, surprised at my question.

"Why do you ask? What have you heard?" he said.

"I haven't heard anything. Don't look so alarmed. It was seeing you playing with Nathan that prompted me to ask you, that's all."

"Oh! I have a confession to make."

"What! What confession?"

"I don't know how to say this… I've been secretly in love with a Greek girl, for two years. I thought for a moment that I'd been found out."

"Oh, my dear Marko!"

"I know. Mother and Father would be shocked and devastated, if they ever found out that I wanted to marry a 'foreign' girl." Time stood still for a second. I had been in that place, where Marko was now. I knew very well what he was going through. I must ease his torment.

"You would be against it too, wouldn't you?" he asked.

"No! Not at all, Marko. Times have changed, anyway. A mixed marriage is not anathema anymore."

"I'm not too sure about that. An only son and all that…"

"But what about the girl in question. Is she prepared to wait indefinitely?"

"We agreed to wait a little longer. I know that I have to make a decision, sooner or later." My heart went out to him. I had been prepared to wait too…

I heard Father's key in the door and went to meet him. Marko was with him. They went to see how Mother was faring. In the meantime, I prepared a simple lunch for us. None of us was hungry, so we decided to have some bread, cheese and a slice of cold watermelon. The only thing Mother wanted was a slice of watermelon. I helped her get out of bed and took her to the bathroom. Washed and refreshed, she settled back on her pillow and ate the cold watermelon.

Just then, Stepan and Nathan came, on their way to school. Mother's face lit up, when she saw her grandson. She loved all her grandchildren and they adored her. Nathan was taken aback to see his *Nene* (grandmother) in bed. He was shy at first, not knowing how to deal with this unexpected situation. He approached her slowly, and stood by her side, waiting.

"Why are you in bed, *Nene*?" he asked.

"Because I feel tired, my *Pasha*," she said and smiled. "I'll be up and about tomorrow, I promise you." Nathan seemed satisfied with her explanation and went to school happily, holding his satchel firmly in his hand. But Mother did not get out of bed the next day, or the day after that. Her skin looked more orange now. Dr. Michailides came to see her, and confirmed our worst fears. There was definitely a lump there, he said, and he made arrangements for Mother to go into hospital.

That evening, I telephoned my three sisters about Mother's illness. Lillie and Nonnie came to see her the next day and Sara came at the weekend. It was a sad gathering of the sisters. There was nothing any of us could do, except to make Mother feel comfortable. It was Father we could not face. In a few short days, his life had turned upside down. He could not bear it. He shut the shop early and sat at Mother's bedside, without saying a word.

We waited anxiously, on the day of the operation. It was a devastating blow, to be told by the hospital surgeon that the cancer in the pancreas had spread to the liver and beyond. He said that it was much too late to be able to do anything. It was a matter of weeks. Mother was told nothing about it, but she was too wise not to have guessed the truth. There was a member of the family with her at all times. Auntie Roza had to be dragged away from the hospital room. Mother was her only close family left. She couldn't believe that she would be losing her sister. She put on a brave face – chatting away in her usual inimitable way, as though by doing so she might delay the inevitable end.

Mother died, eighteen days after the operation. She was the bravest of us all. She was in considerable pain. I don't know how she did it, but she always looked calm and serene when we were with her, hiding her pain behind her smile. Only once, did she hint that she knew she was dying. All four of us girls and Marko were at her bedside, unable to hide our sorrow.

"Do not be sad, my beloved children," she said, in a soft and gentle voice. "It is right and proper for a parent to go first. It is the natural and divine order."

Father lingered only eleven months after Mother's death, before he joined her. The light went out of his eyes and never came back. He could not bear the empty house and stayed at the coffee shop until closing time. Gradually he gave up. He did not try to rebuild the crumbling walls of his world. Fortunately, he did not suffer. He died peacefully in his sleep.

Chapter Thirty Two

The seasons came and went. It was summer again, as blisteringly hot as any other. Nathan's school had broken up for the long summer break. He had asked, no, begged his father to be allowed to go to London with his grandparents. Stepan's parents had got into the habit of going to England for two months every summer – July and August - to escape the hottest period in Cyprus. Both Stepan and his parents thought it would be good for Nathan. He would get to know his cousins, Mike and Nora, and also improve his spoken English. He was nine years old now – a good student, he could speak, read and write Armenian, Greek and English.

"Travel expands the mind, it's educational," said Stepan.

"I agree with you. But two months is a long time for him to be away from home," I said. "He will be so home-sick…"

"You mean we shall miss him more than he will miss us!"

"Maybe, but two months is too long…"

"At that age, the promise of adventure is more attractive than staying at home with your parents, isn't it?"

"I suppose so. Especially, if it is for the whole of the school holidays." But even though I tried to make light of it, the thought of not seeing Nathan for so long was heart wrenching.

Nathan's excitement reached fever pitch. His clothes were packed, presents for his cousins were wrapped. He declared he was ready. *Mayrik* had packed a whole suitcase with all the goodies that were now a must for anyone visiting Agnes. Apart from the various nuts, cheese and sweets, she had also packed fresh vine-leaves from her own garden and a kilo of fresh okra – the first of the season.

It was time to say good-bye to Nathan and his grandparents. I was determined not to be emotional. I hugged him and held him close for a moment, and then I let him go. His father lifted him high in the air as he used to do when he was a toddler.

"Enjoy your holiday my son, but don't forget to telephone us - at least once a week."

"I won't forget. Bye-bye Mama, bye-bye Baba." His voice sailed through the air, like a song. All three raised their arms in a final farewell, and then they were gone.

We walked silently towards the car, in the semi-dusk. I looked at Stepan. He is already missing his son, I thought, as he lit a cigarette and wound down the window.

"Shall we find out what the 'gang' is doing?" he said. "I don't want to go home, yet."

"Yes, let's." I said. I didn't want to go home to an empty house, either.

We went round to Nico and Anna's. Sona and Kevork were already there, enjoying a drink before going to a *taverna* for dinner. "Have you seen the family safely off to London?" Nico asked, as he handed me a coke and a Keo beer to Stepan. I nodded. "The boys will miss him this summer. Cigarette?" I took one and he lit it for me. I took a puff and tried to relax. Just then Anna emerged from the kitchen with the appetisers - dishes of nuts, crisps and olives.

"Boys, I'm worried about the continuing tension between the Greeks and the Turks," Kevork said. "When will it end? More to the point, how will it end?" We all looked at each other.

"I wish I knew, Kevork," Nico said. "The tension, the skirmishes and the 'incidents' between the Greek and Turkish communities is not something new. It started a few summers back, if you remember."

"Yes, I do remember. But what about the recent troubles which started in the spring? The rumours that the Turks would invade the northern parts of Cyprus?"

"They are just rumours, my friend. It won't come to anything. The Turks would not dare invade!"

"Nico is right," Stepan, who had been silent up to then, said. "The UN Peace-keeping force won't let anything develop. Don't you remember when the Turks threatened to invade before – in 1964, and again in '67? We all worried then, but nothing happened."

"I don't know... The minorities living in Cyprus, including us, the Armenians, are mere spectators in the events taking place."

"So are we Kevork. I only know what I read in the newspapers. The clashes between the Greeks and the Turks will no doubt continue, but I feel strongly that nothing serious will happen."

"I wish I had your confidence, Nico. It's just that I can't forget what the Turks did to us…"

"But that was years ago. I'm sure the UN will not let something like that ever happen again."

I looked at Stepan. What was going through his mind? He caught my glance and smiled reassuringly.

"Don't look so worried, little one. Nico is right. The UN is here to keep the peace. We can sleep safe in our beds." He offered his cigarettes round, before lighting one for himself. "Now, where are we going for dinner? Reya and I are free agents for the summer and we intend to enjoy every single day of it. We are planning to spend every single week-end up in the mountains."

With Nathan gone, I found I had time on my hands. There was less to do in the house, so I spent more time in the garden. Every morning, I watered the plants, 'inspected' the flowers, the rambling rose and the jasmine. The colourful flowers of the field called *antaram* had somehow found their way into the garden and established themselves there. *Hayrik* had done a brilliant job with the garden, in the five years we had lived in the house. The fruit trees – lemon, orange, apricot, peach and kumquat – which he had planted with loving care, were coming on very nicely. And the grapevine, which is the pride and joy of any Armenian garden, had grown and flourished even better than expected.

Even though I missed Nathan very much and looked forward to his weekly phone calls from England, I nevertheless enjoyed my moments of solitude. To sit under the shade of the vine, to read, to gaze at the *antaram,* mingling happily with their neighbours, and to have the jasmine to intoxicate me with its glorious scent was to be in Eden.

The week-end became the highlight of the week for me. When the shops closed at one o'clock, Stepan picked me up and we headed straight for the mountains. We stopped at a *taverna* half way to Pedoulas to have lunch. It was a long drive to get there, but well worth it. It was wonderful to escape the searing heat of Famagusta and breathe the cool mountain air. We got up very early on Monday morning and drove back to Famagusta. This became the pattern for the summer.

Spending week-ends away from home seemed to make the weeks go by very quickly. We were half-way through August already. It wouldn't be long before Nathan and his grandparents came back from England.

As I had time on my hands, I got into the habit of driving over to Stepan's parents' house to water the garden and make sure that everything was in order. On this particular afternoon, I came home, made myself a cool drink and sat under the shade of the vine and lit a cigarette with my new lighter. I noticed there were lots of leaves ready to be picked and stored in jars, for the winter. I promised myself I would do this first thing in the morning. I was thinking how good I had become in making the traditional Armenian dish of stuffed vine leaves. I never minded the time it took to make it. The insistent ring of the telephone interrupted my thoughts. I put my cigarette out and rushed into the hall to answer it.

"Hello," I said, wondering who the caller was. It was Stepan. He spoke without preamble. I took a deep breath and waited.

"There are rumours that a second Turkish invasion is imminent, Reya." My heart sank. Things had escalated since the day we had seen Nathan and his grandparents off at Nicosia airport. Nico had been wrong. A few weeks before, on the 20th July, the Turks had invaded the northern parts of Cyprus.

"My God," I said. "Not another invasion."

"Yes – and this time, they are saying that they will invade Famagusta. There was a news bulletin… But we can't talk now. Listen - what I want you to do is pack a small suitcase with a few clothes, passports, bankbooks, any cash in the house, all the important documents and your jewellery."

"Does this mean we might have to leave…?"

"I don't know *hokis,* I don't think so. But we must be ready for any eventuality."

"Yes. I understand. I'll do it right away." With a sinking heart, I sat down in the nearest chair, to digest what I had just heard.

A shiver ran down my spine. Both Stepan's parents and mine had found themselves in a similar situation, many years before. They hadn't believed that they would ever flee their homes in Turkey, but in the end they had to. That was how they had come to Cyprus, in the first place. I could hear my father's voice ringing in my ears – "The British will never leave Cyprus, never…" But the British had left, and now there was conflict again.

I had barely finished packing when the telephone rang again.

"I shall close the shop a bit early tonight," said Stepan. "Have you finished the packing?

"Yes."

"Well done. Nico said we should not be on our own tonight. He asked us to go over to their house later. I'll be home soon…"

When I heard Stepan's car in the drive I rushed out to meet him. "Any news?" I asked breathlessly.

He got out of his car and put his arm around me and we walked to the back verandah. Stepan sank into the wicker chair without saying a word. He looked tired. "Any news?" I asked again.

"No, *hokis*, the same rumours circulating, that's all."

"We should phone London tonight."

"Yes, we will. We'll let Nathan and the family know that everything is alright for the moment. We must put their minds at rest." He sighed and lit a cigarette.

"What's the matter?" I asked.

"I felt very uneasy all day," he said, and inhaled deeply.

"Why?" I stammered.

"I don't know why. I still feel uneasy. I brought the new consignment of watches and some uncut stones home, for safe keeping."

"Good. Your father would have approved of that."

The possibility of a Turkish attack dominated the conversation as soon as we got to Nico's house. By the end of the evening we had more or less convinced ourselves that an invasion was unlikely. We were simply taking precautionary measures in case of an unforeseen emergency. It was better to be safe than sorry. It was past midnight when we got home.

I opened my eyes. Stepan was in his swimming trunks. Beach towel under his arm, he blew me a kiss and with a wave of his hand and 'see you in an hour' he was gone. He never missed his early morning swim. I heard the front door closing. I turned on my side and promptly went back to sleep. Not for long. The shrill ringing of the telephone woke me. The little bedside clock showed quarter past six. Who could be phoning at this hour I thought and lifted the receiver. I heard Marko shouting "Put the radio on, the Turks are going to attack!"

"What did you say…"

"Where is Stepan? Let me speak to him, quick, there's no time to lose."

"He's not here Marko. He's gone swimming…"

"Holy Mother of God! Get dressed quickly and as soon as Stepan comes home, leave…

"Where to?" I cried, shaking uncontrollably. It had come. The moment we had dreaded had come. We were being attacked.

"To the British base at Dhekelia! Ring me as soon as Stepan gets home." The phone went dead. With shaking fingers I put the radio on. The newsreader was confirming what Marko had just said. Panic set in. In between running to the front door to see if Stepan was coming and listening to the radio, I managed to get washed and dressed. Then to my horror, I heard loudspeakers crying 'leave your homes, the Turks are going to attack', 'leave your homes now, the Turks are going to attack' over and over again. Still no sign of Stepan. What to do? I took several deep breaths and willed my heartbeats to slow down. I closed the windows and then went into Nathan's room. It was spotlessly clean and tidy, waiting for him. On an impulse I took the framed photograph of him taken on his last birthday and put it in the suitcase and put it by the front door. The house was oppressively hot with all the windows shut. My throat was so dry it hurt. I went into the kitchen and drank a glass of water. I was ready but where was Stepan? I opened the front door one more time and looked out. This time, to my unutterable relief, I saw Stepan's car turning the corner. The car screeched to a stop. He jumped out, leaving the door open, the engine running. "Thank God you are back..." I cried. "I'll phone Marko and tell him we're on our way, while you change..."

"No time *hokis,*" he said and began dialling Marko's number. "You get in the car." As I grabbed my handbag and rushed out of the door, I heard him say 'we're on our way'.

Stepan practically threw the suitcase into the boot, got in the car and slammed the door shut. "Let's go," he said. As I looked out of the car window, I could see similar scenes being played out up and down the street. People bundling bags and children into their cars, before they drove off to join the growing stream of traffic trying to get out of Famagusta.

"Can you hear the planes?" I asked, as Stepan waited to pull out onto the main road.

"They are probably bombing the harbour," he said. He looked dishevelled in his crumpled shorts and shirt, sandals on his bare feet, unshaven, his hair damp and unruly. He turned to look at me. "Don't worry little one," he said, softly. "We shall be in Dhekelia in no time." But his grim face told a different story. His dark eyes were burning with an unfamiliar passion. I couldn't tell whether it was annoyance, anger or fear – or a mixture of all three.

I turned my head back to look at the house, but we were turning the corner and it was already out of sight.

Chapter Thirty Three

Two weeks had passed since the Turkish invasion. Two weeks since the mass exodus of Famagusta. We had a new identity – we were refugees - refugees crammed into the British base in Dhekelia. We were grateful for their kind hospitality. They had given us food, blankets, shelter and above all safety.

I don't think anyone slept that first night in Dhekelia. Stepan and I certainly didn't. We tossed and turned and clung to each other, going over the unbelievable, unstoppable events that had overtaken us. I felt again and again the stab of fear that had clenched my heart, as I locked the front door and fled. I relived the long journey, which had ended in this place of safety.

With the morning came the news that the bombing had stopped. Everyone cheered. Everyone assumed we would be going back to Famagusta. Stepan's first priority was to find a telephone and let his parents and Nathan know that we were safe and well looked after in the British base and that they were not to worry. Next, I phoned my sisters and assured them that we were well and would soon be going back to our homes.

Not surprisingly the Armenian families grouped together. By the third day we had formed a close kinship. In the evenings we talked about our plight, far into the night. Everyone asked questions but no one could come up with an answer.

Nonnie and Lillie came to see us in the base. They brought with them sheets, towels, toiletries and food. "Reya, why don't you and Stepan, Marko, Christina and the children come and stay with us?" Nonnie asked. "Between us, Lillie and I have plenty of room for all of you. By all accounts it shouldn't be too long before the situation is brought under control."

"You are welcome to stay with me for as long as you like," said Lillie.

"Think of it as a visit," Nonnie continued. "We haven't been together as a family for ages. What do you say Reya?"

"Thank you both for you offers," I said. It was tempting to accept their invitations and spend the 'waiting period' in their lovely homes. But I knew that Stepan would not leave his friends in the base. "I think we'll wait a bit longer and see how things develop."

"How about you Marko?"

"It's nice of you both to offer. But at the moment I feel I should be as close to Famagusta as possible. You never know when we might be asked to go back..."

"But it's not very nice staying in this place, Marko," Lillie said. The understatement of the year, I thought wryly, but made no comment. Our lovely Lillie would never have set foot in 'this place' as she put it. She would most likely check into the best hotel in Larnaca.

"It's not too bad. We manage don't we Reya?"

"We do. There is camaraderie here," I said. "Most of our friends are here, and we have made some new friends too. It won't be for long anyway." I suddenly thought of my parents when they had spent forty days in quarantine. They had made new, lasting friends there. In a strange way, the British base was our 'quarantine'. We shared the agony of waiting.

Slowly, painfully, one day followed the other in the same anxious and yet listless way. There wasn't much to do in the base, except to think of our present life in 'exile'. But thinking could be dangerous. It could take you to places best not to go. My way of not thinking was to read anything I could lay my hands on. It wasn't easy, but I tried.

"I see your sister Sara came to see you today," Sona said. I put down the newspaper I was reading. "It proved to be very emotional," I said. "She took one look at Marko and me – the 'children' of the family – in our dishevelled state, and she burst into tears."

"It's so upsetting isn't it? Sometimes I feel like pulling the sheet over my head and forget everything... I don't want to see anyone or talk to anyone outside this place..." she said, her voice breaking up.

"Stop it!" I said. "You'll have me sobbing in a minute. Here, have one of Sara's home made biscuits with your coffee." I opened the huge tin Sara had brought and offered it to Sona. "Very nice," she said pensively, biting into it.

"She also brought a fruit cake, we'll have that tonight," I said and helped myself to a biscuit. We munched in silence for a while.

"Sara brought me this book of poems too. More accurately, she lent it to me. She said I was to return it to her 'the moment' I went back home!"

"I know what my answer would have been..."

I smiled. "Yes. I said it would give me the greatest of pleasures to hand it back to her – if and when that day comes. I know it sounds silly, but the very thought of it lifted my spirits."

"Wishful thinking… Who is the author anyway?"

"Bedros Tourian," I said. This Armenian poet was my all time favourite. I had so cherished my copy of his book. "You can borrow it if you like. It will take your mind off things."

She shook her head. "I can't concentrate on anything at the moment, let alone Tourian's poems…"

"I was thinking how lucky Sara was for not living anywhere the 'green line' in Nicosia. At least they are safe in the Greek neighbourhood where they live."

"It must be the fate of the Armenians to get caught up in any conflict that breaks out, in any part of the world," Sona continued, in the same vein of hopelessness. "I've heard that quite a few Armenian families living near the 'green line' have lost their properties, and quite a few of them have gone to England. Sometimes things get unbearably depressing."

"I know they do. We have to wait and see what happens."

"Wait, wait, wait… That's all I do!"

At first a languorous waiting had settled over us. We had been optimistic that we would be back in our own homes soon. We had coped with living in the crowded base - even though we missed all the things we had taken for granted - grateful to be allowed to stay there. But at the end of the two weeks everyone's patience was wearing thin. Our lives seemed to revolve round the news bulletins, the radio being the link to our destiny.

"We all read the newspapers, and we try to understand what they are trying to say, but, we still don't know what the situation is, do we?" Kevork asked, later that evening.

"Well, with every passing day my hopes of returning to Famagusta are diminishing," answered Bedros. "If this goes on much longer, I shall send Roxi and the children to Beirut."

"I feel as though the life we had known has come to a standstill," Sona said, wiping her tears. "How long do we have to wait to be told what is to become of us…"

"It won't be for long Sona," Stepan told her reassuringly. "I think the waiting is getting to us. Why don't we go to Larnaca tomorrow? We need to get some things anyway don't we, Reya?"

"Yes, we do," I said, trying to sound happy, glad to get away from the base for a while. "Maybe we girls could have our hair done. I'm sure Anna would like to come too. That will surely lift our spirits up." How I longed to have a shower in the privacy of my own home, to have my hair done, to put on one of the dozen summer dresses hanging in my wardrobe.

Having our hair done certainly made us girls feel a lot better. But when we walked along the unfamiliar streets of Larnaca, watching the people getting on with their normal, everyday lives, it brought home to us the terrible plight we were in, more forcibly than anything else could have done.

"I've never been so inactive in all my adult life," complained Stepan. "I'm getting frustrated with waiting." He threw the newspaper he was reading on the table and lit a cigarette. I agreed with him, but there was nothing we could do. "What did Aram have to say?" I asked, instead.

"He said what he's been saying ever since we came here – that the best thing we can do is to go to England until the 'waiting' is over."

"Aram is right. At least the family would be together," I said. I was hoping that Stepan would consider this option. "If the newspapers are to be believed, it might be many weeks, or months even, before we can move back…"

"You might both be right. When the crisis is over, I suppose I could be back in Cyprus fast enough, to sort things out."

"When I talked to Nathan, I could tell by his voice that the novelty of his holiday away from us had long since worn off. He said he missed us, he missed his toys, his bicycle…"

"I know. Whether we stay here or go to England, it will be a drastic change from the life we had before the invasion," said Stepan, looking at me with troubled eyes. "You do realise that don't you, little one?"

"I do *hokis*," I said, trying to be brave. "I also know that we can't live in the past. But we are luckier than a lot of other people. We have a house in Ealing…" I hadn't appreciated that I would be eternally grateful to Aram for persuading Stepan to buy the house in Ealing. I had been against the idea at first – even resented it – because I had to wait for my 'dream house' for such a long time. But now I had to admit that it had been the best investment Stepan could have made. Not only had the value of the house risen, but it had provided him with an additional source of income, which was not affected by events in Cyprus.

"The news gets worse each day, doesn't it?" Stepan continued. "Thousands dead or missing. The rumours are even worse…"

"Rumours exaggerate," I interrupted. I had never seen him so upset, so agitated. I had heard the rumours too. There was talk that our homes and shops were being looted and vandalized. The very thought that strangers might have violated my home sent shivers of anger down my spine. That strangers could walk into Nathan's room and take his toys, his clothes was unthinkable. "All the more reason why we should seriously think about going to England. Both Lillie and Nonnie have again asked us to stay with them for the 'duration' as they call it, but I'd rather be with Nathan, wouldn't you?"

"Of course I would. I think Aram is right. We shall go to England – hopefully for a short while," Stepan said and smiled, for the first time that day. "We can watch developments in Cyprus from there." That night, for the first time since the invasion, I slept an uninterrupted sleep.

"I've got the tickets," Stepan said. "We leave on Saturday. We have to sail to Greece as the airport is closed, and from there we fly to London. At last this infernal waiting is over." He heaved a great sigh of relief and reached for his packet of cigarettes. It worried me that he was smoking more and drinking more. The pattern every night seemed to be smoking, drinking and talking far into the night. I too, was a true smoker now – at first I had enjoyed a cigarette with tea, coffee and my evening drink. But now in these unsettled times of stress and worry, I *needed* to smoke.

The 'gang' was breaking up. The night before we had a 'farewell' party. Bedros had sent Roxi and the children to Beirut, and he had gone to Limassol to find out if he could make a new start there. "I have to earn a living. People will always want their cars serviced and repaired, won't they?" were his parting words.

Kevork was looking for a job in Larnaca, hoping to be able to rent a flat there. Nico hadn't yet decided what he would do. He was still hoping to go back to Famagusta.

"What will you do Marko? Have you decided yet?" I asked.

"We'll wait a little while longer. If we can't go back, then I would like to start a small grocery store in Larnaca. Christina agrees with me."

"You can't go wrong with food, Marko," Stepan said. "I'm sure you'll make a go of it. Look at Aram. The grocery business will make a millionaire of him yet!" I looked at Christina, the lovely Greek girl my brother had married after the death of my parents. Their love for each other will sustain them in these difficult times, I thought. I looked at the baby in her arms and the toddler by her side. I prayed that they would succeed, for the sake of the children.

I was glad that my parents were not alive to see this human tragedy, glad that they had been spared the second time. I was also relieved that Nathan and his grandparents were safe in England. They had been spared too. One had to be grateful for small mercies.

At the end of the fourth week we left Cyprus. My heart was full of sorrow as I said my farewells. My father, just like Stepan's father, had struggled for years to give his children a better life. Now, by some quirk of destiny history was repeating itself. All their hard work was lost and might never be recovered. 1974 had changed our idyllic lives, maybe forever.

Chapter Thirty Four

Agnes and Aram were kindness itself, from the moment Stepan and I stepped foot in England. They welcomed us into their home, with open arms. Living conditions were cramped – with six adults and three children living in close proximity, it was not easy - but they didn't mind. "It's the least we can do, after what you've been going through," Aram told us time and time again.

It was wonderful to be reunited with Nathan. Unable to hold back the tears, I let them break loose, and they streamed down my face. I clung to him for long moments, before I let him go. I hoped and prayed that some semblance of normality would return to our shattered lives, now that we were together again.

The days turned into weeks. Stepan phoned me from Aram's shop one afternoon. "Good news, little one," he said. "The tenants are moving out at the end of the month!"

"Wonderful," I cried. "When can we move…?"

"Not so fast, *hokis*," he said. "Aram thinks the house will need cleaning and redecorating from top to bottom. I'm told it's very costly to bring in painters and decorators. So, I told Aram I shall have a go at it myself, even though I've never held a paint brush in my hand before." I could hear the enthusiasm in his voice.

"Well, as it happens, I *can* use a duster and a mop," I said. "Between the two of us, we can restore the house to its former 'glory'."

"I'm sure we can. It will give me something positive to focus on. We can discuss it later. I have to go now, duty calls!"

Soon, the family adapted to the new circumstances. We each knew what our duties were. Stepan and his father went to Aram's shop, to help out in any way they could. Agnes took the children to school and did the daily shopping. *Mayrik* took charge of the kitchen and the preparation of meals, while I did the cleaning and the laundry. It was important to have a routine, in order to be able to cope with the unforeseen events that had overtaken us.

In the evenings, after the children went off to bed, the conversation inevitably revolved around the Cyprus situation. The same questions were asked, but remained unanswered. How long would the forced partition of Cyprus last? When would negotiations begin to bring the two communities together again? On and on we went. We each had different views on the matter. Stepan was optimistic that we would be able to return to Famagusta sooner rather than later. But his parents were not so hopeful. They were talking from experience.

"When we left our homeland and went to Cyprus, we were as optimistic as you are now. We thought we would go back too..."

"But things are different now Father. No country, no power came to your rescue. But now we have the UN who will speak and act on our behalf."

"Yes my son, things seem different now, but are they?" His hand went to his temple, massaging it, as though the thoughts in his head were pressing on him.

"I agree with Stepan," said Aram. "The UN will not stand by and do nothing, I can't believe that Famagusta will not be given back to the Greeks!"

"I hope you're both right. I hope we shall go back... sometime. For now I'm thankful that the family is safe, with a roof over our heads. As the old saying goes: you can reclaim bricks and mortar, but you can't reclaim life." *Hayrik* couldn't hide the sadness in his eyes.

Just then the *News at Ten* started. Everyone was quiet and listened to the newsreader, to see if there was any news on Cyprus. But Cyprus was seldom mentioned now, other events, other places on the globe were making the headlines.

One evening, Aram announced that he had spoken to Kevork and Sona, and had offered to help them.

"Kevork was at his wit's end. He said he needed to get a job pretty soon, or else..."

"Poor Kevork, poor Sona," said *Mayrik*. She had a special affection for Sona, she was like a daughter to her.

"I know, *Mayrik*," continued Aram. "I've offered Kevork the job of Manager in my supermarket in Thorne Road, off the High Street."

"Bravo, my son," exclaimed *Hayrik*.

"Well, Kevork needs a job and I need a manager. The new supermarket is doing very well but I don't have the time to run both of them. Besides, there is a flat above the shop, where they can live – for the time being, anyway."

"What did he say?" Agnes and I said, in unison.

"Both he and Sona accepted my offer. They said the flat would be infinitely better than the camps. I know Kevork has no experience of the grocery business, but neither had I, when I started on my own. A small matter like that doesn't put an Armenian off, does it?"

"No, it doesn't! We jump in at the deep end of the lake, and only then worry about swimming ashore in the icy water!" said Stepan and we all laughed. It was true enough though. Armenians *were* enterprising as well as hardworking. They didn't wait long for things to happen. They embarked on new ventures and most of the time, they succeeded.

"So, when are they coming?"

"They should be here by the end of October." We fell silent, each one considering this new development. The atmosphere in the room had changed perceptibly. Our spirits had lifted. There was light at the end of the tunnel. There would be changes, maybe drastic changes, if we were to survive in our new role as refugees. We had to change direction, adopt new ways…

My thoughts flew back to another place and time when we children gathered round the *mangal* (charcoal brazier) begging my father to tell us, yet again, the story of my parents' early life in Cyprus.

"Agnes is asking if you want a cup of tea, little one." I heard Stepan speaking to me. He nudged me and I came back to the present, with a jolt.

"Sorry, Agnes, I didn't hear you," I apologized and took the mug of tea from the tray.

"You were miles away," she smiled.

"I was thinking about the past," I said, blushing as I always did when I sensed people looking at me. "I was thinking how our parents sought refuge in Cyprus and created a safe haven for us, yet, ironically, we have been forced to flee that safe haven – leaving everything behind. It is twice as hard for you *Hayrik*. It is the second time for you…"

"I know, my daughter," he said. "But, there is nothing we can do to change our destiny. I remember how I struggled to learn Greek when we first went to Cyprus. Now I'm struggling to learn English!"

"I think you two dears are brave, very brave indeed, to cope with everything, the way you do," said Aram.

"We get by, don't we Rubina? There is a bit of spark left in us yet, eh!" *Hayrik* winked at his wife and smiled. She, in turn, smiled back at him, her eyes shining with unshed tears. They tried to be cheerful, but they couldn't always hide their grief at the cruel way their lives had been disrupted once again. Would they never find a place, where they could settle and feel secure?

Summer had come to an end. Autumn leaves were collecting in little groups. Every morning, *Hayrik* could be seen sweeping them up and putting them into sacks. It was a losing battle, as by the afternoon another lot would gather. The days were getting shorter. The morning air struck cold and sharp against my face – winter was on its way. It was the start of a new school year, too. The question of Nathan's education had been uppermost in our minds. He couldn't stay at home until the Cyprus question was resolved. Nathan himself was eager to start school. He wanted to go to Grove Road School, where his cousins were to start soon. Much to our relief, he was accepted. He loved his school uniform and within a week he had settled in – taking part in the school activities eagerly, especially sports.

In the meantime, Stepan took to his new role of painter and decorator with missionary zeal. The fact that he had never done this sort of work before did not deter him. As soon as the tenants moved out, he moved in with his Do It Yourself manuals and the paraphernalia that went with them. I followed him with dusters, mops and cleaning stuff.

The house looked as though a hurricane had passed through it. Unwanted clothes, newspapers, books were strewn everywhere. A dirty mattress lay on the floor of one of the bedrooms. The bathroom was not fit to be used. I got more and more depressed, as I went from room to room and saw the state they were in. I didn't know where to start. Maybe I should clean the kitchen first, I thought and went to investigate. I couldn't believe my eyes. It was the dirtiest kitchen I had ever seen. I fled and sat on the stairs. It was all too much. I covered my face with my hands and wept.

I don't know how long I sat there. Gradually, my weeping subsided. I felt a sudden rush of anger rise up from some place in my soul. My mother would not have given up at the first hurdle. I wouldn't either. I wiped my tears and resolved to count my blessings instead of feeling sorry for myself. First things first, I said aloud and went back into the kitchen.

By the time Stepan returned from the hardware shop, I had cleaned the kitchen windows and was half way through cleaning the grease from the tiles and work surfaces. There was no trace of the crisis I had experienced, as I greeted him with a sunny smile. After a short coffee break we set to work.

"Preparation is the key to good decorating," read Stepan from the DIY manual, which was open on the kitchen table. "Let's wash down the paintwork on the kitchen walls together, and then I can start painting while you move on to another room." And so it began. By the end of that first day, we were both bone-shatteringly tired. But we pressed on regardless. I tackled the dirt with such vigour and vengeance that even I was surprised at my new found energy.

By the end of the third week, my hands looked like a washerwoman's hands. But I was rewarded. The house looked like a new pin. The autumn sun beamed through the spotlessly clean windows, illuminating the freshly painted walls. The scrubbed quarry-tiled kitchen floor shone and the parquet floor downstairs gleamed with polish. I made a list of what we needed. The list was endless. What we needed most now was to furnish the bedrooms and the kitchen. The rest could wait.

We all worked hard, but Stepan worked the hardest, as if work was a panacea to his pain. On the surface he looked and behaved in his usual sprightly way, but beneath the cheerful smile, his worries and fears for the future lay hidden. He had changed. I knew he had changed. I would wake up in the night and sense that he was still awake, tossing and turning restlessly, unable to sleep. I was as devastated and worried as he was about leaving behind everything we loved and cherished. To imagine my beautiful home being pillaged was unbearable. To think of strange, greedy hands ransacking Nathan's room, taking his clothes, his toys, his books and magazines was unutterably painful.

The invasion had forced Stepan to contemplate a future of possible financial hardship. This sudden change in fortunes had left him struggling to adjust. He was so used to being up early, with a busy day ahead. Now, he was having to find things to do to fill his days. Hence the decorating frenzy, the hours spent in Aram's shop. Every time I wanted to talk to Stepan, to comfort him and be comforted by him, he would pat me on the shoulder or put his arms around me and whisper, "Don't worry little one, go back to sleep, everything will be alright." I was hurt that he could not share his thoughts with me. I was concerned that he was smoking and drinking more now. Before the invasion, he smoked and drank for pleasure, but now he was drinking and smoking to forget.

This exile was not of our making. I wondered if Stepan, like me, retreated into the past. It was so easy to do so. So easy to be transported from the grey skies of Ealing to the heat of Cyprus, the sun, sea, lush fruit, the vineyards shimmering in the sun. It was the season for grapes. I imagined the vine in our garden. It must be groaning under the weight of the huge bunches of ripe purple grapes. My heart ached with longing for my home, for Famagusta, for Cyprus.

We moved into 12 Bedford Lane, as soon as the painting and cleaning was done. We had been a burden on Aram and Agnes long enough. There were new curtains at the windows, new furniture and a new television set. We gave the biggest and best bedroom, overlooking the garden, to Stepan's parents. There was enough room for a settee, so they could sit there comfortably, if they didn't want to watch television.

We settled in comparatively easily. There was a new routine now. *Mayrik* was in charge of the kitchen once again. *Hayrik* took over the garden and did odd jobs in the house and I did the cleaning and the laundry. Stepan did the food shopping and helped Aram in the new supermarket.

Sona, Kevork and their daughter Sevan were due to arrive in England, in two days time. Aram, the saviour of the family, went out of his way to make their move to England as painless as possible. And Stepan too - as soon as he had finished in our house, he took his new found painting and decorating skills to the flat which was being prepared for them.

Agnes and I cleaned, scrubbed and polished, until our arms were ready to drop off. There were new curtains at the windows and a new rug by the fireside. The furniture was old-fashioned but in quite good condition. A few colourful cushions livened up the sofa. All that the flat needed was Sona's personal touch, to make it a home. The added bonus with the flat was that it had a separate entrance from the shop. It would be nice for Kevork to go up to the flat at the end of the day, away from the workplace.

Agnes and I stepped back and admired our handiwork.

"It was worth the effort, wasn't it?" I said, going over the coffee table with my duster one last time. "I could get a job as a cleaning lady, couldn't I?"

"We both could, after all the cleaning we've done," she said, examining her hands. They looked as bad as mine – with broken nails and chapped fingers. "I'll get a couple of plants and some fresh flowers for Sona, tomorrow. That will cheer her up."

"And I'll make her a date and walnut cake!"

"Good. We all like your date and walnut..." Just then, we heard the front door open and Aram and Stepan came up the stairs. They each carried a box of groceries and put them on the kitchen table.

"I'll get the other box," said Stepan and rushed down the stairs. "Just a few bits and pieces to make their first days here more comfortable," said Aram. There was no end to his thoughtfulness. There was rice, sugar, flour, pasta, salt, a jar of coffee, and tea bags. There were bottles of cooking oil and olive oil, cans of baked beans and peeled tomatoes, and various tins of sardines and salmon as well as bottles of orange squash. Agnes put the groceries in one of the cupboards.

"And this box is for the fridge," said Stepan, as he came into the kitchen. I emptied the box of its contents of milk, butter, cheese, ham, eggs and salad stuff and stored them in the fridge.

"I hope I've thought of everything," said Aram. He opened the cupboard under the sink and looked inside. "Good, good. There's some cleaning stuff here," he said. We followed the boys, as they went from room to room – well pleased with the results of our labour. We were all thinking the same thing - this flat was a far cry from Sona's lovely house in Famagusta. We hoped and prayed that her family's stay here would be temporary.

"Well done girls, you've done a good job here," said Stepan. "It's time we went home, early start tomorrow."

The reunion with Kevork and Sona at the airport was emotional, to say the least. Especially when Sona first set eyes on her new home. She broke down and wept. She clung to Aram and said, "I don't know what we would have done, without your help..." over and over again.

"You would have done the same for me, wouldn't you?" Aram told her with mock surprise. "After all, we are family. And no more crying, for tonight we shall celebrate your safe journey to England." And celebrate we did. After dinner, we talked until the early hours of the morning. Stepan and I were hungry for news of our friends, the political situation in Cyprus. Although we were in touch with the 'gang', it was much more reassuring to hear of their well being from Kevork.

"Bedros and Araxi have moved to Limassol. Bedros has rented a small garage and started his own business. He said he was doing alright, when I phoned him a couple of days ago, to say goodbye."

"What about Nico?" asked Stepan. "Last time I spoke to him, he was about to start on his own too."

"Yes. He rented a shop in Larnaca – off the main road – and started selling children's clothes, as well as dress material." Kevork reached into his pocket and took out a letter. "This is for you. He wants to make you a business proposition. All the details are in it."

"A business proposition?" asked Stepan as he took the letter and looked at it for a long moment, before opening it. There was a look of surprise on his face, but it changed to something close to elation, as he started reading the letter. We were all watching him.

"Well what do you know! I knew it wouldn't take Nico long, before he started a business again." I saw, for the first time in many weeks, the dull pain of his unwanted stay in England turn into hope and expectation. "Nico seems to think that Larnaca will take the place of Famagusta, as a tourist attraction, soon. The Cypriots are optimistic that they will overcome the effects of the invasion and that the Cyprus economy will recover and flourish again."

"What is Nico's business proposition?" asked Aram. I was glad he asked the question. I was curious to know what Nico had in mind.

"Well… He says the shop he has rented is big enough to provide space for me, if I wanted to start the jewellery business again. He says I could start with repairing watches and items of jewellery at first, and go on from there…" There was silence, as we digested this unexpected news.

"What will you do, Stepan?" asked Agnes in a low voice, echoing my own thoughts.

"I don't know… All kinds of thoughts and ideas are running wildly through my mind. I've done nothing but *think* these last few months. My head is so heavy with them, that I sometimes fear it's going to explode…" He took his head in his hands, as if to squeeze out some of the thoughts that were pressing in on him.

I reached out and touched his hand. Fear struck at my heart. It was worse than I thought. The sleepless nights were taking their toll. If only I could help him in some way. What would I do, if it were left to me? I knew straightaway. I would adopt the country that had taken us in and make the best of what we had. Stepan could get a job and so could I. The money in the bank would not last forever…

"What is really troubling you, my son?" Stepan's father asked. "I'm disappointed that you don't want to share your thoughts and your anxieties with the rest of us." He looked across the richly patterned rug to where *Mayrik* sat, knitting a cardigan for Nathan. She looked up at her husband, with an expression of helplessness on her face. Then she looked at her son, her heart going out to him, knowing the dilemma he was in. They were both proud of Stepan, who had grown into a fine man - their son, who now bore the responsibility of the family's future on his shoulders. Stepan ground out his cigarette and looked up at his father.

"My trouble is that I can't see myself living here indefinitely, until things are sorted out in Cyprus. I can't bear this idle life, anymore."

"But you've been working so hard with the painting and decorating…" interrupted his mother.

"I know Mother. If it hadn't been for that and helping out at Aram's shop, I would have gone crazy. Now that we're settled here and Nathan is happy at his new school, I have to start earning a living. I'm aware of your concern for me, Father, but the question is - what can I do to make a living? The only business I know is the jewellery business. The only job I can get here is as a salesman in a jewellery shop or as a repairer. I've only ever worked in our own business, the thought of working for anybody else is so alien to me…" His voice trailed off.

We all sat together in silence. The clock on the mantelpiece ticked loudly, and it seemed a long time before Stepan spoke again.

"I've been thinking of nothing else but Nico's business proposition. And the more I think about it, the more sense it makes to me. I'd like to discuss it with you of course, Father, but I think it is the only way I can start again."

"What about starting a business here, my son? Aram could help you…"

"No. I've thought about it, but leasing a shop here is complicated, to say the least. I don't want to tie myself to a long lease. Besides, the rents are very high. And as you know, Father, it's so much cheaper and easier to make a start in Cyprus."

"I agree with you there, but what about Reya? Have you talked it over with her?" Stepan was taken aback by his father's questioning, as though it was unnecessary. "I haven't actually talked about it with her yet, but she is my wife and she would agree with me. Wouldn't you, little one?" he asked, turning to me and looking at me with pleading in his eyes.

Did I have a choice? I didn't. More than anyone, even more than his parents, I knew the turmoil he was in. The sleepless nights and the chain-smoking told their own story. It seemed to me that the letter from Nico had come at the right moment. It had acted as a catalyst. I wouldn't – couldn't – stand in his way.

"I would agree with you, if that's what you really want to do," I said, forcing a smile to my lips. "I have to go wherever he wants to go," I said, to no one in particular.

"Thank you *hokis*, I knew you would support me. This is my plan. I shall go to Larnaca, immediately after the Christmas festivities, and see for myself how things are developing there. If I decide to stay and go in with Nico, I shall give myself three months. If the business goes well, then I shall rent a flat and you and Nathan can join me. If it doesn't…" He shrugged his shoulders and put his hands up. "Then I shall come back, and think of something else."

"I think that's very fair," said his father. "We shall wait and see. As the old Turkish saying goes – who knows what unexpected things may come to light, before a new day is born."

"I *have* to do this Father, I must *try*… before I can be reconciled to living anywhere, but my beloved Cyprus."

That night, for the first time in many weeks, Stepan fell asleep before his head touched the pillow. Whereas I lay awake, going over everything that had been said. I was glad about one thing, at least – Stepan's spirit was no longer anchored to the past. He was ready to embark on the future, no matter how uncertain it looked, at the moment. And I was ready to give him all the help and support I was capable of. When sleep came at last, it came in quick spurts, from which I emerged giddy, with thoughts swirling in my head, thoughts I could not single out or direct.

Chapter Thirty Five

It was the 5th of January – the day before our Christmas. Agnes and Aram had invited the 'family' – which now included Sona, Kevork and Sevan – to have Christmas dinner with them.

"I'm quite anxious about how the family will react to the meal," she confided to me, as she prepared the dessert. "After all, it is the most important feast in our calendar. I'm not going to make the traditional Armenian meal, this year. We are all trying to come to terms with life in England, so I have decided to try my hand at cooking the classic English Roast Beef with all the trimmings."

"What makes you think they will object?" I asked. "I'm looking forward to it, already. It's quite different from our cooking, where so much can be done in advance. A roast dinner requires a lot of planning and preparation, and on top of that, there is the last minute rush to make the gravy, while you keep everything hot. But you are such a good cook - I'm sure it will be a great success. There's no need to worry."

"I wasn't worried at first, but when Mother raised her eyebrows at me, when I told her, I knew I was in trouble!"

"I know the look you mean. My mother had it too. Come to think of it, I use it myself, with Stepan and Nathan. It comes in useful, when you want to make a point without uttering a word!" I smiled, remembering many such moments. Agnes finished making the trifle and put it in the fridge. I lit both our cigarettes and we smoked and drank our tea.

"I think Mother was planning to come in here at the crack of dawn and prepare everything, before she went to church. I couldn't make her understand that I'm not betraying our Armenian tradition by cooking the beef. It's simply that now that I live in England, I thought it would be a good idea to combine Armenian tradition with a classic English meal."

"You were right to think that way. After all we celebrated the New Year with the traditional Armenian feast. That's enough tradition isn't it?"

"I think it is. And we are all going to church tomorrow! By the way, you and Stepan don't have to come home early, just because we do. Why don't you take Nathan somewhere for a treat - he will miss his father when

-us. He worships him, doesn't he?"

ᐧnately, he doesn't go back to school until the 7th. But,

ᐧo long before we join Stepan in Larnaca."

, after a leisurely breakfast, we went to the Armenian

ᐧn. Stepan's parents went in Aram's new Rover – a

to himself - and Stepan, Nathan and I squeezed into what

ᐧd Kevork's 'company' car – the Morris van that he used for

ᐧss. He dropped Sona and myself in front of the church and

dr. ᐧ with Stepan and Nathan, to find a parking place not too far from the church. Being a weekday, the traffic was quite bad, and it had taken us twice as long as usual to reach our destination. The service had already started – we could hear the choir singing.

The small Church was full. People stood by the main door, trying to get in while others – mostly men – stood in small groups in the grounds of the church, talking. Sona and I squeezed in through the side entrance. We found two empty seats and sat down to follow the liturgy. St. Sarkis Church was built in the shape of the cross. It had high ceilings, with a crystal chandelier hanging from the centre, where the nave and transepts crossed. I tried to concentrate on the service. My eyes roamed around the church – there were so many beautiful decorative features. They finally came to rest on the marble altar, with its lovely flowers, and the icon of the Mother and Child behind. The expression on the Holy Mother's face was doleful, her limpid blue eyes gazing at the child in her arms, as if she knew the fate that awaited him. The bishop's baritone reverberated across the aisle, mesmerizing the congregation with his impassioned sermon.

The pure voices of the choir singing *Sourp* (Saint) - the most moving of all Armenian hymns - together with the pungent smell of the Jerusalem incense transported me back in time to another church, in another place. There it was that Stepan had first set eyes on me. It was there that he had decided he would marry me. I smiled inwardly. I remembered how I had rejected him at first, even resented him for putting an end to my 'dreams'. And later – much later - my surprise and wonder when I realized how much I loved him. And now, we would be apart for the first time in our life together. I didn't count the times we were apart when he went to Beirut on business – they were flying visits. This time, however, it would be a long parting - months before I could join him and we could be together again.

I heard the bishop's last Amen. The service was over. I joined the queue of people waiting to kiss the bishop's hand and receive his blessing. Turning round, I saw Stepan and Nathan waiting too. Good, I thought, all three of us will receive the blessing - God knows we need it. Afterwards I went over to the alcove, where people were lighting candles. When my turn came, I put some money on the lace-covered tray, and chose three candles, one for each of us. As I lit them, I prayed silently for Stepan's safe journey to Cyprus and for strength to sustain us all in the coming months.

It was difficult to spot the family, when Sona and I left the church. The size of the congregation surprised us both. We didn't realize there were so many Armenians living in England. I hardly knew anyone, but Sona did and she started to talk to people she hadn't seen for some time. When I did spot the family, I pushed my way to where they were standing, waiting for us.

"Mummy, Mummy! Daddy is going to take us to Wimpy for hamburgers!" said Nathan, excitedly. He spoke to us in English now, but we answered him in Armenian. We wanted him to be able to speak both languages, equally fluently. It was the same with Agnes's children. They had started to speak in English, when they started school. But all three children still spoke to their grandparents in Armenian – it came naturally to them, just as it had done to us, when we were children and used to talk to our grandmother in Turkish. "And that's not all," Nathan continued. "Afterwards, we're going to the toy department in Barkers, for my Christmas present."

"But you've already had presents…"

"But today is our *real* Christmas, isn't it?" I looked at Stepan and I understood. He wanted this day to be special, to create a lasting memory for them both, as he would be away from Nathan for so long.

"Of course it is, *hokis*," I said. "Aren't we lucky, to have two Christmases to celebrate!"

"Your Mama can look for bargains in the sales, while we spend time in the toy department." But I shook my head. That was the last thing on my mind. I wanted to spend as much time as possible with my husband.

"What about afternoon tea, in the roof gardens?" he suggested. Dear Stepan – he knew how much I loved afternoon tea – English style – with dainty sandwiches and scones with strawberry jam and thick cream. I beamed at him. "That would be wonderful!"

It always makes me smile, to see how good food and feasting puts people in a light-hearted mood, making them shrug off worries and unwanted thoughts, and easing them into a spirit of celebration. The magic was working now. The family was sitting round Agnes's roomy table, in her large dining room. The embroidered tablecloth from Lefkara graced the table and she had brought out her best china and cutlery to complement the splendid meal she had cooked. We were drinking Othello wine – a rich red wine of Cyprus - from exquisite crystal glasses. Agnes had gone to so much trouble, to make her family feel happy on this special day. She looked flushed from cooking, but she was delighted to see that everyone was enjoying the roast beef and all its trimmings.

"You've done us proud, my daughter," said her father. "Where did you learn to cook such a wonderful meal? Even Yiannis could not always roast beef to perfection in his *fourno*. This is so tender."

"From a cook book, Father."

"And the potatoes, the vegetables…" said her mother, eyeing the crisp, golden potatoes. I caught Agnes's eye and we smiled. *Mother was happy.* We ate in silence, which is always a good sign that the food is fit for a king. As for the Sherry Trifle – that was so delicious, it vanished in a twinkling. As Aram opened the fourth bottle of *Othello*, we all agreed that the Christmas feast was a brilliant success.

I looked at Stepan across the table, as he drank his wine, joking and laughing with everyone. He was so happy. Catching my glance, he raised his glass and winked at me. I hoped and prayed that his decision to go back to Cyprus and start again would be successful. My gaze shifted to Sona and Kevork. It was ironic that they should have decided to start a new life in England, while we were planning to return to Cyprus. They seemed happy with their decision and were settling nicely in their new environment. Sona had plans to work from home – using her skills as a seamstress. She would start by doing alterations and making curtains. I admired her spirit and wished her luck. Their daughter Sevan, who had grown into a very attractive girl, had already started work, at a High Street travel agent's.

For the umpteenth time that evening, I tried to understand why Stepan couldn't or wouldn't try to settle in Ealing. It was true that a number of Armenians, who had fled to England at the beginning of the troubles, had gone back and started anew. But those who stayed were doing well. If I had the choice, I would stay too. I missed Cyprus sorely, but I was adapting to life in England. Throughout our history, Armenians have always been able to adapt to living under different situations and in different countries.

Dinner was over. It was time to make the coffee.

Chapter Thirty Six

"You've certainly made a good job of turning this room into your *atelier*," I congratulated Sona. She had spent some of the money she had saved 'for a rainy day', to set up in business, on her own account. She had bought an industrial sewing machine, a large table, and a full-length mirror, and had taken out an advertisement in the local paper. She had also made pretty curtains for the window and I had helped her hang a few pictures on the walls. Although Sona was not a trained dressmaker, she was a good seamstress. She made her own and her daughter's dresses, she was good at making alterations and she had a flair for making curtains. Her business venture took off. It had been slow at first, with a few enquiries and an alteration or two, but now she had so much work, that she was grateful for any help I could give her.

I had got into the habit of visiting Sona two or three mornings a week, to help her with the sewing. I was hopeless with the sewing machine, but my hand sewing was neat and even. When she was busy with fittings, I answered the phone and made appointments for her. Sona was a good friend and I enjoyed helping her, it got me out of the house and stopped me thinking of Stepan - I missed him so much. I made the coffee and took the tray in.

"Coffee-break," I announced. Sona put her scissors down and stretched her arms. "You look tired," I said. "Do you still help Kevork in the shop?"

"Only with the cleaning. After all that rain yesterday, the floor of the shop looked filthy. I couldn't bear it, so I cleaned it thoroughly, before I started cooking the dinner."

"You're working too hard."

"I know I am. But I have to, if we are to make a success of things, here in England. I don't intend to live above the shop forever. I've told Kev..." She stopped short, as she saw my quizzical look. "That's what people call him at work, these days. Anyway, I told him that I want to save enough money for a deposit on a house, sometime in the near future. I have to think of Sevan's future too..."

"You worry too much about Sevan. She is a lovely, intelligent girl. She will make her own future. And she will meet a 'nice' young man without any help from anyone." Sona didn't seem to realize that times were changing. Young Armenian boys and girls were a lot less restricted than our generation. They went out in groups to parties and clubs, and they had more chance of meeting people at work than we had.

"Enough about us," she said. "Have you heard from Stepan, this week? How is he doing? It must be more than a month, since he went…"

"Five weeks and four days," I said. "He phoned us last night."

"How is he? Tell me all the news." I took a sip of my coffee and lit a cigarette.

"He is well. At least, he sounded well and happy. He said he has found a flat for us – two bedrooms - in a newly built block of flats, not too far from the shop. I don't know Larnaca at all, so it could be anywhere, really."

"What about the business?"

I shrugged my shoulders. "I don't really know. He said he is doing some repair work as well as selling watches, silverware and 'trinkets', as he calls mass produced stuff…"

"You don't want to go back to Cyprus, do you? Would you rather Stepan had stayed and started a business here?"

"To be honest, I would. We have a house here. Nathan is happy in his school here - he's made friends. And I could easily get a job, or retrain for something different, couldn't I?" Sona thought for a moment.

"I'm sure you could, my dear Reya. But don't you see that it isn't 'business' that has taken him back to Cyprus?"

"What then?"

"He's gone back because he misses the life-style he had in Cyprus. anyone could see he was not happy here."

"But he liked England. He enjoyed his holidays here, as much as I did…"

"That's just it. He was not on holiday this time. The thought of living here for the foreseeable future – and maybe even for the rest of his life - must have lowered his spirits no end."

"But it won't be forever! I'm sure we shall all go back one day, and our life will be as it was before."

"I don't know about that. But I'm pretty sure Stepan felt trapped."

"You could be right, I suppose. He is an outdoors person. The cold and wet weather we're having, would have been unbearable to him."

"If you ask me, he won't be happy until he goes back to his beloved

Famagusta."

"I'm sure thousands of Cypriots feel the same way. What about Kevork? Why doesn't he complain? He enjoyed the same life-style. He lost his job…"

"It's not quite the same for Kevork. He has never worked for himself, so he had to find another job. As it happens, there are more opportunities for him here in England at the moment. But, I think there are more commercial prospects in Cyprus for Stepan."

"But, don't *you* miss Cyprus?"

"Of course I do! I miss my house even more. I shall be one of the first to go back, when the dispute is settled. But for the time being, I'm content to bide my time and save some money!"

"I do admire your optimism, Sona. I feel I'm drifting, waiting for Stepan, when I could be doing something useful."

"But you are doing something useful. You're looking after your son, aren't you? Not forgetting the never-ending housework and washing and ironing, as well as helping me the way you do, eh?"

"But it's not enough. *Mayrik* is in charge of the kitchen, like in the old days, and *Hayrik* – bless him – does the odd jobs around the house, as well as taking care of the garden. So you see…"

"But, you do get on well with them, don't you?"

"Of course I do. They are wonderful and they adore Nathan. But I feel so frustrated at times, I could scream!"

"I know what it is! Your bed is cold without *him!*" I laughed. She had a unique way of saying things that never failed to cheer me up. Just then, the phone rang.

"There! I made you laugh," she said, as she picked up the phone.

On the way home, I went over what Sona had said. I suppose if I were to be honest with myself, I could see why Stepan had yearned to go back. To lose at a stroke, everything he held dear, everything he had taken for granted all his life, was not easy to come to terms with. But, most of all - to see his ageing father driven from his home, his beloved garden, his friends and his coffee shop. That was breaking his heart. Stepan simply had to go back. He had to give his all, to recapture that life.

The last few months, before I went back to Cyprus, were the longest of my life. Stepan phoned me one evening and said that the flat he had found for us was ready for occupation. The landlord had new furniture put in.

"It has a balcony with a 'half' view of the sea. You'll like it," he had announced, cheerfully.

"I'm glad the waiting is over," said Agnes, as she handed me a mug of tea. I had gone over to her house, to help her prepare the dinner for tonight. It was to be a farewell dinner, for me. For, tomorrow I would leave for Cyprus. My bags were packed and ready, standing in the hall.

"I'm glad, too - not to say relieved," I said, lighting a cigarette. "I'm also glad that Stepan has started to make headway with the business."

"I know my brother. He will move heaven and earth, to *make* it work. It will be difficult for you, at first – living in a strange town, knowing few people. At least, you'll be together. Stepan will have a home life again after all this time."

"Yes. But I'm not sure if I've done the right thing, in agreeing to let Nathan stay, until school breaks up in July. This thought is looming in my mind, overshadowing all others."

"You're not worried about our Nathan, are you? He is such a happy soul. He's got lots of friends, besides my own two. You know that his grandparents and I will take care of him for you …"

"I know. I wasn't thinking of that, at all. Do you think it is right, for a boy his age to be away from his father, for so long?"

"What was Stepan's reaction, when you talked to him about it?"

"He didn't seem to mind. In fact, he said it would give me time to fix the flat and find my way around Larnaca." Agnes didn't answer for a moment. She drank her tea and smoked her cigarette instead.

"Well," she said, grinding her cigarette in the ashtray. "My brother and I went to boarding school and so did you and your sisters and your brother. It didn't do us any harm did it? On the contrary it made us more independent. And Nathan won't even be at boarding school. He'll be living with his grandparents."

"You're right, of course. It's just that I shall miss him so much."

Shortly afterwards, Sona and Kev arrived – the name had stuck.

"Here is something for you," said Sona, handing me a parcel. Surprised, I opened it to find two pretty aprons.

"I made them, out of some remnants I had," she said. "For your new kitchen. It's time you took up the reins of domesticity, once more!"

"I expect you to cook hearty meals for Stepan," said Kev, trying hard to keep a straight face. "He has suffered long enough, going without proper food for so long."

"Stepan going without food! Ha, ha, ha," we three girls shrieked, in unison.

"I wouldn't be surprised, if the poor boy has lost a lot of weight in all this time!" said Aram. He handed out drinks for everyone and sank down on the sofa. "Let's drink to Reya's new life in Larnaca."

"Don't forget, we shall all want to visit you, when Stepan makes his fortune!" said Sona. Everyone was trying to be light-hearted about my going back. They knew how I felt - one half of me was glad to be going back to join Stepan, but the other was sorry to be leaving my son behind, no matter for how short a time. But, they didn't know how afraid I was of what I would find, when I got there. Nor did anyone guess how nervous I was, to be travelling on my own, for the very first time in my life. But these thoughts were for later. For now, I buried my anxieties, smiling and thanking them all for their kind wishes.

"Of course," I told them. "I can't wait for you all to come to Cyprus to visit us."

Chapter Thirty Seven

I looked at my watch. Only ten minutes, before we landed. I looked out of the window at the familiar coastline. The island spread before me, beautiful, enchanting, nestling in the warm waters of the Mediterranean, but now crippled. Is it possible, I thought, that this island is now divided and that my beloved Famagusta – the Eden of my childhood – is a ghost town?

There was a lump in my throat, as the plane touched down at Larnaca International Airport. It seemed so small, compared to the big, bustling airport in Nicosia. It was hot and humid and I was already perspiring, by the time I retrieved my two suitcases and started to walk towards immigration and passport control. I needn't have worried about travelling by myself. Aram had kindly taken me to Heathrow and helped me to check in my luggage. Only then, had I really been on my own. Somehow, I had managed to deal with all the formalities of travel – even going to the Duty Free Shop, to buy a bottle of whisky and a carton of cigarettes for Stepan - without any mishap.

The officer looked at the picture in my passport and then at me. He smiled and – in Greek – asked me if I had come for a visit.

"No, not for a visit," I said. "I've come to join my husband, in Larnaca. He has started a new business. We are from Famagusta…"

"Oh! So you went through all the trauma of the invasion?" I nodded. "Good luck," he said, as he handed me my passport. I moved on, walking into a babble of noise and confusion. I scanned the crowds, looking for Stepan. I couldn't see him anywhere and then all at once he was standing next to me, enveloping me in his arms. I clung to him, tears of relief and joy running down my cheeks.

"My car's outside. I'll take you home."

"Your car looks good as new," I said. I got in and sank into the soft leather seat, while he put my suitcases in the boot. Stepan got in and we drove off.

"She's still a beauty, isn't she?" he said, as the big car purred away. "Nico took good care of my car for me. He stored it in his garage, but never drove it once, even though I told him he could, whenever he wanted.

How was your flight?"

"It was uneventful, but very long."

"How is Nathan? Is he looking forward to coming back to Cyprus, at the end of term?"

"Yes, he can't wait for the start of the summer holidays. He misses swimming in the sea, as much as you did." Parting from Nathan had been tearful for me, even though it was only for a short time. I had sensed that a part of him wanted to come with me, but another part wanted to stay and continue his schooling in England. I hoped it wouldn't be too difficult for him, to change schools again and make new friends, when he eventually joined us.

I looked out of the window, seeing, for the first time, the unfamiliar streets of Larnaca. There was a lot of building work going on. Larnaca had always been known as the 'sleeping village'. But now it was waking up from its deep slumber – thanks to the influx of refugees from Famagusta. Stepan stopped in front of a three-story block of flats. His Mercedes looked incongruous, parked in front of the nondescript building, with its dull green shutters.

"We're on the second floor," he said cheerfully. We climbed up the two flights of stairs. Stepan opened the door and I followed him into the flat. He put the suitcases down in the tiny hall and led me into the living room. It was hot and humid. As he opened the window, I wiped the perspiration off my face.

"Come here, little one. I want to look at you. I missed you so much." Stepan took me in his arms and held me close, running his fingers through my hair. "You look different. I don't know what it is, but you look different, somehow... Ah, I know what it is. It's your hair!" he cried, as if he had solved a great mystery. I smiled, happy that he had noticed my new hairstyle. Only last week, I had gone to Agnes's hairdresser and told her to 'chop' off my long hair. She had obliged and given me a new hairstyle – a bob - with a fringe. I had walked out of the hairdressing salon feeling good and confident about myself. And I had even felt – for some unaccountable reason – liberated!

"Do you like it?" I asked shyly, hoping that he would approve.

"I do. It suits you. Although, I think I still prefer you with long hair. Come, I'll show you the rest of the flat."

There were two bedrooms. The bigger one was ours and the small one would be Nathan's. The flat was sparsely furnished. "And this is the kitchen. It's small, but enough for our requirements, isn't it? The washing machine was delivered only yesterday. And this is the balcony I told you about," he said, opening the kitchen door and stepping out. It was a good-sized balcony - the only redeeming feature of the flat, I was to discover, later. From here, we could see the back of the apartment block opposite, and beyond that, the sparkling blue sea – as Stepan had described it, on the telephone – a 'half' view of the sea! There were two chairs and a round table. He looked for his cigarettes. "Damn! I left my cigarettes in the car."

"It's alright, I've got a packet in my bag. I got you some duty free ones and also a bottle of whisky." I said, going inside to get them.

"Well done, little one." We smoked in silence for a minute, on the balcony. It was cool, there.

"I see what you mean about the sea-view," I said.

"Do you like the flat?"

"It's very nice," I said, trying to hide my disappointment.

"This is only temporary, you understand. Next year, we'll move to a bigger and better place, eh?" Stepan looked at his watch. "I better go back to the shop. Why don't you have a rest first, and then unpack your clothes and get acquainted with your new home? I'll be back at six, and you can tell me all the news from the family. Nico and Anna are coming to see you later, and then we're all going out to dinner, to celebrate your homecoming." And with that, he was gone.

The front door clicked shut. I was alone in the flat. I felt a great weariness sweep over me. I missed Nathan already. It seemed such a long time, since I said goodbye to him. But it wasn't just that. I felt sad, homesick almost. I should feel happy and elated, I thought - after all, I've come home, home to Cyprus. I'm here with my husband, and my son will join us soon. But the feeling of homesickness did not go away. I felt like a stranger, in a strange place. I desperately yearned to be in my own home. I was confused. I could hear an inner voice, asking me - which home are you thinking about? The home you left behind this morning, or the one you were forced to flee? With a struggle, I pushed these bewildering thoughts to the back of my mind and set to work.

It was even hotter in the bedroom. I opened the window for some air, but all I got was the noise of the traffic below. I was to find out that this was the warmest, noisiest part of the flat, while the kitchen and balcony, at the back of the building, were less so. Once I had unpacked, I put the cases on top of the wardrobe. The noise was so bad that I closed the window, before lying down on the bed, exhausted. It was not until late in the afternoon that I awoke, drenched in perspiration and feeling very thirsty.

"I do like your new hairstyle!" cried Anna, after we hugged and kissed and hugged again. "It makes you look like a gamine. Does Stepan like it?" I shrugged my shoulders.

"He liked it, but he said he prefers my hair long. It will grow soon enough, though, won't it?"

"Of course it will. Do you remember Roulla, my hairdresser? She opened a salon not long after we came to Larnaca. You can go there, with me. It's so nice, going to a hairdresser you know and trust, isn't it? Anyway, how do you like your new home? I know it is small, but it's only temporary. Everything is temporary, until we go back to our beloved Famagusta."

"I don't mind it being small. It means less housework for me!" I said, trying to sound cheerful. "To be honest, I haven't really looked at the place, properly. I felt so tired, I went to bed and slept like a baby. Have you adapted to the enormous upheaval..."

"We had to *agabimou*. There was no option. We just got on and did the best we could, and we survived. Would you believe it, we are called 'refugees', by the locals. If you ask me, they should be grateful to us, for forcing this dull and sleepy town to wake up!"

"Do you really think we shall soon go back to Famagusta?"

"That's what I pray and hope for every morning, when I wake up. In the meantime, we carry on, for without that hope..." Anna's eyes shone with unshed tears. She dabbed at them with her handkerchief and was silent for a while. Then, taking a deep breath, she assumed her usual cheerful persona. She must have sensed my apprehensions, my worries. "The children can't wait for Nathan to come," she said. "They have found new playgrounds, new coves to swim in. Come on, let's join the boys on the balcony. It's cool there. I fancy a drink, before we go out to dinner."

Dinner turned out to be a jolly affair. We went to *Chris's Taverna*. Chris was a refugee from Famagusta, himself. He had always been in the restaurant business and, when he came to Larnaca, he opened a small take-away Kebab place. His fellow refugees supported his new venture and, in no time at all, the business flourished. The restaurant had come to be known as the *Famagusta Tavern*. It was now one of the best and busiest *tavernas* in Larnaca – right on the sea front.

Chris gave us a table overlooking the sea. The silvery water shimmered in the light of the full moon. We could hear the gentle wavelets lapping the shore. It was easy, in this enchanting setting, to forget for a moment nagging thoughts of the past and future, and enjoy the present.

"This is a lovely view," I said. "It's like..."

"It's like being in Famagusta, isn't it?" Anna finished the sentence for me.

"We love coming here. It has become a meeting place for old friends and business acquaintances," said Nico.

"Wait till you taste the food!" This was Stepan's contribution. Giving me one of his impish smiles, he put his arm around my shoulders, in the playful way he always had. "What would you like to eat?" he asked.

"*Meze* of course," I said, with no hesitation. My mouth started to water at the thought of it. "You don't know how much I've missed it." I sipped my drink of ouzo - with ice and water. It was delicious. Then, I looked around me. The place was buzzing with people enjoying themselves. Beginning to relax, I noticed, for the first time, that my three companions at the table had also changed. The two men had grown even closer now. They seemed to be living for the moment, happy to celebrate the fact that they had survived the invasion and had picked up the threads of life. The phrase 'when we get back home' came up in the conversation, time and time again, like a mantra. As for Anna, outwardly she was her charming, flirty self, but in unguarded moments I saw her frown deeply and a faraway look come into her eyes.

The waiter came with the food - and lots of it. The table was soon covered with a variety of appetizers, but these were only to whet our appetite, for there was more to follow - mouth-watering kebabs, grilled red mullet and many other delicacies.

We lingered over the *meze*, savouring the subtle flavours of each dish. The breadbasket was replenished more than once. The contents of the bottle of ouzo on the table gradually disappeared. It's true that alcohol loosens the tongue, I thought - we were laughing, joking and chatting away happily, seemingly without a care in the world. I, for one, was feeling quite light-headed, enjoying the almost forgotten gourmand experience. It was past midnight, before we got home.

"It's been too long, without you," said Stepan, softly. I nodded, not trusting my voice. He gathered me in his arms and carried me into the bedroom.

Chapter Thirty Eight

My first morning in Larnaca arrived, in a blaze of sunshine. I had forgotten that the sun shone almost every day, here. Sitting up in bed, I took the cup of coffee Stepan had brought me.

"What will you do, today?" he asked. He sat down at the foot of the bed and sipped his coffee. I didn't answer for a moment. I had a splitting headache and could hardly keep my head straight. I peered into his face. I envied him his ability to feel alert and cheerful, the moment he opened his eyes. I needed time, to really wake up.

"I shall probably clean the flat, do some washing and cook the lunch," I said, without thinking and sipped my coffee. I thought of the day – it seemed like centuries ago, now - when we had our first breakfast in the 'secret' garden. Stepan must have been thinking the same thing, for he smiled and said: "Breakfast is ready and waiting for us on the balcony. Remember our first breakfast in the 'secret' garden?"

"This is wonderful," I said, when we were sitting on the balcony. The noise of the traffic was muted on this side of the building. The cool, fresh air eased my headache a little. "I didn't think I would be able to eat anything this morning, after the feast of last night. But the smell of the sesame-seed bread has changed all that." There was cheese, apples and apricots to go with the bread.

"If I continue to eat like this every day, I shall get fat!" I said biting into a ripe apricot. "We both shall," I added. I couldn't help noticing that he had already put on weight, since coming back. I guessed that eating out, not to mention the drinking every night, had been responsible for that. But I didn't say anything.

"I shall still love you," Stepan said, smiling. He lit two cigarettes and handed one to me. "I'll take you to the shop, this afternoon." We smoked in companionable silence, enjoying the 'half' view of the sea.

There is something gratifying, something reassuring, about cleaning one's house. That is to say, it used to be so, until now. For the first time in my life, I was living in rented accommodation. Living in a flat was a new experience for me, and I knew that it wasn't and never would feel like home, no matter how much time I spent cleaning and caring for it. Nevertheless, out of habit, more than anything else, I cleaned and tidied the place and mopped the tiled floors, tirelessly. I was hanging out the washing, when I heard the doorbell. I opened the front door, to find Marko on the doorstep.

"How wonderful to see you," I said, my voicing cracking with emotion, and gave him a big hug. I suddenly realized how much I had missed my side of the family, in the months I had been away.

"I came to see if you had settled in," he said and followed me into the kitchen.

"Tell me all the news, while I make the coffee," I told him. "How are the sisters?"

"They are all well. I don't see them all that often."

"Not even Sara?"

"Sara is different isn't she? I make a point of keeping in touch with her. I see her, whenever I can."

"How is the new business?" I asked.

"It's alright. But, like everybody else, I've pinned my hopes on the new wave of tourism. My 'supermarket' is in a good locale – very near the seaside – but I have to stay open until eight o'clock at night, in order to catch the late shoppers. It's hard work." He looked tired. He had lost a lot of weight.

"Have you got anyone to help you?"

"Christina helps me as much as she can. In fact, I couldn't have done it without her. We work hard but we don't mind, because it is for the children. It's their education, their future we have to think of now." He ground out his cigarette and got up to go. "Nice to see you, Reya. Come and see us at the shop. We are not far from Stepan's."

"I will, just as soon as I find my way around Larnaca." I was happy for my 'little' brother. He had had to wait so long to get married. I sighed nostalgically...

The doorbell rang again. I opened the door. This time it was a woman of about my age or so, standing on the doorstep. "My name is Lenia and I live in the flat below yours," she said, smiling. I asked her in and introduced myself.

"I just got some *koulourakia* from the bakery," she said, handing me a plate of the slightly sweet, sesame cookies.

"Thank you. Would you like a coffee?" I asked. She nodded and followed me into the kitchen. I made coffee, for the second time in the past hour, and we sat on the balcony. I dipped a cookie in my coffee – in the time-honoured custom – and put it into my mouth.

"It's delicious. I didn't know there was a bakery, nearby," I said.

"There is a grocery store, as well as the bakery. When you come out of the main entrance of the flats, you turn right and after a few minutes' walk, you can see the shops. It's very handy, if you run out of everyday things. The market is a long way away from here."

"I only came yesterday, so I don't know my way about, yet. Thank you for telling me."

"That's alright. We moved in at about the same time as your husband. He told us you would be joining him soon. Well, I'd better be going. If you need anything, just ask. Come and have coffee with me tomorrow, if you're free and I'll take you to the bakery."

"Thank you, I will," I said. I looked at my watch. It was twenty to one. Stepan would be home soon and I hadn't even thought about lunch. I went to the fridge to investigate. There were a few bottles of water and beer but not much more. I opened the cupboard. There were a few tins of sardines and prawns. It was too late to go in search of the grocery shop, my kind neighbour had told me about. In any case, I didn't have a key. Nor did I have any Cyprus money. It will take some time, to get used to having my main meal at lunchtime, I thought. I missed my lovely supermarket in Ealing. I missed the way *Hayrik* and I went to our local supermarket on a Friday morning, and did the shopping for the whole week.

I looked helplessly round the kitchen for inspiration. What to do? I needn't have worried, because just then I heard Stepan's key in the door.

"Hello, little one!" he called out. I went into the hall to meet him. He was laden with bags of shopping. "I've got *Kleftiko* for lunch. Can you get me a cold Keo and make a salad, while I put the groceries away?" During lunch, Stepan explained that he had come across *The Kouzina*, a restaurant where they excelled in homemade 'take-away' food. "You should see their menu. They cook everything from boiled beans to fish and roasts. As you can imagine, I'm a good customer. Sometimes it's not worth cooking for two, is it?" I had to agree with him.

"The lamb simply melts in your mouth, and as for the potatoes…" I said, relishing the unexpected treat. Over coffee and cigarettes, I told Stepan about my visitors. "I went to Marko's shop for the groceries. He told me he came to see you. We 'refugees' stick together and support each other."

"That's the spirit."

"The couple in No. 12 are very friendly. You must invite her back for coffee."

"I will. All in all, it's been a busy morning."

"It will be a busy afternoon, too. I'll take you to the shop. Later, Anna will take you round the town and show you the sights."

Stepan parked his car on a side street. He took my hand and we crossed the busy road and walked over to the shop. The sign above it said *Nico's Novelty Shop* in big letters and underneath, in smaller letters, Cyprus Souvenirs, Silver, Gold, and Jewellery.

The shop was long and narrow. The section that Stepan occupied was at the front. My heart sank, when I saw his 'workshop'. It consisted of an old work-bench, two chairs and one single glass-cabinet, displaying a selection of watches, inexpensive gold and silver jewellery, silver frames in various sizes, and the like. It was a far cry from his elegantly designed and well-stocked jewellery shop, where the precious stones sparkled and winked under the lights - an exclusive establishment in the heart of Famagusta.

"I shall put a bigger glass-cabinet here, and display silver trays and crystal vases and ash-trays, and things like that. What do you think?" It was not often that Stepan asked my opinion on anything to do with business. For generations an invisible line had existed, separating the sphere of domesticity from the unfathomable realm of commerce. The question took me by surprise.

"I think it's a very good idea," I replied. "A bigger cabinet here will create a separate section from the shop. With lights above the glass cabinet…"

"Lights? Of course, I'll put lights," he said and ruffled my hair. "But it won't be long before I have my own shop, I promise you."

The rest of the shop was taken up with Nico's souvenir items. On a long table, bales of cotton, towels, sheets, pillowcases, tablecloths, kitchen towels, aprons, knick-knacks and many souvenir items were laid out. Next to the table, there were two stands, on which bales of dress and suit materials were displayed. It was a utility shop, geared towards tourism and necessity. It had none of the exclusivity of his shop in Famagusta. I sighed, feeling sad at the way things had turned out. Don't be so silly, I told myself. What these two men had done was remarkable, to say the least. They were to be commended, if anything.

"Hello! I've come to rescue you," Anna said, as she walked in with her usual aplomb. She was wearing a pretty cotton dress and she had tied her hair back with a ribbon. "I made the dress myself, out of a remnant from the shop," she said proudly, when she saw me looking at it.

"It's very pretty. You are a clever girl, Anna." She nodded her head and smiled. "I'll make you a dress, if you like. There are plenty of remnants, at the back."

"I'll hold you to that," I said.

The shopping area was small. We walked along the shops; we went to the Municipal Market and then to the seafront. There were cafés, *tavernas* and hotels, overlooking the sea. "The seafront is called *Finikoudes*. It's a popular spot for the locals, as well as visitors. It gets very crowded on Saturday afternoons and Sundays. People put on their best clothes and walk up and down before going to a café or a restaurant."

"I see why it's called *Finikoudes*," I said. The line of mature palms had given the promenade its name. It was a lovely spot. The sea was calm and sky blue. I stood there for a moment, breathing the fresh sea air. I looked at the sea, longingly. This was the nearest I could get to Famagusta.

"Shall we have a cup of Nescafe over the road, at that nice new patisserie *Paloma*?"

"Lets," I said. "But, I don't want a coffee, I've had four already. I would love a cup of tea, though."

"A pot of tea for you, then."

"This is very nice" I said, sipping my tea. The place was full. There was a tantalizing display of every kind of cake one could think of.

"It's a popular place to meet friends, for morning coffee and tea." Afternoon tea was another thing I missed from England. I used to make a big pot of tea, as soon as Nathan came home from school. It became a ritual - tea, bread and butter, and homemade cake. Even the grandparents enjoyed it. We would sit round the kitchen table, and listen to Nathan, as he told us about his day at school. I looked at my watch, they would have finished with their tea by now, I thought. England and Nathan seemed a million miles away.

My happiness was complete when Nathan came to Cyprus, for the summer holidays. He was becoming more like his father, every day. He was self-assured and self-reliant, wanting to excel in everything he did, and most of the time, he succeeded. Both Stepan and I were proud of him. He had not only done very well in his school in Ealing, but he had also sat for the eleven plus examination and passed! He was eligible to go to grammar school. The sense of achievement was overwhelming and we had a little celebration that day.

But this triumph meant that Nathan would have to go back to England, if he were to take up the offer. That evening, the three of us sat on the balcony and discussed the subject far into the night.

"This is an opportunity not to be missed," said Stepan. "I would have given my right arm to go to a Grammar school in England." I looked for objections but found none. While Stepan was philosophical about Nathan going to school in England, I was quietly sad. The last thing I wanted was to be parted from my son. I could put up with anything, I could reconcile myself to any hardship, as long as I had my family around me. Despite all the heartache that the invasion had caused, this summer was proving to be one of the happiest we had had as a family. The weekends were dedicated to the pursuit of pleasure. We went swimming on Saturday afternoons and we got up very early on Sundays and just drove off, to wherever the fancy took us.

Nathan's pale skin was turning to bronze under the hot Cyprus sun. I loved watching him with his father, swimming and frolicking in the sea. He had resumed his friendship with Anna's two boys, Chris and Michael. He talked to them more in English than in Greek, but they didn't mind, because it was an opportunity for them to improve their English.

"Why don't we ask Nathan about his views on the matter," I suggested.

"What do you think, my son? Would you really like to go to school in England? Or would you prefer to go to the American school, here in Larnaca. The one I went to, as a boarder, when I was your age."

"I do so want to go to grammar school, Dad," said Nathan. "I'm sure Tony and Phil – my two best friends - will be going there, too. You know them, don't you Dad?"

"But won't you be homesick?" I blurted out, naively. I held my breath. A frown flitted across Nathan's forehead. He looked at his father and then at me, and back at his father again, questioningly. He is trying not to hurt my feelings, I said to myself. The word 'homesick' sounded like something out of a melodrama. I felt foolish. I thought of the day when I had gone to boarding school. After a few days of missing home and Mother's cooking, I had settled in quite happily.

"I won't go, if you don't want me to, Mum," he said, his voice full of disappointment. He stood up and went into the kitchen, for a drink of water. When he came back, he leant in silence against the rail of the balcony. Stepan lit a cigarette and inhaled deeply. The silence continued. Even the noise of the traffic below had died down. Choking back the tears, I got out of my chair and went over to Nathan and took him in my arms.

"Of course you'll go to grammar school, *hokis*. Your future is more important than anything else in the world. At any rate, we have a home in Ealing, haven't we? And Nene and Dede will look after you, like they have always done."

I remained on the balcony, long after they had gone off to bed. I sat in my chair and stared into space. The midnight air was cool. The sky above was ablaze with stars. Where are you now, my lucky star? I whispered. Why have you deserted me? There was no comprehending the twists and turns of fate. One minute, I had everything and the next I had nothing. All I wanted was to have my son with me. Surely, it was not too much to ask. One thought swirled in my head, over and over again. If only the invasion hadn't happened, if only we could go back.

The stars were waning when I got into bed. Stepan was awake. He cradled me in his arms.

"Everything will be alright, little one," he whispered. "Nathan will be alright and so will we."

As the days went by, I got used to the idea of not having Nathan with me. Stepan decided that I should go back to England with Nathan for a while, to see to his new school uniform, as well as anything else that was needed.

"When you have made sure that he is happy and settled, then you can leave him to the care of his grandparents. You know how much they dote on him," he said.

"I know. It will give them something positive to do."

"Exactly. At any rate, he'll come here at Christmas and the summer holidays. Who knows what might happen, when the business really takes off. When I move into my own shop..." I could find no objections to what he was saying. But, there was one thing that I had wanted to bring up with him all summer. I felt that now might be the right time to do so.

"I agree with everything you say, but there is one condition..."

"Condition! Did you say *condition*?" He looked puzzled at first, and then a look of delight - almost merriment - came into his face. He is going to humour me, I thought.

"Well, I want to do something useful when I get back," I started, before he made a joke of it. "I have too much time on my hands, not enough things to do. You said the other day that you might rent one of the shops, being built on the seafront. You will need someone to help you. I want to be that person." I stopped for breath. The words didn't come out the way I had rehearsed them, but it had the desired effect. He sat up and took notice. He was silent for a moment – too long for my liking.

"I'm touched, little one, really touched by what you said. But you know how I feel about you working. I know I can't give you everything you had before the invasion. Not yet, anyway…"

"But that's not what I'm talking about. I want to be by your side. I want to work with you, so we can rebuild the future - *together*. I don't want to see you struggling on your own. I don't want to feel useless, any more." I looked at my hands – I didn't want to look at his face - I might not like what I saw there.

"Useless! You feel useless! What in the name of all the saints in heaven are you talking about? Can't you see that you are my tower of strength? I would have crumbled into dust this past year, if it wasn't for you."

"ME?"

"Yes, *you*, my angel. Calm, serene, undemanding, unquestioning. Always there, waiting for me. Can't you see that you are the oasis to my desert?" I was dumbfounded by what I heard. I looked into his eyes. He looked solemn, not a trace of playfulness on his face. His eyes glistened, the long lashes moist. I moved nearer to him. In the same instant, he gathered me into his arms and held me tight. All too soon the siesta hour was over.

Chapter Thirty Nine

"I had a dream last night. A vivid, colourful dream," I said to Stepan. We were having breakfast on the balcony.

"Oh yes. What was your dream this time, my sweet?"

"I dreamt that I was walking along a riverbed, hand in hand with a man who was supposed to be you, but he didn't look like you, at all."

"You'll find that not many men look like me." That playful look I knew so well came into his eyes, as he lit a cigarette and handed it to me. I took a puff and went on.

"After a while, we came to a fork in the road. Suddenly, you let go of my hand and walked away from me. I stood there and watched you in alarm, as you walked away from me and disappeared from view."

"And then what happened? I'm impatient to find out…"

"I shall ignore your sarcasm. As it happens in dreams, I saw you reappear and dive into a lake and swim to the other side. You saw me, and waved your arms and beckoned me to go to you. I started to walk towards you, but at that point, a noise startled me out of my dream and I woke up."

"All your dreams are vivid and colourful, as well as long-winded," said Stepan. He liked to tease me about my dreams and superstitions. "Only Freud can interpret your 'meaningful' dreams, little one! I certainly can't!"

"I know I'm superstitious. But then, as children, our lives were ruled by ancient and irrational superstitions. I suppose they still lurk in our psyche, affecting the way we think and act and our attitudes to life."

"I know. My grandmother was very superstitious. The number of times I was told off for whistling after dark. 'Don't you know that Satan will hear you and disrupt your life?' she would scold me." He shook his head and laughed at the memory.

"My grandmother told me never to look in the mirror after dark. Because I would see Satan's image in it! I must confess I have never tried, just in case …"

"But, why would anyone want to look in the mirror in the dark?" he asked and burst out laughing again. "Anything else?"

"Even you must believe in the absolute power of the 'evil eye'. You ignore it at your peril. You must remember the special blue stone – the 'blue eye bead'. They used to pin it on a newborn baby to ward off evil eyes and evil spirits. I remember, I wore one on my vest, for years and years!"

"You didn't pin one on Nathan's vest, did you?"

"No… but your mother put one in his cot – only as a precaution, you understand!"

"Incredible!"

"Everybody believes in them. I noticed that they are sold in souvenir shops now, as key rings, and so on." I made a mental note to buy one and hang it, somewhere in the flat. "Anyway, coming back to my dream - I believe in the interpretation of dreams, because they can foretell the future. I miss my 'dream book', but from what I remember, I'm pretty sure last night's dream is a good one. Water - be it sea, river or lake - means good fortune. I'm happy with my dream," I announced.

"Thank God, for that!"

Stepan was still shaking his head in disbelief and smiling broadly, when he took his car keys from the hall table, blew me a kiss and left for work. It is true though, I thought. We were seduced by old wives' tales. There were certain things to do and certain things to avoid, in order not to tempt fate. There were religious beliefs and superstitions too. I remembered one such belief. Every Saturday afternoon, Mother would burn the dry olive leaves, which had been blessed in church on Palm Sunday, in a small earthenware pot, and then go into every room in the house, saying a special prayer. This act would ward off evil spirits and bring back the blessing of God. We never stopped to question these rituals. They were culturally accepted. It was easier to succumb to their powers, than to doubt them. My generation did not follow these rituals any more, but I still believed in dreams.

It was hard to believe that two years had passed, since I had come to join Stepan in Larnaca. Two years of living in a curious state of resignation, hope and frustration. Hopes rising - when talk circulated of negotiations to end the partition and bring the two communities together. Resignation and frustration - when these talks came to nothing. But this did not dampen Stepan's spirit. It was always, "This time next year, we shall be back in Famagusta." I didn't always share his optimism. Sometimes, it took every ounce of resolve, not to dwell on the past.

The economy of the island was recovering. The Greek Cypriots were overcoming the disastrous effects of the invasion. They were rebuilding their lives. Larnaca had come alive, with the arrival of the refugees. Nico and Stepan's business venture was doing well. They could pay the rent and make a decent living.

"We can start looking for a bigger and better flat, if you want," Stepan said. "Buy our own furniture. I can afford it."

"We don't really need a bigger place, do we? Nathan is only here on school holidays."

"Are you sure, little one? I don't want you to be unhappy."

"I'm quite happy here. I've got nice neighbours. There's the bakery too…"

"It won't be long before I move to the new shop on Evagora Street. I know exactly how to set it up. I shall need your help …"

"I can't wait! I've been idle for too long. I want to be kept busy."

"You will be, my sweet. So make the most of your leisure time. How long before Nathan goes back to school?"

"He's got another three weeks." These two years had been punctuated by Nathan's visits. He came to Cyprus at Christmas, Easter and the summer holidays. It was always the same – happy reunions and tearful goodbyes. He was growing up, fast. He seemed taller, with every visit. Stepan said that we would go to England at Christmas. We hadn't seen the family in two years. That was something to look forward to.

"That's a promise," he had said. He always kept his promises.

I had got into the habit of getting together with Anna and my neighbour Lenia, from No. 12, for coffee. Today, it happened to be my turn to be the 'hostess'. Earlier in the morning, I went to the local bakery and selected the little cakes and *koulourakia* (little biscuits) to go with the coffee. The conversation invariably turned to the homes we had left behind and, of course, to the latest rumours about negotiations to end the partition. Anna was feeling nostalgic, this morning. When one of us felt like that, then the other two tried to cheer her up.

"I miss our orange groves, as much as my house, would you believe it?" bemoaned Anna. She finished her coffee and put her cup absent-mindedly on the tray.

"Of course, we believe you. I miss the copybook I had, with all my Armenian recipes," I said, in an effort to cheer up. "It took me ages to write each recipe down meticulously, with precise measurements and cooking times. It's such an insignificant thing, but I miss it more than all my other books."

"It's understandable, because they were your mother's recipes. It has sentimental value, hasn't it?" said Lenia. "I try not to think of what I had before, but concentrate on what I have now. Otherwise, I couldn't bear it."

"Oh, I try, but sometimes, I just can't help it..." Just then, the doorbell rang, interrupting Anna's sentence. I went to open the front door. I was surprised to see Nico standing on the doorstep.

"Hello, Nico. Come in," I said. "Do you want to see Anna?"

"Yes - I mean, no – I've come to get you..." Anna sprang from her chair, like a shot. "What is it Nico-*mou*?"

"I've to take Reya to the hospital. Stepan was taken ill..."

"*What?*" I said, in disbelief. "He has never been ill, in his life. What happened?"

"We were having our coffee, when all of a sudden, he said he didn't feel well and collapsed..."

"Oh my God!"

"No time to waste. We'd better go." I looked around me, in confusion. "Nathan..."

"I'll look after the boys. You go with her, Anna," said Lenia, taking charge. "I'll be here, when you get back. Go with God." Taking my hand, she walked with me to the front door, where Nico was waiting.

On the way to the hospital, the word 'collapsed' rang in my ears like a church bell. I prayed that when we reached the hospital, everything would be alright, the anxiety I was feeling would melt away. Nico drove like a mad man, hooting his horn and cursing under his breath - "Come on, come on, you idiots, move!" - at pedestrians, as well as drivers.

"He'll be alright, won't he Nico?" Anna kept on saying, but she got no answer from him. I sat at the back of the car, trying to be calm. At last, we arrived at the hospital.

When I saw Marko, walking towards us, alarm bells started to ring. An icy wind enveloped me and I froze. I felt like a sleepwalker, about to fall from a great height. Marko put his hand on my shoulder, but said nothing. Then a nurse appeared, and led the four of us into an empty waiting room. "The doctor will see you, shortly," she said and left. We waited. After what seemed like a lifetime, the doctor came. "I'm Dr. Elias. Which one of you is the wife of Mr. Manoukian?" he asked, looking at Anna and me.

"I am," I said. He sat down in the empty seat, next to me. "Your husband had a massive heart attack, Mrs. Manoukian. He died on the way here. There was nothing we could have done. I'm so very sorry." The doctor's words hung heavy in the air of the silent room. I didn't want to hear them. In the midst of the silence, I heard a scream piercing the air.

"It's not true! It's not true!" I looked around me, to see who it was. With a shock, I realized that it was my own voice. I got up from my chair and, as I did so, the room started to go round and round while a black cloud threatened to envelop me.

When I came to, I felt Anna's arms around me. The doctor had gone. Nico and Marko stood in the middle of the room, their faces frozen in shock.

"You fainted, *agabimou*, it's the shock," I heard her say. "The doctor said you can see Stepan, after you calm down." See Stepan? Does that mean the news I had just heard was wrong? I prayed that it was so.

"Somebody, please tell me it's not true…" My voice fell to a whisper.

"We've lost him, sister. We can't believe it, either. The doctor said, if Stepan had survived the attack, he would have ended a vegetable. You wouldn't have wanted that, would you?"

"I can't bear it. I want to die, too…"

"You have to be brave, Reya-*mou*. Very brave… for Nathan's sake," said Nico, tears running unashamedly down his cheeks.

"Nathan!" I cried. "How can I tell him that his father is dead?"

"We'll help you. But first, you must go and see Stepan." I nodded. I had to say goodbye to my husband.

He looked so peaceful that I thought he was asleep. He almost had a grin on his face, as if he was going to sit up and start laughing. I touched his hand. It was still warm. I took it in both of mine and held it to my face. Only a few short hours ago, we were having breakfast together, sitting on the balcony and enjoying the 'half view' of the sea. I could still hear the jangle of his car keys, as he picked them up. I could see him, blowing me a kiss and calling out, "I'll see you at lunch, little one." But, there wouldn't be any lunch, not now.

I don't know how long I sat there. There were so many things I wanted to tell him. I kept looking at his smooth, sun-kissed face. I won't cry now. I won't disturb him with empty words, I thought. I won't tell him that I love him. I won't tell him that I'm hurting. I won't tell him that I don't know how I shall cope, without him. I shall only tell him, 'Goodbye, *hokis*, fly to the western fields, for peace everlasting…'

The door opened. I was still holding Stepan's hand. It had gone cold.

Someone took my hand away and led me quietly and softly, out of the room. The door shut behind me. The message got through to me then that I would never see Stepan again. Anna and Nico helped me into the car. On the way home, I noticed Stepan's gold lighter on the dashboard. It was then that the tears came, the grieving process began.

Nothing had prepared me for the void of Stepan's sudden death. When I had come into his orbit, my life had altered. Like my father before him, Stepan had shielded me from the pitfalls of life, and now, like my father, he was suddenly gone. Now, I stood at the mouth of the pit – alone and afraid. Where Stepan had been there was an aching emptiness. The world was an unsafe and precarious place, without him.

Those first terrifying moments, after leaving the hospital, were the beginning of a period of unutterable pain and sorrow. Dressed in compulsory black from head to foot, I turned to stone. I entered an alien planet. I was adrift, in a world I no longer understood. There was a procession of people – my sisters, my brother, friends, children, neighbours – all milling around, talking in whispers, providing coffee, food and sympathy. They all seemed to move in slow motion – like sleep walkers.

The daylight of the following morning seemed to lift the black fog, which had clung to me so tenaciously all of the previous day and most of the night. The phantoms of the night receded. For the time being, the only way I could cope with my loss was to hide my feelings behind a mask of composure. Outwardly, I would try and look calm and accepting of the fate that had befallen me. My duty was to be by Nathan's side, to comfort him in this most painful time of his young life. My thoughts went to Stepan's parents, to his sister Agnes. Only by thinking of others, would I be able to hold myself in one piece. Only at night, in the privacy of my bedroom, would I allow myself to take off the mask and wallow in my sorrow.

No brother could have been more helpful, no sister more comforting. No friend could have been kinder, no neighbour more understanding. Together, they carried me through the painful ordeal of the funeral. It was the worst day of my life. I listened to the priest perform the ritual. I gazed transfixed at the coffin. It was not right that Stepan should be lying in that small space - he who loved the wide open spaces.

Between them, these kind people took care of the thousand and one things that needed to be done. When I gave in to despair – which came in great waves - their support was there, steady and unchanging and reassuring.

I went into the hospital, a young woman, untouched by the world. But I came out as an adult, who had to take up the reins of her own life for the very first time.

PART THREE

Chapter Forty

"I have decided to go back to England, Agnes," I said. "There is nothing to keep me here, now. My first priority is Nathan." Agnes took the news in silence, only nodding her head in acknowledgment. She looked pale. The shadows beneath her eyes had deepened. Her loss was no less than mine. When Nico phoned her to tell her about her brother's sudden death, she was the one who had to break the news to her parents. I could only imagine the level of their grief, I could only imagine what they were going through. Naturally, they wanted to come to the funeral, but the shock had been so devastating that the doctor had put both of them on tranquillisers, so Agnes had come over to Cyprus by herself. Aram had stayed behind to look after the children and keep an eye on the parents.

"What about the flat, the shop, all the paperwork?" She dabbed at her eyes, the tears were never far from the surface.

"To vacate the flat is not a problem. Nico says that one month's notice is all that's required. As for the paperwork - Mr. Ermides, your father's friend and lawyer of many years will deal with all the financial matters. He said I should give power of attorney to Nico. He and Stepan were like brothers."

"I know. That's alright, then. I'm sure Stepan had a life insurance policy. Father would have seen to that."

"I don't know anything about that. Stepan never told me anything about the family's financial situation. I shall leave all that to the lawyer and Nico, and, of course, to your father."

"Good. I don't want you to worry about anything. Aram and I will help you in any way we can. You know that, don't you?" I nodded. How quickly grief was overtaken by the reality of survival. I took a cigarette from the packet on the table and lit it with Stepan's lighter. Just holding it in my hand, seemed to bring him close to me. In a strange way, it comforted me. I offered the pack to Agnes, but she refused.

"I have to go back on Saturday," she continued. "There is so much I have to do, before the children go back to school. I'm worried about Father too. The shock has devastated him. When do you think you'll be ready to leave Cyprus?"

"We should be ready in a week or so. If we can leave by the first of September, I shall have a few days to get Nathan's school uniforms and so on. It will give him time to get used…" I couldn't finish the sentence. Nathan would need time to adjust to a life without his father.

"Shall I make the arrangements, for the memorial service?"

"Can't it wait till I get there?"

"Yes. Of course it can, dear," she said and patted my arm.

With Agnes gone, the flat was even quieter. And at night, after Nathan went to sleep, there was only silence. There was no laughter, no bursting into song, no surprises, no teasing… My life loomed before me like a long, dark tunnel.

"We can't leave Cyprus without saying good-bye to Famagusta," I said to Nathan. He agreed. We took a taxi and told the driver where we wanted to go. There was a house by the border, whose owner had opened his roof to the public. You could go up there and look through binoculars at the ghost town that Famagusta had become, since the invasion. We climbed the stairs, up to the roof. It was only a few yards from the UN Peace Keeping Force. We could see the soldiers, guarding the dividing line. We looked through the binoculars and gazed at the buildings of Famagusta. The heat haze made the town look eerie, almost spectral, like a mirage.

"Our house is somewhere over there, somewhere in that ghost town," I said to Nathan. So was my car, my lovely little Morris. A shiver ran down by back. I prayed that one day, I would come back, to claim what was rightfully Stepan's – and now, rightfully Nathan's.

We were packed and ready. We had said our good-byes, to family and friends. We spent our last night at Anna's house. We all tried to put on a brave face, but it was difficult to hide our emotions.

"I had no trouble selling some of the stuff to a jeweller, Stepan used to know," said Nico, as he handed me a cheque. "This will tide you over, until the lawyer sorts out the rest."

"I can't find the words to thank you," I said. "I don't know what I would have done, without you two…"

"It's nothing. About the car, what do you want me to do? Shall I sell it for you?"

"I don't know, Nico," I said. I didn't want to think about it. It was Stepan's car. For some reason, I didn't want anyone else to have it. It had been his pride and joy, a symbol of his success, and later, it had acted as a spur to start again, after the devastating aftermath of the invasion. Suddenly, I had a thought. "Why don't you keep it, Nico?" I asked. "Stepan would want you to have it. You were the brother he never had."

"I appreciate the gesture, Reya-*mou*, but I can't accept it."

"I don't want to sell it. It would be the final parting from him."

Nico scratched his forehead and thought for a long moment. "In that case, this is what I shall do. I'll store it for him, like I did before and when the time comes, I shall buy it. I know how much this car meant to him."

"No. He would want you to have it now. And, when the 'good times' are here again, you can 'buy' it." It was agreed.

"Are you sure you don't want us to take you to the airport?" asked Anna, who had been silent up to now, dabbing at her eyes every so often.

"Quite sure Anna-*mou*," I said. "We shall take a taxi." I didn't want to prolong the agony of parting with Stepan's best friends. It was the end of an era.

There was one last thing left for me to do, before the taxi came for us. Clutching several bunches of *antaram*, I walked to the cemetery. It was peaceful, in the grounds of this small cemetery. A few visitors were tending the graves of their loved ones. Others were placing flowers. I removed the dead flowers from Stepan's grave and replaced them with the *antaram*. I hoped that he approved of my plan to leave his beloved Cyprus, to start a new life in England. "It's the best thing for Nathan, *hokis*," I whispered. "And as for me, I have to find a way to cope without you."

I sat down on a nearby bench and waited – as though for a sign. I knew it was silly, but I waited just the same. The sun was getting hot. Then a sudden breeze cooled my forehead. It rustled softly, through the cypress trees silhouetted against the sky, the branches nodding, whispering. I had a strange feeling that Stepan had heard me, and that he approved - understood. I got up from the bench and walked over to where Dai's, Grandmother's and my parents' graves were and placed the rest of the flowers on them. This was my final goodbye to them. 'Look after my beloved', I whispered.

Leaving the cemetery, I walked along the seashore one last time. The sea was calm and a bright blue. I breathed in deeply – I had been holding myself in tight all the time I had been in the cemetery. I let out a great sigh of relief. For the first time since Stepan's death, I felt calm and courageous enough to face the world again.

Chapter Forty-one

It was raining when we landed at Heathrow airport. The sky was a sad, grey blanket keeping the sun well hidden from view. There was a lump in my throat, as Nathan pushed the trolley through customs and into the arrivals lounge. "There's Uncle Aram!" he cried. Fortunately, Aram had come on his own to pick us up from Heathrow. He hurried over, as soon as he spotted us. Without a word, he bent down and put his arms around Nathan and held him tight.

"Hello, Aram," was all I could utter without choking. He arms went round my shoulders like a warm blanket, as he whispered, "It's alright, it's alright." My resolve not to cry in front of Nathan held. Aram took hold of the trolley, and we proceeded to walk to where his car was parked.

It was Nathan who broke the silence on the drive home. "Can I see Mike and Nora when we get home, Uncle?" he asked.

"Of course, my boy," Aram replied. "They are waiting for you. I expect you have a lot of catching up to do. Auntie Agnes is taking all three of you to the zoo, tomorrow. It's a special treat, before you go back to school. You'd like that, wouldn't you?"

"Oh yes! I haven't been to the zoo for ages, have I, Mum?"

"That's true, *hokis*. I hope the weather will be nice for you." Nathan settled back in his seat and watched the traffic speed by. His passion was cars like his father. He knew every make and every detail of the current cars in production and on the road.

"Would you like to go to the match on Saturday, Nathan? Arsenal is playing at home."

"I would love to, Uncle. I can wear my new No. 7 shirt." Football was the second of his passions. There was that lump in my throat again. I swallowed. Between them, Aram and Agnes were trying to make Nathan's first weekend back as happy as possible.

My hands shook, as I got out of the car. The front door opened and the children rushed out to meet us. Agnes, *Mayrik* and *Hayrik* followed. I wished there was a way I could have stemmed the flow of tears that ran down my cheeks, the moment I came face to face with Stepan's parents.

We stood on the doorstep, clinging together, my tears mingling with theirs, my pain joining their agony.

The children lost no time in escaping to Nathan's room, where they stayed most of the afternoon and evening. Aram took the suitcases upstairs and then he made his exit. Agnes disappeared into the kitchen to make tea. This was the moment I had dreaded. I was alone with Stepan's parents. They looked at me, with pleading eyes, as if to say, "Is it true? Have we really lost our beloved son?" I looked at them, helplessly. I swallowed. I cleared my throat. I wanted to say something – anything – but my tongue seemed stuck to the roof of my mouth. Somehow, I found my voice.

"That morning was just like any other morning," I began. "We had breakfast on the balcony, as usual. He left for work, happy as a lark and said he would get a takeaway for our lunch – *Kleftiko* – as we all like it so much. But, he never came back…" I sobbed, reliving every moment of that last morning. Once the words came rushing out from my parched throat, there was no stopping them.

"It was such a horrible shock. It happened so quickly. Nico said, one moment he was laughing and joking, and the next he was gone…" It was only then, when I finished talking, that I looked at them, properly. Stepan's parents had both aged, since the last time I saw them. Their world had collapsed around them. Stepan's father had crumbled at his son's death. He had been an upright, dignified man, but now he stooped and looked old. The pain was etched on his face.

"It is so unfair. Fate has upset the natural order. My son should be grieving for me, not the other way round," he said. He slumped into the nearest chair, as though his emotional outburst had exhausted him. Stepan's mother tried to bear her grief with a dignified resignation.

"Don't torture yourself, dear. It was God's will that he should be taken away from us, so soon. It was my boy's destiny to die young…" At last, Agnes came in with the tea tray. We drank the tea in silence.

"You look tired, Reya," she said. "Why don't you go upstairs and have a rest, before dinner. I've asked Sona and Kevork to come. I thought it would be nice to have company tonight. Is that all right with you? If you don't feel up to it…"

"That's fine with me," I said. "I would like to see them. Thank you so much, Agnes. You've thought of everything, you've done everything. I think I will go to my room and lie down for a while, before I start unpacking and sorting things out." Poor Agnes, I thought - she had taken on all the responsibilities of the family. She had put aside her own grief, and comforted her parents in their sorrow. Not only that, she had taken charge of my house, cleaned it from top to bottom, stocked up the fridge and was about to prepare dinner for us all. It was high time I took control of my life. It was now my responsibility, to look after Nathan and Stepan's parents. I owed it to him. I resolved to take up the reins of duty, as of tomorrow.

I steeled myself, to enter my bedroom. It was just as I had left it, a lifetime ago. I looked out of the window at the trees dripping with rain. I looked at the pale watery sky. All I wanted to do was curl up beneath the covers and sleep my way out of my misery. Instead, I started unpacking and putting away my clothes. I wouldn't want to wear these pretty and colourful dresses for a long time, if ever. I would continue to wear black for the period of bereavement, which would last for at least a year.

Suddenly, overcome with tiredness, I sat on the edge of the bed. Waves of panic rose up, from some dark place in my soul. You left me too early Stepan, a voice from my centre cried out. How will I cope? Where do I begin? I feel I'm going to climb a mountain, barefoot.

With a great effort, I controlled my panic. I wiped the tears that were rolling down my cheeks. No more tears, I scolded myself. I must be strong, because Stepan would expect it of me. I continued to unpack.

When I came down the stairs, two hours later, I felt calm and collected. No trace of panic was visible on my face. I walked purposefully into the kitchen and started to help Agnes with the evening meal.

"There's only the salads to make," she said.

"I'll make those and then I'll set the table," I told her. I was prepared for the ordeal of seeing Sona and Kevork. 'This also will pass,' I told myself, as I got down to work with my kitchen knife.

After a tearful reunion with Sona and Kevork, we sat down to dinner. During coffee, I brought up the subject of the memorial service. Forty days after a loved one died, a memorial service was held in church, where the priest read out the name of the newly departed and said a special prayer, so that his spirit would rest in peace. Afterwards, the priest and the congregation were invited to share a lunch - the 'soul food' - in memory of the loved one.

"I would like to hold Stepan's memorial service on Sunday fortnight, if it's alright with you all," I announced. "And the memorial lunch, at the church hall." If they were surprised by my decision, they did not voice it, but agreed that the date was fine.

"I can phone the priest and make the necessary arrangements," said Aram. I accepted his help gratefully.

I never thought for a moment that one day I would return to England, without Stepan, and make it my home. During the weeks that followed the memorial service, life took on a new turn. Nathan was settled and happy in his school, while the rest of us adapted to our new routine, as best we could.

The few friends and acquaintances we had made came to visit, offering words of comfort. Words that were meant to lift our spirits, sounded like platitudes, sometimes. It was cold comfort, to be told that others had gone through the same traumas as myself. Did they think that knowing of other people's loss would bring me relief?

"When a door closes, God opens another one," sounded in my ears, like an empty refrain. I had to find that door, myself, and make my own passage through it. I had to find a niche, into which I could fit. I didn't say anything, of course. I listened to everything they said, and nodded my head at the appropriate moments.

In due course, Stepan's financial affairs were settled. He did have a life insurance policy. One day, a cheque arrived from the family lawyer. *Hayrik* was too wrapped up with his grief, to offer any advice with regard to investing the money. *Mayrik* knew even less than me, about financial matters. After days of thinking about it, I still had no idea about investing the money. In the end, I decided to ask Aram's advice, for he had become the unofficial guardian of the family. I went to see him, in his shop. He was sitting behind his desk in the 'office', doing his accounts. It was a quiet time in the shop.

"Hello, my dear," he said and got up to give me a hug. "It's so nice to see you out and about. You're just in time for coffee."

"Shall I make it?"

"No. You sit down and get warm. I won't be a minute." While he made the coffee, I remembered the times when Stepan helped in the shop, fetching and carrying, making the coffee and washing up. Aram returned with the coffee and a plate of Morning Coffee biscuits. He offered me a cigarette and lit it for me.

"How are you?" He took a sip of his coffee and looked closely at me. "Are you taking care of yourself?"

"I'm alright. I've come for advice. The cheque from Cyprus came last week. I'm not sure what I should do with it." I handed him the cheque. He looked at it. He inhaled deeply, and thought for a moment.

"I think the best thing to do is to invest the money in a building society, which will give you a small annual income. Interest rates are quite good at the moment."

"Are they? I'll do that right away, then."

"The good thing about investing in a building society is that you can withdraw money from it, if you should need it – provided you give them three months' notice."

"I see," I said, paying attention to everything he was saying.

"Now, let's see. At present you have your widow's pension from Cyprus and your father-in-law has his own pension. Are you managing alright on that?"

"Yes," I said, a little too quickly. I didn't want to tell him that I drew money from my bank, to pay the household bills.

"I'll help you, of course…"

"No! You've done more than enough for us - all this time. All that fruit and the vegetables, not to mention other things you bring to us every week…"

"Don't be silly. They are perishable goods - they wouldn't last until the Monday. I share them with the staff. Sometimes Agnes gets fed up with the same things, so she gives them to her next-door neighbour and friend. So there! Anyway, would you like me to come with you, to the building society? I've got the time."

"No, thank you Aram. I must learn to do these things myself, now. I've got to stand on my own two feet - sooner or later. You've been so good to us. I can't begin…"

"I loved him too, you know. Do you think he wouldn't do the same for me? Apart from which, you are part of my family. Promise me you'll come to me, if you need anything."

"I promise," I said.

The next day, I took the cheque to the building society. I had butterflies in my stomach, as I pushed the door open and walked in. I stood at the back of the queue and waited for my turn. I needn't have worried. The transaction took less than half an hour. I signed, where I was asked to sign. I clutched the savings book in my hand and walked out into the cold November morning, flushed but feeling proud of myself, almost euphoric.

This time next year, we would have some extra money! I'm learning fast, I thought, as I crossed the road.

Thus emboldened, I went to my bank and asked for a balance of my account. I couldn't wait for the quarterly statement – I had to know exactly how much there was in the account now, because I had some accounting to do. I gave the woman my account number. After a few minutes, she wrote a figure on a piece of paper and handed it to me. I looked at the figure. There wasn't much money left.

That evening, after everybody had gone to bed I sat at the kitchen table and worked out the outgoing expenses, against the money coming in. The two figures did not balance. I was determined not to touch the money in the building society. That was for Nathan, for his future. I'll have to get a job I said to myself, shaking off the cloak of apathy and despair.

At first, it was the pain of losing Stepan, the 'end' that had dominated my life, but now, suddenly, there was the question of the future – survival. For the first time in my life, I felt the mantle of responsibility on my shoulders. It weighed heavy, but I had to learn to carry it.

Chapter Forty-Two

The next morning, after seeing Nathan off at the bus stop, I walked resolutely to the job centre. It was early, so there was only one other person in the place. I read the notices, to see what jobs were on offer. There were several local jobs for copy-typists and secretaries, but they wanted experienced people. That rules me out, I thought, I haven't worked for years. Disappointed, I started to walk out, when a voice behind me said, "Can I help you?" I turned round, to see who it was. A pleasant looking woman, sitting behind a desk, gestured to me to sit down.

"Are you looking for a job?" she asked.

"Yes, I am. But they want experienced people. I haven't worked for years…"

"I see. Well, you might be in luck. The Adult College is running courses, for people who want to get back to work. What kind of employment were you in?"

"I was a clerk/copy typist. I learnt short-hand at school, but I never used it."

"That's alright. There is a secretarial course that lasts for twenty-five weeks. You might be eligible for it. There is a test you have to sit for. Why don't you go to the college and find out more about it?"

"I will. Thank you very much for your help. I'm so grateful." I was too.

"That's alright. Good luck. I hope you get a place." She smiled. I smiled back at her.

During the bus ride to the college, I went over what the friendly clerk had told me. If I could get a place and did the course, I would surely be able to get a job, and then all my financial problems would be at an end. I would be independent… My spirits lifted. The bus stopped, almost opposite the college. I went to the information desk and enquired about the course. I was given an application form to fill and was told to come back the next day for an interview. I had begun.

The next afternoon, I was nervous as a kitten, but my interview with the course co-ordinator went very well. I handed my application form to her.

She read it through.

"That's fine," she said. "The only thing left is a spelling test. It's nothing fearsome. I don't think you'll have a problem with it." I didn't.

"The course starts in February," she said. "It's a twenty-five week course. You'll get a letter of confirmation, in a week or so. You'll also get a student's pass and have access to the common room and the library."

"Thank you," I said. A whole new world was opening up for me.

"You will be entitled to get financial assistance, while you are on the course. When you get your letter of confirmation, you have to take it to the Department of Social Security and they will tell you how much you are entitled to. It's a weekly payment, to help students with their daily living expenses. You'll also get a free bus or train pass."

"A weekly payment?" I could hardly believe my own ears.

"Yes. They will give you the details. Any other questions?"

"No. Thank you very much." She shook my hand, smiled and walked briskly back to her office. I felt almost hypnotized, by what I had just heard. I sat in the empty interview room, to collect my thoughts and get used to the good fortune that had come my way. "Weekly payment, weekly payment," was ringing in my ears, as I hopped onto the bus, to go home. This meant I would be able to manage, without dipping into the savings account.

I don't know why I started walking in the opposite direction, when I got off the bus. It was probably the sense of achievement, and the desire to share the news of my good fortune with a friend. I didn't want to go home yet. I looked at my watch. It was only eleven thirty. I would go to Sona's house, for a quick coffee, and tell her my exciting news.

Sona was surprised to see me on the doorstep. I hadn't been to visit her, after coming back from Cyprus. "I can't believe my eyes," she shrieked with delight. We went straight into the kitchen and she made the coffee. We had both got into the habit of drinking Nescafe in the mornings, instead of the small cups of Greek coffee. I lit a cigarette and told her all about the extraordinary 'events' of the last two days. For once, Sona was speechless!

"Well done, my girl! So you start the course in February, next year. You are serious about getting a job, then?"

"Yes, I am. It's not that we can't manage, on our income. We do, but I want Nathan to have everything he would have had, if his father had been alive." Pride did not allow me to admit even to Sona – who was as close to me as a sister – that I really had to work, in order to have a reasonably comfortable life.

We finished our coffee and went to Sona's workroom. She took up the dress she had been working on, and started to finish off the hem.

"You are right, of course," she said. "Why do you think I work, all the hours God gives me? So we can buy a house and live a better life. You won't have any problems, finding a good job. Sevan has just been promoted, where she works. If you are conscientious and hard working, you can get on, in this country. You know what, Reya, the longer I live in England, the more I like it."

"I feel the same, but then we are still young, we can adapt more easily. It's the older generation, I feel sorry for. Look at my parents-in-law, especially *Hayrik*. He was doing all right, in the beginning, taking an interest in everything around him. But the light went out of him, the day his son died. Now, nothing seems to matter to him."

"What about Stepan's mother? I've been so busy with work. I haven't been to see her, for at least two weeks. How is she?"

"She is very brave. I admire her stoicism. She gets up at her usual time, every morning and carries out her duties, as calmly and efficiently as ever. Only her eyes betray her pain and loss. As for Agnes, not a day goes by without her dropping in, to see that everything is alright."

"I'm glad she is close by. How is Nathan getting on, in school?"

"He is doing very well. I'm so proud of him. Whenever I feel dispirited, down in the dumps, I look at him and think to myself - 'if he can bear it, then I must too'. He is such a comfort to his grandparents. Look at the time! I better get going."

"Why don't you stay for lunch? I've got left-over stuffed cabbage leaves, in the fridge."

"No thanks, Sona. I'm too excited to think of food."

"Come and see me again, soon."

"I will." I walked on air, all the way home. I stopped by at the bakery and bought five chocolate éclairs, hoping that Agnes would drop in - a treat for the family. When I came within sight of the house, I suddenly felt apprehensive. How would the family react to my impulsive decision to go to college?

I waited until Nathan came home from school, before I broke the news. I made the tea and took the tray into the living room. This was the best time

270

of the day for us. The house came to life, the moment Nathan walked in through the door. In the very same way as when Stepan used to breeze in, filling the house with his presence.

"Anyone for tea and chocolate éclair?" I called out. Just then, the doorbell rang. It was Agnes. Good, I thought - I can get this thing over with, in one go.

"There is something I'd like to tell you all," I said. My statement had the desired effect. Everyone seemed interested. Even *Hayrik* stopped reading and looked up. I told them what I had decided to do, in a calm and matter-of-fact manner. Nathan was the first to react.

"You mean, you will be going to school, Mum?" he laughed. "Wait till I tell my friends!"

"It's only for a few months, *hokis*," I said. "Just so I can improve my office skills." Agnes came to my rescue.

"What a good idea," she said, with enthusiasm. "It will do you good, to go out and about, and to find a job. You can't spend the rest of your life, cooped up in the house. Don't you think so, Mother?" I was expecting a protest, but her mother accepted the idea calmly.

"My dear girl, destiny sometimes forces us to do things that would have been unthinkable, before. Reya must do what she feels she has to. Your father and I will do everything we can, to help her." She was wiser than I thought. Although she never took part in financial matters, she knew why I had to do this, and she understood. We looked at each other, across the room. Unless I was mistaken, the sadness in her brown eyes was tinged with pride.

Chapter Forty-three

They say the first year of bereavement is the most painful and the most difficult to get through. It is so true - the first birthday, the first name day, the first Christmas, the first Easter without Stepan - they were all unimaginably sad and desolate.

The long Christmas break was the most difficult to endure. For Nathan's sake, *Mayrik* and I prepared for it in the usual way, as though nothing was any different from last year. Even *Hayrik* came out of his apathy, and helped Nathan with the Christmas tree. He even wrapped the presents for his grandson and put them under the tree, himself. If it had been left to me, I would gladly have spent it quietly, at home, reliving the memories of other Christmases. But Agnes wouldn't hear of it.

"We have to think of the children," she argued. "Unfortunately, life does go on. We can't bring him back by hiding away from reality – I only wish we could…"

"I know, I know. When I asked Nathan, what he would like for Christmas, do you know what he said?"

"What? What did he say?"

"He said, 'I don't really want anything, Mum, because the only thing I want, I can never have.' He looked at me with sorrowful eyes and burst into tears."

"Oh, dear God. How sad…"

"It was like a knife going through me. I felt so helpless, so inadequate. We held each other and wept together for a long time…"

"The poor boy. I feel angry, too. Why did he have to die so young? I ask myself, over and over again. I can't find an answer…"

Somehow, we got through the festive season, without breaking down emotionally. The New Year came, bringing with it a spell of icy cold weather. And then one day, towards the end of February, buds suddenly appeared on the trees in the garden.

Spring was on the way. And so was I – on my way to college, on my way to a different life. My first day at the adult college was bewildering, to say the least. The morning went in a daze. There were fifteen of us in the class -

fourteen women and one solitary male. Everyone attempted to be friendly, introducing themselves to the person sitting next to them. I was relieved to find that I wasn't the only 'foreigner' in the class. There was a French woman, Colette, married to an Englishman, and a young South African woman, Dina, with English parentage.

At lunchtime we all trouped out of the classroom, to go to the common room for lunch. I stood at the back of the queue, wondering what to have. In the end, I opted for a ham sandwich and a cup of coffee and sat down at the refectory table. One of the women from my class came over, to where I was sitting.

"Hello! I'm Jennifer. Do you mind if I join you?" She sat down opposite me, without waiting for an answer.

"Please do," I said. She was an attractive blonde, with a distinctive voice.

"It was all very exciting, wasn't it?" she said. "I'm sorry, I didn't catch your name."

"My name is Reya, short for Mareyam."

"That's an unusual name. I noticed your accent. Where are you from?"

"I'm Armenian. I don't suppose you've met an Armenian before."

"I haven't, but I've heard of Armenia. Where exactly is it, on the map?"

"It's somewhere between Russia and Turkey."

"Oh! When did you leave Armenia?" I smiled. I was about to confuse her.

"Actually, I was born in Cyprus. My family came to England after the Turkish invasion." Sure enough I had confused her. She looked puzzled and all she said was, "I see." It was so difficult to explain, to someone I had just met, that my ancestors had been driven from Armenia, many years ago and had found themselves in Adana, in Turkey. I remembered, with nostalgia, how I had told Paul my family history. I remembered how fascinated he had been... We finished lunch and I searched in my bag, to find my cigarettes.

"Here, take one of mine," said Jennifer. I looked at her open face and thought of the old Armenian saying which, roughly translated, means, 'If you can't accept a gift gracefully, then you can't give anything back.' I accepted her offer. Jennifer lit my cigarette, and then her own. She left the packet and the lighter on the table. I noticed it was an expensive lighter.

"Thank you, they are the brand I smoke. I know I must give them up, but not just yet." I shrugged my shoulders resignedly and took a puff.

Jennifer and I became good friends. I hadn't had the opportunity or the inclination to make new friends. Agnes and Sona were the only people I interacted with, outside my home. But going to college changed all that. It was like a breath of fresh air that blew away my emotional cobwebs. My school days were nothing like this. There was freedom here, freedom to be oneself, to express personal opinions without being criticized.

Jennifer and I were of the same age. She was separated from her husband and she was in the throes of an acrimonious divorce. She didn't go into the grim details of it. I could see she was still raw with pain and anger, but it seemed as though it was mostly a financial battle. She had two children, a boy of thirteen and a girl of eleven.

"Alan is having the kids this week-end, so I'm free! Would you like to go to the cinema with me on Saturday and then for a pizza, afterwards?" she asked.

"I don't know..." I stammered.

"Bloody hell, Reya!" she said. Jennifer swore a lot, or used colourful language, as my mother would have said. "I'm not asking you to go to a bloody strip club!" The surprise on my face must have been so great that she looked at me in alarm. "I'm sorry, if I shock you with my swearing," she said. "You never swear, do you?"

"I'm not a puritan! I don't swear, because 'bad' language was absolutely forbidden in our house. Only Father indulged in a few colourful swear words, but coming from him they sounded funny, not at all offensive."

"It was alright for him, but not for you?"

"Exactly. It was acceptable for the man of the house, but did not extend to the rest of us. Mother used to say, 'there are plenty of adjectives in every language. We don't need to use swear words to emphasize a point.'"

"Your parents were strict, then?"

"You can say that again! We were not allowed to smoke or go out with boys, either. But, as you can see, some things have changed." I said, lighting a cigarette.

"Why did you look so surprised then, when I asked you to go to the cinema with me?"

"It was just the unexpectedness of it. I have never gone out on my own before..."

"You mean you don't go out, at all?"

"I only go to my sister-in-law's house and a few other close family friends."

"Would they mind if you went out with me? We can ask Clare to come, too. Safety in numbers, eh?"

"I honestly don't know how the 'family' would react to my going out, Jennifer."

"I can't believe this! You mean you have to ask their permission?"

"No, I wouldn't put it like that. I shall ask them, out of courtesy. It's a mark of respect." Jennifer was speechless for a moment.

"Would there be a problem with Nathan?" she asked, determined to get to the bottom of what she obviously saw as a totally bizarre situation.

"No. I'm sure he would want me to go out. He adores his grandparents and they love him just as much. So, the answer to your original question is yes, I would love to go out with you and Clare. I haven't seen a film, in ages. There is a Pizza place on the High Road. We could go there after the film, if you like."

"Thank God, for that!" she said, raising her eyes heavenward. "I take my hat off to you, Reya. I couldn't live with my mother, let alone my in-laws. Can't they live on their own?"

"No. It wouldn't be right or fair. I wouldn't let them anyway. They are very nice people. They were such good friends of my parents. In any case, they have as much right – if not more – to live in that house. After all, it was Stepan's father who created the wealth in the first place."

"So be it!" she said, shaking her head.

"You must come to dinner, one night and meet them. You'll like them. You must bring the children too, of course, so they can meet Nathan."

Once again, I was surprised by *Mayrik's* approval to my going out with my new girl friends. "You must feel free to go out with your friends, sometimes. It's not good for you, to be cooped up in the house, night after night. As it happens, Agnes and Aram are going to a friend's house, so the children are going to spend the night here."

"That will be company for Nathan. Thank you *Nene*," I said. I had got into the habit of calling my mother-in-law *Nene* (Grandmother) and my father in law *Dede*, (Grandfather) like Nathan did. "You'll like Jennifer and Clare. They're coming to pick me up on Saturday. I would like you to meet them."

"That would be very nice my dear. I'm glad you've started to make new friends."

Chapter Forty-four

My first outing as a single woman went off very well. After the film, we went to the Pizza place and shared a bottle of wine between us. We three seemed to find so much to talk about. Clare was the eldest. She had lost her husband ten years before, in a tragic car accident. It had taken her years to get over his death, as they had been very happy together. She had had a few relationships, but none of them had worked out.

"But why did you want to meet somebody, if you were happy with your husband?" I wanted to know.

"It was precisely because I was happily married that I wanted to try and have a second chance at happiness. But so far I haven't met anyone."

"Have you been to any of these 'Singles' clubs, that seem to be the rage at the moment?" asked Jennifer.

"Yes, I have. That's where I met Simon – the last 'relationship' I had."

"What went wrong?" Jennifer and I spoke at the same moment.

"You could say he double-crossed me. He was charm, personified. We went out a few times. We even went on holiday together. He said he was single, never been married. And then I discovered that he was not only married, but he also had two children!"

"What! The bastard! What was he up to?"

"He was cheating on his wife - that's what he was up to. I was his bit on the side. It was a devastating experience, I can tell you."

"How awful!" I said. A cold shiver ran down my spine. How could a man treat a woman in that deceitful way?

"You've given up going to Singles clubs, then," said Jennifer.

"I did for a while. But, there's a new one started up, aptly called *Rendezvous*. I was going to ask you two, if you'd like to go there with me, one night." Jennifer and I looked at each other. I could tell she was interested. I shook my head.

"You can count me out," I said.

"Why, for heaven's sake?" said Jennifer.

"I understand," Clare said. "She is not ready yet. When the time comes…" I shook my head. "To meet a man is the last thing I want.

Anyway, I've finished with all that. I've locked my heart and thrown the key in the deepest ocean."

"You sound like a character in a Victorian novel," Jennifer laughed.

"Nonsense!" said Clare. "You'll find the 'key' when you meet the right man, one day."

"You mean 'the right man' will find the key to her heart and open it!" Jennifer found the statement so funny that she couldn't stop laughing. The people sitting nearest to us turned to look at her and smiled. I wondered if they had overhead everything.

"Well," I said, determined to have the last word, "if you really must know, I was unlucky in love - that's why I have no desire to meet another man."

"Ah! We are beginning to get the picture aren't we, Clare?" Jennifer said, raising her eyebrows and nodding her head in a knowing way. They both leaned closer - eager to listen to my confession of loves lost. They waited. I looked at my watch.

"Please do not look so disappointed, girls," I said, in a dramatic whisper. "You'll have to wait for another day, if you want to hear any sad love stories. It's getting late. Shall we head for home?"

Jennifer went to the new singles club with Clare, the following Saturday night. She phoned me the next day, to tell me all about it. "It was a good night out. We had a few drinks and danced a few dances…"

"You mean strange men asked you to dance!" I teased her.

"They introduced themselves first, silly!" she retorted. "Anyway, it was a friendly atmosphere. The disco was very good, too. We made friends with some of the women there. They said they go there every week, they enjoy it so much."

"Did Clare enjoy herself?"

"She did. Listen, do you want to make some money in the summer?"

"Yes, if I can."

"I found out through a friend of mine that the local council is looking for families, who can put up foreign students in their homes. You've got a spare room, haven't you?"

"I've got a spare room. What's the deal?"

"Well, these foreign students come to England to improve their English. They stay in your house, and you treat them as one of the family."

"How long do they stay?"

"They stay for three weeks, then another lot comes. It's usually from France or Italy. I thought it would be a painless way of making some money until we find jobs."

"That's brilliant Jennifer. I can put up a student. What do I have to do?"

"I'll give you the number to ring. You tell them how many you can put up and then somebody – an assessor, I think - comes to look at the room and have a chat with you. That's all."

"Thanks ever so much. I'll phone them first thing tomorrow."

All too soon, we came to the end of the course. The exams were over. All we had to do now was to write our curriculum vitae. Some of us in the class didn't even know what curriculum vitae meant. We hadn't even heard of a CV. It was, we were told, an outline of one's educational and professional history, which was important for job applications. Writing the CV proved to be more difficult than I imagined. I couldn't remember the exact dates of some of the exams I had passed, it was all so long ago. Fortunately, the tutor rewrote the whole thing for me and it read quite well. I typed it up on the only electric typewriter in the classroom during my lunch break, ready to be sent off with job applications.

According to Mrs. Simmons, one of our tutors, it was more or less guaranteed that everyone in the class, who finished the course and passed the exams, would find a suitable job almost immediately. She advised us to apply for jobs, even before the exam results came out.

I spent the next week scouring the local newspapers for jobs. I also paid several visits to the job centre. In the end, I applied for five jobs. None of them were within walking distance. I made a few decisions. I needed a car, but before that I had to pass a driving test. I remembered the first time Eleni and I took our first driving lesson - the thrill of getting behind the wheel and starting the car, the panic on the day of the test and later, the excitement of passing. But most of all, I remembered the supreme moment when I drove, on my very own, the little Morris Stepan had bought for me. This time, it was necessity, not pleasure that was making me go through the same mixed emotions, once more.

On the last day of college, I walked into the local driving school and booked six lessons, to start the following Monday morning. When I told Agnes what I had done, she beamed at me. "Believe me, when I say it is easier to drive here than in Cyprus."

"Easier? I can't believe that…" I said. I had met her in the high road, by chance and asked her to have tea with me, at the *Copper Kettle*, the little coffee shop we both liked. I lit our cigarettes and took a sip of my tea.

"As long as you're in control of the car and know where you're going, of course," she said. "You shouldn't need too many lessons."

"No. It's the test I'm dreading."

"Well, don't. Just keep your nerves under control. I remember my heart sank, when I saw my examiner. He was a dour man. I ignored him and pretended he wasn't in the car. To my surprise, he smiled, when he told me I had passed the test! Have you any idea what car you want?"

"I don't really know - a Mini, perhaps? They are small cars and very economical, aren't they? I shall need it mainly for work, and also it will be so much easier and quicker to do the shopping. Your father is getting frail. I don't want him carrying home the shopping in all weathers."

"I keep offering to take him to the supermarket, but he refuses. It breaks my heart, to see how fast his health has deteriorated."

"I know. I suppose he wants to be independent for as long as he can."

"Maybe. I'll tell Aram that you're looking for a car. He'll find you something. As you know, once you get used to having your own car, you can't do without it. I wish I could get a job, but Aram won't hear of it. He says I have enough to do, as it is."

"I suppose he doesn't want the routine to change," I smiled. It had been the same with Stepan. He had hated the idea of me going to work. Now I had to.

"You mean he wants his dinner ready, when he comes home from work! Which reminds me, I'd better go home and start preparing the evening meal. Do you want a lift home?" I shook my head. I wanted to walk and clear my head. With that, Agnes got behind the wheel of her car and sped away.

Of the five jobs I had applied for, only one – a pharmaceutical company - asked for an interview. Two replied, saying that I was not suitable and the other two did not reply at all. This deflated my new found confidence, somewhat. Nevertheless, I went for the interview. I had only ever had one other job interview. And that had been in Cyprus, many years ago. One of our tutors told us that interviews were conducted quite differently, now.

We were given tips as to how to dress, what to say, and how to behave with the interviewer. Unfortunately, everything I had been told went clear out of my head, the moment I came face to face with my 'interrogator'- a Mr. Phillips.

To my surprise, Mr. Phillips was more interested in my ethnicity and the political situation in Cyprus, than the job I had applied for. He was a good-looking man in his fifties, with grey eyes and thinning grey hair. The waistcoat of his dark blue suit failed to cover his paunch. We talked for what seemed quite a while and then he said, "And now, I'll take you to the office so you can meet Maureen, my secretary. She'll put you in the picture."

I followed him into a pleasant little office, overlooking the car park. Maureen got out of her chair and came forward to meet me. We shook hands. She explained what my duties would be. I thought she would give me a typing test, but she didn't. I suppose the secretarial course I had attended and the successful test results were credentials enough. They wanted two references, however, and a medical.

"Can you start next week?" Maureen asked. "My last assistant left in rather a hurry." I looked at the empty desk opposite hers and told her that I could.

"Welcome to Sidon Pharmaceutical Co.," she said. "I hope you'll be happy here."

I couldn't believe how painless the interview had been. Nor could I believe that I had actually secured a job and that I would start in just a few days. Have I been lucky? I wondered, or were they just desperate for a typist? On the other hand, an employment agency could have provided them with a temporary typist without any difficulty at all. I stopped wondering about it, when the letter of confirmation arrived the next day.

Everything seemed to click into place after that. The French student was arriving on Saturday. His imminent arrival had galvanized the family into action. I cleaned the house, from top to bottom, while *Nene* cooked a special meal, in the boy's honour. Even *Dede* perked up, offering help and even working in the garden – something he hadn't done for ages. A rare smile replaced the gentle melancholy of his eyes.

The boy's name was Armand. He knew very little English. There were hilarious moments, when he and my in-laws tried to communicate. Nathan came into his own as translator and host. At weekends, he took Armand sightseeing. By the end of the three weeks, Armand's English had improved considerably. We were sad, when he left. The house seemed empty, without the boys' laughter and the extra activities. Three days later, a huge bouquet of pink and white roses arrived from Armand's mother. She telephoned that evening, to thank us for looking after her son so well and making his stay with us so pleasant. I assured her that we had enjoyed having him, just as much.

Nathan and Armand became good friends. They wrote to each other for years, visiting each other's countries numerous times.

Chapter Forty-five

The *Rendezvous* singles club was very crowded and noisy on this Friday evening. Jennifer, Clare and I pushed our way through the throng and found our way to the bar. We joined the queue of people, waiting to be served. Clare elbowed her way to the front and got our drinks. The disco music was so loud that it was difficult to talk. It was even more difficult to find a table, so we stood and sipped our drinks, watching the couples on the dance floor. The arrangement was that we would each do our own thing, but meet at the bar at 11.30.

Jennifer had continued to invite me to the singles club and this time I had agreed. It was to be a kind of celebration. At long last, her divorce had gone through and the bitter financial dispute was finally settled. She looked lovely, tonight. The strained look on her face had gone. She knew where she stood now, so she had begun to rebuild her life. Before long, she was whisked off to the dance floor. I spotted Clare at the bar, talking to a man.

I was left on my own, but I didn't mind. I surveyed the crowds of people, again. Everyone seemed to be having a good time. The air was thick with cigarette smoke. I had given up the habit, some six months previously, without too much difficulty, but now I craved a cigarette badly. I finished my drink and was looking for a table for my empty glass, when a young man approached me and asked me for a dance. Before I had time to answer him, he took the wine glass from my hand and I found myself on the crowded dance floor with him. I'm here now, I thought - I might as well enjoy myself!

Talk was impossible, so we shuffled, pushed and pulled around the dance floor. The man seemed as relieved as I was, when the music stopped.

"My name is Thomas," he said.

"And I'm Reya," I answered. We shook hands.

"Now, let me see if I can guess your country of origin. You are either Italian or French."

"Neither. Guess again."

"I see. Greek?"

"No, but you're getting close."

"Yugoslavian?"

I shook my head and smiled.

"I give up!" He put up his hands in mock surrender. "Put me out of my misery."

"I'm Armenian. I bet you haven't heard of it."

"Yes I have! It's my job to know about ethnic minorities in this country."

"Your job?"

"I work for a periodical. Now that we have established your nationality, how about a glass of wine?"

"Thank you."

"Red or White?"

"Red please. Thanks." Thomas came back, with two glasses of wine. He spotted an empty table and we sat down. He took out his packet of cigarettes and offered me one. I looked at it longingly for a second, but shook my head.

"I gave them up, six months ago," I said. On closer inspection, Thomas didn't look as young as I thought he was.

"I've been trying for years," he said. He shrugged his shoulders and took one from the pack and lit it. "In my case, it is stress that makes me want to smoke. I give it up for a day or two, and then I start again."

"Stress?" I repeated, not quite understanding what he meant.

"The stress of life, today," he explained. "The strain of coming to a place like this, on a Friday evening, in the faint hope of meeting someone interesting to talk to - didn't you find that stressful?" He smiled for the first time and his eyes crinkled, with a mixture good humour and apprehension.

He either has an odd sense of humour or he is sad and lonely, I thought. For some unaccountable reason, I felt sorry for him. You had to be lonely, to come to a singles club. Wasn't that the reason I was here?

"Not really," I said, with feigned indifference. "Maybe, because I only came out for a night out with my girl friends. It's my first time, and probably my last." I was grateful for the dim lights, because I felt a deep blush creeping over my face. I felt so gauche and unsophisticated. What was I doing here, sitting opposite a strange man, in 'a place like this', as he had put it?

"It's my first time, too. After fifteen years of marriage, I found myself a bachelor again." Thomas looked serious now. He lit another cigarette and inhaled it, deeply. Should I believe him? I remembered how Clare had once been duped, by a man who had pretended to be single, but was not.

"Oh… how awful," I said, failing to find the right words to express sympathy for his situation.

"It's alright. I'm getting used to being on my own. What is your story?"

"I lost my husband, some years ago."

"I'm so sorry. How did it happen?"

"Heart attack."

"It's the best way to go, but it leaves the most painful void to the ones left behind."

"Yes, that is so true. I remember watching the sun come up the morning after he died. 'How dare you shine today, sun? When my beloved is dead?' I shouted at it."

"How awful … how painful it must have been."

"The sun does shine and the snow does fall. And you have to go on."

"That's the spirit."

"We think and talk about him, but we have to keep going or the family would collapse."

"You're very brave."

We were silent for a few minutes, and then he said, "Would you like another drink?" My glass was half full. "No thanks," I said. "Two is my limit."

"Do you mind if I have one, myself?" I shook my head.

"Don't go away," he said and went over to the bar. I took a sip of my drink and felt the need for a cigarette. Why, in the name of the Holy Mother, had I bared my soul to a complete stranger? I must have been mad. In the midst of this noisy but happy crowd, I felt terribly lonely. A sudden sharp pain pierced my heart. I yearned for the past. I longed to see cherished faces and places that were now consigned to oblivion.

I had come a long way since the day my world had collapsed around me. I had grown up. I had changed. Here I was - a woman in control of her life, nurturing her independence. A woman, who was not worried in the slightest that she was on her own - up to now that is. What would Stepan think - if he saw me now? Would he be proud of me, for taking these first tortuous steps to rebuild my life? Or would he be shocked and disappointed - to see me in a singles club, dancing and having a drink with a strange man?

I had been so engrossed with my own thoughts that I didn't notice Thomas had rejoined me.

"You were deep in thought, there. Are you alright?" he asked.

"Everything is fine," I said, but the mood of the evening had changed. A dull despair was all I felt. I wanted to get out of this place. The noise was too much to bear.

"I know," he said, pressing his fingers to his temples. "The noise is getting to me too. But, before I go, I would like you to know how much I enjoyed your company. Would you like to come out with me, sometime? For a drink maybe…" he let the sentence hang in the air. I was taken by surprise, at what he said. After all, we hadn't spent more than a couple of hours together. He flicked the ash from his cigarette into the overflowing ashtray and waited for my answer. What vague excuse could I offer up, for not wanting to go out with him?

"I'm so busy these days…" I stammered.

"What is it that takes so much of your time?"

"I have started to write down Armenian recipes, handed down from my mother and grandmother." I said the first thing that came into my mind. "It takes up most of my free time." This wasn't a complete lie. I had begun to collect recipes and I was writing them in a copybook, to replace the one I had left behind.

"I see. How very interesting." Thomas fished into his jacket pocket and took out a card, which he handed to me. "Call me, if you change your mind. I mean - if you find the time. I would love to see you again – in a more convivial atmosphere." He smiled, collected his cigarettes and lighter from the table, shook my hand and left.

Out of curiosity I looked at the card. I could barely read the writing in the dim light. It said Thomas Barker, Features Editor, *The New Wave* and under it a telephone number. I dropped the card in my handbag. I knew I would not ring him.

Time softens the harsh edges of grief, but it gives no remission from it. We learned to live with it. December was the cruellest month for the family. Somehow the 24th of December was more poignant not only because it is Stepan's name day and birthday, as if that were not enough, but also because it is the beginning of the festive season. It is hardest for Stepan's parents. Parents never recover from the loss of a child. So we talked about Stepan and celebrated his day. We had to - otherwise the family would have fallen apart.

But December this year, proved to be a little different from past years.

One morning, a letter arrived from Nico. We kept in touch by phone, but not usually by post. I opened the envelope, to find a letter - written in English – together with a cheque and two return tickets to Cyprus, in the name of Mr. & Mrs. Manoukian. We knew that the new wave of tourism in Cyprus had been good for the economy of the island, but we hadn't realized how good.

Nico wrote that he, like most of the refugees in Larnaca, had done fantastically well in the last couple of years. They had moved into their new house, only two weeks ago. Anna was busy buying new furniture and the boys were delighted with their new, big garden. The cheque was for Stepan's Mercedes – he had bought it, as he had promised he would. Nico finished the letter, by saying that he and Anna would be honoured if 'Mother' and 'Father' would come to Cyprus and stay in their house, as their guests.

When I finished reading the letter, my eyes welled with tears. I placed the letter on the kitchen table and looked at *Nene* and *Dede*. They were crying too. I left them to their own thoughts and got up to make the coffee. When I came back into the living room, they seemed to have recovered.

"I think you should accept Nico's invitation," I said. "They were such good friends…"

"Closer than brothers, even," interrupted *Dede*. "You are right daughter, we would like to go back home. See Cyprus, one more time." All three of us knew the real reason, why they wanted to go back. They wanted to see their son's grave and say their goodbyes. Only then, could they find peace. Only then, could they reconcile to the will of God. Nothing was said, of course. There was no need to put it into words.

Two days after Nico's letter, there was a second surprise. Having spent the entire morning, looking for Christmas presents for the family and failing miserably, I headed for the *Copper Kettle*, for a cup of coffee and a sandwich. I was ready to leave, when I heard a man's voice: "You never phoned me. You must have been so busy that you didn't find the time." I looked up, not knowing who the man was addressing. He looked vaguely familiar. Suddenly, with a jolt, I recognized him. The singles club!

"Oh, hello Thomas," I said, trying to regain my composure. "What are you doing in these parts?"

"I live in Ealing."

"What a coincidence. I live in Ealing too."

"You remembered my name! May I join you?"

"Yes." He sat down and looked at my empty coffee cup. "Would you like another cup of coffee?"

"I would love another cup, thank you."

"So, how have you been keeping? It must be at least six months since we met?"

"Is it as long as that? Did you go to the singles club again?"

"No. I've been very busy at work. What about you?"

"Same here." Just then the waitress came with the coffee. Thomas took out his packet of cigarettes.

"Still not smoking?" he asked.

"Still not smoking," I said feeling very self-satisfied.

"Very commendable," he said and lit a cigarette. He was silent for a moment. "What are you doing over Christmas?"

"We are having a family get-together at our house on Christmas Eve, and on Christmas day we are going to my sister-in-law's. What about you?"

"I am spending Christmas day with John and Ginny – childhood friends – and on Boxing Day, my daughters are coming to stay with me for the rest of the week."

"That's nice. Thank you for the coffee. I have to go. I'm determined to finish my Christmas shopping today." I got up to leave.

"It was nice seeing you again. Maybe we can see each other sometime in the New Year. Can I phone you?"

"Well... I'll give you my office number."

"Maybe we can have lunch together."

"That would be nice. My lunch hour is from one to two o'clock." I wrote my office number on a piece of paper and handed it to him. We came out of the café, shook hands, wished each other a happy Christmas and New Year and went our separate ways.

I convinced myself that it was all right, to give Thomas my office number. It was such a surprise, to meet him by chance like that and discover that he lived in my neighbourhood. He seemed a nice enough man. Nor would I mind having a snack with him, once in a while. I saw the 'girls' less and less, these days. Clare had met the love of her life, at last, and he had moved in with her. As for Jennifer, she too had a boyfriend now, and she naturally wanted to spend her evenings with him. Occasionally, the three of us went out to the cinema or for a pizza, but that was all.

Having Thomas as a friend would be all right, but I didn't want any complications in my life – no emotional entanglements. Being on my own didn't bother me. There was nothing I liked more, than going home after a day at work and spending the evening with Nathan and the family. After dinner, I liked to watch television. It was a pleasant escape from the reality of life. Since childhood, I had found it difficult to get off to sleep. Now, I was an insomniac. While the world slept, I read and read. I took up the writing of my recipes in earnest. I wrote them neatly in a copybook, adding little notes to some of the recipes, explaining what some of the ingredients were, and so on. I didn't want the next generation of Armenians to forget their traditional style and manner of cooking. I'd had a long apprenticeship, watching and learning from my own mother, and then from my mother-in-law, before finally taking control of my own kitchen. I was now confident enough to call myself a reasonably good cook.

I went back to my Christmas shopping, with renewed enthusiasm. In no time at all, I finished all my purchases and headed for home. As I got behind the wheel of my car, a thought crossed my mind. This month was the last payment on the car. Aram had come to my aid, once again. As soon as Agnes told him that I wanted to buy a car, he had come up with a lovely Mini Clubman. It was black, a year old and in pristine condition. What's more, he had loaned me the money for it and I had been paying him back, each month.

The cheque from Nico was safely in the building society. That money was for Nathan's future, not to be spent. My salary was not much, but it was adequate. I was so careful with money, now – making use of 'special offers' in the supermarket and filling up the freezer. And I also waited for the sales, in order to buy clothes and household necessities. Who would have thought, that I – a spendthrift all my life – would turn into a penny-pincher? In fact, I was verging on mean. But my efforts had paid off. The future did not look as bleak as it had a few years ago. Please God, I prayed - let this year be the end of our dark days. Let the cluster of recent 'happenings' be a sign, for happier times to come. I welcomed the New Year, like I would welcome the sun on my face on a cold winter day.

Chapter Forty-six

I was alone in the house. My parents-in-law were in Cyprus, and Nathan was spending the night with his cousins, in Agnes's house. It had been strange at first, to come home in the evenings and not be assailed by the wonderful aroma of *Nene's* cooking. I had spoken to her on the phone, a few times. They were being looked after splendidly, by Nico and Anna. It seemed a good opportunity to invite Jennifer and Clare, with their respective boyfriends, to an Armenian dinner. Having been to their homes several times, I thought it was the right time to reciprocate. I had also invited Thomas, so he could meet my friends. He had phoned me several times, since our surprise meeting and had taken me to lunch a couple of times. But now, I was having second thoughts about it.

I spent the afternoon cooking. I made *Bourek* (water dipped pastry with cheese filling), *Sempoug* (Baked aubergine with lamb), *Derev* (stuffed vine leaves) and *Kofte* (cumin flavoured lamb sausages with potatoes). Then, it was just the usual salads and relishes. Unfortunately, I didn't have *Raki* – the anise drink – that would have been ideal with the food. We would have to drink wine, instead. For dessert, I made my own quick and easy version of *Paklava* - just as good as the authentic recipe. A choice of black coffee or cinnamon tea would complete the meal.

Thomas was the first to arrive. He had a bottle of wine in one hand and flowers in the other. He stepped into the hall and kissed me on the cheek.

"For the gracious hostess," he smiled and handed me the bouquet of pink and white carnations.

Oh my God! I thought. What if my family should walk in, right now and see me 'entertaining' a strange man! They would surely think - while the in-laws are away, the widow plays. A merry widow I was not, but at this moment, that is how it would have looked.

"Would you like me to open the bottle now?"

"Yes, thank you," I said. "I'll get the corkscrew." I went into the kitchen and he followed me.

"Something smells good," he said, sniffing appreciatively. The cooking smells pervaded the kitchen, if not the whole house. "Need any help?" He handed me a glass of wine.

"No thanks, everything is under control. The good thing about Armenian cooking is that almost everything can be prepared beforehand. There isn't any last minute 'drama' in the kitchen! I hope everybody will enjoy it."

"I'm sure they will. *I* certainly will, I can assure you." Just then the doorbell rang.

After the flurry of introductions, we sat down on the comfortable sofas and sipped our pre-dinner drinks and helped ourselves to the dishes of pistachio nuts, crisps and cheese sticks, I had arranged on the coffee table. Next to the ashtrays and lighters on the two small occasional tables, were two packets of cigarettes – to complete the time honoured custom of Armenian hospitality.

When everyone was seated at the table, I explained a few things to them. "We Armenians take our meals in the traditional way, wherever we live. That is to say, we place all the prepared dishes for the meal on the table – as you can see - at the one time, so that everyone can have as much or as little of what they like."

"What a good idea," said Thomas.

"There is no standing on ceremony, either. Please try everything. And help yourselves to whatever you liked most. *Bon apetit.*" I relaxed. Everyone seemed to be enjoying the food, except Clare's boyfriend Simon. He must be a "meat and two vegetables" man, I thought. He had a small piece of the *Bourek* and a small helping of the *Kofte*.

"These stuffed vine leaves are delicious, so tender," said Thomas, helping himself to a few more of them. "Where can you buy them?"

"You can buy them in Greek shops. But, we have our own vine, in the garden," I told him. "We pick the leaves in the summer, when they are at their freshest and then store them, so they can be enjoyed all the year round."

We lingered over the meal. When everyone said they had enough, I got up to clear the table for dessert and coffee. Jennifer helped me carry the plates to the kitchen.

"I like your Thomas! How are you getting on with him?" she asked, as soon as we were out of earshot. "Do you like him? He seems to be taken with you…"

before you get carried away, he's not *my* Thomas. I like him, but ᴀᴜy as a friend. This is the first time he's been to my house."

"Well, we shall see," she whispered, with a knowing look in her eyes. I quickly transferred the leftover food – what little there was – onto smaller plates, covered them with foil and put them in the fridge. Food was never wasted in an Armenian kitchen. Nathan liked 'leftovers', anyway. He would have them on a tray in the living room, while he watched television. It was long after midnight, when the party broke up. I knew sleep would not come any easier, this evening. I spent the next two hours pottering around downstairs - washing up, cleaning and tidying, until everything was back to normality.

Feeling delicate from the night before, I stayed in bed far longer than I usually did, slipping in and out of sleep. The shrill sound of the telephone penetrated into my dream and woke me up. Reaching over, I picked up the phone on my bedside table. It was Thomas.

"Good morning, or is it good afternoon," he said. He sounded cheerful. "Thank you, for last night. Thank you, for introducing me to new and exotic gastronomic delights!"

"I'm glad you enjoyed yourself," I said, feeling fuzzy from my late morning doze.

"You told me - a while back - that you write your recipes down, in a copybook. Have you finished writing them all?"

"I'm in the process of writing down the recipes for cakes and desserts, preserves and so on. Why do you ask?"

"Well… I'm thinking that your recipes should be published. Judging by the food last night, those recipes shouldn't be hiding in your kitchen drawer. They should be introduced to the public at large, not just to discerning gourmets like myself!"

"You are joking, aren't you? Who would want to publish them anyway?"

"We'll worry about that, when the time comes. First, you must finish writing them. I've been thinking - maybe you can add little anecdotes, or give some idea of the special occasions when certain dishes would be served - to give it an authentic feel…"

"Wait a minute! I don't think I can manage to write anecdotes in English. You forget that English is not my mother tongue."

"And you forget that I'm a journalist. You write it and I'll edit it for you."

"I'll think about it," I said.

"Can you bring your recipe book with you, on Thursday? I would like to take a look at it."

"Thursday?"

"You haven't forgotten lunch on Thursday, have you?"

"No, of course not. I'll see you then." I put down the phone and sat on the edge of my bed.

It sounded such a preposterous idea and yet, my interest was aroused. Maybe, it was that streak of independence that had grown in me, since Stepan's death, or the thought of becoming involved in something challenging that caught my imagination. Whatever it was, it made me think and I decided to have a go at it.

Thomas was waiting for me when I got to the *Copper Kettle*. I put my copybook on the table, while he ordered the food.

"What neat handwriting," he said. He leafed through the pages, pausing now and then, to look more closely at a particular recipe. "Are all these recipes tried and tested?"

"Yes, they are."

"Good. Try to write a few captions, a brief explanation or a comment beside each recipe. Do you understand what I mean?"

"I think so. You mean write about certain foods that we have in Lent, or the origin of this or that tradition…"

"That's the idea! Don't worry about the style, or anything like that. I know you can do it."

"I'll try," I said. My only experience of writing had been letters to my pen friends and later, my long letters to Paul. Just then our toasted sandwiches and coffee arrived. We ate in silence for a few minutes.

"How is everything with you?" I asked.

"Not too bad at the moment. I see the girls every weekend. And Frances is a lot more friendly towards me. She even invited me to Sunday dinner. We had a wonderful time. It brought back memories of the past."

"I'm so glad for you Thomas. I won't be surprised if you get back together one of these days."

"It's doubtful, but who knows, eh?" He shrugged his shoulders and ground out his cigarette in the ashtray.

In the days, weeks and months that followed, my spare time was taken up with the 'book'. First, I finished writing the recipes. Then, I began to write

- tried to write - the introduction to the book. This was to be a short but comprehensive history of communities in the Armenian Diaspora. I looked upon it as a project, an opportunity to explain why Armenian people were spread so far and wide, and how Armenian exiles had managed to adapt to the customs and traditions of their adopted countries, while holding steadfastly to their own culture and their own cuisine. It was difficult, at first, to put my thoughts down on paper in English, but with practice and reams of wasted paper, it began to make some sense. In time, it became an obsession. I wrote and rewrote a sentence a dozen times or more, until I was satisfied with it. I couldn't wait for my parents-in-law to come back from Cyprus, so that I could ask them to fill in the gaps.

My enthusiasm for the 'book' gradually rubbed off on them. No sooner had they unpacked their suitcases, than I began to bombard them with questions. They exchanged significant glances at first, wondering what had come over me. Their holiday in Cyprus had worked wonders. They both looked healthy. The Cyprus sun had worked its magic, bringing colour back into their cheeks and spark into their eyes. Visiting their son's grave and saying a proper farewell had at last brought serenity into their souls. They were finally reconciled to Stepan's death and at peace with God.

Dede proved to have a thorough knowledge of Armenian history and his help was indispensable. It made my task so much easier. While *Nene* explained to me the art of making the perfect dough, the sense of achievement of making jams and preserves. I remembered the summers of my childhood, when Mother spent hours and hours preparing for the winter. The food store had to be replenished. Fruit was plentiful in the summer and every effort was made to make the most of this bounty. Walnuts, apricots, cherries, peaches, and apples were all preserved. The glass jars took pride of place in Mother's pantry.

"I miss the custom we had in Cyprus, of offering *Anoush* (preserved fruit) to visitors, don't you, *Nene*?" I said, one Saturday morning over coffee.

"I do, daughter," she replied. "My favourite is the walnut."

"I loved them all, but my favourite is the apricot. It has that tart taste, which balances the sweetness of the syrup." We both smiled, remembering the custom. The *Anoush* was served in a small glass or silver dish, with a silver spoon or fork. It was accompanied by a glass of iced water – very necessary - as it is very sweet.

"Foreign visitors were always intrigued, when they were offered *Anoush*, weren't they?"

"Yes. I remember the English neighbours, we had once - the bewildered expression on their faces - when Agnes brought in the tray and offered the *Anoush* to them!"

"Did they like it, though?"

"They did. They said it was very refreshing."

Another fruit, which is plentiful in Cyprus, is the watermelon. This has a double usefulness. The white part of the watermelon (the pith) is used to make preserves, and the seeds are washed, boiled in salted water, and then dried in the sun. It is a pleasant pastime, to crack the seeds open and eat the kernels – salty but delicious!

"It was all work for women in the summer months, wasn't it?"

"You can say that again. We had to make the tomato puree. It was a lot of work, but the result was beautiful. It was so concentrated that you only needed half a teaspoon, to get that lovely red colour. The tomato puree we use nowadays, from tins and jars, is nothing compared to home-made…"

"My generation is lucky. We buy most things already prepared."

"Yes, but they are not the same. I remember cracking green olives, with my wooden mallet. I had to soak them in water, for a week – changing the water every day of course – to get rid of the bitter taste. Then they had to be stored in salted water, in huge jars."

"The way I've always liked olives is when they are marinated in lemon juice and olive oil, with cracked coriander seeds and a clove of garlic. To dip your bread in the dressing – mouth watering!"

"Yes. Then, there was the bulk buying of the essentials… I could go on and on. I have so much time on my hands, now."

"Time on your hands! With all the sewing and knitting you do? It's time you took things easy, *Nene*."

"Those things are relaxation, daughter, not work." She smiled and picked up her knitting.

Even Nathan became interested in the project. Every evening, after dinner he joined the rest of us, in the ritual of 'questions' and 'answers'. There were no answers to some of my questions, though.

"Why is it that Armenians living in Lebanon use olive oil in bulgur salad and not tahini, like we do?" I asked *Nene*, one time. She shook her head. "I don't honestly know," she said. "Maybe, they couldn't get tahini, when they first went to Lebanon and so they substituted olive oil. It's the same with *Patcha* soup and salads. We use lemons, but Armenians in other countries use vinegar."

"Lemons are so plentiful in Cyprus that maybe Cypriot Armenians preferred it," suggested *Dede*.

"Well, I prefer lemons to vinegar," said Nathan.

"We know that! Heaven help us, if we forget to put a dish of sliced lemons on the dinner table!" I said, raising my eyebrows and shaking my head from side to side. He laughed his infectious laugh, so like his father's that, for a split second, I felt Stepan's presence in the room. I shivered and my eyes scanned the room involuntarily, and in vain.

"It's the same when I make *Harissa*," continued *Nene*. "I can't get *yarma* (a special wheat) here, so I use barley instead. To adapt is to survive."

At last we finished the book. I say 'we' because, without the help of my family, I could never have done it. I gave a huge sigh of relief, when I finally felt confident enough to hand it over to Thomas. But I also felt a great sense of achievement.

Chapter Forty-seven

There was something that worried me, something that persistently disturbed my conscious. I was living a double life again, as I had done before my marriage, when I was seeing Paul. Keeping things from my family and even from Nathan. I hated lying to them. I hated the fact that I couldn't tell them I had gone to a singles club and met someone, who had become a good friend and confidant. I could never tell them that I had given a dinner party – secretly – while they were in Cyprus. Sometimes, I felt like a prisoner, locked in a situation I couldn't possibly escape from.

"I don't know why you torment yourself, Reya," Clare said. "Tell them! It's not as if you're doing anything wrong, for heaven's sake! You and Thomas are two lonely souls, who have found solace in each other." She couldn't keep the exasperation out of her voice.

"I know. We are just friends, nothing more. Thomas would dearly love to get back with his wife, one day. But, I still can't tell anyone in the family."

"I need another drink. Do you want a refill?"

"No, thanks." Clare came back with her drink and sat down. The *White Horse* pub was not busy tonight, as it was mid-week. This pub was where we three girls met. Thomas joined us, sometimes. We met regularly here, to catch up with each other's news.

Just then, Jennifer walked in. She looked tired. She flopped on the seat and shut her eyes for a moment.

"What's up?" Clare and I chorused.

"Oh I don't know. I'm fed up with my job. My car wouldn't start this morning. I'm just fed up with everything."

"Is it alright, now?"

"It will be tomorrow, when I pay the bill – two hundred and seven pounds."

"These things catch you when you least expect them. I'll get you a drink." Clare got up and went over to the bar.

"How is the family?"

"Not too bad. The trip to Cyprus has been good for them. I was telling

Clare, just before you came in, how guilty I feel about keeping secrets from them…"

"This will make you feel better, Jennifer," said Clare. She put the glass of white wine on the table, in front of her. Jennifer took a sip of her wine and lit a cigarette. Her mood brightened instantly.

"Thanks, Clare - enough about my troubles. Reya, you should tell your family about Thomas, you know. I'm sure they will understand. They must know that platonic friendships, such as yours, do exist!"

"That's exactly what I told her."

"I'm not sure about that. But anyway, you can imagine how I felt when *Dede* suggested that there were several Armenian publishers in Beirut who might be interested in the book. I was so shocked that I was lost for words. I couldn't tell him that it was Thomas's idea to write the book, in the first place, and that *he* was helping me with the publication of it."

"How could you, when nobody knows of his existence."

"I remembered Father's words 'beware of lying because one lie leads to another'."

"What did you tell him, then?"

"I said that I knew someone at work, who had a friend who might be able to help. If he was disappointed in my response, he didn't show it."

"Did he say anything?"

"All he said was, 'You never know, daughter,' and we left it at that."

The White Horse is always busy on a Friday night and this Friday was no exception. It was only six o'clock but the place was full of people, eager to start the weekend on the right note. This pub had proved to be such a convenient place for me to meet my friends, as it was on my way home from work. I spotted Thomas waiting for me, at our usual corner table.

"There you are," he said, getting up from his chair, to greet me. "The usual?" he asked. I nodded. He had a sour look on his face, as though he had just bitten into something very sharp. It was unusual for him to look so grumpy.

"What's the matter?" I asked, before I took a sip of my drink. He lit a cigarette.

"It's Sophie. Apparently, she didn't go home last night. She had an almighty row with her mum and walked out of the house, in tears." He sighed and absentmindedly fidgeted with his cigarette lighter.

"What was the row about?"

"It seems that Frances doesn't like Sophie's new boyfriend, so he is not allowed to stay the night. I went over to the house, as soon as she phoned me. Fortunately five minutes after I got there, Sophie turned up, full of remorse…"

"Everything is O.K. then. Why do you still look so low, so fed up?"

"I don't know. Something like this brings all the pain and frustration back." He was quiet for a moment. I felt so sorry for him. I had seen pictures of his wife and daughters, in their lovely home. It was plain to see, how much he still cared for them. Surely, I thought, family upsets like this will bring Thomas and his wife back together again.

"Enough about my domestic problems," he said. "How have you been? It must be about three weeks, since I saw you last."

"It must be. I was going to give you the finished…"

"You've finished the book! Well done. Have you got it with you?"

"Yes. But maybe, this is not the right time, as you've got other matters to worry about."

"Nonsense. It will take my mind off things. Can I have a look at it?"

"Only if you're sure…" I reached down into my bag and took the manuscript out. He read the introduction. I waited anxiously for his comments.

"I like the title - *An Armenian Kitchen*. We'll keep it," he said. And so we did.

An Armenian Kitchen was published some eighteen months later. But it didn't gain much of an audience, or much in the way of commercial reward. At first, it was displayed quite prominently on the shelves of bookshops. But, as the weeks went on, it was put further and further to the margins, until after a few months, it disappeared off the shelves without trace. I was sad that so few copies had sold. Months of hard work have come to nothing, I thought. But my family disagreed.

"You must put it down to experience, daughter," *Dede* told me. "An interesting project."

"I think it's much more than that," said *Nene*. "It's a legacy that future generations of Armenians will be thankful for and appreciate. Your work was not wasted at all, daughter."

"Look at it this way, Mum. The world is not yet ready for our glorious food! For once, the Armenians are ahead of the times!" Nathan's cheeky grin, so like his father's, did the most to cheer my spirits. The rest of the family and close friends made similar comments. They were delighted with their copies of the book.

Thomas was more disappointed than I was. "All your time and effort wasted," he said, time and time again, passing his hand over his face and shaking his head, as though it were his fault that people were not interested in Armenian cooking. "Glossy pictures would have helped, of course..."

"You mean like Delia Smith's books?" I smiled, trying to make light of the whole thing.

"Why not? Your recipes are as good as anybody's. But Mark Saunders had such a tight budget to work with, that pictures were out of the question. I wish I could have done something..."

"Don't take it so seriously," I pleaded, even though deeply touched by his belief in me. "I enjoyed the time I spent on it. It gave me something to do. I have so much time on my hands now that I'm thinking of going to evening school in September."

"Good for you. But I'm still disappointed that your exotic recipe book isn't the big success it ought to be."

The next day I was at lunch, when the telephone call came. As soon as I came back, Maureen told me that there was a message for me to ring Agnes, and she gave me a number to ring. It was an unfamiliar number. My heart stopped. Agnes never phoned me at the office, unless it was absolutely necessary.

"It's Father," she said. I could tell from her voice that something was very wrong. "He's had a stroke. He was taken to St. Mary's hospital. Mother and I are waiting to see the doctor..." her voice trailed off.

"Is it serious?" I asked in alarm.

"I don't really know, but at his age... I thought I'd better let you know."

"Of course. I'll meet you at the hospital, as soon as I can." My hands were shaking, as I put the phone down. I took a moment to collect my thoughts, before I looked at Maureen across the office.

"I couldn't help overhearing," she said. "Give me a moment, to make myself a coffee and then you can go."

"But it's your lunch hour. I'll wait..."

"That's alright. You go now."

"Thank you, Maureen. I'll pick up Nathan on the way."

"Drive carefully," she called after me, as I picked up my handbag and rushed out of the office.

They were waiting for us, when we walked through to the reception area. Agnes was staring into space and *Nene* was dabbing at her eyes with a handkerchief.

"Oh *Nene*!" cried Nathan, rushing to hug his grandmother. "I can't believe what I've heard. My *Dede* can't have had a stroke! He was as healthy as anything, this morning. Just before I left for school, he was talking about our game of backgammon. And he was joking - 'Be warned,' - he said - I won't let you win, this time!' "

"I know *hokis*, I heard him too. It happened so suddenly… Let's hope and pray that God will be merciful."

"Any news yet?" I asked Agnes.

"He is still unconscious. The doctor said a stroke is often followed by paralysis or an embolism. I don't exactly know what that is, even though he tried to explain it to me."

Dede never regained consciousness. The family was at his bedside, when he slipped away three days later. Had he recovered he would have been paralysed and that would surely have been worse than death for an active man like him. We comforted ourselves that God had been merciful. *Dede's* death was another link in the chain of events since 1974 that further reduced the size and force of the family. No sooner, it seemed, did we get over one loss, than another descended.

After *Dede's* funeral, *Nene* went downhill fast, both physically and emotionally. To make matters worse, one winter morning, she slipped and fell on the icy ground and broke her right arm.

"It's as if Mother has given up," mourned Agnes.

"Breaking her arm was probably the last straw," I said. "She can't bear being inactive."

"Aram and I are very worried about Mother. We've thought long and hard about her fragile state of health and we're agreed – with your approval of course – that she should come and live with us…"

"Oh Agnes!" I cried. "Is it wise to uproot her - especially at her age? This house has such memories for her. She belongs in this house. I shall look after her."

"I don't doubt that for a moment, my love. We did think about the upset to her routine, but then we thought, maybe she needs to get away from her memories. Anyhow, she certainly does need looking after and I've got the time, whereas you have your job to think of. And now Nathan is going to university, there's even less reason for you to be tied to the house." She shrugged her shoulders, indicating that there was no alternative, anyway.

She was right of course. But that didn't stop me feeling sad and helpless at the same time. I felt that I was letting Stepan down, by not being able to look after his beloved mother in her hour of need. My eyes filled with tears.

"Don't feel sad, Reya. I know you feel it is your duty to look after Mother, but it is my duty also – after all, I am her child too." There was no answer to that.

I could hardly believe that I was the mother of a nineteen year old. Nathan had grown into a tall, good looking young man, with his father's dark eyes and cheeky grin. He was wearing the uniform of the college student – jeans and t-shirt – and soon he would be leaving, to spend three years at Southampton University. I could hardly bear the thought of it. I felt as though the whole family was deserting me.

Agnes and Aram had decided that Nathan should have a proper send-off. We would drive to Southampton, to the halls of residence, where Agnes and I would help him unpack his staff and make sure that he had everything he needed. Nathan and I were ready, when they came to pick us up. We settled ourselves in the back seat of Aram's luxurious car, beside *Nene*. We stopped at a hotel on the outskirts of the town and had a sumptuous lunch.

"I expect this will be my last proper meal, until I come home at Christmas," said Nathan, rubbing his stomach appreciatively.

"Oh, my poor boy!" lamented *Nene*. "Won't they feed you properly, at university?"

"I'm joking, my darling *Nene*. There's a very nice cafeteria and judging by the boxes of food Uncle Aram has got in the boot of the car, I won't go hungry!"

Nene was visibly relieved. She couldn't have a grandson of hers go hungry!

Aram went to inspect the grounds of the university, while the rest of us crowded into Nathan's room, to unpack his stuff. I put away his clothes and Agnes stored the tins of food in the tiny cupboard and helped me make the bed. Nathan arranged his books and magazines on the small table, where he would do his work.

"I'll hang my pictures later," he said. He was clearly excited and ready to start his new life. It was time to leave.

The car park was crowded with parents, either departing or arriving - mothers fussing around their 'children', kissing them goodbye, fathers giving stiff hugs, trying to hide their feelings. I felt my throat tighten, as the time came to say goodbye to my own 'child'. I wished Stepan could have been there, to see him. I swallowed hard and put a brave smile on my face. I managed to keep it there, until I had got into Aram's car and waved a last goodbye through the window.

Chapter Forty-eight

Life settled into a routine once more, an unutterably lonely routine this time. I learned to cope with it. I got used to coming home to a dark and empty house every evening, after work. I found comfort in having my dinner on a tray, in front of the television. It was comforting to watch the 'soaps' and escape to another world. But the loneliness of the soul was something else. I lived in an emotional wilderness that had no bounds and no horizons. If I got lost here, I would never find my way back again. There was the occasional respite from my own company. Jennifer sometimes called, to invite me to go to the cinema with her, or even to the theatre. And Thomas would ask me to have a drink with him, once in a while, on a Friday evening after work. I always accepted these invitations, and grew to value my new friends even more.

I was expected to spend Sundays with the family. Agnes and Aram insisted on it. I went to church with them and stayed to Sunday lunch. I was grateful for their support and concern, but sometimes I felt suffocated by their well-intentioned protectiveness. Had I become an object of pity? I lived alone, but I wasn't allowed to be independent. There it was again – I was living a lie. I did have a life of my own, during the week – but I couldn't admit to it. Sometimes, I got so frustrated, that I felt like abandoning all responsibilities, absolving myself of all tasks, and taking flight. But where could I go? And what would I do, when I got there? I came to dread the end of the week. Another Friday, another weekend, another lie.

The phone rang the moment I put my key in the door. I had spent a pleasant evening with Thomas, at the pub. It was Agnes.

"Where have you been? I've been phoning you all evening," she said, with obvious concern. I looked at my watch. It was only eight o'clock.

"I'm sorry," I said. "I was having a drink with the girls. You know, some Fridays, I meet Jennifer and Clare. We had a bite to eat, afterwards. That's why I'm late." Lying came so easily to me, now. So far, I had kept my 'secrets' well hidden from the family and close friends and even from

Nathan. One of these days, I would be found out…

"I see. Anyway, I'm phoning to remind you about tomorrow night. Can you come a bit early and help me…?"

"Of course I will," I interrupted. "I made the cake last night. Tomorrow I'll make the *bourek*. Shall I come about five?"

"Five o'clock is fine. See you then." She rang off, and I gave a sigh of relief. I took off my coat, made a cup of tea and flopped into an armchair. I didn't really like going to family parties, any more. They asked me the same old questions and I gave them the same answers. But tomorrow night's party was different. It was *Nene's* birthday and the whole family and all our friends would be there - everyone except Nathan, that is. He had phoned to say that he had so much work to do, that he wouldn't be able to come. Typical of the young, I thought, thinking only of themselves. It wouldn't have been a great hardship, for him to make the effort - after all, he had his own car now. I would never forget the joy on his face, when I told him that he would find his Christmas present in the garage. I don't know which was greater, the surprise or the happiness. He enveloped me in his arms and we danced around the car, in joyous abandon. Yes, he could have made the effort - if only to please his *Nene*.

"But never mind," I said aloud – I was definitely spending too much time on my own, these days. "*C'est la vie*, I have learned to take disappointments like these, in my stride."

The next morning, I was drinking my second cup of tea, when I heard the postman. I picked up the bundle of envelopes and looked at them disinterestedly. It was the usual assortment of bills, circulars and 'special offers'. The telephone bill was high this quarter, I noticed. But this did not surprise me, what with Nathan's collect calls from university. There was a postcard from Clare - she was enjoying her holiday in Majorca with her recently widowed mother. There was a letter, as well. I couldn't tell whose handwriting it was, even though it looked vaguely familiar. I looked at it more closely and my heart started to beat furiously. The handwriting was very familiar now. I tore the letter open and my eyes searched for the name at the end of the single sheet. It couldn't be - but it was! The signature was Paul's. How on earth had he found me? Any why, after such a long time?

My hands were shaking, as I sat on the kitchen chair and started to read Paul's letter. He wrote that he had come across my cookery book by chance. He felt compelled to get in touch with me. He hoped I didn't mind. He so wanted us to meet, 'so much to say, so much to catch up on'. He was free to meet me, at a time and place that suited me. He hoped I would. His address was printed at the top of the page - he still lived in Surrey.

It was hard to believe that he had found me, after all these years. I hadn't thought of Paul in such a long time. I had been too busy, rebuilding my life after Stepan. Too burdened with responsibilities, to journey back into the past. My heart sang, at the thought of seeing him again, but would I recognize him? Even his features had become blurred in the mists of time. Several times during the day, I took out Paul's letter from the pocket of my apron and reread it, mainly to reassure myself that I wasn't dreaming, for I already knew the contents by heart. But why has he written to me after all this time, I asked myself, a dozen times. Why did he want to meet me? What was the point? I read it one more time, kissed it and put it under my pillow, just like I used to, so that I could read it again, first thing in the morning.

By four o'clock, I was ready for the party. House tidy, *bourek* made, *Nene's* present – a grey silk scarf – wrapped and labelled. I put on my coat and looked at myself in the hall mirror. I hoped no one would notice the sparkle in my eyes.

Nene's birthday party was in full swing. She looked very nice, in her new charcoal grey dress. Her hair was completely silver now, but it was still thick and shiny as ever.

"I can't get used to birthday celebrations, at my age," she said shyly, as she opened her presents. The beautifully wrapped gifts were many and varied: chocolates, sweets, perfumed toiletries, scarves, and items of clothing from her favourite store – Marks and Spencer. *Nene* loved the silk scarf I gave her and she put it round her neck, straightaway. It went very well with her dress.

I walked on air all evening, trying to contain my excitement. I smiled and chatted to everyone, emptied ashtrays, replenished drinks and helped Agnes to make sure that everything went smoothly. But Paul's letter dominated my thoughts, all the while. I couldn't wait to get home, so I could read it one more time.

We were about to cut the birthday cake I had made for *Nene*, when the doorbell rang. To everyone's surprise, especially mine - it was Nathan. I became moist-eyed, at the sight of him. I thanked God that he had turned out so well. He seemed to be well adjusted and confident.

"I simply could not miss *Nene's* party," he said and went straight to where she sat and gave her a big hug. "Happy birthday, darling *Nene*," he smiled, handing her a huge bouquet of white and pink roses, her favourite flowers. Nathan was his father's son all right, doing things with generosity and flair. I was so proud of him.

The party broke up not long after midnight. Nathan followed me home in his car. I made two mugs of tea and we sat at the kitchen table, talking. I was determined to tell Nathan about Paul's letter, as soon as the appropriate moment came. It was time to stop having secrets from him.

"It was very thoughtful of you to make the effort to come to the party, *hokis*," I began. "You made *Nene* very happy." Almost from babyhood, there was a special bond between Nathan and his *Nene*. She had been a constant in his life. I was glad that the bond was still strong.

"Well, she is a very special lady. But I have to leave early tomorrow morning…"

"I understand, my son. You have a lot of studying to do."

"Yes, but that's not the only reason. You see… I've got a new girl friend and I'm going to meet her parents tomorrow. They have invited me to lunch…"

"Oh!" was all I could say. This girl was the second or third 'girl friend', since he started at university. I hadn't realised my son was a Casanova! I found my voice at last. "She must be special, if she wants you to meet her parents."

"She is very special, Mum. She is the most beautiful girl I have ever seen and we are in love. And guess what, her name is Tara! You know, from the film, *Gone with the Wind*."

"As if I could ever forget! Is Tara a student, too?"

"No. She did a Business Studies Course and now she works as a secretary in her father's textile business."

"Oh!" I said, for the second time. I didn't want to ask too many questions.

"Would you like to meet her? I know you'll like her."

"Yes, of course I would, *hokis*. Bring her to lunch, one Sunday. Do you think she will like Armenian food?"

"I'm sure she will." I looked at my son in wonder. He was overflowing with excitement, like a pot about to boil. He had made the transition from boy to man. He was in love. I didn't tell him about the letter. The right moment never came.

How swiftly my disposition changed. Only yesterday, I had been in a sorry state, unable or unwilling to extricate myself from the vacuum that was my existence. But, the arrival of Paul's letter lifted my spirits no end. My first instinct was to find his phone number in the directory and phone him, to hear his voice again. But I hesitated. He hadn't put his number on the letter - perhaps he didn't want his family to know about me. But why had he written to me? Why did he want to meet me? I asked myself these questions, over and over again. More to the point - why should I want to see him again, after all this time?

Nevertheless, that very evening I wrote back to Paul, agreeing to meet him. I posted the letter – affixed with a first-class stamp - on my way to work, the next morning.

Chapter Forty-nine

I'm early, I thought, as I parked the car and switched off the engine. My hands were sweating. I hadn't felt as nervous as this, for a very long time. I had chosen a quiet hotel for my meeting with Paul. Thomas had taken us girls there, for a celebratory drink once. The hotel had a nice lounge, overlooking pleasant gardens. I didn't want to meet Paul in the smoky and noisy atmosphere of a pub.

In the mirror that morning, a strange face had stared back at me. I had peered closer, noting with dismay, the number of silver hairs appearing among the dark ones. I hoped the colour rinse at my hairdressers would make them fade - temporarily at least. I had stood and stared into my wardrobe, agonizing over what to wear, not wanting to choose anything too casual or too formal. I wanted to look nice for Paul. In the end, I had settled for an olive green dress with a matching jacket. A single row of pearls and matching earrings – Stepan's last gift to me before the invasion - completed the outfit. I looked well groomed, smart and desirable, once more. Desirable - desirable to whom, I asked myself, with a shock. Feelings of guilt, which I had pushed to the back of my mind, surfaced. I twisted my rings round and round on my wedding finger. Was I being unfaithful to Stepan's memory? His mother and sister would certainly think so, if they were to see me now - secretly meeting a man that I had loved, more than twenty years ago.

With an effort of will, I smothered my feelings of guilt. I took a deep breath and went in through the revolving doors of the hotel. Sunlight streamed through the low windows and reflected on the bottles behind the bar. The smell of freshly sliced lemons lingered in the air. Before I had time to notice my surroundings, I saw a tall man walking towards me. For a moment, I could do nothing but stare at him, transfixed. It can't be, I thought. Then, I knew beyond doubt that it was Paul. We stood face to face, almost touching.

"It *is* me," he said. "I recognized you, instantly." He took both my hands in his and smiled disarmingly, his eyes crinkling at the corners. I found myself sitting opposite him, at a table by the window, with a glass of wine in my hand. We gazed at each other, spellbound, taking note of the changes that the passage of time had caused. Then we smiled, pleased with what we saw. The thrill of seeing him was not instantaneous – rather, it came in waves. I almost felt as if I was imagining the whole thing. There were laughter lines, around his blue eyes. Grey hairs had appeared at his temples. His boyish good looks had metamorphosed into something more handsome, more distinguished. He was a mature man now. He was not the bronzed, fresh-faced Corporal who had stolen my heart. Paul was the first to break the spell.

"I'm so glad you agreed to meet me." He looked straight at me, in the same attentive way I remembered.

"How did you find me?"

"It wasn't difficult. I must confess I made a few enquiries…"

"Enquiries?" I echoed, surprised.

"Several times, I went to St. Sarkis Church in Kensington, in the hope of seeing you. I wanted to verify that the Reya Manoukian of *An Armenian Kitchen* was really you." So the book had brought him to me.

"Did you see me?"

"No. But one Sunday, after the liturgy, I asked to see the Bishop. He was very kind and helpful. He told me everything. If your husband had been alive, I would not have written to you. I would have been content, to know that you and your family had survived…"

"When I look back at those nightmare days and nights, I wonder how I came through it all, without breaking down."

"It's your irrepressible Armenian courage and resilience, that got you through. I haven't forgotten the stories you told me, about your parents' struggles when they first went to Cyprus."

"Sadly, history has repeated itself."

"I know. But there was an article in the newspaper the other day, saying that negotiations or talks have started to bring the two communities together again. There is hope, isn't there?"

"There's always hope." I sighed, not feeling very hopeful. We were silent for a moment, each lost in thought. We sipped our wine and Paul lit a cigarette. I looked at him in amazement. I wondered how it was - against all the odds – that we had found each other.

"It must have been the hand of destiny that made me walk into that charity shop and spot your cookbook, amongst the pile of old books, mustn't it?"

"It must have been," I answered. "But, I never thought you would want to see me again, after the way I hurt you…"

"Yes, I was hurt. I tore up your last letter into tiny pieces. And angry too - so angry, that you didn't love me enough to stand up to your parents. That's why I never wrote to you again. But it was a long time ago."

"I'm so sorry. If you only knew how painful it was to write that letter."

"I didn't understand it then, but I can now. Anyway, I tried to forget you and in time, I did. Only when I saw the awful events happening in Famagusta in 1974, splashed across my newspaper, did I remember you again. It all came back. The way we met - you all shy and sweet, me all big smiles and boisterous energy and optimism. The arrogance of youth…" He shook his head and was quiet for a moment. He took a sip of his drink and went on. "You came back into my life, then. You were real again. I listened to every piece of news, on the radio and television. I read every word written on the subject. I couldn't believe that Cyprus was partitioned - Famagusta a ghost town - and the beaches, our beautiful sandy beaches, deserted. I know how much you have suffered, how much you have lost."

Dusk was falling. The lights came on. The lounge had begun to fill up with people. The clink of glasses and the quiet, desultory conversation of others lapped gently around us.

"I've travelled a long way, since the last time I saw you on that glorious Sunday afternoon at my Sergeant's house – both literally and metaphorically. Would you like to hear it?" I nodded, not trusting my voice.

"In that case, would you like to have dinner with me first?" Old habits die hard. I looked at my watch. It was almost eight o'clock. I panicked. What if… Relax, I told myself. There's nobody waiting for you, at home. After a second's hesitation, I threw caution to the wind. I might not see Paul again, after today. I would not begrudge him or me, a few more hours together. Our wineglasses were refilled and our lives unravelled.

"Did you become an aeronautical engineer?" This was a question I was burning to ask him. His handsome face crinkled into a smile, again.

"No I didn't. There was no point. I resigned from my job instead and my father helped me buy a ticket to Sydney. I wanted to get as far away from England as possible."

"But did you have any friends or relatives there?"

"I had an uncle – Father's older brother - who had emigrated to Australia on an assisted passage scheme, some years back. Uncle Harry welcomed me into his home and treated me like a son. His daughters, Sandy and Sophie, introduced me to their circle of friends. It was exactly what I wanted and needed." Paul rubbed his forehead and looked out of the window. "Predictably, I married the first girl I came across." I waited for him to continue.

"I don't know whether it was the wrong time or the wrong decision, or a mixture of the two. Anyway, the marriage collapsed, within the year. By this time, I wanted to leave Sydney, but I couldn't because there was a baby on the way. As it happened, there were two babies. I had to stay and provide for the twins and try to make a go of the marriage."

"I'm so sorry," I said. The words sounded so hollow, so inadequate. Yet my heart went out to him. The waitress came, just then and refilled our coffee cups.

"The twins were ten years old, when I came back to England. My father was dying with cancer. I wanted to be with him. I wanted to be there for Mother, too. She would need help and support. I hadn't realised, how much I had missed England. How much I missed the seasons. It was springtime. England has always been a magical place for me, in the spring. It is the time for rebirth isn't it? After Father passed away, I was faced with making decisions."

"What kind of decisions?"

"Well, there was Father's business for a start. I could either sell it or take it over, myself."

"What about your mother? Didn't she have a say in the matter?"

"She left the decisions to me. As the days turned into weeks, I found myself settling effortlessly back into a life in England. The tight band of disappointment and failure, that had almost strangled me these past years, loosened and fell away."

"So you never went back to Sydney again?"

"I did. I made one last attempt to save the marriage. I thought I was doing it for the right reasons, but primarily it was for the twins. I asked Polly if we could start again, this time in England. I thought we could patch things up. Unfortunately, Polly didn't want to leave her native land. And who can blame her. With hindsight, I should never have asked her."

"Everything seems easier with hindsight."

"So you see, my life hasn't exactly been a success. Although, there have been some good times and, of course, the twins. They have taught me to enjoy the moment and to take things as they happen." I nodded. That was exactly what I was doing - enjoying the moment with Paul. But now, it was time to take my leave of him. The lounge had emptied. He must have read my thoughts.

"It's getting late, you want to go home."

"Yes. It's been a lovely evening. Thank you for dinner…"

"It was wonderful, to see you again."

"I'm glad we met, even though I didn't know what to expect."

"For me, it went better than I'd hoped."

"As though the years in between never happened?"

"Exactly. Can't you stay a bit longer?"

"I'd like to stay longer, but I don't like driving late at night."

"I'll walk you to your car, then." Neither of us moved. Paul leaned across the table, his face close to mine. "I don't want this evening to end. Do you?" he asked softly. I swallowed and looked at my hands – I couldn't risk looking into his eyes. He gently lifted my chin, so I could not avoid looking at him.

"Do you? Do you want this evening to end?" he repeated softly. I looked deeply into his eyes. He was smiling in the same way; open and relaxed. I trusted him just as I had trusted him before. And I knew that I didn't want the evening to end. He had stirred something inside me, something that I had almost forgotten. I shook my head. He took my hand and we left the hotel. It was later than I thought. The moon was up and it cast silver shadows over the greenery. The warm air wrapped around me and made the world grow soft and pure.

"Where are we going?" I asked, not really caring. I just wanted to enjoy each moment we spent together.

"To watch the sun rise," said Paul. We reached his car and he opened the door for me. I heard a little inner voice – my conscience, maybe – 'Have you gone completely mad, my girl,' it said. 'Getting into his car and going off, to wherever he chooses to take you.' I refused to listen. But the voice would not go away - 'the wine has loosened your tongue and fuddled your brain. What if he's got a girlfriend, or a wife even…' But I had finished with 'what-ifs'. I got into the car and Paul drove off. I felt liberated, as though something heavy that had been pressing on my conscience for years had been released.

The drive took on a dreamlike quality. No doubt, the wine and my close proximity to him all evening contributed to my euphoric state of mind. But I didn't care. For once in my life, I wanted to follow my heart. With a delicious sense of truancy, I shrugged off the mantle of duty and reason and threw it out of the window. We seemed to be gliding over deserted country lanes. The sky was lightening, with the promise of a new day, as we pulled up, in front of what I presumed to be Paul's house.

"Look over there, darling," he said. I looked. The sun was rising spectacularly from behind the hills, ushering in the new day. The splendour of the spectacle took my breath away. "I promised you this, didn't I? Do you remember?"

"I remember."

We were in the semi-dark hall. Paul put his car keys onto the table. He took a step towards me and he reached out his arms. I slid into them like I belonged there. He held me close, almost crushing me. The intensity of his passion matched my own. I could hear the beat of his heart. His lips touched mine and wiped out everything from my vision. My arms went around his neck, longing to surrender. Our love took wings and we soared, higher and higher, as though we were being swept away by a warm air-current, somewhere beyond the horizon, somewhere we had never been before.

When I awoke the next morning, I felt disoriented. The rumpled pillow beside me was the only testimony to the night before. Throwing caution to the wind was one thing, but this was something entirely different. To my surprise, I didn't feel remorse or guilt, only a warm feeling of peace and tranquillity. I heard kitchen sounds, coming from somewhere in the house. Paul came into the bedroom, with two huge mugs of tea. He opened the curtains, to let the sun in.

"Good morning, my love," he said and bent down to kiss me. "When I woke up this morning, I thought last night was a dream. But, when I saw you next to me…" He sat on the edge of the bed. He was wearing a loose, open-necked shirt and jeans. He looked even more handsome this morning.

"It's not a dream." I saw my own happiness, reflected in his eyes. I snuggled up to him and drank the refreshing tea.

"Where are we?" I said.

"This is *Erewhon*, my hideaway. My cottage in the Malvern hills."

"You mean we drove all that way, last night?"

"It doesn't take long, at that time of night. It was worth it though, wasn't it? It was worth seeing the sun rise majestically from behind the hills, just for us, wasn't it?"

"Yes. It was just like you said it would be."

"You must have slept a little. You look as radiant as I feel."

"I did manage to sleep and I feel wonderful," I said and lay back on the pillows.

"Good. No regrets?"

"None."

"Fantastic. I'll rustle up breakfast. The bathroom is through there."

I found Paul's bathrobe hanging behind the bathroom door and put it on. I smelled the perfume of his aftershave, still lingering in the room. Through the open window, I saw the dew glistening on the grass. It was a glorious day. A good omen, I thought. The smell of toasted bread led me to the kitchen.

"It's only toast and marmalade, I'm afraid. I never dreamt... I'll make more tea."

"It is unbelievable isn't it? Only yesterday, I was nervous as a kitten at the thought of meeting you. This morning, I'm wearing your bathrobe."

"My darling, we have both endured so much sadness and loneliness. It would be foolish, not to accept this gift of a second chance, wouldn't it?"

"You are right Paul. By some miracle, we have stumbled upon utopia. But now, reality beckons."

"I can't deny that there are things to be sorted out, but they are like specks of dust, *sirelis* (my beloved)." I was so surprised to hear the Armenian word he had spoken, that I was speechless for a moment.

"You remember your Armenian words!"

"Only that and one other word - I remember the name of the flower, *antaram* – undying, like the memory of you. I could never forget that. Will you teach me some more words and phrases?"

"I will. But before that..."

"Before that, I want to show you the garden and the rest of the cottage."

After breakfast, Paul took me round the cottage. It was an idyllic place to get away from everything.

"How did you find this place?"

"Quite by chance. I wanted somewhere, where I could be on my own." He smiled when he saw the puzzled look on my face.

"When my father died, I stayed on in my parent's house. I didn't want Mother to live by herself. But eventually, I hankered for a place to call my own and retreat to. This is where I spend most weekends."

"How is your mother?"

"She is getting frail now, but still insists on doing everything herself."

"Have you told her about me? About our meeting?"

"Of course, I have. She said she would love to meet you."

"She has waited a long time, hasn't she?" At the back of the cottage there was a walled garden, with a lawn, roses, honeysuckle and apple trees.

"As you can see, the garden needs a lot of attention. There is a lot to be done in the house, too. And here is the patio. It's the sunniest spot in the garden. How about a coffee?" While he busied himself in the kitchen, I sat on one of the wicker chairs on the patio, staring into space. As we drank our coffee, a cat appeared from nowhere and rubbed itself against Paul's leg. He put out his hand and stroked it.

"Ginger has adopted me. She knows when I'm here and comes over for her bowl of milk." He loves animals, I thought. There was so much we didn't know about each other.

A sweet smell came from the honeysuckle. I remembered my garden in Famagusta. I remembered the jasmine that covered the roof of the pergola. I remembered the day after Stepan's funeral, when I went to the edge of the sea and watched the waves rushing in and crashing on the shore, spent of their fury. How I had wished that I could get rid of my anger, in a similar way. My anger is gone, I thought. I am my own person - the sweet smell of jasmine belongs to a time and place that is gone, forever. For once, my inner voice was in agreement with me.

"Now that I have found you again, I shall start on the alterations to the cottage with renewed energy." Paul got up from his chair and stood uncertainly, a few feet away from me. Then, he knelt by my chair and faced me. Taking the coffee cup out of my hand, he placed it, together with his own, on the table. He took my hands in his. There was no mistaking the love in his eyes. "I would like us to get old and doddery together. I would like us to retire here, one day."

"Are you suggesting that we are teetering on the edge of old age?" I frowned at him, in mock reproof.

"Give or take a few years! What do you think?" His eyes crinkled their smile at me. The years of sadness and loneliness had vanished. The ghosts of yesterday were laid to rest. For the first time in my life, I was going to put my feelings first. I would make my own decisions, right or wrong. I met his eyes, unable to keep the smile from my face. "Is that a proposal of marriage or a proposition, Corporal?" I asked.

MADDIE :
retour sur une enquête controversée !

LEVI FERNANDES

A Katia et Chloé...

Jamais une disparition n'a eu une telle répercussion mondiale ! Les recherches pour retrouver la petite Madeleine McCann ont mobilisé ses proches, de nombreuses personnalités et gouvernements. L'affaire a été suivie par les médias du monde entier. Plus de dix ans plus tard, la disparition de cette fillette reste un mystère.

Que s'est-il passé le soir du 3 mai 2007 dans l'appartement de l'Ocean Club, dans le sud du Portugal ? Malgré ce retentissement mondial, une mobilisation de moyens unique et une couverture médiatique sans précédent, le mystère reste bel et bien entier.

Journaliste à Lisbonne pour l'Agence France Presse au moment des faits, j'ai été malgré moi l'un des premiers journalistes étrangers à couvrir cette disparition et les premières recherches.

Je garde intact le souvenir de ce coup de fil de ma rédaction en chef à Paris. C'était un vendredi matin. On m'appelle pour me prévenir que Sky News passait en boucle l'histoire d'une fillette disparue la veille, en Algarve, au sud du Portugal. On me demande de vérifier l'information. A ce moment-là, aucun média portugais n'en parlait encore. Je passe quelques coups de fils, je cherche sur internet, sur les sites des journaux portugais... Mais personne n'en parle.

Finalement, j'obtiens confirmation auprès de la gendarmerie portugaise. J'ai juste assez d'éléments pour écrire une petite information d'un peu moins de deux cents mots.

**

Portugal-GB-disparition-enquête

Disparition d'une fillette anglaise de trois ans au sud du Portugal

LISBONNE, 4 mai 2007 - Les autorités portugaises enquêtent sur la disparition mystérieuse d'une fillette anglaise âgée de trois ans dans la région touristique de l'Algarve, au sud du Portugal, a indiqué vendredi la gendarmerie portugaise.

Les enquêteurs écartent pour l'instant l'hypothèse d'un enlèvement.

La disparition de l'enfant est survenue alors que la fillette dormait dans la chambre d'hôtel de ses parents avec deux autres enfants, tandis que les parents étaient sortis pour dîner.

A leur retour vers dix heures du soir, la fillette avait disparu. Les parents ont raconté avoir trouvé la porte de la chambre et la fenêtre ouvertes.

La famille originaire de Leicester (centre de l'Angleterre) passait des vacances à la plage de la Luz, près de la ville de Lagos (sud-ouest).

**

L'intérêt suscité par cette affaire ne fait que croître et augmenter les heures et les jours suivants. Les médias britanniques sont évidemment les premiers à s'emparer de l'affaire. La presse portugaise ne tarde pas à suivre. Et la machine médiatique s'emballe.

Au fur et à mesure de la couverture, je me rends compte que je ne suis pas devant un fait divers ordinaire. Tout est exceptionnel: les réactions, la mobilisation, la couverture médiatique.

J'ai rapidement compris qu'on était face à une affaire d'une ampleur singulière. J'ai voulu m'intéresser de plus près à l'enquête qui m'a occupé pendant plusieurs mois, avec un type de couverture inédite. Elle se révèlera effectivement riche en rebondissements.

Le problème des sources s'est rapidement posé. La presse publiait pléthore de détails, mais la police ne confirmait quasiment jamais, à l'exception de rares conférences de presse. Je m'aperçois que pour avoir accès à l'information, il faut entrer dans un cercle de journalistes proches des enquêteurs. Approcher ces réseaux est le seul moyen d'avoir accès aux derniers développements de l'enquête. C'est la raison pour laquelle la presse portugaise publiait tous les jours son lot de révélations qui correspondent la plupart du temps à ce que savaient les enquêteurs.

J'ai alors entrepris de prendre des notes quotidiennement sur l'affaire pour essayer de comprendre comment un fait divers en apparence banal a pu se hisser parmi les affaires les plus médiatisées de l'année 2007. Le nom de Maddie est aujourd'hui connu dans le monde entier.

J'ai voulu reproduire ici les grandes étapes de l'affaire Maddie de manière chronologique, raconter comment elle a été vécue au Portugal, qui est devenu le décor de cette histoire dramatique.

L'affaire reste à ce jour non élucidée. Mais continue toujours autant de passionner. Aujourd'hui deux thèses s'affrontent toujours : mort accidentelle ou enlèvement ? Personne n'est en mesure d'apporter une réponse. Cet ouvrage retrace les premiers pas de l'enquête. Il recueille les nombreux témoignages et les démarches de la police. Je reste convaincu que la réponse se trouve dans les éléments recueillis les premières heures.

« They've taken her ! »

"They've taken her!, they've taken her!" (Ils l'ont enlevée!"). Affolée, pâle, la mine décomposée, Kate appelle son mari. Gerry est assis à la table du restaurant Tapas, à une cinquantaine de mètres de l'appartement. Seul quelques arbustes, des palmiers et la piscine du complexe hôtelier les séparent. Le dîner d'amis s'arrête. Tout le monde se lève de table à l'exception de Diane Webster, qui rejoindra le reste du groupe cinq minutes plus tard.

"Ils l'ont enlevée, ils l'ont enlevée!", ne cesse de répéter Kate. La tranquillité et la douceur de ce soir de printemps, du 3 mai 2007, sont brusquement interrompues. Devant toute cette agitation, le complexe hôtelier Ocean Club sort de sa torpeur. Personnel, voisins, amis, tout le monde est alerté. Des groupes s'organisent et les recherches commencent.

Il est un peu plus de 22 heures. Les amis pénètrent dans l'appartement. Vérifient, cherchent. Sur le lit, seul les draps défaits et la peluche de la fillette témoignent de la présence encore récente de l'enfant. A côté, les jumeaux Sean et Amelie, deux ans, continuent de dormir. Aucune trace d'effraction. La fenêtre est entrouverte, les volets sont légèrement levés, mais n'ont pas été forcés.

Qu'a-t-il bien pu se passer ce soir-là? Seule certitude : Madeleine Beth McCann, qui aurait eu quatre ans dans une semaine, a disparu. Des avis de recherche de la fillette aux yeux bleus verdoyants avec une petite tâche brune à l'oeil droit coulant de la pupille vers l'iris, mesurant un peu moins d'un mètre, sont lancés en fin de soirée dans les médias anglais. Il est possible de reconstituer la soirée d'après les témoignages des McCann et de leurs amis.

DERNIERS MOMENTS AVANT LA DISPARITION

Une journée de vacances à la plage

La journée du jeudi 3 mai 2007, les McCann passent une partie de l'après-midi à la plage avec leurs enfants et amis. Ils font une pause au bar Paraiso, tourné vers l'Océan. La joyeuse bande y déjeune. Maddie commande des spaghettis, puis s'amuse longuement dans la balançoire de la plage avec son père. Le bar est équipé d'un système de vidéo surveillance, qui captera les dernières images de la fillette. On la voit choisir une glace.

En fin d'après-midi le groupe quitte la plage et rentre à l'Ocean's Club. Ce qui est arrivé ensuite est toujours un mystère. Selon la version des McCann, ils préparent ensuite leurs enfants à aller dormir, puis les couchent.

Maddie est heureuse. Elle confie à sa mère avoir vécu la meilleure journée de sa vie. Après avoir enfilé son pyjama rose et blanc aux petites fleurs, Kate couche sa fille et les deux jumeaux. Maddie s'endort avec son petit doudou, un petit chat en peluche, dont elle ne se sépare jamais.

Comme tous les soirs depuis leur arrivée à l'Ocean's Club, les époux McCann ont rendez-vous au restaurant Tapas avec leurs amis, situé au bord de la piscine du village de vacances, à une cinquantaine de mètres de leur appartement. Kate et Gerry sont les premiers à arriver vers 20H40. Puis, il y a le couple Oldfield, proche de la quarantaine. Rachael, et son mari Matthew ont une fille de 18 mois. Matthew et Gerry se sont connus dans l'hôpital de Leicester où ils ont travaillé ensemble. Il y a également le couple Payne. David et Fiona, tous deux médecins

11

également, marié depuis sept ans. Ils ont deux enfants qu'ils surveillent grâce à un système émetteur récepteur de surveillance.

Les McCann

Gerald McCann, Gerry comme le surnomment ses proches, est Ecossais. Il est cardiologue, tandis que sa femme Kate, originaire de Liverpool, est médecin généraliste. Ils ont 39 ans tous les deux. Ils résident dans une zone pavillonnaire de Rothley dans le Leicestershire, centre de l'Angleterre. Ils sont décrits par les voisins comme une famille calme et discrète. Le couple est marié depuis huit ans. Ils se sont connus en Ecosse dans les années 90 pendant leurs études de médecine. Après ses études, Kate trouve un premier travail en Nouvelle Zélande. Tombés fous amoureux, Gerry décide de la suivre.

Quelques années plus tard, Kate et Gerry rentrent finalement en Angleterre et se marient en 1998. Le couple rêve d'avoir des enfants, mais Kate ne parvient pas à tomber enceinte. En mai 2003, naît enfin la première fille du couple, Madeleine, grâce à une fécondation in vitro. Un an plus tard, c'est autour des jumeaux Sean et Amelie. De confession catholique, les McCann sont très croyants et pratiquants. Le dimanche, la petite "Maddie", comme la surnomme sa famille, a l'habitude de porter le petit panier des offrandes à l'église.

En plus des McCann, on trouve aussi dans le groupe le couple Tanner, Russel O'Brien, également médecin, et sa femme Jane. Le couple a deux enfants, dont un du même âge que Maddie. Ils sont très proches du couple Payne. Puis, il y a Diane Webster, la soixantaine, mère de Fiona Payne. Elle est la plus âgée du groupe. Les McCann ne sont pas les seuls à laisser leurs enfants couchés pendant la soirée. Huit enfants dorment dans les appartements, pendant que leurs parents dînent. Régulièrement, toutes les vingt minutes environ, l'un des membres du groupe est chargé de faire le tour des chambres et de vérifier que les enfants vont bien.

Praia da Luz

Originaire du nord de l'Angleterre, la famille McCann est arrivée au sud du Portugal cinq jours plus tôt, le 29 avril, pour un séjour de deux semaines. Ils sont accompagnés d'un groupe d'amis. Neuf adultes et huit enfants au total. La famille loue au rez-de-chaussée l'appartement 5-A de l'Ocean club, entouré d'un petit jardinet, avec vue sur la piscine du village de vacances. La porte, en chêne massif foncé, contraste avec le reste de la façade entièrement peinte en blanc, un rez-de-chaussée, à l'intersection de deux rues paisibles de la station balnéaire de Praia da Luz, à l'ouest de l'Algarve.

Avec ses maisons traditionnelles blanchies à la chaux et ses plages de sable fin, Praia, réputé pour être un endroit calme, est particulièrement populaire parmi les familles. Cela fait plus de cinquante ans que les Anglais ont adopté ce petit port de pêche. Les Portugais représentent une minorité d'habitants dans cette commune. Un curé anglican vient même toutes les semaines célébrer la messe dans l'église catholique de Praia da Luz.

Les Britanniques sont de loin le principal contingent de touristes en Algarve, la région phare du tourisme. Ils représentent selon plusieurs études près de 40% du nombre total de touristes de la région. On trouve également une communauté britannique importante ayant fui les terres de sa majesté pour se réfugier sous les palmiers et le doux soleil de la région, séparée à peine par quelques centaines de mètres d'Océan Atlantique des côtes marocaines.

LA DISPARITION

Le dîner

Le dîner commence à être servi vers 21 heures. Russel O'Brien n'est pas présent. On demande au serveur du Tapas de garder son repas, pendant qu'il s'occupe de sa fille malade dans la chambre. Mattew est l'un des premiers à se lever. Il écoute à la porte de l'appartement des McCann, mais n'entre pas. Aucun bruit. Il se dit que tout va bien et repart. Gerry se lève quelques minutes plus tard. En chemin, il croise Jeremy Wilkins, un producteur de télévision anglais séjournant à l'Ocean Club dont il a fait la connaissance quelques jours plus tôt. Ils parlent ensemble une dizaine de minutes.

Jane se lève à son tour pour aller voir ses enfants. Elle raconte avoir remarqué un homme, traversant la rue d'un pas pressé, portant un enfant dans les bras. Elle fixe l'homme, mais ne reconnaît pas Maddie. Gerry et Jeremy diront plus tard qu'ils ne se rappellent pas avoir vu Jane, ni l'homme qu'elle dit avoir vu passer dans la rue étroite et peu éclairée. Vers 21H25, Gerry revient au Tapas. Russel reste plus d'une heure avec sa fille de l'âge de Maddie, qui a vomi à plusieurs reprises. Peu avant 22 heures, Russel revient au restaurant, tandis que Kate se lève quelques minutes plus tard pour s'assurer que les enfants vont bien.

Elle entre dans la chambre et sent un léger courant d'air qui effleure son visage. Elle remarque que la fenêtre est légèrement entrouverte. Puis elle s'approche du lit où elle avait couché la petite Maddie et constate qu'elle n'est plus là.

La panique

C'est la panique. Elle crie, fait des grands gestes. Elle appelle son mari assis à la table du Tapas avec leurs amis anglais. Pamela Fenn, la voisine du dessus s'approche de la fenêtre lorsqu'elle entend Kate crier. Elle lui propose de l'aide, d'appeler la police. Kate la remercie mais décline, puis rentre dans l'appartement.

C'est un employé du restaurant qui appellera la police une demi-heure plus tard. Les gendarmes ne tardent pas à arriver sur place. Ils ne parlent pas anglais et ont du mal à se rendre compte de la situation. Ils interrogent les employés portugais du complexe touristique et des responsables de l'Ocean Club.

Face à l'éventualité d'avoir à faire à un enlèvement, les militaires de la GNR préviennent la police judiciaire. Alors que Kate ne quitte pas l'appartement pendant les premières heures, Gerry arpente les rues de Praia criant le nom de Maddie. Désespéré, il retourne au bar Paraiso où il avait passé l'après-midi avec ses enfants et s'arrête devant l'église de Praia.

Les gendarmes et les agents de la police judiciaire sont sur place depuis quelques heures. Ils se sont déplacés avec une équipe de chiens spécialisés, à qui leurs maîtres on fait renifler la petite couverture rose dans laquelle dormait la fillette. La police procède à l'audition des premiers témoins, mais ne pense pas immédiatement à protéger l'appartement afin de préserver d'éventuelles empreintes ou autres indices. Ce n'est que vers 02H00 du matin, que les McCann sont invités à changer d'appartement. Le couple prend les affaires dont il a besoin, tandis qu'une amie du couple va chercher les jumeaux, qui continuent de dormir profondément.

DISPARUE DEPUIS 10 HEURES

Premières recherches

Le lendemain, les McCann vont être entendus par les enquêteurs dans les locaux de la Police judiciaire de Portimao. Les parents sont convaincus dès les premiers instants qu'il s'agit d'un enlèvement. Ils insistent. La police n'en est pas aussi sûre. Elle pense à plusieurs hypothèses. La fillette aurait pu se lever et sortir de l'appartement par ses propres moyens à la recherche de ses parents, tomber dans un puits ou d'une falaise. Les premières recherches sont orientées vers la côte, les plages et l'océan.

Les premières heures passent. La fillette reste introuvable. L'inquiétude monte. On ébauche différents scénarios. La porte de l'appartement n'a pas été forcée, les fenêtres non plus. Il n'y pas eu de vol. Pas de casse à l'intérieur de l'appartement. Les jumeaux n'ont pas été réveillés. Les voisins n'ont rien entendu. L'absence d'indices fait craindre la thèse du rapt prémédité. La police de sécurité publique de Lagos se joint aux efforts des gendarmes de la GNR. Toujours aucune trace de Maddie.

Les représentants des autorités britanniques au Portugal prennent conscience de l'ampleur de l'affaire. L'ambassadeur britannique, John Buck, ainsi que le consul britannique en Algarve, Bill Anderson, se rendent sur place dès le lendemain. M. Buck annonce aux médias qu'une équipe de policiers britanniques spécialisée dans les questions d'enlèvement est attendue dans les prochaines heures.

Une course contre la montre

Les recherches ne se sont pas interrompues la nuit de vendredi à samedi. Plus de dix heures après la disparition de la fillette, toujours aucun indice. Le temps presse. Il faut agir vite. S'engage alors une véritable course contre la montre. Un important dispositif est déployé. Un hélicoptère de la protection civile survole la région. Sur le terrain des dizaines d'agents de police, des équipes cynophiles, des pompiers sillonnent la petite commune de Praia da Luz. Un bateau de la police maritime surveille la côte et les falaises.

Les abords des routes, les plages, les piscines, les puits, les jardins du quartier sont passés au peigne fin. La police frappe à toutes les portes des appartements de l'Ocean Club. Ils sont fouillés. Les portes qui ne s'ouvrent pas sont aussitôt ouvertes par un fonctionnaire du complexe qui accompagne les enquêteurs avec un énorme trousseau de clés. Badauds, touristes ou résidents, des dizaines de personnes se joignent aux efforts de la police, des gendarmes et des pompiers. Des touristes anglais, la photo de la petite Maddie à la main, parcourent également Praia et ses environs demandant aux passants s'ils ont vu la fillette. D'autres collent des affiches avec le portait de la petite fille sur lesquelles est écrit en portugais et en anglais: "*Alguèm viu esta rapariga?*" (Quelqu'un a vu cette fillette?).

Dans l'après-midi de vendredi, la police scientifique en uniformes blancs et des masques sur le visage pénètre dans l'appartement pour relever d'éventuelles empreintes et recueillir toute sorte d'indices.

L'appel

Vendredi soir, au comble du désespoir, le père de Maddie lance un premier appel au ravisseur présumé, lu devant les caméras, aux côtés de sa femme:

"Laissez-la rentrer, dit-il. Que celui qui a notre fillette, la laisse revenir auprès de sa mère, de son père, de sa soeur et de son frère. Ne lui faites pas de mal. Essayez de comprendre notre douleur. Nous ne pouvons décrire notre souffrance. Nous demandons à toute personne qui dispose d'une quelconque information, de contacter la police".

Les policiers portugais lancent également un appel à leurs collègues espagnols, à l'Organisation européenne de police Europol spécialisée dans le crime organisé et le trafic humain, ainsi qu'à l'organisation internationale de police criminelle Interpol.

L'Algarve s 'inquiète et se défend

La région de l'Algarve, qui vit essentiellement du tourisme britannique, s'inquiète des éventuelles répercussions pour le secteur. La région est réputée sûre. Le scandale pourrait porter un coup rude à cette réputation, alors comme pour essayer de se dissocier de ce drame, les responsables portugais de la région ne tardent pas à critiquer les parents.

"Ils ne peuvent pas nier leur responsabilité dans le fait d'avoir laissé leurs enfants seuls. Il s'agit d'une erreur d'inattention de la part des parents et non d'un problème de sécurité dans la région", lance dans la presse portugaise, dès le lendemain, un responsable du tourisme de la région.

Même attitude du côté des responsables de l'Ocean Club. Le gérant du complexe hôtelier rappelle que les parents n'ont pas fait appel pendant la soirée au service de baby-sitting mis à disposition par l'établissement.

Toutefois de nombreux témoignages publiés dans la presse présentent les McCann comme des parents responsables. La police affirme n'avoir jamais douté de la version des parents. Un cas similaire avait déjà eu lieu en Algarve, en 1990. Une fillette également britannique, Rachel Charles, âgée de neuf ans, avait disparu. Son corps avait été retrouvé trois jours après sa disparition. L'enquête avait conduit à un Britannique de 39 ans: Michael Cook. Rachel avait été assassinée à Vale Navio dans les environs d'Albufeira. Deux ans plus tard, le coupable avait été condamné à 19 ans de prison pour homicide qualifié.

Les premières critiques des forces de police portugaises surgissent dans la presse anglaise. La police est notamment accusée de ne pas avoir mesuré l'importance de l'affaire et d'avoir perdu un temps précieux les heures qui ont suivi le signalement de la disparition. Les frontières n'ont été alertées que le lendemain de la disparition, soit près de douze heures plus tard, ce qui aurait laissé largement le temps à un ravisseur de quitter le pays.

Première conférence de presse de la police

Devant l'émotion suscitée par cette affaire, il devient de plus en plus difficile pour les enquêteurs de reporter plus longtemps une communication à la presse. Le responsable de la Police judiciaire de Faro, Guilhermino Encarnaçao, décide donc d'organiser une conférence de presse. C'est un fait assez rare au Portugal, voire inédit pour la PJ portugaise, dans une affaire dont l'enquête est en cours, qui obéit normalement à la règle stricte du secret de l'instruction.

"Nous n'aurions pas pu agir plus rapidement, se défend tout d'abord M. Encarnaçao. Nous disposons d'éléments semblant corroborer l'hypothèse du rapt", précise-t-il. L'enlèvement est donc la piste privilégiée par les enquêteurs, mais les thèses d'un prédateur sexuel et d'une possible demande de rançon ne sont pas non plus écartées. La police se dit convaincue en outre que la fillette se trouve toujours en Algarve.

Un portrait robot du ravisseur présumé a été établi. Ce dessin présente le principal suspect de dos. On aperçoit davantage la nuque et les cheveux que ses traits de visage. L'homme mesure 1,70 mètre environ. Il est mâte. Il a les cheveux courts et porte un blouson bleu et un pantalon blanc en lin. De stature moyenne et enrobée, l'homme est d'apparence nordique.

La police refuse toutefois de diffuser publiquement le portrait pour ne pas mettre en danger la vie de la fillette. Les enquêteurs expliquent que le ravisseur pourrait se sentir menacé si son portrait était rendu publique, et décider de se débarrasser de l'enfant. Certains estiment que le refus de dévoiler le portait pourrait obéir à une stratégie de la police, qui chercherait ainsi à mettre la pression sur le ravisseur présumé et le conduire à commettre la faute qui mettrait les enquêteurs sur une piste.

DISPARUE DEPUIS 2 JOURS

Périmètre des recherches élargi

Dans la journée de samedi, les recherches s'intensifient. La police installe un cabinet de crise dans un appartement de l'Ocean Club. Une nouvelle conférence de presse est convoquée pour la fin de la journée. Le périmètre des recherches est élargi et couvre à présent un rayon de trois kilomètres. Autour de l'Ocean club, tout est passé au crible.

Munis de plans des maisons, des villas, des hôtels, les policiers frappent à toutes les portes. Jardins, puits, citernes et les abords de la nationale 125 qui conduit à Praia da Luz sont également inspectés. Des barrages routiers sont dressés. Les automobilistes sont contrôlés et les voitures fouillées. Police judiciaire, police maritime, gendarmes, police de sécurité publique, agents de la protection civile et pompiers, plus d'une centaine de personnes sont mobilisées à la recherche de la petite Maddie.

Des policiers britanniques au Portugal

Trois policiers britanniques arrivent en Algarve pour aider les policiers portugais dans l'enquête. Leur rôle sera également de soutenir la famille et faire le lien entre les forces de police des deux pays. Des éléments de la Direction centrale de lutte contre le banditisme de Lisbonne viennent également prêter main forte à leurs collègues en Algarve.

Malgré les efforts, les recherches n'apportent rien de nouveau. La PJ, qui n'a pas de nouveaux éléments à communiquer, décide finalement d'annuler à la dernière minute la conférence de presse destinée à faire le bilan de deux jours de recherches.

Les McCann, main dans la main, avec leurs deux enfants, se laissent filmer et prendre en photos par les dizaines de journalistes qui ont envahi Praia da Luz. Gerry lit une nouvelle déclaration devant les caméras de télévision. Il fait appel à toute personne ayant des informations sur Maddie de les communiquer à la police.

Il est rejoint dans cet appel par le responsable des enquêteurs. Guilhermino Encarnaçao s'adresse au ravisseur présumé à travers la presse: "Il est temps de remettre la fillette. Je demande à celui qui a la fillette en ce moment de la rendre ou bien de communiquer l'endroit où elle se trouve". L'avis de recherche de la petite Maddie est venu s'ajouter à la liste des huit enfants portés disparus figurant sur le site internet de la PJ portugaise. L'émotion grandit.

La presse britannique s'intéresse de plus en plus à l'affaire, qui occupe désormais les premières pages des journaux et domine les titres des bulletins radio et des journaux télévisés. La chaîne britannique Sky News a été la première à s'emparer de l'affaire. Dès le lendemain de la disparition, elle ouvre ses journaux du matin avec cette information. Les médias britanniques dans leur ensemble suivent. The Guardian, The Independent, The Sun, Sky News, la BBC, ont tous envoyés des correspondants sur place. Les récompenses pour aider à retrouver Maddie se multiplient. Le tabloïde The Sun est l'un des premiers à proposer une récompense de 15.000 euros contre toute information faisant avancer l'enquête. Le quotidien demande à ses lecteurs résidant en Algarve de télécharger sur son site une photo de la fillette portant l'inscription "Let her come home to mummy and daddy" (laissez là rentrer à la maison pour rejoindre sa maman et son papa).

DISPARUE DEPUIS 3 JOURS

La fête des mères

Trois jours après la disparition de Maddie, on célèbre la fête des mères. Un jour qui rend l'absence de la fillette encore plus cruel pour les parents. De confession catholique, le couple se tourne vers la foi où ils confient puiser leur force. Accompagnés de leurs proches, les McCann se rendent en ce dimanche matin dans la petite église blanche et jaune de Praia da Luz. Ils prennent place à l'avant dernière rangée.

"Nous sommes avec vous. Courage, courage!", proclame le curé catholique de la paroisse, père José Pacheco, dans un sermon bilingue, en anglais et en portugais, avant de demander à ses paroissiens de continuer de prier pour le retour de la fillette. "Il est important qu'ils sachent que nous sommes avec elle ainsi qu'avec toutes les mères qui souffrent, dit le curé en s'adressant à Kate. Il nous faut beaucoup d'espoir et de courage, car la petite Maddie est entre les mains de Dieu".

Emilia, une adolescente de 14 ans, se lève et remet à la mère un bouquet de roses rouges et jaunes. A la fin de l'office religieux, les mères déposent les bouquets offerts par leurs enfants aux pieds de la statue de la vierge. En fin d'après-midi, le curé rend visite aux parents dans leur appartement.

Les McCann s'adressent une nouvelle fois à la presse, qui campe désormais 24 heures sur 24 devant leur appart'hôtel. Ils remercient la population locale et leur demandent de continuer de prier. Ils saluent également le travail des policiers. C'est la troisième fois que les parents s'adressent aux médias qui les suivent.

"Cette messe m'a donné beaucoup de force pour m'aider à traverser cette étape terrible", déclare la mère devant les caméras, serrant entre ses mains le *cuddle cat* de Maddie, la peluche préférée de sa fille disparue.

Les recherches s'intensifient

Du côté de l'enquête, rien de nouveau. Personne ne peut garantir que Maddie se trouve toujours en territoire portugais. Un inspecteur du Service des étrangers et frontières (SEF) rappelle qu'une fuite du ravisseur vers l'Espagne par exemple serait "impossible" à éviter. Nous sommes dans l'espace Schengen, si bien qu'il existe le droit à la libre circulation entre les deux pays.

Les recherches se poursuivent sous une chaleur écrasante. Elles sont élargies aux villages voisins, à un périmètre d'une dizaine de kilomètres. Les opérations sont méticuleuses, assure la police. "Pour que rien ne nous échappe, nous plaçons une équipe sur une largeur d'une centaine de mètres et avançons en ligne", explique Antonio Silva, chef de l'une de ces équipes, aidées de nombreux chiens.

Les voitures sont également arrêtées pour des contrôles, ce qui provoque des embouteillages monstres. Les éboueurs sont mis à contribution. On leur demande d'être attentifs et vigilants aux égouts et aux ordures. Dans les même temps, la police fait appel aux services secrets portugais pour leur demander de contrôler les organisations pédophiles.

Les enquêteurs étudient d'autres affaires d'enlèvement afin d'essayer de trouver des similitudes et de mettre en lumière des points communs qui permettraient d'avancer dans l'enquête. Les témoignages, surtout de Britanniques, affluent sans qu'ils soient très précis. Joyce, qui habite un appartement non loin de l'Ocean Club, raconte avoir aperçu le soir de la disparition une voiture noire faisant marche-arrière. George Burke, un autre Britannique, raconte quant à lui avoir aperçu vendredi, à l'aube, "au détour d'une rue, un couple en compagnie d'un enfant, marchant rapidement".

La communication des McCann en marche

Les McCann organisent leur vie en fonction des recherches de leur fille. Ils se plient aux besoins des médias. Ils posent en compagnie de leurs enfants, acceptent d'être filmés, publient des communiqués, font des conférence de presse, nourrissent le travail des professionnels de la presse pour que l'affaire ne tombe pas dans l'oubli. Ils ont toutefois passé un accord avec les médias: une fois ces images en boîte, les journalistes doivent respecter leur vie privée.

Les jours suivant la disparition, les McCann s'adressent plusieurs fois au ravisseur présumé de leur fille, à travers les médias toujours plus nombreux campant devant leur hôtel. Cinq jours après la disparition, le couple sort de l'Ocean Club et s'arrête devant les caméras.

"Rendez-nous notre fille, lance Kate en portugais, la photo de Maddie à la main. Je vous en supplie. Ne lui faites pas de mal. Faites-nous savoir comment nous pourrons retrouver Madeleine ou conduisez-la vers un local où nous pourrons la ramener à la maison". Une courte déclaration est remise par écrit aux autres médias présents. Le couple se tient par la main. L'air triste et grave, ils baissent la tête. Kate tient un téléphone portable et le petit doudou de Maddie dans ses mains. Des images réfléchies pour les télévisions, des mots qui feront la Une des journaux le lendemain. Se met en place la machine de communication des McCann.

Dans le même temps, la police poursuit son travail. Les indices recueillis, comme les empreintes, semblent peu utiles. Elles ont été contaminées par le passage de dizaines de personnes dans l'appartement les heures qui ont suivi la disparition. Les inspecteurs de la PJ retournent une nouvelle fois dans l'appartement. Les lieux sont à nouveau minutieusement inspectés. Sur le terrain, le périmètre des recherches est élargi.

L'enquête se concentre également sur la vie des McCann. Les pistes d'un enlèvement perpétré par un proche ou par un pédophile, font partie des hypothèses analysées. Les enquêteurs s'intéressent à un rapport des services secrets datant de l'année 2000 qui fait figurer le Portugal parmi les destinations des réseaux pédophiles, comme celui de Jean-Pierre Roffi, découvert en 1987, qui produisait des photos et des films avec des enfants dans la banlieue de Lisbonne.

Premières tensions avec les enquêteurs

Sous la pression des médias britanniques, habitués à avoir des liens plus directs et transparents avec leurs enquêteurs, la PJ décide de convoquer une nouvelle conférence de presse. L'heure est sans cesse reportée. Elle est finalement fixée à 20 heures dans le salon d'honneur de la mairie de Portimao. Prise de cours par cette affaire, la police doit trouver rapidement un porte-parole anglophone. L'inspecteur Olegario de Sousa parle anglais. Il présente bien. Il semble convenir parfaitement pour ce rôle, si bien qu'il se trouve sans trop avoir le temps de réaliser ce qui se passe, propulsé sous les projecteurs.

Olegario commence la conférence de presse en rappelant l'engagement de la police à retrouver la fillette.
- La fillette est-elle toujours vivante? demande un journaliste dans la salle.
- Nous n'avons aucune information indiquant que la fillette est morte, répond Olegario.

Après la conférence de presse, la PJ publie un communiqué qui n'apporte pas beaucoup de précisions: "Les différentes pistes suivies dans cette enquête ont permis de recueillir des informations pouvant revêtir un intérêt particulier dans l'enquête. Les autorités nationales bénéficient du soutien permanent et de la collaboration des autorités policières étrangères comme Interpol et Europol".

Fausses alertes

Les jours qui suivent la disparition de Maddie, les fausses alertes se multiplient. Les témoignages sont nombreux, mais toujours rien de concret. Pas de demande de rançon. La police commence à douter que le ou les ravisseurs présumés se trouvent toujours au Portugal. Pour l'instant seules de fausses alertes. Les enquêteurs s'attardent toutefois sur le récit de personnes ayant aperçu un homme, accompagné d'une femme, photographiant des enfants une semaine précédent la disparition de Maddie, dans la région de Sagres, à quelques dizaines de kilomètres de Praia da Luz.

Selon les témoignages, cet homme a même tenté de forcer un enfant à entrer dans une voiture. Maria Bandeirinha raconte que sa fille a fait l'objet d'une tentative d'enlèvement par ce couple d'une quarantaine d'années. Selon elle, cela s'est passé à Lagos quelques heures avant la disparition de Maddie. Alerté par leur comportement suspect, le grand-père de la fillette est intervenu. Et le couple a pris la fuite. La description du suspect correspond au portrait robot, selon eux.

"L'homme mesurait 1,70 mètre environ et la femme était blonde. Mon père m'a dit qu'ils ont fixé attentivement ma fille après avoir fait un signe discret de la tête", raconte cette femme au quotidien portugais Diario de Noticias. Une autre femme encore appelle la gendarmerie pour leur dire qu'elle a vu une fillette ressemblant à Maddie monter dans un train en direction de Faro. Les propriétaires du café Polly, dans le quartier de l'Ocean Club, ont été interrogés par la police qui leur a montré le portrait robot du ravisseur présumé. Ils affirment avoir aperçu un homme, correspondant à la description du suspect, se promenant la semaine précédent la disparition dans les rues de Praia.

La presse se précipite pour passer derrière la police et

recueillir ces témoignages avant de les publier le lendemain dans leurs colonnes. La police vérifie, mais les témoignages ne débouchent sur rien. Dans cette psychose générale, toutes les familles accompagnées de fillettes blondes en bas âge sont interpellées dans la rue. Près de Lagos, à Odiaxere, une femme accompagnée de sa nièce, âgée de 4 ans, ressemblant à Maddie, est arrêtée par deux inspecteurs de la police. Effrayée, la fillette commence à pleurer. La femme n'avait pas ses papiers d'identité sur elle. Elle a été raccompagnée par les deux policiers jusqu'à son domicile où elle a dû leur montrer des documents prouvant le lien de parenté.

A Nelas, dans le district de Viseu, au centre du Portugal, la police arrête un homme ressemblant au portrait robot: grand, maigre, les cheveux attachés en arrière, en queue de cheval, le front dégarni. L'alerte a été donnée par Carlota, une employée de supermarché. Lorsqu'elle aperçoit cet homme, accompagné d'une fillette blonde, au comportement étrange, achetant des fruits, du pain et des yaourts, elle prévient aussitôt les autorités. "Il était accompagné d'une fillette portant un chapeau de paille qui ne cessait de me regarder", raconte-t-elle.

Un peu avant, d'autres témoins avaient aperçu la fillette assise sur le banc arrière d'une Peugeot 307 de couleur grise immatriculée en Espagne, en compagnie de cet homme faisant le plein d'essence dans une station de service. La fillette semblait triste. Elle avait l'air de vouloir s'échapper, racontent les employés. La police agit rapidement et dresse des barrages sur les autoroutes de la région. Arrivés sur place, les policiers ne trouvent personne, mais récupèrent des images captées par le système de vidéo surveillance de l'établissement. Après vérification, la police annonce qu'il ne s'agissait pas de Maddie. Il s'agissait tout simplement d'un étranger de passage au Portugal se promenant avec l'une de ses deux filles.

Une autre piste est également signalée dans le sud,

près de Lagos. Les employés d'une station de service alertent les autorités. Il leur semble avoir reconnu Maddie. La petite était accompagnée d'une femme lui ayant demandé de remercier la caissière de la boutique en portugais. L'employé raconte avoir trouvé la relation entre les deux très étrange. "On dirait que la fillette voulait dire quelque chose, qu'on l'avait forcée à être là", confie une employée. La police vérifie mais une fois encore, cela ne donne rien.

Toujours dans la région, les policiers s'intéressent à une voiture abandonnée sur la route nationale qui conduit à Praia da Luz. Rapidement, les agents de police constatent qu'il s'agit juste d'une voiture appartenant à un touriste français de passage dans la région, s'étant arrêté là pour se reposer.

Le portrait robot ne semble pas être d'une grande aide, selon les personnes interrogées par la police. "On voit à peine les traits du visage. Il n'a pas d'yeux, pas de bouche, pas de nez bien définis. Le visage est un peu long. Les détails ne permettent d'identifier qui que ce soit", soupire Simon Russel.

L'enquête avance, clame la police. Dans un communiqué, la police judiciaire indique que quelque 500 appartements ont été inspectés, 350 pistes vérifiées, des centaines de portugais et étrangers interrogés. La police évoque la piste "d'un crime grave".

De leur côté, les policiers anglais fournissent aux enquêteurs portugais une liste d'une douzaine de noms de pédophiles condamnés au Royaume-Uni. La PJ tente de localiser toutes les personnes figurant dans la liste et s'étant rendu au Portugal les dernières quatre semaines. Au fur et à mesure que le temps passe, les pistes de la fugue ou encore du réseau d'adoption international sont écartées. "A partir des nombreux éléments recueillis, nous avons abandonné plusieurs hypothèses, affirme le porte-parole de la PJ lors d'une nouvelle conférence de presse. Mais nous continuons de travailler sur d'autres pistes qui peuvent nous aider à déterminer ce qui s'est passé". En bref, la police se résume à indiquer que l'enquête continue. Mais concrètement, rien de nouveau, aucun détail.

Le Portugal s'inquiète de son image

Faute de nouvelles avancées, une polémique surgit dans les médias portugais. De nombreuses critiques s'élèvent pour dire que la police n'aurait pas déployé une telle mobilisation s'il s'agissait d'un enfant de nationalité portugaise. Ils étaient accusés d'en faire trop en raison de l'ampleur internationale suscitée par cette couverture. "Nous aurions déployés exactement les même moyens quelle que soit la nationalité de l'enfant", assure l'inspecteur responsable de l'enquête.

Mais c'est avant tout l'"image du Portugal à l'extérieur qui inquiète de plus en plus les entités portugaises. Il faut rappeler que le secteur du tourisme représente alors près de 10% de la richesse nationale.

Tout d'abord, l'Institut du tourisme portugais (ITP) se propose de prendre en charge les frais de séjour de la famille McCann pendant toute la durée de l'enquête. L'ITP décide également d'annuler la présentation publique de la campagne de promotion de l'Algarve en Grande-Bretagne, "Allgarve", avec cette année une sonorité très british. La présentation était prévue au Royal College of Art, et devait compter avec la présence de l'entraîneur vedette portugais Jose Mourinho, qui entraînait alors Chelsea. "Nous attendons que les conditions soient à nouveau réunies" pour lancer la campagne, explique le président de l'organisme, Luis Patrao.

L'affaire gagne une telle ampleur, que même les responsables politiques au plus haut niveau sont amenés à réagir. Le président portugais Anibal Cavaco Silva sort de sa traditionnelle réserve pour affirmer qu'il "accompagne avec inquiétude" l'enquête. "Je suis sûr que les policiers portugais, aidés des autorités internationales, font de leur mieux, observe-t-il lors d'un sommet sur le tourisme à Lisbonne. Il aurait été difficile de faire davantage. Le

Portugal est un pays sûr, reconnu comme tel", tient-il à souligner.

Tony Blair, alors Premier ministre de la Grande-Bretagne, manifeste également son inquiétude. Il est "naturellement préoccupé", selon son équipe. "Nous remercions les Portugais pour leur travail", déclare un porte-parole du Foreign Office.

Mobilisation de stars

Les appels à l'aide pour retrouver Maddie se succèdent. Un mail commence à circuler au Portugal. "Aidez! Faites comme s'il s'agissait de votre soeur, votre fille". La PJ lance également un appel sur son site: "Aidez-nous à retrouver cet enfant". Les stars du ballon rond se mobilisent à leur tour. L'attaquant vedette, qui jouait au Manchester United, Cristiano Ronaldo, lance un appel à travers la télévision de son club. Les images sont reprises par de nombreuses autres chaînes de télévision. "Je suis très inquiet de la disparition de Madeleine. Je demande à toute personne ayant des informations de se manifester", lance Cristiano.

Près d'une semaine après la disparition de Maddie, la mobilisation des médias est totale. L'intérêt de la presse est à son comble. Des hélicoptères loués par des chaînes de télévision survolent la zone pour avoir les meilleures images aériennes de la station balnéaire.

La mobilisation des stars et des vedettes du sport se poursuit. Après l'appel très médiatisé de Cristiano Ronaldo ou encore de Paulo Ferreira, un autre joueur portugais de Chelsea, entre autres stars du ballon rond, c'est autour de David Beckham de lancer un appel. "Si vous avez aperçu cette fillette, je vous en prie, contactez les autorités locales ou la police. S'il vous plaît, s'il vous plaît, aidez-nous", dit-il en exhibant une affiche avec la photo de Madeleine.

Les joueurs des équipes écossaises Aberdeen et Celtic portent des rubans jaunes, couleur de l'espoir en Grande-Bretagne, pendant une rencontre du championnat anglais à Glasgow, en Ecosse, à la demande de la famille McCann. Le montant des récompenses ne cessent également d'augmenter avec des offres provenant de plusieurs milliardaires comme l'Ecossais Stephen Winyard, Richard Bronson, le célèbre patron de Virgin, ou JK Rowling auteur d'Harry Potter.

En plus de ces personnalités, de nombreux anonymes lancent également des initiatives. Parmi celles-ci, Jenny Murat, une septuagénaire britannique. Cette ancienne infirmière retraitée, aujourd'hui veuve, a été mariée à un Portugais. Elle est à l'origine d'une initiative pour le moins originale et qui suscite l'intérêt des médias. Elle a décidé de monter un stand, dans la rue principale qui conduit à la plage de Praia da Luz. L'objectif est de recueillir les témoignages de tous ceux qui ne se sentiraient pas à l'aise pour s'adresser à la police, comme "les immigrants illégaux travaillant dans les chantiers", dit-elle. Elle promet "une totale confidentialité". Sous un parasol jaune, elle dresse une longue table sur laquelle elle pose des portraits de la fillette disparue. Trois chaises sont disposées autour. Puis, un bloc note trône dans un coin. "Celui qui enlève un bébé se terre dans une maison et ne se pavane pas dans la rue. Tout le monde doit être attentif", explique-t-elle.

Fait exceptionnel dans la presse portugaise, le quotidien sportif Record, une institution dans le milieu du sport, fait sa Une avec Maddie: "Tous pour Madeleine". Record publie l'appel de plusieurs stars du ballon rond parmi lesquels Eusebio, la légende du foot portugais des années soixante. Le quotidien propose 15.000 euros contre toute information faisant avancer l'enquête.

DISPARUE DEPUIS UNE SEMAINE

Les 4 ans de Maddie

Ce samedi 12 mai, c'est l'anniversaire de Madeleine. Maddie a ou aurait eu quatre ans aujourd'hui. Elle a disparu depuis un peu plus d'une semaine. Pour l'anniversaire, les parents avaient prévu une petite fête. Ils avaient commandé un gâteau d'anniversaire inspiré de Dr Whoo, personnage de la série télévisée préférée de Maddie. Pour cette journée particulière, les parents choisissent la discrétion. Ils se réfugient dans un endroit loin des regards indiscrets et des objectifs des caméras. Kate envoie un texto à sa famille leur demandant de garder le gâteau pour plus tard. "Je vous remercie pour tout le soutien, mais je veux vous demander que le jour d'anniversaire de Madeleine ne soit évoqué qu'en famille, sans entretiens à la presse. Gardez le gâteau pour son retour. Que Dieu vous bénisse. Merci".

Neuf jours après la disparition de la fillette, l'enquête piétine. Très peu de témoignages solides. Le mystère demeure. Les enquêteurs n'excluent pas la possibilité que la fillette ait pu être emmenée en Espagne, puis vers le nord d'Afrique et notamment vers le Maroc. Une affiche appelant à l'aide pour retrouver Maddie en arabe est diffusée.

Au Portugal, l'enquête s'intéresse à quelques employés et hôtes ayant séjourné ou travaillé à l'Ocean Club la dernière semaine. La police doit faire appel à des interprètes et doit les auditionner un par un, séparément.

Les parents de Maddie sont entendus une nouvelle fois par la police. Ils ont été confrontés à des dizaines d'images, de photos, d'images recueillies dans des stations service, des distributeurs de billets, des centres commerciaux. Gerry rentre à l'Ocean Club à l'aube. Après avoir passé plus de 14 heures dans les locaux de la PJ à Portimao.

Fin de vacances pour les amis des McCann

Pour le groupe de Britanniques qui accompagnait les McCann, les vacances arrivent à leur terme. Avant leur départ, les autorités portugaises souhaitent les auditionner à nouveau pour verser leurs témoignages au dossier. C'est une course contre la montre qui s'annonce le deuxième week-end de mai.

Ils vont être entendus par le juge d'instruction criminelle de Lagos. Ces dépositions doivent se faire en présence de traducteurs. Le fait d'entendre ces personnes, ne veut pas dire qu'elles sont soupçonnées de quoi que ce soit, précisent les enquêteurs. "Il n'y a pas de suspects pour l'instant, affirme le porte-parole de la PJ. L'objectif est de faire appel à leur mémoire, pour qu'ils livrent leurs témoignages, racontent ce qu'ils ont fait, ce qu'ils ont vu. La capacité de perception est très différente selon les personnes. Ce qui est important pour l'une ne l'est peut être pas pour une autre. A présent, nous devons croiser toutes ces données. Un travail difficile et long nous attend", explique-t-il.

« Nous souhaitons à présent passer à la vitesse supérieure. Nous avons des dizaines d'inspecteurs sur le terrain, qui se relaient car la fatigue se fait sentir de plus en plus et l'enquête s'annonce longue", prévient le chef de l'enquête.

Les McCann restent. Ils sont dans l'attente. Ils se rendent régulièrement à l'église depuis la disparition de leur fille. Dix jours après le drame le couple reçoit une visite particulière. Le curé qui les a marié et qui a baptisé leur fille a fait le déplacement depuis l'Angleterre pour les soutenir.

Premières rumeurs contre les McCann

Le couple est victime des rumeurs les plus folles. La presse portugaise les relaye. Barra da Costa, célèbre criminologue recruté par la télévision portugaise pour commenter le déroulement de l'affaire Maddie, fait des déclarations pour le moins curieuses. Les McCann seraient adeptes du "swing", échange de couples, et cette pratique pourrait être liée à la disparition de leur fille selon lui. Il plaide pour un nouvel interrogatoire du couple avec un détecteur de mensonge. "Le swing est par nature atypique, entraînant une grande promiscuité. Ces échanges peuvent entraîner une vengeance qui pourrait expliquer la disparition de la fillette", déclare-t-il.

Ces déclarations provoquent la colère des McCann. Un proche de Kate réagit aussitôt. "Je ne sais pas comment il est possible de dire cela. Leur couple est le fruit d'un amour pur. Ils se sont soutenus quand ils tentaient d'avoir des enfants et qu'ils n'y parvenaient pas. C'est tout simplement cruel de dire ces choses là!". Barra da Costa, qui confiera avoir puiser cette information dans un blog anglais, finira par présenter ses excuses au couple.

Malaise chez les enquêteurs

Le malaise des enquêteurs est palpable notamment lors des conférences de presse. Les policiers portugais n'ont pas l'habitude de ce contact si direct avec les médias. Contrairement à leurs collègues britanniques, la PJ portugaise a l'habitude de travailler dans une certaine discrétion. En Grande-Bretagne, la gestion de l'information est différente de celle qui est faite au Portugal. La méthode anglaise est plus ouverte dans la phase d'investigation avec le système "Child rescue alert", qui permet d'émettre des alertes publiques dès le signalement de la disparition avec par exemple la description du suspect. Au Portugal c'est le contraire. La police mise davantage sur la discrétion dans la première phase de l'enquête.

La méthode de travail des Portugais entraîne de vives critiques. Un journaliste de Sky News évoque les affaires d'enfants disparus au Portugal jamais résolues, la plus célèbre étant celle de Rui Pereira en 1998. Le journaliste rencontre les parents du garçon qui font part de leur déception à l'égard des enquêteurs. Dans le reportage, Sky évoque également le méga scandale pédophile de l'institution pour enfants Casa Pia et dit que les autorités portugaises auraient fermé les yeux sur ce scandale car il impliquait des personnes influentes.

Le responsable de l'enquête se doit de réagir. Il souligne que dans aucun autre pays on aurait mobilisé autant d'hommes. Près de 150 inspecteurs travaillent sur l'affaire. "Quelqu'un a déjà interrogé les parents pour savoir comment ils ont pu laisser trois enfants en bas âge seuls? Les policiers ne peuvent pas faire de miracles. Nous faisons tout notre possible", confie un enquêteur requérant l'anonymat.

Jamais les enquêteurs n'avaient organisé autant de conférences de presse pour s'exprimer sur une enquête en cours. Jamais la PJ n'avait eu un porte-parole pour une affaire spécifique. Le secret de l'instruction interdit à la police de révéler des détails sur une enquête en cours. Les journalistes contrevenant à cette règle sont passibles de poursuites judiciaires. La loi reconnaît toutefois une exception: les affaires ayant une répercussion publique. Exception rarement utilisée avant Maddie. Les Britanniques ont du mal à comprendre ces règles. En Grande-Bretagne, c'est la police qui décide de la stratégie de communication à adopter. Elle choisit dans la plupart des cas d'informer la presse tout au long d'une l'enquête en donnant un maximum d'informations pour faire participer le public aux recherches.

Nourrir la presse en images

Les actes symboliques occupent une place importante pour alimenter les images qui seront ensuite diffusées par les médias. Ils sont nombreux par exemple à répondre à l'appel du curé portugais José Pacheco qui demande au plus grand nombre d'allumer une bougie à l'occasion d'une veillée à Praia da Luz pour évoquer la fillette.

Près de 300 personnes, dont une grande majorité habillé de vert, la couleur de l'espoir au Portugal se sont se rassemblés à l'église de Praia. Gerry et Kate sont également présents. Kate porte un t-shirt vert sous une veste blanche. En plus du *cuddle cat* de Maddie, elle serre entre ses mains une autre peluche. Gerry porte un polo vert. Ils arrivent à l'église de Praia da Luz escortés par deux gendarmes et un policier britannique, après avoir traversé la foule massée à l'extérieur de l'église. Ils entrent dans l'église sans adresser un mot aux médias.

La foule est si nombreuse que tous ne peuvent rentrer dans la petite église. Nombreux sont ceux qui assistent à cette messe à l'extérieur, malgré de forts vents qui balayent la côte. L'émotion est grande. Des larmes coulent sur certains visages. La nappe blanche qui recouvre l'autel de l'église a été remplacée par un tissu de couleur verte, sur laquelle ont été posées des bougies et une bible. Sur le mur blanc à l'intérieur de la chapelle, a été accrochée une affiche verte où l'on peut lire: "nous allons allumer une lumière d'espoir". Juste au-dessous un coeur rose renferme une photo de Madeleine.

"Où qu'elle se trouve nous sommes avec elle et sa famille", dit le curé, tandis que Gerry s'adresse aux personnes venues assister à la messe. "Je remercie cette vague de solidarité qui a dépassé les frontières". Le couple quitte l'église sous une salve d'applaudissements en guise de solidarité, quelques bouquets de fleurs à la main, et des ballons rouges dans les mains.

Une britannique, mère de trois enfants vivant au Portugal depuis une vingtaine d'années, décide de prêter main forte au couple McCann. Elle dresse un mémorial à la sortie de l'Ocean Club. Elle place sur une grille en fer des affiches avec le désormais célèbre portrait de Maddie entouré de rubans jaunes, des peluches, de bouquets de fleurs et de dizaines de cartes avec des messages.

DISPARUE DEPUIS 12 JOURS

Création du Fonds Madeleine

Douze jours après la disparition de Maddie, les McCann organisent une nouvelle conférence de presse, un lundi matin. Ils tiennent à clarifier auprès de l'opinion publique la raison de la présence d'avocats à leurs côtés.

"Depuis que les avocats sont arrivés, ils nous ont ôté un poids, ce qui nous permet de nous concentrer sur notre bien-être physique et émotionnel, déclare Gerry. Nous avons reçu beaucoup de propositions de soutien de la part de personnes qui souhaitent nous aider à retrouver Madeleine. Nous acceptons volontiers ces offres, mais jusqu'à présent nous ne savions pas comment les gérer. Nous avons appelé nos avocats pour nous aider à déterminer la meilleure manière d'utiliser ces dons". Et Kate de conclure: "Jusqu'à preuve du contraire, nous pensons toujours que Madeleine est en vie. Je ne peux pas envisager l'hypothèse de rentrer à la maison actuellement. Cela ne me traverse même pas l'esprit".

Quelques jours plus tard, le fonds Madeleine est créé. Il a pour objectif de promouvoir et orchestrer une campagne internationale pour retrouver la fillette. "Remuer ciel et terre pour retrouver Maddie", est le slogan choisit.

L'association se propose de recueillir des dons pour aider les McCann dans leurs démarches. Un site internet est également créé: www.findmadeleine.com. Il met en ligne des photos de la fillette et permet aux internautes d'y déposer des dons. Le site fait rapidement fureur et comptabilise près de deux millions de visiteurs en deux jours. "Nous avons reçu beaucoup de propositions d'aide, aussi bien de la part de petites entreprises que de multinationales. Mais nous avons besoin de votre soutien pour accroître la couverture en Europe", précise le porte-parole du couple.

Les promoteurs de l'initiative estiment que quelque 450 millions de personnes ont eu connaissance de la disparition de Maddie à travers 160 pays depuis le début de l'affaire.

Une piste, un premier suspect

Coup de théâtre le lundi 13 mai après-midi. La police passe près de treize heures à fouiller une villa, la "casa Liliana", située à une centaine de mètres de l'Ocean Club. Les enquêteurs travaillent en toute discrétion à quelques mètres à peine des dizaines de journalistes massés face à l'Ocean Club, où John Buck, l'ambassadeur britannique, fait une conférence de presse au cours de laquelle il souligne "le travail exceptionnel" des policiers portugais.

Dans le même temps, les policiers quittent la villa avec des sacs plastiques remplis de matériel vidéo et informatique. Une personne est interrogée pendant des heures. Il s'agit de Robert Murat. L'homme aux cheveux châtains clairs, mesurant 1,70 mètre environ et portant des lunettes carrées. Il porte un oeil de verre à la suite d'un accident. Patron d'une agence immobilière près de Lagos, ce trentenaire, qui est né au Portugal a la double nationalité luso-britannique. Sa mère Jenny est anglaise, tandis que son père, décédé dans les années 80, est Portugais.

Son agence est spécialisée dans la location de maisons et appartements dans la région de l'Algarve. Divorcé, il a une fille de quatre ans, du même âge que Maddie, vivant avec son ex-femme en Grande-Bretagne. Le couple, a vécu au Portugal. Son ex-femme est rentrée en Grande-Bretagne après le divorce. Depuis sa séparation, Murat vit avec sa mère dans la villa Liliana. L'ex-madame Murat, ainsi que deux associés de l'agence immobilière, ont également été entendus par les policiers. Sa maison en Angleterre, prise d'assaut par des hordes de journalistes, a dû être placée sous surveillance.

Murat est apprécié de ses voisins en Angleterre et au Portugal, qui le décrivent comme un homme poli, sociable, sympathique, un "homme normal", qui "adore les enfants". "Il s'entend bien avec tout le monde", raconte un agriculteur de 71 ans, un ancien voisin en Angleterre. Il se rendait régulièrement au pub où il plaisantait tout le temps. Je n'ai jamais rien remarqué de suspect avec des enfants", dit une autre voisine.

Pendant les jours qui ont suivi la disparition de Maddie, Robert Murat a été très serviable avec les journalistes. Il a proposé ses services comme traducteur, a servi de l'eau à ceux qui faisaient le pied de grue devant l'Ocean Club. Son comportement éveille toutefois des soupçons notamment chez une jeune journaliste d'une trentaine d'années travaillant pour le Sunday Mirror. "Quand il parlait de Madeleine, il disait toujours que c'était trop tard, qu'elle devait déjà se trouver en Espagne, raconte Lorie Campbell. Il faisait souvent référence au travail des policiers et à l'enquête. Il se présentait en outre comme un proche de la famille, ce qui était faux". Ce comportement, le fait de s'intéresser de beaucoup trop près à l'enquête, lui rappelle l'affaire Soham. L'affaire s'est passée en Angleterre en 2000. Deux soeurs, Holly et Jessica, sont retrouvées mortes près de leur maison dans la forêt toute proche, deux semaines après leur disparition. L'assassin avait réussi à infiltrer le cercle de l'enquête. D'autres journalistes portugais ont également fait part de leurs soupçons à la police.

Robert Murat a un casier judiciaire vierge. Il s'explique dans des déclarations au quotidien portugais 24 Horas. "J'ai aidé les autorités comme j'ai pu. Dans la mesure où j'ai été traducteur des enquêteurs, j'ai forcément créé des liens de proximité avec la famille".

La police judiciaire portugaise précise qu'elle soupçonnait déjà Murat, qui a pourtant travaillé pour eux comme traducteur accrédité. Après 14 heures d'audition dans les locaux de la PJ, Murat ressort en liberté surveillée et se réfugie chez des amis. "Nous n'avons recueilli aucun élément de preuve permettant de le placer en détention préventive", indique la PJ.

Sa mère Jenny Murat, une infirmière à la retraite, avait dressé quelques jours plus tôt un stand à Praia da Luz pour recueillir des informations auprès d'éventuels témoins. Les rumeurs les plus folles sur Murat circulent: des images pornographiques violentes auraient été trouvées sur son ordinateur. Sa photo est à la Une de tous les journaux portugais le lendemain de son audition. Murat, lui, clame son innocence. "Le seul moyen de m'en sortir est de retrouver les vrais coupables, déclare-t-il. Cette affaire est en train de ruiner ma vie ainsi que celle de ma famille".

La police se concentre sur Murat et ses proches, son associée allemande et un informaticien russe Serguei Malinka. Ce dernier, qui tient une boutique informatique à environ 40 kilomètres de Lagos, a vu son appartement également fouillé par la police. Il vit avec ses parents au Portugal depuis leur arrivée dans ce pays il y a sept ans. Ce technicien informatique a réalisé le site de l'agence immobilière de Murat. Après une perquisition dans son appartement, la police repart avec un sac plastique noir contenant du matériel informatique. Serguei est également entendu dans ses locaux de la PJ pendant plusieurs heures. Les enquêteurs veulent déterminer la nature exacte des liens entre les deux hommes. "Ils cherchent des bouc-émissaires", confie la petite amie du jeune russe. Ses voisins prennent sa défense également. Ils le décrivent comme une personne "sociable et poli".

Malinka raconte dans la presse comment sa vie "a été chamboulée". "Je n'ai rien à voir avec la disparition de la fillette. J'ai juste été entendu comme témoin. Rien de plus. Je n'ai pas de casier judiciaire, ni au Portugal, ni en Russie, contrairement à ce qu'ont publié certains journaux. C'est un tissu de mensonges. Mes liens avec Murat sont strictement professionnels. Je me suis donné à fond depuis sept ans au Portugal pour m'assurer un bel avenir. J'espère juste que toute cette affaire ne va pas me gâcher la vie".

Les soupçons de la police reposent sur des déclarations contradictoires des deux hommes. Murat affirme avoir passé la soirée du 3 mai avec sa mère. Or, la police conclut que les deux hommes se sont appelés plusieurs fois au téléphone ce soir là. Par ailleurs, près d'une semaine après la disparition de Maddie, Robert Murat a eu un comportement qui a éveillé les soupçons. Le jour de l'anniversaire de Maddie, il a loué une voiture, une Hyundai bleue. Il a appelé avec insistance à l'heure du déjeuner, raconte l'employé de l'agence. Il semblait très pressé. Dans le formulaire de location, il a donné son ancienne adresse en Grande-Bretagne. Fait étrange, car Murat possède déjà deux voitures. Un ami explique à la presse, que Robert Murat et sa mère partagent les deux véhicules, mais que l'un d'entre eux était tombé en panne, si bien qu'il avait dû en louer un autre.

Les témoignages se poursuivent dans la presse. Cette fois c'est autour de l'architecte ayant dessiné la villa Liliana de contacter les enquêteurs pour leur donner des éléments sur la maison. M. Taylor, octogénaire, ingénieur civil anglais, habite au Portugal depuis les années 70. Il vit à une dizaine de kilomètres de Praia da Luz. Cette maison, il l'a dessiné à la demande d'un ami britannique dont la femme s'appelait Liliana.

Il décrit à la police les différentes pièces de la maison, mais surtout il attire l'attention sur deux endroits moins visibles et qu'il faudrait penser à fouiller. "A côté de la piscine, se trouve une fosse sceptique. Par ailleurs, la maison a été construite sur un terrain en pente. Il y a par conséquent, un trou sous le sol de la salle à manger. Dans la partie la plus haute, l'endroit mesure plus ou moins un mètre. Une personne peut s'y déplacer à genoux avec un accès par le sol de la salle à manger. L'endroit a été recouvert, mais il suffit de taper sur le sol pour se rendre compte qu'en dessous il y a une cavité", indique l'ancien architecte. A la mort de M. Smith, Jenny Murat a acheté la maison.

Tensions entre médias britanniques et portugais

En revanche la tension entre la presse britannique et les enquêteurs portugais ne retombe pas. Un célèbre journaliste britannique, qui a souhaité conserver l'anonymat, fait état de nombreuses critiques à l'égard des enquêteurs portugais dans la presse portugaise.

"Il y a eu tant d'erreurs depuis le début de l'enquête! Tout d'abord, l'appartement d'où a disparu la fillette n'a pas été isolé tout de suite après sa disparition. N'importe qui aurait pu y pénétrer et effacer d'éventuelles preuves", proclame-t-il.

L'autre aspect concerne le délai écoulé entre la disparition de la fillette et le moment où les frontières en ont été alertées. "Nous n'avions pas de support légal pour le faire", répond la PJ par presse interposée. L'accord Schengen ne permet ce genre d'alerte immédiate, à l'exception de cas bien précis comme le hooliganisme et le terrorisme, rappellent les autorités portugaises.

Les enquêteurs en profitent pour pousser un coup de gueule contre la manière dont les télévisions en particulier couvrent cette affaire. Ils leur reprochent de ne pas préserver l'anonymat des inspecteurs de police dans les reportages télévisés. "C'est une honte! Ils mettent en péril le travail mes collègues. Ce n'est pas du journalisme", lance Olegario de Sousa, porte-parole de la PJ, visiblement agacé.

Pour tenter de calmer les esprits, le ministre des Affaires étrangères, Luis Amado, déclare que son homologue britannique Margaret Beckett l'a appelé pour lui faire part de "sa reconnaissance pour le travail des enquêteurs". Le procureur de la République reçoit l'ambassadeur britannique, John Buck, pour aborder l'affaire, tandis que de son côté, le ministre de la Justice Alberto Costa réaffirme une "totale confiance" dans le travail des policiers.

Les gouvernements s'emparent du dossier

L'enquête est évoquée au parlement. "Comme tous dans le pays, nous attendons et prions pour le retour en sécurité de Madeleine", dit le vice-premier ministre John Prescott. La soeur de Gerry, Philomena McCann, s'entretient quant à elle avec Gordon Brown, ministre des Finances, sur le point de succéder à Tony Blair à la tête du gouvernement. "J'ai été impressionnée, car il m'a paru très sincère", a-t-elle souligné à l'issue de l'entretien.

Démentant des informations publiées en Grande-Bretagne, le cabinet du Premier ministre portugais Jose Socrates, tient à démentir "toute pression politique" de la part des Britanniques. "Sur le terrain, il y a une coordination entre les forces de police des deux pays", explique le gouvernement lusitanien.

A Strasbourg, l'affaire Maddie s'invite au parlement européen. L'eurodéputé britannique Gary Titley lance un appel à ses collègues européens pour leur demander de rendre publique cette affaire dans leurs pays et de contribuer aux recherches, dans la mesure où l'on pense que Maddie aurait pu avoir quitté le territoire portugais.

Maddie sur la scène internationale

Les grands événements, qui attirent des millions de spectateurs, sont des occasions rêvées pour parler de Maddie. Les jours qui suivent la disparition de la fillette, les grands rassemblements vont offrir une tribune idéale aux McCann leur permettant d'atteindre des millions de spectateurs. La finale de la Coupe de l'UEFA entre l'Espanyol de Barcelone et Séville, est un moment important. "A la recherche de Maddie", proclame une affiche géante dans le stade de Hampden Park, à Glasgow, en Ecosse.

Des photos de Maddie en français et anglais sont également distribuées à Cannes pendant le festival de cinéma, à l'initiative de l'association Crimestoppers. Des grands groupes manifestent leur intention de participer à l'effort des recherches: le réseau de stations services BP Shell, McDonalds, Carrefour, British Airways, la banque espagnole Santander. Ils s'engagent à exhiber des portraits de la fillette dans leurs établissements. L'opérateur de télécommunications britannique Vodafone propose d'envoyer des messages à ses clients.

Faux témoignages

La police n'a pas rendu public le portrait robot du ravisseur présumé, mais elle aurait en réalité réalisé trois croquis, sous trois angles différents: de face, de profil et de dos. Avec trois coupes de cheveux différentes: cheveux frisés, courts et longs, selon des sources proches des enquêteurs. La stratégie de la police consiste également à fournir de fausses pistes et des informations afin de détourner l'attention du ou des ravisseurs présumé, par exemple en déclarant que les recherches à Praia da Luz avaient été ralenties. Le but est de faire commettre une imprudence au coupable, confie un responsable de l'enquête.

La police organise une nouvelle conférence de presse, mais n'annonce rien de nouveau. Elle refuse de dévoiler des détails de l'enquête et se contente de dire qu'elle poursuit son travail. Les analyses du matériel informatique de Murat et Malinka n'ont rien donné. Si Murat est mis en examen, Malinka a juste été entendu en tant que témoin.

De nombreux témoignages continuent de parvenir aux enquêteurs. On raconte avoir aperçu la fillette dans les environs de Lisbonne, en Espagne, en Suisse, en Grèce. "Tous les témoignages sont vérifiés, assurent les enquêteurs. Malheureusement pour nous et pour la famille McCann, ils n'ont rien donné jusqu'à présent. Le fait qu'il y ait une récompense de plusieurs millions doit y être pour quelque chose. Beaucoup sont à l'affût de l'argent facile".

Toutes ces fausses informations font perdre un temps précieux. L'enquête piétine et les médias commencent à démobiliser. Sky news, qui au début de l'affaire avait une équipe de 32 personnes sur place, a réduit ses effectifs à 8. Avec 20 personnes au début, la BBC ne compte plus que 12 journalistes et techniciens. Sky news est un peu la chaîne qui donne le ton de la couverture.

DISPARUE DEPUIS 2 SEMAINES

L'enquête au point mort

Cela fait un peu plus de deux semaines que Maddie a disparu. Nous sommes le 19 mai. Une messe est organisée dans la petite église de Praia da Luz. Devant l'église, les journalistes forment une haie d'honneur. Caméras, objectifs, micros sont tendus. A l'intérieur, Kate et Gerry se recueillent. La presse n'est pas autorisée à rentrer. Sous un arbre à l'extérieur de l'église, une statue de la vierge a été dressée.

L'enquête avance lentement. La police, qui cherche toujours à déterminer le mobile du crime, manque cruellement de pistes solides, mais assure que l'enquête avance "à bon rythme". Après avoir parlé dans un premier temps d'enlèvement, les policiers reviennent à la formulation plus prudente de "disparition".

La piste Murat est celle qui est privilégiée par la police. Selon l'un des scénarios évoqués par la police, Murat aurait repéré la fillette quelques jours avant sa disparition. Mais les premiers résultats de l'analyse des comptes bancaires de Murat et Malinka ou encore de leurs ordinateurs n'ont révélé aucun élément solide.

Les effectifs mobilisés pour retrouver la fillette sont considérablement réduits. Des quelques 150 agents travaillant au début de l'affaire, seuls 50 sont maintenus sur le terrain.

Un portrait robot rendu public

A l'issue d'une réunion avec les McCann, la PJ décide de rendre public le portrait robot du ravisseur présumé. Il s'agit d'un homme blanc, de 35-40 ans, entre 1,70 et 1,75 mètre, les cheveux courts sur le devant, mais longs jusqu'aux épaules, couvrant le cou à l'arrière. Il porte un blouson foncé, pantalons clairs, chaussures noires. D'après la police, le suspect a été aperçu rôdant dans les environs de l'Ocean Club le 3 mai au soir portant dans les bras ce qui pourrait probablement être un enfant. L'objectif de la police en publiant ce portrait est d'éliminer certains témoignages, explique un inspecteur.

La PJ lance un appel au ravisseur présumé à l'occasion d'une nouvelle conférence de presse. Elle lui demande de ramener la fillette. La police pense que l'homme aurait traîné dans le quartier de l'Ocean Club la semaine de la disparition. Dans le même temps, les enquêteurs lancent également un appel à témoin à tous les touristes ayant séjourné à Praia da Luz, les jours qui ont précédé la disparition. Ils leur demandent d'envoyer leurs photos de vacances, espérant qu'elles permettront de trouver d'éventuels indices.

Dans le même temps, la police reçoit de nombreuses propositions de collaboration. Plus curieuses les unes que les autres. Des voyants affirment avoir eu des rêves, des visions sur l'endroit où se trouverait la fillette, des détectives proposent leur aide.

La campagne internationale bat son plein

La campagne internationale pour retrouver Maddie est bien lancée. Une équipe de plus en plus professionnelle entoure les McCann.

Un film sur la fillette est projeté au stade Wembley à Londres lors de la finale de la Coupe d'Angleterre, opposant Chelsea à Manchester. Des photos défilent sur fond musical, sur le titre du groupe Simple Minds: "Don't you forget about me" (Ne m'oublies pas).

Pour les besoins de la campagne, les McCann décident de raconter une de leurs journées type et de poser pour les photographes, répondant ainsi à une curiosité du public. Les premières photos de leur quotidien sont dévoilées par les agences d'information internationales. Elles montrent notamment le couple jouant avec leurs enfants dans l'appartement. Les McCann se réveillent vers 6H30. Ils prennent le petit-déjeuner en famille, en compagnie de leurs proches ou amis, se trouvant en Algarve. Vers 9H-9H15, ils déposent Sean et Amelie à la crèche de l'Ocean Club. Le couple revient dans l'appartement pour des réunions avec leur équipe: porte-parole, conseillers, avocats ou policiers.

A midi, ils vont chercher leurs enfants à la crèche du village de vacances pour le déjeuner, avant de les déposer une nouvelle fois en début d'après-midi. Kate et Gerry passent un peu de temps ensemble. Ils se promènent, se recueillent à l'église. En fin d'après-midi, ils vont chercher leurs enfants. Ils prennent le thé avec d'autres couples britanniques séjournant à l'Ocean Club, avant de faire dîner les jumeaux, leur lire une histoire et les coucher vers 20H. Les McCann dînent avec leurs proches, puis se couchent vers 23H30, après avoir prié ensemble pour le retour de Maddie.

Les jumeaux posent beaucoup de questions sur leur soeur disparue, raconte Susan, la mère de Kate. "Ils avaient de très bons rapports avec leur soeur. Ils étaient très proches. Ils n'ont que deux ans, mais ils sont très intelligents. Kate m'a raconté, émue l'autre jour, qu'ils lui ont demandé où se trouvait Maddie. Elle leur a répondu que leur grande soeur était partie faire un voyage, mais qu'elle reviendra et qu'elle les aime beaucoup".

Les témoignages de sympathie affluent également. Le site findmadeleine.com a enregistré 75 millions de visites en une semaine. Près de 16.000 personnes y ont laissé des messages de soutien. D'autres envoient des lettres à la famille. Beaucoup de ces lettres ont pour seule adresse: "Famille McCann, Portugal". Elles finissent malgré tout par être remises à leur destinataire. Elles sont toutes lues, assure l'entourage des McCann. "Nous prenons une ou deux heures tous les jours pour lire notre courrier. Une tâche que nous nous partageons entre nous: les deux personnes du service de presse, les parents, d'autres membres de la famille et amis".

Gerry fait un voyage éclair en Grande-Bretagne. Il doit régler les derniers détails du fonds Madeleine avec ses avocats basés à Londres. A son retour, Gerry ramène de nouvelles photos et vidéos de sa fille pour les besoins de la campagne.

Pèlerinage à Fatima

Les jours qui suivent, le couple se rend au sanctuaire de Fatima, à une centaine de kilomètres au nord de Lisbonne. Sur place, ils sont chaleureusement accueillis. Regards tendres, mains tendues, accolades, bouquets de fleurs, Gerry et Kate sont très touchés par les nombreuses marques de sympathie. Les parents allument des bougies et assistent à l'office religieux à l'intérieur de la chapelle des apparitions. Kate serre entre ses mains le *cuddle cat* de sa fille et une rose jaune. Dans le même temps, l'évêque de l'Algarve, Manuel Neto Quintas, lance un appel sur les ondes de la Radio catholique Renascença, la radio portugaise la plus écoutée. Il se propose de jouer un rôle de médiateur dans l'affaire Maddie, entre le ravisseur et les parents. "Pensez à la souffrance des parents, pensez à cela et rendez Madeleine", déclare-t-il.

Le 24 mai est la journée internationale des enfants disparus. Les McCann écrivent une lettre publiée dans la presse portugaise pour redonner espoir à tous les parents vivant le drame de la disparition d'un enfant. "C'est un jour très important car tous les enfants disparus à travers le monde sont évoqués aujourd'hui".

Après quelques jours d'une couverture médiatique intense, les parents craignent que l'attention médiatique ne retombe. Gerry commence à rédiger un journal sur un blog. Les époux McCann décident d'accorder de nouvelles interviews à la presse portugaise, où ils livrent un témoignage touchant.

"Personne ne peut se sentir plus coupable que nous de ne pas avoir été là le soir de l'enlèvement. Mais nous ne pouvons laisser dire que nous avons négligé nos enfants. Le sentiment de culpabilité ne nous quittera jamais. Nous sommes des parents responsables et non négligents. Nous avons toujours été vigilants. Nous aimons nos enfants. Nous sommes dévastés et n'imaginons pas rentrer à la maison sans Madeleine. Si nous pensons à tous les millions de personnes qui se rendent dans le sud de l'Europe pour des vacances, les chances pour qu'une situation comme celle-ci se produise est d'une sur cent millions. Nous avons essayé de penser de manière raisonnable. Ce qui s'est produit est un fait. A présent nous devons aller de l'avant. Nous tirerons des leçons à l'issue de l'enquête. Cela ne sert à rien de se retourner, de regarder en arrière".

Périple européen

VATICAN

Les McCann se lancent corps et âmes dans la campagne pour retrouver leur fille. Fin mai, commence le périple européen qui les conduira dans plusieurs pays. Le Vatican, à Rome, est la première destination. Le couple y sera reçu par le pape. La rencontre est organisée par les autorités britanniques. Un jet privé est mis à leur disposition par un milliardaire britannique, Sir Philip Green, présenté comme la quatrième fortune de Grande-Bretagne. Le 20 mai, les parents de la petite Maddie prennent l'avion à Faro. Les images de leur départ sont retransmises en direct par la principale chaîne de télévision portugaise d'information. Les jumeaux restent à Praia da Luz avec les proches du couple. "Nous aimerions beaucoup parler avec le pape en privé, mais c'est déjà un grand privilège d'aller au Vatican", confie Gerry dans l'avion.

Place Saint Pierre, le couple assiste à la messe de Benoît XVI installés au premier rang, normalement réservé aux hauts dignitaires de l'église. Kate porte un tailleur noir, un chemisier blanc et des rubans jaunes et verts dans ses cheveux attachés en arrière. Gerry porte un costume noir. Ce matin là, quelque 32.000 personnes assistent à la messe pontificale. A l'issue de l'office religieux, le pape se dirige vers les premiers rangs. Après avoir salué plusieurs personnes, Benoît XVI s'arrête quelques instants devant le couple. Il prend les mains de Kate. Elle lui demande de bénir la photo de sa fille qu'elle serre fort. Leur rencontre dure quelques secondes à peine.

A l'issue de l'office religieux, le couple organise une conférence de presse à l'ambassade britannique. Gerry est le premier à prendre la parole: "le Pape a voulu nous montrer son intérêt et nous faire part de son soutien spirituel. Il nous a assuré qu'il prierait pour notre fille, des mots qui nous ont touché et donné beaucoup de force. C'était la première fois que nous rencontrions le pape. Les circonstances malheureusement ne nous ont pas permis d'apprécier ce moment si exceptionnel à sa hauteur".

Et Kate, émue, d'ajouter: "Pour nous catholiques, la rencontre avec le pape est un moment important, mais aujourd'hui nous étions traversés par des sentiments contradictoires. Nous ne pouvions oublier que notre fille n'était pas avec nous. Nous sommes en Italie, non seulement pour rencontrer le pape, mais parce que de ce pays partent de nombreux touristes vers le Portugal".

Pendant ce temps à Praia da Luz, deux publicitaires écossais dressent une énorme affiche publicitaire, six mètres sur douze, avec deux portraits de Maddie. L'équipe des McCann rend public une petite vidéo de Maddie, captée via un téléphone portable. On y voit la fillette, avec son frère et sa soeur, montant dans l'avion qui les emmènera en Algarve.

A ce stade de l'enquête, Robert Murat est toujours le principal suspect. Les enquêteurs s'intéressent à la ressemblance entre Maddie et la fille de Murat, Sophie, résidant en Angleterre. L'ex-femme de Murat pose pour le Sunday Mirror. Elle s'affiche en Une avec sa fille tenant un portrait de Maddie.

MADRID

Après Rome, les McCann se rendent à Madrid. Après une brève escale à Praia où ils embrassent leurs enfants, le couple prend la voiture en direction de Lisbonne en compagnie de son équipe habituelle. Ils prennent un vol commercial cette fois-ci. Kate tient toujours le *cuddle cat* entre ses mains. Les rubans jaunes et verts qu'elle porte d'habitude dans ses cheveux, sont accrochés à la taille cette fois-ci. L'Espagne a été choisi non seulement par sa proximité géographique avec le Portugal, mais également parce que le pays accueille de nombreux touristes. Le couple est accompagné au cours de ce voyage par quatre journalistes britanniques et un photographe. Après l'Espagne, les McCann rentrent à Praia pour préparer leurs prochains voyages.

Clarence Mitchell est devenu le nouveau porte-parole du couple. Cet ancien journaliste de la BBC, membre du cabinet de communication du gouvernement de Tony Blair, est devenu un personnage clé dans l'entourage des McCann. "Ma principale fonction est de faire le lien entre le ministère des Affaires étrangères anglais, la police britannique et la police portugaise", explique-t-il.

Il sera chargé de mettre en place la campagne des McCann, organiser leur périple européen, penser leurs apparitions publiques, mettre en scène les promenades du couple au bord de la plage, ... Il doit s'assurer que la presse dispose d'informations publiables tous les jours, afin que les recherches de la petite Maddie ne tombent pas dans l'oubli.

Début juin, les McCann se rendent en Allemagne et aux Pays-Bas. Ce déplacement est important pour eux dans le cadre de leur campagne. Les Allemands et les Néerlandais sont les deux plus importants groupes de touristes après les Britanniques séjournant en Algarve.

ALLEMAGNE

Ils voyagent une nouvelle fois en jet privé, en compagnie de huit personnes, dont cinq journalistes et leur porte-parole Clarence Mitchell. A Berlin, le couple organise une nouvelle conférence de presse. Main dans la main, l'air grave, Gerry et Kate avancent dans le couloir du centre de presse du gouvernement allemand, s'installent devant une table où se tiennent des dizaines de micros et s'adressent aux journalistes.

"S'il vous plaît, informez la police locale en premier lieu si vous croyez avoir des indices", lance Gerry, qui demande également aux touristes Allemands ayant séjourné en Algarve en mai dernier de télécharger leurs photos de vacances afin qu'elles soient analysées par la police.

"Ce n'est pas une tournée européenne, se défend Gerry. Nous venons dans les capitales où nous pensons trouver des éléments qui pourront faire avancer l'enquête".

Le visage ravagé par le chagrin et les mains tremblantes, Kate brandit un pyjama sous les flashs des photographes, le même que portait Madeleine le soir du 3 mai. Le pantalon du pyjama rose fleuri arbore un petit âne brodé devant. "C'est le pyjama d'Amélie", la petite soeur de Maddie, "mais Madeleine avait le même", lance Kate, tout en serrant très fort la peluche rose de Maddie.

Après quelques minutes de conférence de presse, les McCann sont confrontés à une question surprenante, et un peu gênante à la fois, posée par une journaliste allemande de la radio nationale, Sabine Mueller. Elle leur demande ce qu'ils pensent de ceux qui les accusent d'être en partie responsables de la disparition de Maddie, dans la mesure où ils ont laissé leurs trois enfants seuls pour aller dîner le soir du drame. Kate, un brin interloquée, prend la parole. Sans perdre son sang froid, elle assure que ces critiques ne sont formulées que par "une minorité de personnes". "Nous sommes des parents très responsables, qui aimons infiniment nos enfants", dit-elle.

La presse britannique s'est émue de cette question et prendra la défense de Kate dans ses colonnes dès le lendemain. Deux quotidiens, The Sun et Daily Mirror, critiquent la journaliste allemande pour avoir osé poser cette question. "Une Allemande accuse les parents", "Mère de Maddie insultée", "Question méprisable", "Insinuation choquante", "Insensibilité incroyable", les titres et les unes des journaux britanniques réagissent avec véhémence à ce qu'ils considèrent comme un affront. La journaliste allemande se justifie en expliquant qu'elle faisait juste son travail.

PAYS-BAS

En Allemagne, le couple est également invité à une émission de télévision très regardée. Le présentateur leur remet la lettre de soutien des grands-parents de Felix Heger, un enfant disparu depuis janvier 2006, du même âge que Maddie. "Ne perdez pas espoir", dit la lettre que les parents de Maddie lisent les larmes aux yeux devant les caméras. "Nous tirons notre force du fait d'être actifs", souligne Gerry se disant "heureux que l'enlèvement de Madeleine ait permis de parler d'autres cas d'enfants portés disparus".

A la fin de leur séjour, le couple est reçu par le maire de Berlin Klaus Wowereit. A l'issue de cet entretien, les McCann s'apprêtent à repartir pour Amsterdam, lorsqu'ils reçoivent un appel anonyme d'une personne affirmant disposer d'informations sur Maddie. Le vol est retardé. On découvrira plus tard que l'appel a été passé depuis l'Argentine, à partir d'une carte prépayée. L'auteur de ce coup de fil a d'abord appelé la police espagnole, refusant de fournir son identité, et a insisté pour parler aux McCann. Il a affirmé disposer d'éléments confirmant l'enlèvement de Maddie par un réseau pédophile international. Les informations semblent peu crédibles. Le voyage est finalement maintenu et le couple s'envole vers les Pays-Bas. La presse argentine évoquera l'oeuvre d'un "escroc professionnel" qui tentait d'extorquer un million de dollars aux McCann.

A Amsterdam, le programme est identique. La conférence de presse est l'étape incontournable de ces séjours éclairs. Les McCann font également appel aux Néerlandais. "Nous sommes là pour demander de l'aide, déclare Gerry dans un salon d'un grand hôtel d'Amsterdam où il a convoqué les médias. On ne sait toujours pas qui l'a enlevée, on ne connaît pas le mobile et on se sait pas où elle se trouve".

De nouvelles initiatives

Les initiatives se multiplient. Les proches des McCann continuent de distribuer des posters, affiches et autres T-shirts avec des portraits de Madeleine. Sur les T-shirts distribués on peut lire: "S'il vous plaît, retrouvez notre fillette. Elle peut être près de vous. S'il vous plaît observez attentivement!".

Le groupe de travail entourant les McCann veut frapper fort. Il approche le moteur de recherche américain Google pour qu'il reproduise les yeux de leur fille dans les deux "O" du mot Google à l'occasion d'une opération spéciale.

De son côté, J.K. Rowling, l'auteur d'Harry Potter, a également été contactée pour que des marque-pages avec le portrait de Maddie soient glissés dans le septième et dernier tome de la série "Harry Potter" intitulé "Harry Potter et les reliques de la mort", dont la sortie est prévue dans quelques semaines au Royaume-Uni.

DISPARUE DEPUIS 1 MOIS

Des moyens exceptionnels

"Tout ce qui devait être fait a été fait", indique la Police Judiciaire. Un mois s'est écoulé depuis la disparition de Maddie. En Algarve, la patrouille de la gendarmerie chargée de surveiller l'appartement des McCann à Praia da Luz, d'où a disparu Maddie, est démobilisée. Le ministère public autorise l'Ocean Club à louer l'appartement à de nouveaux clients.

La presse portugaise s'émeut des moyens exceptionnels mise en place aux frais du contribuable portugais. "Jamais une enquête n'aura coûté aussi cher", écrit la presse. Le directeur national de la PJ, Alipio Ribeiro, intervient dans le débat et assure que la PJ n'enquête pas "en fonction des coûts d'une opération" et que l'enquête va se poursuivre au "même rythme".

De son côté, le porte-parole de la PJ fait un point sur le travail des enquêteurs. "Nous continuons de croire que la personne qui a enlevé l'enfant aurait pu vouloir demander une rançon. Il est possible qu'il ne l'ait pas fait, car il a eu peur de la médiatisation de l'affaire. Qui oserait demander de l'argent en échange d'une fillette dont le portrait est connu dans le monde entier ?, s'interroge-t-il. Le ravisseur peut toujours cacher la fillette près d'ici. En revanche, si nous avons à faire à un prédateur sexuel, il se peut qu'après avoir assouvi ses désirs, il ait cherché à se débarrasser du corps", ajoute-t-il.

La dernière hypothèse évoquée, enfin, est celle d'un enlèvement à des fins de "pornographie infantile". "Si c'était le cas, il serait difficile que les films produits avec la fillette soient introduits dans le circuit de la pornographie infantile en raison de sa notoriété", estime-t-il par ailleurs.

Voyage au Maroc

Par ailleurs, les médias évoquent une piste marocaine. Des journaux britanniques rapportent que les services d'espionnage ont intercepté des conversations en arabe faisant référence à une fillette blonde au Maroc. Pour les McCann, cette thèse a du poids. Après leur périple européen, ils se tournent vers le nord de l'Afrique. Ils annoncent leur intention de se rendre à Casablanca et à Rabat. Ils empruntent un vol commercial à Lisbonne. A leur arrivée à Casablanca, le couple prend la route en direction de Rabat, où il passe la nuit. A Rabat, ils rencontrent trois ONG, ainsi que le chef de la police et le vice-ministre de l'Intérieur.

A l'issue de ces entretiens, le couple se plie une nouvelle fois à la traditionnelle conférence de presse. "Nous sommes venus au Maroc pour demander l'aide de la population, car en dépit d'une vaste enquête ces dernières six semaines, nous sommes toujours dans l'incertitude sur l'identité du ou des ravisseurs, déclare Gerry. La principale raison de notre venue au Maroc est la proximité de ce pays avec le Portugal. Les frontières entre le Portugal et l'Espagne, ainsi que les ports n'ont été contrôlés que douze heures après la disparition de Madeleine. En raison de l'absence d'indices au Portugal, Kate et moi, pensons qu'elle aurait pu avoir été conduite en Espagne et peut-être au Maroc", explique Gerry avant de conclure. "Le ministre de l'Intérieur nous a assuré que les autorités feront tout leur possible pour nous aider à retrouver Madeleine et qu'elles vont coopérer avec les autorités internationales. Kate et moi sommes convaincus, après avoir rencontrés des responsables marocains, que si Madeleine se trouve au Maroc, elle sera retrouvée".

Piste marocaine

Leur déplacement au Maroc coïncide avec le témoignage d'une Norvégienne de 45 ans, Mari Olli. Cette femme, qui se trouvait au Maroc en vacances au moment de la disparition de la fillette, affirme avoir aperçu Madeleine dans une station service du sud de Marrakech six jours après sa disparition. Elle fait parvenir son témoignage par mail à la PJ et au quotidien portugais 24 Horas.

"J'ai la certitude que c'était elle dans la station-service de Marrakech le 9 mai dernier, commence-t-elle par écrire. C'était une fillette très douce qui me semblait perdue". Puis, elle raconte: "Mon mari et mois avons pris quelques jours de vacances le 30 avril et sommes rentrés le 9 mai. A notre retour, nous nous sommes arrêtés à une station service au sud de Marrakech. J'en ai profité pour dépenser les derniers dinars qui nous restaient. J'ai acheté de l'eau et des lingettes dans cette station service. J'ai vu une enfant avec un homme. Elle avait des yeux verts. Elle était blonde. Le visage ovale, un peu pâle. Les cheveux mi longs jusqu'à l'épaule. Elle portait un pyjama bleu. Elle avait l'air de s'être réveillée depuis peu.

Quant à l'homme qui l'accompagnait, il mesurait 1,78 mètre environ. Je dis 1,78 mètre, car je mesure 1,74 mètre et mon mari 1,80 mètre. Il était plus grand que mon moi, mais plus petit que mon mari. Il était maigre, âgé de 34 à 40 ans. Il avait l'air négligé, des cheveux courts et bruns. Il portait un T-shirt large, gris clair avec des jeans bleus. Il avait le visage allongé. Il portait un sac à dos qui paraissait vide. Il avait l'air d'attendre quelqu'un. Il avait l'apparence d'un Anglais ou d'un Allemand. Il parlait avec un accent. Peut être écossais. Je n'ai aperçu aucune voiture pouvant leur appartenir. La situation était étrange. C'était bizarre de voir une fillette blonde, là toute seule debout.

Elle était si petite qu'il aurait été normale qu'elle eût

été portée par un adulte ou du moins tenue par la main. Elle lui tournait le dos. Paraissait triste. J'ai regardé son visage. Elle m'a regardé également. Puis elle s'est retournée vers l'homme et lui a demandé quelque chose comme: « «Can we see mummy soon ? » (Peut-on voir maman bientôt?). Je ne pense pas qu'il ait répondu. Je me suis retourné à mon tour pour payer mes achats: deux bouteilles d'eau et des lingettes. Je suis rentré dans ma voiture et j'ai continué de les observer pour voir s'ils avaient une voiture, mais je n'ai rien remarqué. J'ai voulu en parler à mon mari, mais je ne l'ai pas fait. Nous avons continué notre chemin jusqu'à Tanger, on nous devions prendre le bateau".

En rentrant chez elle, au sud de l'Espagne, près de Malaga, Mari Olli apprend en lisant les journaux, la disparition de Maddie. Cette ancienne thérapeute, dont le mari est Anglais, prend alors son téléphone pour raconter ce qu'elle a vu à la police espagnole, mais personne n'y accorde de l'importance, car elle ne parle pas bien espagnol, raconte-t-elle. Elle s'adresse au Missing Child Bureau du Royaume-Uni, un organisme chargé des enfants disparus, qui ne donne pas suite à son témoignage non plus.

Le 13 mai, elle contacte alors la Police judiciaire portugaise, qui lui demande de lui faire parvenir son récit par écrit. Cette Norvégienne affirme ne pas comprendre pour quelles raisons elle n'a pas été invitée à témoigner et pourquoi on a pas dressé un portrait de l'homme qu'elle a aperçu. "Je ne cesse de penser à cette situation. J'ai besoin de savoir si quelqu'un a pris en compte mon témoignage. Je suis sûre que les Marocains qui se trouvaient dans la station service pourront vous confirmer tout cela. Si je peux aider encore, S'IL VOUS PLAIT dites-le moi!", conclut-elle dans le mail envoyé aux autorités portugaises.

Les enquêteurs vérifient cette piste. Ils demandent aux autorités marocaines de leur faire parvenir les images vidéo des caméras de surveillance de cette station service du sud de Marrakech. "Si le ravisseur est entré au Maroc, il y a de fortes chances qu'il l'ait fait par voie maritime, à bord de l'un des ferry qui fait la traversée dans le détroit de Gibraltar", affirme un responsable des forces de police marocaines.

Des journalistes portugais se sont rendus dans la station service de Marrakech, où la petite Maddie aurait été aperçue, mais les employés affirment ne se souvenir de rien.

« El francès »

Quelques jours plus tard, la police portugaise est contactée par un Espagnol originaire de Valence, affirmant être journaliste, spécialiste des questions pédophiles. Antonio Toscano assure connaître l'identité du ravisseur de Maddie. Selon lui, l'enlèvement a été commandité depuis le Royaume-Uni. Le ravisseur est un homme de nationalité française, connu dans les milieux pédophiles sous le nom de "El francès". Il aurait été aperçu à Séville une semaine avant la disparition de la fillette. Il a raconté dans son entourage qu'il devait se rendre en Algarve pour voir des amis.

"El Francès travaille avec des complices. Ils auraient pu avoir fait appel à un couple pour enlever Maddie, explique Toscano à la presse portugaise. L'homme parle plusieurs langues et n'a plus été aperçu dans les circuits pédophiles européens depuis l'enlèvement. Il attend probablement que l'affaire se calme un peu pour agir. Il attend des instructions tranquillement, car les pistes avancées ne le mettent pas en cause. S'il se sent encerclé, il abandonnera la fillette et prendra la fuite. Il sait que s'il la tue, il sera poursuivi".

Les parents peuvent jouer un rôle clé, dit Toscano, qui cherche à rencontrer les McCann à tout prix. "Il ne s'agit pas d'une piste supplémentaire, mais c'est bien la seule qui peut conduire à Maddie et les parents l'ont ignorée jusqu'à présent, affirme-t-il. N'oubliez pas. Chaque jour qui passe l'espoir de retrouver la fillette en vie s'amenuise. " Les enquêteurs portugais le reçoivent, l'écoutent et vérifient ses informations, mais les informations paraissent peu crédibles.

La tension monte d'un cran

La tension entre la presse anglaise et la police portugaise monte d'un cran. La presse britannique accuse les inspecteurs de la PJ de ne pas être sérieux dans leur travail, de faire de longues pauses déjeuner bien arrosées. Le quotidien Times écrit que l'inspecteur chargé de l'enquête a été vu par les clients d'un restaurant, riant à gorge déployée pendant que la télévision de l'établissement diffusait une conférence de presse des McCann à Berlin.

Le porte-parole de la PJ s'empresse de réagir rappelant que les agents de police ont une vie privée et qu'ils sont libres de faire ce qui leur plaît pendant leurs pauses. "Les inspecteurs doivent également manger, boire et se reposer", argue-t-il dans des déclarations au Times.

Alipio Ribeiro, directeur national de la PJ, ressent le besoin de se justifier pour la énième fois également. "Ce qui nous importe, c'est l'opinion de la police anglaise, qui ne cautionne pas ces jugements. Il est important aussi de dire aux parents de la fillette que nous continuerons de travailler sur cette affaire, en coopération avec la police anglaise". Quelques jours plus tard, un photographe anglais qui tentait de prendre en photo des inspecteurs de la PJ à leur sortie d'un restaurant est interpellé et conduit au poste de police.

Après le périple européen et le voyage au Maroc, les parents sont de retour à Praia da Luz. Une pause bilan s'impose. "Nous allons prendre un temps de réflexion avant de décider ce que nous allons faire. La campagne et les recherches de Madeleine vont se poursuivre. Avec l'aide de tous nous la retrouverons. Restez avec nous", écrivent les parents à la mi-juin sur le site findmadeleine.com.

Une lettre fait renaître l'espoir

Une piste parvenue aux enquêteurs portugais début juin fait renaître un peu d'espoir. Tout commence par la publication d'extraits d'une lettre anonyme dans les pages du quotidien hollandais Telegraaf. Son auteur donne des précisions sur l'endroit où se trouverait le cadavre de Maddie. Il écrit que le corps se trouve à quelque 15 kilomètres de l'Ocean Club dans un "endroit désertique, à six ou sept mètres de la route, sous des branches et des pierres".

La lettre est accompagnée d'une carte sur laquelle est indiquée une localisation précise. Selon le Telegraaf, l'auteur est "très probablement la même" personne qui a envoyé au quotidien l'année précédente une lettre pour signaler le lieu où se trouvaient les corps de deux fillettes disparues en Belgique, Stacy Lemmens et Nathalie Mahy, de sept et dix ans.

Les deux demi-soeurs avaient disparu en juin 2006, près de Liège. Les indications, figurant sur la lettre, envoyées au quotidien avaient permis de les retrouver, mais pas d'arrêter le coupable. Les deux fillettes avaient été étranglées et l'une d'entre elles violée.

L'information sera étudiée avec sérieux, comme toutes les autres pistes, assure la PJ. Une dizaine d'inspecteurs se rend sur le lieu indiqué pour un premier repérage. D'après la police, la carte est un peu vague et les recherches risquent de ne pas être simples. Elles pourraient durer plusieurs heures.

Des journalistes mènent une enquête parallèle. Deux chiens de l'association à but non lucratif de l'équipe canine de sauvetage de l'Algarve sont recrutés par ces journalistes. L'initiative provoque la colère de la PJ, qui craint que des preuves soient détruites au cours de ces entreprises privées.

La police restreint donc l'accès de la zone pour écarter les curieux. L'association dira plus tard avoir été trompée et explique avoir accepté de participer aux recherches, car elle pensait que les personnes ayant fait appel à eux collaboraient avec les enquêteurs.

Les McCann n'ont pas apprécié non plus l'initiative du Telegraaf et accusent le quotidien d'avoir eu un "comportement irresponsable", "cruel" et "insensible" en publiant une lettre anonyme. Sur son blog, Gerry reproche au quotidien d'avoir rendue publique la lettre sans que sa crédibilité ait été vérifiée auparavant, et sans que la police ait été prévenue. Après plusieurs heures de travail, avec l'aide de quatre chiens, les recherches ne débouchent sur rien. La police abandonne cette piste.

Nombreux témoignages mais l'enquête n'avance pas

Le directeur de la PJ de Faro, Guilhermino Encarnaçao, s'entretient toutes les semaines avec le couple McCann pour faire le point sur l'enquête. Sept semaines après la disparition de Madeleine, les enquêteurs n'ont rien de nouveau. "Nous n'avons trouvé aucun indice semblant indiquer que la fillette a été tué", dit la PJ. La police a promis un communiqué depuis plusieurs jours, mais il tarde. Les analyses des empreintes recueillies par la police scientifique dans l'appartement où dormait Maddie, n'ont rien donné. Amis, famille, employés, plus d'une vingtaine de personnes sont rentrées ce soir-là dans la chambre avant que la police scientifique ne fasse son travail, ce qui a pu entraîner la destruction d'éventuelles preuves, expliquent les enquêteurs. L'appartement de l'Ocean Club, d'où a disparu Maddie, est finalement loué à de nouveaux occupants à la mi-juin.

Les enquêteurs continuent d'être submergés par de nombreux témoignages parvenant d'un peu partout en Europe. Cette fois-ci, c'est à Malte. Deux touristes racontent avoir vu une fillette blonde à La Valette. Selon eux, elle ressemble beaucoup à Maddie. La police portugaise est alertée et les policiers maltais enquêtent.

Quelques jours plus tard, on affirme avoir vu Maddie dans un avion desservant Lisbonne depuis Genève. La police suisse prévient aussitôt ses homologues portugais et l'avion est fouillé dès qu'il se pose au Portugal. Fausse piste. Il s'agissait une fois encore d'une fillette blonde ressemblant à Maddie. Des témoignages comme celui-ci se multiplient également en Espagne, en Grèce, en Argentine ou en Belgique.

Les récompenses milliardaires n'attirent pas que de

gens bien intentionnés. Un couple, qui voulait soutirer une récompense contre de faux renseignements sur la disparition de la fillette, est interpellé au sud de l'Espagne. L'homme, Danilo Chemello, est Italien. La femme, Aurora, est de nationalité portugaise. Ils ont tenté d'entrer en contact avec les parents de Madeleine pour toucher la récompense promise contre des informations. Le ministère de l'Intérieur espagnol précise dans un communiqué que tout semble indiquer qu'il s'agisse "d'escrocs" et ouvre une enquête.

Les policiers ont trouvé dans leur appartement des dizaines de coupures de journaux sur l'affaire Maddie. Danilo Chemello est visé en outre par un mandat d'arrêt international délivré par la justice française pour association de malfaiteurs. L'Italien a déjà accompli en France une peine de 18 mois de prison pour mauvais traitement sur mineur, en l'occurrence sur sa propre fille, toujours selon le ministère espagnol. L'homme, âgé de 61 ans, est finalement écroué sur ordre d'un juge de l'Audience nationale. Les McCann réagissent à cette arrestation. Ces opérations prouvent que les forces européennes de police travaillent en coordination, se félicitent-ils.

22 juin 2007. Cinquante jours sont passés depuis la disparition de Maddie. Les parents de Maddie veulent marquer cette date anniversaire. Des milliers de ballons jaunes et verts, aux couleurs de l'espoir en Angleterre et au Portugal, sont lâchés dans les airs à travers le monde. En plus de l'Europe, des pays comme El Salvador, l'Inde, les Philippines ou encore l'Afghanistan, participent à l'opération.

"Nous avons eu une réponse formidable. Il y a eu des lâchers de ballons dans environ 300 lieux différents, dans plus de 200 pays", déclare Gerry en guise de bilan. "Nous allons continuer les recherches. Nous demandons au public de ne pas oublier Madeleine, ni les autres enfants disparus".

DISPARUE DEPUIS 2 MOIS

Les McCann à la télévision

Deux mois après le drame, le couple McCann accorde un entretien à la télévision portugaise pour empêcher que l'enquête ne tombe dans l'oubli et rappeler à l'opinion publique que les recherches se poursuivent. Ils font le point sur les semaines écoulées.

Gerry est le premier à prendre la parole. "Nous voulons faire en sorte que le plus grand nombre de personnes soit au courant de la disparition de Madeleine, que le plus grand nombre connaisse sa photo. Il y a des millions de personnes à travers le monde qui la recherchent. Nous voulons continuer d'encourager les gens à se souvenir d'elle. Nos voyages en Europe avaient des objectifs spécifiques. L'Espagne pour sa proximité. L'Allemagne et les Pays Bas pour lancer un appel au grand public. Mais, elle a été enlevée ici (à Praia) et il y a de fortes chances pour qu'elle se trouve dans la région. De toute façon, nous nous sentons plus proches de Maddie au Portugal.

Les premiers jours, les Portugais, notre foi, nous ont beaucoup aidé et nous ont apporté beaucoup de force. Nous aimerions remercier tout le monde pour ce soutien. Nous continuons de recevoir beaucoup de lettres. Certaines doivent être traduites, car notre portugais n'est pas très bon pour le moment. Mais, l'apprentissage de la langue est notre prochaine étape. Pour l'instant, nous ne nous sentons pas capables de reprendre nos emplois de médecin. Il nous reste beaucoup à faire. Nous ne voulons surtout pas, dans trois ou quatre mois, regarder en arrière et nous dire que nous aimerions avoir fait telle ou telle chose.

La communication entre la police et nous est très

bonne. Nous les remercions par la manière dont ils nous ont traité. Les rapports de travail sont excellents. Ensemble, nous avons la même détermination de vouloir retrouver Madeleine. Quant à la couverture médiatique, elle est entourée de beaucoup de spéculation, ce qui nous blesse parfois. Nous essayons de nous focaliser sur des éléments concrets, sur ce que nous disent les autorités et sur ce que nous savons.

Nous regardons les médias, mais nous ne lisons pas tout ce que rapporte la presse et internet. Chaque jour qui passe est très, très difficile. Il y a des jours positifs. Par exemple, quand nous réussissons un grand événement de notre campagne, avec une grande couverture médiatique. La seule chose qui importe vraiment c'est de retrouver Madeleine. Nous espérons que toutes nos démarches favoriseront les recherches".

Kate prend la parole à son tour. "Nous envisageons chaque jour à la fois. Dans l'avenir immédiat nous resterons au Portugal. Notre activité principale est de tout mettre en œuvre pour retrouver Maddie. Il y a une possibilité qu'elle ait été enlevée, qu'elle ait quitté le territoire portugais. Mais nous nous sentons plus proches d'elle ici. Le soutien des Portugais a été extraordinaire, réconfortant. Ils nous ont beaucoup aidé. Ils nous font sentir ici chez nous. Nous sommes certains que la police fait de son mieux pour retrouver Maddie. Il n'est pas encore trop tard. Rendez-nous Madeleine".

Le fonds « remuer ciel et terre » grossit

Les dizaines de jouets offerts aux McCann, et déposés devant leur appartement ou dans leur commune en Grande-Bretagne, sont remis à différentes institutions caritatives. Les parents veulent que ces objets aillent aux enfants défavorisés. A l'accueil de l'Ocean Club, les McCann y ont déposé une boîte bleue pour recueillir des dons. Dans un petit texte, écrit à la main, fixé sur la petite boîte en carton on peut lire: "Tous les dons iront au Fonds Madeleine - remuer ciel et terre. Merci. Kate et Gerry McCann".

Des bracelets jaunes et verts en caoutchouc et en tissu sont également mis en vente pour 3 euros. Plus d'un mois et demi après sa création, le Fonds atteint déjà plus d'un million d'euros. Justine McGuiness, la nouvelle porte-parole du couple, précise publiquement que l'argent récolté est géré par un groupe indépendant, qui obéit à des règles très strictes. Le montant des récompenses, contre toute information faisant avancer l'enquête, atteint plusieurs millions.

Cette récompense attire inévitablement les escrocs. Cette fois, c'est un Néerlandais trentenaire, au chômage, qui affirme avoir des informations sur Maddie. Il envoie plusieurs mails aux McCann à partir d'un ordinateur d'une agence pour l'emploi et d'un cybercafé. Il réclame deux millions d'euros contre des informations importantes. Les policiers néerlandais identifient l'homme et font parvenir les messages à leurs collègues portugais. Il finira par avouer qu'il avait tout inventé. Il est finalement interpellé à Eindhoven, dans le sud des Pays-Bas. Les McCann réagissent dans un communiqué, où ils se disent très perturbés par cette histoire, mais heureux de constater que toute information ou témoignage fait l'objet de vérifications de la part de la police.

Praia da Luz : la clé de l'énigme ?

La police se concentre toujours sur la piste Murat à Praia da Luz. Les enquêteurs sont convaincus que la clé de l'énigme se trouve dans cette petite station balnéaire. Les témoignages apparus dans plusieurs pays d'Europe ont été vérifiés, mais n'ont rien donné. La piste marocaine est abandonnée également. Après plusieurs semaines, les autorités marocaines répondent à leurs collègues portugais. La très mauvaise qualité des images vidéo des caméras de surveillance de la station service de Marrakech, ne permet pas de les exploiter. La police marocaine ne prend même pas la peine de les transmettre aux autorités portugaises.

Le 10 juillet, Robert Murat est entendu une nouvelle fois par les enquêteurs. Il arrive vers onze heures, en compagnie de son avocat Francisco Pagarete. Il restera dans les locaux de la PJ de Portimao pendant plus de sept heures. C'était la première fois qu'il était interrogé après sa mise en examen en mai. La police cherche d'éventuelles contradictions. Trois amis des McCann, ayant passé des vacances avec eux à l'Ocean Club, sont également entendus. Murat a-t-il quitté son domicile le soir de la disparition de Maddie? C'est l'une des questions à laquelle tentent de répondre les enquêteurs. La police organise un face à face entre Robert Murat et les amis des McCann affirmant l'avoir reconnu. A leur sortie, l'avocat de Murat refuse de répondre aux questions des journalistes rappelant qu'il est tenu de respecter le secret de l'instruction.

Les trois anglais quant à eux publient un communiqué lu par le porte-parole des McCann dans lequel ils se disent "très satisfaits d'avoir pu aider la police". Murat réagit dans la presse britannique quelques jours plus tard. Il affirme que la police judiciaire n'a pas de preuves pour l'incriminer. "Qu'ils m'accusent, ou qu'ils me laissent en paix!", proclame-t-il tout en clamant son innocence. Il ajoute que la loi portugaise permet de le maintenir en examen, malgré l'absence de preuves, pendant plusieurs années. "La loi au Portugal date de l'époque fasciste", lance-t-il. Toute la presse britannique s'arrache les confessions de Murat. Certains titres proposent jusqu'à 45.000 euros pour l'interviewer.

Retour des McCann en Angleterre

A la mi-juillet, les McCann s'absentent quelques jours. Ils se rendent en famille pour la première fois en Grande-Bretagne. A leur retour, le couple reprend la campagne pour retrouver Maddie et accorde un nouvel entretien aux médias. Côté portugais, seule la chaîne publique RTP est invitée. Gerry et Kate confient à quel point cela été difficile de rentrer en Grande-Bretagne sans leur fille. Ils refusent de répondre à des questions concrètes sur l'enquête. "Nous ne voulons pas mettre en péril le travail des enquêteurs", observe Kate. Interrogés sur les conseils qu'ils pourraient donner aux parents partant en vacances l'été, ils répondent un peu gênés: "Ce que nous avons fait, nous avons estimé que c'était responsable. Mais, il est très difficile pour nous de donner des conseils".

En juillet, il faut signaler la commercialisation d'un curieux petit objet. Surfant sur les peurs provoquées par ce triste fait divers, une société lance un système GPS pour suivre ses enfants à la trace. C'est la ruée sur ce petit gadget. Succès qui s'explique peut être par l'impact de l'affaire Maddie.

Du côté de la campagne, les McCann réussissent un grand coup. Le portrait de Maddie sera glissé dans le nouveau Harry Potter. Le septième et dernier roman des aventures du petit magicien sort le 21 juillet dans le monde entier en anglais. Le livre bat encore des records. En 24 heures, plus de 2,6 millions d'exemplaires sont vendus.

Voyage aux Etats-Unis

Après avoir parcouru l'Europe, Gerry est invité aux Etats-Unis. L'affaire y bénéficie également d'une large couverture. Comme en Allemagne, Gerry est confronté à des questions parfois gênantes de la presse américaine: Existe-t-il une possibilité de poursuites judiciaires pour négligence, pour avoir laisser des enfants seuls dans l'appartement?

"Les autorités nous ont assuré que nos actes n'ont fait preuve d'aucune négligence. Madeleine a été victime d'un prédateur sexuel", assure Gerry sur CNN. Il est invité également dans la célèbre émission "Good morning america". Le présentateur lui demande pourquoi ils n'ont pas eu recours au service de baby-sitting de l'Ocean Club. "Nous ne l'avons pas jugé nécessaire. Nous dînions à quelques mètres à peine. Nous pouvions entrevoir l'appartement de là où nous étions", se justifie Gerry.

DISPARUE DEPUIS 3 MOIS

La piste belge

L'été avance à bon rythme. Les températures grimpent. Les touristes Britanniques arrivent en masse à Praia. L'affaire Maddie ne semble pas avoir de conséquences sur le tourisme de cette station balnéaire baignée par l'océan Atlantique. Madeleine a disparu depuis trois mois.

De manière inattendue, un nouveau témoignage ravive les espoirs. Le parquet de Tongres, en Belgique, ouvre une enquête à la suite d'un témoignage faisant état de la présence de la petite Maddie dans une ville dans ce pays. Une psychologue pour enfants raconte avoir reconnu la fillette sur une terrasse de café, accompagnée d'un couple, un homme d'une quarantaine d'années et une femme d'un peu plus de 20 ans. Un portrait robot de l'homme est diffusé sur la base du témoignage de cette femme. L'homme a les cheveux bruns et mesure 1,80 mètre environ.

Le substitut du procureur de Tongres, Katia Vanderen, s'adresse aux médias pour lancer un appel : "Un portrait robot a été dressé sur la base des déclarations du témoin. Nous demandons à toute personne qui détient des informations de les transmettre ou aux deux adultes en question de se faire connaître". La police récupère la bouteille de l'enfant, abandonnée sur la table d'une terrasse de café, ce qui permettra de prélever de la salive sur la paille, puis de le comparer avec l'ADN de la petite Maddie. Les résultats sont connus quelques jours plus tard. Il ne s'agit pas de Maddie, mais d'un ADN d'un individu de sexe masculin, indique la justice belge.

L'enquête se poursuit toutefois. "Cela ne signifie pas que la présence de Maddie est d'emblée exclue. Il est possible que l'homme qui se trouvait aux côtés de la fillette ait terminé la bouteille et laissé sa salive sur la paille", souligne le parquet. Mais cette piste se révèlera infructueuse.

Tournant dans l'enquête : la mort de la fillette ?

Début août, le couple se rend à Huelva. La ville espagnole se trouve juste de l'autre côté de la frontière portugaise. Les McCann ont décidé d'y aller distribuer des tracts avec des photos de Maddie, alors que la thèse de la mort est évoquée avec de plus en plus d'insistance.

L'hebdomadaire portugais Sol parle d'un tournant dans l'enquête. Le procureur général de la République reporte une interview qu'il devait accorder à la BBC sur l'affaire, ce qui nourrit davantage encore les spéculations.

"Madeleine aurait été tué dans l'appartement", titre Correio da Manha le 4 août, soit trois mois après la disparition. Quelques jours plus tôt, deux chiens de la police britannique, Eddie et Keela, ont débarqué dans l'appartement 5-A de l'Ocean Club. Keela devient rapidement nerveuse. Elle signale des traces de sang non visibles à l'oeil nu. Les deux chiens inspectent également les affaires des McCann, qui occupent une villa sur les hauteurs de Praia depuis plusieurs semaines.

Ils s'arrêtent sur l'ours en peluche de Maddie, une chemise et des pantalons en jean appartenant à Kate. Les services des deux springer spaniel, assurés pour plus de 6 million d'euros, sont facturés 800 euros par jour.

Les jours qui suivent c'est le quotidien Jornal de Noticias qui évoque la présence de sang dans l'appartement: "Du Sang dans la chambre des McCann". Le titre retentit comme un coup de tonnerre dans l'opinion publique. Les recherches avec les deux chiens ont permis de repérer des traces de sang sur l'un des murs de la chambre. La police centre son enquête à Praia da Luz. L'appartement se retrouve à nouveau au centre des recherches après avoir été occupé par d'autres clients depuis le 3 mai. La thèse de la mort par homicide ou accident est à présent privilégiée par les enquêteurs. Pour que les chiens détectent une odeur de cadavre, les spécialistes disent que le corps a dû rester au moins deux heures dans l'appartement.

Les enquêteurs décident également de retourner un week-end dans la villa Liliana de la famille Murat. Un périmètre de sécurité est dressé à l'extérieur. La arbustes et plantes du jardin sont coupés. Munis de longs tuyaux en acier, les enquêteurs les enfoncent à plusieurs endroits dans le jardin. Des chiens sont là également pour vérifier si des odeurs de cadavre se dégagent. Murat assiste à ces opérations en compagnie de son avocat. Les enquêteurs expliquent qu'ils cherchent à exploiter toutes les pistes liées à Murat.

Nouvelle thèse : les parents ?

Après l'appartement, la police s'intéresse à plusieurs voitures, parmi lesquelles celle de Robert Murat et des McCann. Elle bloque le dernier des quatre niveaux du parking de la place centrale de Portimao, juste devant les locaux de la PJ. Comme dans l'appartement, les deux chiens Eddie et Keela sont sollicités pour rechercher d'éventuels indices. La Renault Scenic grise louée par les McCann 25 jours après la disparition de leur fille est passée au peigne fin.

Cette fois-ci, les enquêteurs travaillent sur une nouvelle thèse impliquant le couple McCann dans la disparition de leur fille. L'étau se resserre autour du couple. Après ces révélations, le malaise chez les McCann et leurs proches est palpable. Pour la première fois depuis le 3 mai, ils cherchent clairement à fuir les médias, après avoir tout fait pour attirer leur attention. Comme à son habitude, Kate va chercher ses enfants à la crèche de l'Ocean Club. Après les avoir récupérés, elle se dirige d'un pas pressé vers la voiture. Elle couvre le visage de ses enfants, qu'elle serre contre sa poitrine. Elle baisse la tête, puis les installe rapidement à l'arrière tout en tentant de fuir l'objectif des caméras. Gerry accélère le pas également lorsqu'il aperçoit les objectifs des appareils photos.

Ils ont l'habitude jusque là de s'arrêter quelques minutes tous les jours devant les journalistes pour que les photographes et télévisions puissent recueillir leurs images. Le porte-parole des McCann demande aux journalistes de ne pas filmer le couple. Pour mieux fuir les médias, les McCann décident de ne plus emmener leurs jumeaux à la crèche de l'Ocean Club, qu'ils continuent de fréquenter après avoir quitté le village de vacances. Ils l'annoncent dans un court communiqué. Le couple se dit "inquiet de l'impact négatif que leur fréquentation de l'Ocean Club pourrait avoir sur l'ensemble des autres familles en vacances".

Les enquêteurs continuent d'avoir des doutes sur l'emploi du temps qui a précédé la disparition de la fillette. Ils cherchent à comprendre ce qui s'est passé ce 3 mai, en fin d'après-midi. Entre 18 et 21 heures, les parents sont les seuls à avoir vu Maddie en vie.

Les témoignages du couple et de leurs proches manquent de précision. "Beaucoup d'éléments ne collent pas. Nous ne sommes jamais parvenus à établir l'heure exacte de la disparition", confie un enquêteur. La PJ souhaite entendre le couple une nouvelle fois.

Kate se confie à la télé

Dans le même temps, des journaux anglais publient un nouveau témoignage confession de Kate. Elle revient sur le soir du 3 mai. "Le soir de la disparition, pendant une vingtaine de minutes, je n'y ai pas cru. Je me suis dit que ce n'était pas possible. Après, ce fut la panique. Nous avons tous paniqué. Je n'ai pas cru une seconde qu'elle ait pu quitter la chambre par ses propres moyens.

A aucun moment, je n'ai douté qu'elle avait été enlevée. Après cela, vient le sentiment de culpabilité. Le désespoir. A chaque heure qui s'écoule, je me demande pourquoi je me suis dit que l'endroit était sûr? Si je m'étais arrêté une seconde pour réfléchir sur le fait de savoir si je devais laisser les enfants seuls pendant le dîner, je ne l'aurais pas fait. Mais cela ne s'est pas produit. Je me suis sentie en sécurité. Nous l'avions déjà fait plusieurs fois la même semaine.

Le soir où Madeleine a disparu, quand on est allé se coucher, elle m'a dit qu'elle avait eu la meilleure journée de sa vie et qu'elle s'était beaucoup amusée. Je me sens comme la personne la plus malheureuse au monde. Le souvenir de cette nuit est toujours dans ma tête. Il me hante et ne me quitte pas. Je suis sûr que d'autres tireront des leçons de nos erreurs. Mais, nous n'avons commis aucun crime. Quelqu'un d'autre en a commis un. Il ne faut pas l'oublier.

Madeleine était très enthousiaste à l'idée de venir en Algarve. Elle a été très sage pendant le vol. Pendant les vacances, les enfants ont nagé, fait de la barque, joué à la plage, fait de la peinture. Madeleine est à un âge où elle peut beaucoup s'amuser ici. Elle a joué au tennis, un jeu qu'elle adore".

Les McCann soupçonnés

La convocation était attendue depuis plusieurs jours. Les enquêteurs cherchent à clarifier certains points de leurs dépositions, qui ne coïncident pas avec les nouveaux éléments recueillis. Après plusieurs heures d'audition dans les locaux de la police judiciaire, le couple quitte les installations par une porte dérobée à l'arrière du bâtiment.

Rachael Oldfield, l'une des amies ayant passé des vacances avec les McCann en mai, témoigne pour la première fois dans la presse depuis que les soupçons atteignent également l'entourage du couple. "Je ne sais pas si cette théorie est une pure invention ou si c'est la police qui nourrit les journaux avec des mensonges, s'indigne Rachael. Hélas, nous ne pouvons pas nous défendre, car la police nous a demandé de ne pas parler pour ne pas compromettre l'enquête".

Rachael et son Mari Matthew Oldfield défendent la thèse du rapt. Pour elle, pas de doute. Les McCann étaient surveillés le soir de la disparition. Le ravisseur savait qu'ils dînaient et a pu pénétrer en toute tranquillité dans l'appartement et s'emparer de la petite fille.

Face à ces nouveaux soupçons, les McCann ajustent leur communication. Le couple décide d'accorder des entretiens aux trois principales chaînes de télévision britanniques (Sky, BBC, ITN). Il se plie à une séance photos exclusivement réservée aux medias anglais, mais fuient la presse portugaise, blessés par ce qui est publié ces derniers jours. Les médias portugais montent au créneau. Ces derniers se plaignent et se disent victimes de discrimination.

Devant cette vague de contestation, le couple décide alors de parler aux médias lusitaniens. Kate confie que lorsqu'elle a constaté l'absence de Maddie elle a tout de suite eu un mauvais pressentiment. "Je ne peux pas expliquer pourquoi, mais je n'ai pas douté un instant qu'elle avait été enlevée", affirme-t-elle.

Les tensions entre la presse britannique et les enquêteurs portugais sont toujours aussi vives. Les journalistes anglais font un rapprochement avec l'affaire Joana, portant sur la disparition d'une autre fillette en septembre 2004, en Algarve également. Le corps de cette petite fille de huit ans n'a jamais été retrouvé mais la mère, qui clame son innocence, a été inculpée et condamnée à 16 ans de prison. Elle accuse la PJ de l'avoir torturé pour avouer le crime. Gonçalo Amaral, le chef des inspecteurs chargé du dossier Maddie, avait travaillé sur cette affaire.

Face à ces accusations, le syndicat des enquêteurs portugais brandit la menace d'attaquer la presse britannique en justice estimant que leurs propos et accusations sont "mesquins" et "ne correspondent pas à la réalité". Carlos Anjos, président de l'Association syndicale des fonctionnaires de la PJ (ASFIC) se défend. "Quand on critique la police portugaise, on critique par la même occasion les policiers anglais, dans la mesure où ils travaillent ensemble", rappelle-t-il. L'idée de faire venir des chiens anglais est une décision qui a été prise en commun, mais suggérée par la police britannique, précise-t-il.

A la mi-août, les McCann parlent une nouvelle fois aux trois principales chaînes de télévision portugaises. Au cours de ces interviews, ils tiennent à faire une mise au point sur un certain nombre d'éléments écrits et rapportés par les médias les dernières semaines. Ils l'affirment et le répètent pour la énième fois: ils sont convaincus que leur fille est toujours vivante. L'absence d'indices semblant indiquer qu'elle ait pu avoir été tuée les en persuade. Ils assurent également qu'ils font totalement confiance à leurs amis, qui les entouraient le soir du 3 mai. Puis, ils se disent surpris d'apprendre qu'ils pourraient figurer dans la liste des suspects. Interrogés sur les traces de sang, retrouvées dans la chambre, les McCann répondent ne rien savoir. "Nous ne savions pas qu'il y avait du sang. Toute cette spéculation nous blesse", affirme Kate. Gerry dément catégoriquement les informations selon lesquelles ils auraient administré des sédatifs à leurs enfants pour les faire dormir. "Absolument pas!", lance-t-il visiblement agacé.

La presse portugaise abonde dans les détails semblant corroborer la responsabilité des McCann. Les médias font régulièrement appel à l'analyse de psychiatres. Parmi les plus cités dans la presse: la pédopsychiatre Ana Vasconcelos. Elle fait le tour des plateaux de télévision en plein été. Mme Vasconcelos précise toujours que son explication relève d'une lecture hypothétique. Sa théorie est que "les parents sont unis dans le profond besoin de croire que leur fille est vivante. C'est une réaction au traumatisme provoqué par la disparition de leur fille. Pour faire face à ce choc, ils entrent dans une phase de négation. Il y a un clivage. Remarquez il n'y a que maintenant, cent jours après la disparition, que la mère confie regretter d'avoir laissé sa fille seule dans la chambre. Elle ne l'avait pas dit avant, car cela reviendrait peut être à remettre en cause l'idée selon laquelle la fillette est vivante. Le regard fixe, le fait de se donner la main, ce retrait par rapport à son mari, tout cela peut paraître étrange mais peut s'expliquer par le fait qu'elle a besoin de croire que leur fillette est vivante. Dans l'hypothèse d'un accident domestique, ce couple réagit ainsi car il n'arrive pas à faire face à la mort de leur fille".

Les initiatives pour retrouver Maddie se poursuivent. Cette fois la campagne "find madeleine" va bénéficier d'un coup de publicité inattendu. Laura Bush, première dame américaine, s'associe à la création d'une section sur le site de partage de vidéos youtube consacré aux enfants disparus. Elle enregistre un message: "Regardez ces vidéos et ces visages, dit Mme Bush. Notre objectif est de retrouver" ces enfants. Le site (www.youtube.com/dontyouforgetaboutme) est géré par le centre international des enfants disparus

(Icmec). Parmi les visages des enfants portés disparus figure celui de Maddie, la plus célèbre des enfants disparus désormais.

DISPARUE DEPUIS 100 JOURS

Triste anniversaire

11 août 2007 - Cela fait cent jours que Maddie a disparu. Pour signaler cette date une messe est organisée dans la petite église de Praia da Luz. Ce samedi matin, Kate et Gerry arrivent main dans la main. Lui porte un T-shirt vert et jaune arborant un portrait de Maddie. Elle, tient un bouquet de fleurs jaunes d'une main, serrant le doudou de sa fille de l'autre.

Des centaines de personnes et plusieurs dizaines de caméras les attendent devant le parvis de l'église. Seul 200 personnes environ peuvent pénétrer à l'intérieur. Ils sont nombreux à attendre la sortie des McCann à l'extérieur. La messe est célébrée par le révérend anglican Haynes Hubbard, qui vit à Praia avec sa femme Susan et ses deux enfants.

Les McCann sont devenus amis avec le couple Hubbard. Pour cette célébration, le contexte est différent. L'enquête semble prendre un nouveau tournant. Les McCann se sentent attaqués. Le révérend Haynes Hubbard commence la messe en prenant la défense du couple. "Le monde souhaiterait que nous croyions à certaines choses, mais je vous demande de ne pas croire à cela et de garder la foi et l'espoir".

Kate prend ensuite la parole pour parler de sa fille: "Je veux vous dire à quelle point Maddie était merveilleuse. Notre vie est incomplète sans elle". Elle s'arrête, fait une pause, baisse légèrement la tête visiblement émue puis poursuit: "Je vous prie, gardez Madeleine dans vos souvenirs et vos prières".

C'est autour de Gerry de se lever et s'adresser à l'auditoire: "Aidez-nous à trouver Madeleine. Madeleine a disparu depuis cent jours, les jours les plus difficiles de nos vies, pour nous, notre famille et nos amis. Nous n'allons pas ralentir nos efforts jusqu'à ce que nous retrouvions Madeleine".

La thèse de la mort gagne du terrain

Dans l'après-midi, un entretien du porte-parole de la PJ à la BBC, fait l'effet d'une bombe. Il évoque pour la première fois en public la possibilité que la petite Maddie soit morte. Il précise toutefois que les parents ne sont pas suspects. "Les développements de ces derniers jours nous ont mis sur certaines pistes semblant indiquer que la fillette pourrait être morte, déclare Olegario de Sousa. Toutes les hypothèses sont sur la table, mais celle-ci semble un peu plus forte que les autres".

Quant aux McCann, "ils sont des victimes, car ils ont perdu leur enfant, et témoins" dans cette affaire, précise-t-il. Le lendemain, de nouvelles révélations semblent renforcer cette piste. La presse parle d'une seconde trace de sang retrouvée dans l'appartement. Après la cérémonie religieuse du matin, les McCann se retirent dans leur villa. Ils ne réagissent pas publiquement aux déclarations d'Olegario de Sousa. Une amie du couple confie toutefois à la presse britannique que les McCann sont blessés et attristés par l'attitude de la police, qui ne les a pas tenu informés de cette nouvelle hypothèse avant de faire des déclarations à la presse. Ils assurent que la police leur a toujours dit rechercher une fillette en vie et non un cadavre.

Les jours qui suivent, Kate évoque pour la première fois la mort de la fillette et la possibilité de rentrer en Grande-Bretagne, dans une interview au magazine Woman's. "Je préfère la savoir morte, plutôt que de vivre dans l'incertitude, confie-t-elle. Je n'ai jamais aimé l'incertitude. Au fond de nous-mêmes Gerry et moi préférions savoir, même que cela veuille dire que nous devons faire face à une terrible vérité. Pour autant cela n'efface pas le sentiment de culpabilité. A chaque fois que je souris avec les jumeaux et que nous mangeons quelque chose qui nous plaît, je me dis que Madeleine aurait aimé cela également.

Quand je me couche le soir, j'espère que ce sera le dernier jour sans elle. Je me suis demandé plusieurs fois ce qui m'a amené à penser qu'il n'y avait pas de danger à laisser les enfants seuls dans la chambre de l'appartement? L'endroit paraissait si sûr. Personne ne pouvait imaginer qu'un ravisseur ferait irruption et enlève notre fille.

Maddie est une enfant très sociable et drôle. Mais elle a un caractère très fort. Elle détestait que nous l'appelions Maddie. Elle répondait toujours contrariée: +Je m'appelle Madeleine!+. Je pense qu'elle doit donner beaucoup de travail à son ravisseur".

Après les nouvelles déclarations de la PJ, les McCann demandent une réunion urgente avec les enquêteurs. Les réunions n'ont plus lieu avec autant de régularité comme au début de l'enquête. Les inspecteurs préfèrent attendre les résultats des analyses des vestiges biologiques et traces de sang retrouvés dans l'appartement avant de fixer une nouvelle rencontre. L'opération est d'une grande complexité et prends plusieurs jours. Les échantillons prélevés sont en très mauvais état et il faut réussir à en extraire l'ADN pour obtenir des résultats. Mais la police assure qu'elle dispose d'autres éléments pour soutenir sa thèse de la mort. Les résultats des analyses sont publiés dans le quotidien The Times.

Verdict : le sang n'appartient pas à Maddie mais à un homme du nord de l'Europe, qui n'a pas de profil génétique dans la base de données de la police, écrit le quotidien. Ces traces de sang ne prouveraient rien. Elles seraient très antérieures au séjour des McCann. Leur degré de fiabilité est de 72%, selon le Times.

Le directeur de la PJ de Faro Guilhermino Encarnaçao ne tarde pas à démentir cette information. Le laboratoire britannique indique également de son côté que les résultats ne sont pas prêts. Et précise qu'il y a de fortes chances qu'ils ne soient pas concluants en raison de la mauvaise qualité des échantillons.

Le directeur de la PJ, très discret d'habitude, s'exprime dans le quotidien Diario Economico. Il apporte une mise au point sur la thèse de la mort : "Nous ne disons pas qu'elle est morte. Cette hypothèse est sur la table. Nous devons l'analyser. Il nous manque toujours un mobile. Il peut être financier, lié à une vengeance, à de la jalousie, de la haine. Pour l'instant, nous n'en savons rien".

Il réfute également l'idée selon laquelle la police aurait été soumise à des pressions de la part de enquêteurs anglais ou des autorités britanniques. Puis, il termine l'entretien sur une note optimiste. "Dans ce genre d'affaires, le taux de succès est élevé au Portugal, affirme-t-il. Il n'y a pas beaucoup d'enlèvements dans notre pays. Ceux dont nous avons connaissances se passent surtout entre des proches. Par exemple, des parents divorcés. Le père qui enlève son enfant à la mère qui en a la garde".

Sur le terrain, la police poursuit son enquête. Les enquêteurs interrogent Pamela Fenn, une septuagénaire britannique, qui séjournait au-dessus de l'appartement des McCann à l'occasion de la disparition de la fillette. Elle dit à la police avoir entendu une enfant pleurer, entre 22 et 23 heures, dans l'appartement des McCann quelques jours avant la disparition de Maddie. La petite a appelé son père plusieurs fois. Le soir de la disparition, elle dit avoir proposé au couple d'appeler la police. Mais Kate avait décliné. Elle raconte également que, quelques jours avant le 3 mai, quelqu'un avait tenté de cambrioler son appartement. Surpris, le voleur avait pris la fuite. Selon elle, l'homme pourrait correspondre à la description du suspect du portrait robot. La police tente de recouper tous ces témoignages avec d'autres éléments. Mais ils ne donnent rien de concluant. Au Royaume-Uni, la police procède à l'audition de quelques touristes britanniques ayant séjourné à l'Ocean Club en même temps que les McCann. Rien également.

Nouvelle piste mais beaucoup d'interrogations

Le mois d'août touche à sa fin. Les derniers rebondissements de l'affaire changent complètement l'axe d'investigation. L'enquête prend un virage en raison de "nouveaux éléments", affirme M. Ribeiro. Pour autant, l'affaire est loin d'être résolue, s'empresse-t-il toutefois de souligner. Après le sang retrouvé dans l'appartement, des résidus biologiques, tels que des cheveux, ont également été retrouvés dans la voiture louée par les McCann après la disparition de Maddie. Cela pourrait donc vouloir dire que le corps de la fillette y a été transporté. Mais vers où? Où se trouve-t-il actuellement? Jeté à la mer, enfoui dans les environs de Praia da Luz, les enquêteurs cherchent à comprendre. Les policiers reprennent l'affaire point par point.

La version des McCann et de leurs proches suscite une série d'interrogations. Premier point relevé par l'hebdomadaire portugais Sol, les McCann et leurs amis ont raconté qu'ils se relayaient régulièrement pendant le dîner au restaurant pour surveiller les enfants. Les employés du restaurant Tapas ne se souviennent pas d'avoir vu les clients de ce groupe se lever de table à une telle fréquence.

Le comportement de Russel O'Brien soulève également des questions. Ce médecin a raconté à la police avoir été absent pendant la plupart du dîner pour s'occuper de sa fille malade qui ne cessait de vomir. Or, d'après les employés de l'Ocean Club personne n'a réclamé de nouveaux draps ce soir-là.

Autre point: comment le ravisseur présumé de la petite Maddie a-t-il pu pénétrer dans l'appartement des McCann? L'appartement ne présentait aucun signe d'effraction.

113

Par ailleurs, Jane Taner, l'une des amis des McCann, a affirmé avoir aperçu, quand elle s'est levée de table, un homme transportant un enfant, qu'elle n'a pas reconnu. Non loin de là, Gerry parlait avec un autre touriste Jeremy Wilkins. Les deux hommes affirment n'avoir rien remarqué d'étrange. Comment l'homme décrit par Jane Taner a-t-il pu leur échapper?

Le journal portugais souligne également que lorsque les McCann se rendent compte de la disparition de leur fille, ils appellent d'abord Sky News avant de prévenir la police.

Par ailleurs, comment expliquer le comportement de Gerry le soir de la disparition. Il a réclamé la nuit du drame un curé. Comme aucun n'a fait le déplacement, il s'est rendu dans l'église la plus proche. Pourquoi? Que cache cette attitude?, s'interroge Sol qui s'étonne en outre que les jumeaux ne se soient pas réveillés le soir du 3 mai malgré le bruit et l'agitation régnant dans l'appartement. Les McCann ont-ils administré des somnifères à leurs enfants?

Complot politique ?

Les résidus biologiques recueillis dans la voiture ont été envoyés au laboratoire britannique de Birmingham pour analyse. Les jours passent et les résultats tardent. Toute la presse s'alarme. Les théories les plus folles sont évoquées. La diplomatie britannique tenterait-elle de mettre la main sur l'enquête afin de mieux contrôler l'évolution de l'enquête? Spécialistes, criminologues défilent dans les journaux et plateaux de télévision pour y exposer leurs explications et leurs théories du complot. Manipulations politiques au plus haut niveau, avancent certains. Les résultats ne vont pas dans le sens des intérêts du gouvernement britannique qui défend les McCann depuis le début, affirment certains spécialistes.

D'autres, appellent à la raison. Ils expliquent que les analyses, qui prennent normalement une quinzaine de jours, sont plus longues dans ce cas précis en raison de la qualité des échantillons. Le laboratoire doit également réaliser des contre-analyses pour éviter des erreurs, puis il doit comparer le profil génétique avec celui des membres de la famille et des proches.

L'étau se resserre autour des McCann

Les McCann, qui ont toujours affirmé vouloir rester en Algarve jusqu'à ce que toute la lumière soit faite sur l'affaire, commencent à changer d'avis. Alors que l'étau se resserre sur eux, ils affirment envisager de repartir en Angleterre. Gerry le répète notamment en Ecosse au cours du festival international de télévision à Edimbourg, où il est invité à participer pour expliquer comment il a mis en place, en si peu de temps, une campagne internationale pour retrouver sa fille, avec une telle répercussion mondiale.

"Rester au Portugal peut se révéler contre-productif. Mais émotionnellement, il est très difficile de quitter ce pays à quatre, alors que nous étions cinq quand nous sommes arrivés", confie-t-il. Sur la répercussion mondiale de l'affaire, il se dit surpris. "Nous ne nous attendions pas à une telle médiatisation. Nous nous sommes limités à organiser des événements pour rappeler que Maddie était toujours disparue et que nous étions à sa recherche", souligne-t-il.

A son retour, le couple répond aux sollicitations de la télévision espagnole Telecinco. L'interview serait passée inaperçue sans la réaction inattendue de Gerry à une question sensible. Le journaliste demande tout d'abord pourquoi les jumeaux ne se sont pas réveillés le soir du 3 mai, laissant ainsi planer le doute sur l'utilisation de somnifères. Gerry répond: "Nos enfants étaient très fatigués. Ils sont très petits. Nous ne savons pas s'ils ont entendu quelque chose. D'habitude, nous les couchons entre 19 et 20H00 et ils dorment toute la nuit sans se réveiller.

Sur l'enquête, il se plaint de l'absence d'éléments nouveaux. "Il ne semble y avoir aucun élément nouveau. La police agit de manière très, très discrète". Puis arrive une question sur les traces de sang retrouvées dans l'appartement. Gerry explose. Il se lève, enlève le micro et quitte la pièce, laissant Kate seule face aux caméras. Gerry s'excusera plus tard d'avoir laissé éclater ainsi son exaspération.

La presse anglaise continue de pointer d'un doigt accusateur Murat et dénonce une "campagne de haine" de la presse portugaise à l'encontre des McCann. La stratégie des journaux anglais consiste à critiquer la presse portugaise tout en reprenant leurs informations. De son côté, la presse portugaise adopte un ton très critique à l'égard des McCann. Les journaux dénoncent les liens haut placés de la famille et notamment avec le Premier ministre Gordon Brown. Gerry a parlé plusieurs fois par téléphone avec le chef du gouvernement britannique, selon des proches. L'affaire Maddie a même figuré plusieurs fois au programme des discussions des réunions bilatérales entre les deux pays.

DISPARUE DEPUIS 4 MOIS

Mise en examen des parents

Quatre mois après la disparition, Kate publie une tribune dans le quotidien anglais News of the world. Elle y défend la création d'une base de données européenne dans laquelle figureraient les prédateurs sexuels condamnés. "Gerry et moi ne comprenons pas pourquoi cette information, qui pourrait tant aider à protéger des enfants, n'est pas partagée par les différents pays en Europe", écrit-elle. Elle appelle à faire pression auprès des gouvernements pour la création de cet outil judiciaire.

Sur son blog, Gerry s'adresse une nouvelle fois au ravisseur présumé : "Parfois les gens font des choses qu'ils ne comprennent pas eux-mêmes. Un acte de folie, un accident, tout cela peut avoir des conséquences que personne n'aurait imaginé avant. Si vous avez fait quelque chose, que vous regrettez, il n'est pas trop tard pour faire ce qui est correct. Je vous en prie, faites un signe, rendez Madeleine, déposez-là dans un endroit sûr. Ou alors aidez-nous, laissez-nous savoir ce qui lui est arrivé".

Cette première semaine de septembre, les résultats des analyses tant attendues semblent sur le point d'être remis aux enquêteurs. Le jeudi 6 septembre, la situation bascule. Kate et Gerry ne quittent pas leur villa pour leur jogging matinal. Les McCann ont été convoqués par la Police judiciaire. C'est la cinquième fois qu'ils vont être entendus. La police veut les interroger séparément. Cette fois ils sentent que la teneur de l'audition sera différente. Le jeudi matin, ils se préparent. Après avoir pris leur petit déjeuner, le couple dépose les jumeaux à la crèche de l'Ocean Club sous le regard des journalistes et des photographes qui les attendent à l'extérieur de leur villa. Ils se rendent ensemble à l'église. Puis, ils déjeunent avec la mère et la soeur de Gerry, qui séjournent avec eux à Praia da Luz.

A 14H00, Kate a rendez-vous dans les locaux de la PJ de Portimao. Elle porte un pantalon noir et un sac à dos vert kaki. Sur son haut blanc, elle arbore un badge avec un portrait de Maddie. Elle serre entre ses mains la petite peluche de sa fille. Gerry l'accompagne en voiture jusqu'à la porte de la police judiciaire. Ils s'embrassent, puis elle rentre en compagnie de la soeur de Gerry, mais c'est seule qu'elle affrontera les questions des enquêteurs. Elle n'aura droit pour seule assistance que les services d'un traducteur.

A l'extérieur, Justine McGuiness, porte-parole des McCann, lit un communiqué où les McCann affirment qu'ils vont retrouver Maddie en vie. Kate "est une mère adorable et attentionnée. Elle est l'une des victimes dans cette extraordinaire et terrible succession d'événements. Kate continue de croire que Madeleine est vivante. Elle attend et prie tous les jours pour qu'elle revienne vite". Les McCann se disent en outre "heureux d'aider la police dans son enquête".

A l'intérieur des locaux de la PJ, les enquêteurs lui posent des dizaines de questions sur le soir du 3 mai et plus particulièrement sur les heures qui ont précédé sa disparition. Entre 18 et 21 heures, Maddie n'a pas quitté sa famille.

A quelle heure Maddie a-t-elle disparue? La journée du 3 mai, Maddie n'a pas été aperçue après 18 heures. D'après certains témoignages, Kate a joué avec ses enfants entre 18h30 et 19H dans le salon de l'appartement. C'est là aussi que la police a retrouvé des traces de sang par terre, sur les murs et derrière un canapé. Les enquêteurs font visionner à Kate des images vidéo montrant les réactions des chiens lorsqu'ils détectent l'odeur de cadavre dans l'appartement, ainsi que sur un t-shirt et un pantalon lui appartenant. Des éléments qui semblent mettre à mal la thèse de l'enlèvement, pour privilégier l'hypothèse de la mort dans l'appartement. Kate devient nerveuse. Elle se défend et explique qu'en tant que médecin, il est naturel que les chiens aient eu cette réaction lorsqu'ils ont reniflé ses vêtements, dans la mesure où elle a été en contact avec des cadavres dans l'hôpital où elle travaille, quelques jours avant son départ pour le Portugal.

Par ailleurs, le couple a affirmé qu'il allait voir leurs enfants toutes les 20 minutes, ce qui ne semble pas si exact. Gerry dit s'être levé vers 21 heures pour aller jeter un coup d'œil dans l'appartement. En réalité, il semble qu'il ne se soit pas rentré. Il aurait croisé une connaissance et se serait arrêté pour parler.

D'après les employés du Tapas, au cours du dîner seul deux personnes se ont absentées: Russel O'Brien et Mattew Oldfield. Aucun d'entre eux n'est entré dans l'appartement où dormait Maddie. Les autorités ne savent donc pas si Maddie se trouvait bien dans sa chambre entre 18 et 23H40, l'heure à laquelle les gendarmes portugais, la GNR est arrivée à l'Ocean Club.

Par ailleurs, le témoignage de Jane Tanner, qui dit avoir vu un homme portant ce qui pourrait être un enfant enroulé dans une couverture, est contredit par les employés du Tapas. Jane, selon eux, ne se serait levé de table que lorsque kate est entrée affolée pour crier au secours. De même, Russel O'Brien dit être sorti du restaurant pour voir sa fille malade, qui a vomi. Or, le service de nettoyage indique que personne n'a fait appel à lui pour lui demander de changer les draps. D'après le témoignage de certains gendarmes appelés à l'Ocean Club, le groupe d'anglais semblait être sous l'emprise de l'alcool.

Autant de témoignages qui soulèvent de nombreuses questions chez les enquêteurs. Lors de l'audition de Kate, la police l'interroge également sur les vestiges biologiques

121

semblant appartenir à Maddie, des cheveux notamment en grande quantité, recueillis dans la voiture de la famille louée près de deux semaines après la disparition. La voiture pourrait avoir servi à transporter le corps de la fillette, selon eux.

La police portugaise est toutefois consciente que la réaction de ces chiens ne peut constituer une preuve en tribunal. Elle sert juste à orienter les policiers sur une piste plutôt qu'une autre. Ils insistent, mettent la pression, espèrent obtenir des aveux. Kate maintient sa version. Elle ne ressortira que vers une heure du matin, après onze heures d'audition.

Après plus de 16 heures d'audition sur deux jours, l'information tombe comme un couperet et ouvre les journaux télévisés: Kate est mise en examen. C'est le choc. En quelques heures, elle est officiellement passée de victime à suspecte. Dans le droit pénal portugais elle est déclarée "arguida". Pour cela, il doit exister des indices suffisants de sa participation à un délit ou à un crime.

Selon l'importance des soupçons pesant sur la personne, celle-ci peut être placée en détention préventive, en résidence surveillée, ou se voir interdire de quitter le territoire. Une décision qui nécessite l'intervention d'un juge. Par ailleurs ce statut comporte certains droits et devoirs. En tant que témoin, une personne peut être interrogée sur ce qu'elle a vu mais qu'en tant qu'+arguido+ elle est interrogée sur ce qu'elle a fait. De son côté, la personne peut refuser de répondre à certaines questions et peut être assistée d'un avocat.

Le vent a tourné et l'opinion publique portugaise également. Kate ne bénéficie plus de la sympathie et la compassion du début de l'affaire. Elle est même sifflée et huée à sa sortie des locaux de la Police Judiciaire (PJ).

Gerry arrive à la PJ quelques minutes à peine après que Kate eut quitté les lieux. Ils ne se croisent pas. Il en ressortira vers minuit, mis en examen également.

Maître Carlos Pinto de Abreu, l'avocat portugais du couple, le confirme. "Kate et Gerry ont été mis en examen mais restent en liberté", précise l'avocat en ajoutant "qu'aucun chef d'accusation ne repose sur eux" et que "l'enquête se poursuit avec sérénité". Le couple n'a pas répondu à une quarantaine de questions que la police qualifie d'importantes pour l'enquête. Les McCann ont par exemple refusé d'expliquer la présence de cheveux dans le coffre de la voiture en invoquant leur droit au silence.

Ce sont les premiers éléments de ces analyses, confirmant avec un degré "élevé de fiabilité" la présence dans le coffre de la voiture des McCann de vestiges biologiques, laissés par des corps en décomposition, qui ont entraîné leur mise en examen.

Selon les proches des McCann, les parents sont soupçonnés d'être impliqués dans la disparition de Maddie, morte à la suite d'un accident, et d'avoir ensuite dissimulé son cadavre. Les principaux soupçons reposent sur Kate. Selon l'un de ses porte-parole, David Hughes, c'est elle qui est "soupçonnée d'avoir accidentellement tué sa fille".

De son côté, Philomena McCann, la soeur de Gerry, précise que les enquêteurs portugais ont laissé entendre que "Kate a tué Madeleine accidentellement, d'une façon ou d'une autre, et qu'elle a gardé le corps avant de s'en débarrasser". Philomena affirme également que la police a proposé à Kate une réduction de peine si elle reconnaissait avoir tué sa fille, ce que la police conteste.

Ces soupçons sont "risibles", lance Gerry sur son blog réaffirmant que sa femme est "totalement innocente". Il se dit déterminé à se battre par tous les moyens pour continuer de chercher Madeleine.

Les confessions tant attendues par la police n'ont pas

eu lieu. Mais les enquêteurs décident tout de même la mise en examen des parents. Plusieurs scénarios sont évoqués: surdosage de somnifères, violence sur la fillette? La police est convaincue d'un homicide accidentel, dont Kate serait l'auteur. Le couple se serait alors mis d'accord pour cacher le corps avant de donner l'alerte. C'est la théorie défendu par l'équipe des inspecteurs, qui cherche à comprendre comment le corps a pu être dissimulé pendant près d'un mois.

La mise en examen des McCann, qui porte à trois le nombre de "arguidos" depuis la disparition de la petite "Maddie", a suscité la stupeur à Portimao, où des dizaines de journalistes, parmi lesquels de très nombreux Britanniques, et des badauds étaient massés devant les locaux de la PJ pour tenter d'apercevoir le couple. En plus des journalistes, les touristes sont également nombreux. Beaucoup de vacanciers se trouvant en Algarve font un détour par Praia da Luz, pour tenter d'apercevoir le désormais célèbre Ocean Club.

Des médias en masse

Jamais Praia da Luz n'avait connu une telle concentration de médias. Si ces professionnels se trouvent dans une station balnéaire où tout rappelle les vacances, leur emploi du temps n'a rien à voir avec une partie de plaisir. Certains journalistes britanniques travaillent en groupe et se donnent rendez-vous tous les matins dans le petit café bar Hugo Beaty, transformé pour l'occasion en salle de rédaction.

Ils se lèvent à l'aube pour surveiller la concurrence. Vers 08H30 arrive leur traductrice attitrée, Gaynor de Jesus, avec une pile de journaux et magazines sous le bras. Ils épluchent la presse portugaise et décident des sujets de la journée. Le déjeuner a lieu normalement dans un restaurant de Praia, après l'envoi des premiers papiers.

Sky News a joué un rôle clé dans cette affaire. Les reporters de la chaîne de Rupert Murdoch avaient été les premiers à arriver sur place dès le lendemain de la disparition. Au plus fort de la couverture en mai, les jours qui ont suivi la disparition de la fillette, Sky avait dépêché sur place jusqu'à 36 personnes. Le journal de la chaîne avait même été délocalisé à Praia da Luz, d'où il était présenté en direct par deux présentateurs vedettes de la chaîne.

Martin Brunt, la cinquantaine bien tassée avec plus de trente ans de métier, est l'un de ces journalistes vedettes de Sky News. Il confie au quotidien portugais Diario de Noticias que l'affaire Maddie est "l'histoire la plus compliquée et la plus fascinante en même temps" qu'il a eu à couvrir.

Il raconte son quotidien. "C'est assez compliqué. Je tente tous les jours de comprendre ce qui se passe, mais c'est très difficile car la police ne nous informe de rien. Nous devons alors puiser dans les médias portugais tout en ne sachant pas si ce qui est écrit est vrai. Au début, je me méfiais des journaux portugais, mais aujourd'hui je me rends compte qu'ils reproduisaient souvent ce que la police savait à un moment donné".

Il compare ensuite la couverture de cette affaire au Portugal avec ce qui se serait normalement passé en Grande-Bretagne. "En Grande-Bretagne, la police communique avec la presse, tandis qu'au Portugal elle se retranche derrière le secret d'instruction. En revanche, les informations filtrent quand même et les journalistes portugais ont accès à des détails de l'enquête. C'est complètement contradictoire".

Par exemple, "j'appelais tous les jours le porte-parole de la PJ, mais je n'obtenais jamais de réponse, ou alors des éléments que je connaissais déjà. En Angleterre ce genre d'affaires ce serait passé différemment, fait-il remarquer. Quand un enfant est porté disparu, la police distribue des portraits, fournit des détails spécifiques sur les vêtements qu'il portait. Le public est mis à contribution. Par ailleurs, la police anglaise aurait enquêté sur la famille dès les premières semaines, or ici ce ne fut pas le cas. Ils ont fait les choses dans le mauvais ordre. Par exemple, l'ADN qui a permis de mettre en examen les McCann n'a été prélevé que plusieurs semaines après la disparition de la fillette."

Les McCann rentrent en Angleterre

Le lendemain de leur mise en examen, les McCann ne quittent pas leur villa. Ils rassemblent leurs affaires, sans que les dizaines de journalistes à l'extérieur ne se doutent de ce qui se prépare. Seul les porte-parole du couple s'expriment. Ils assurent que les McCann vont rester à Praia. Mais, samedi soir une rumeur circule parmi les journalistes selon laquelle le couple s'apprête à prendre l'avion le lendemain matin pour rentrer en Grande-Bretagne.

Dimanche à l'aube, il fait encore nuit. Des dizaines de photographes et reporters font déjà le pied de grue devant le portail de la villa des McCann. Vers sept heures du matin, la famille s'installe dans la Renault Scenic de location. Des gendarmes forment une barrière pour contenir les journalistes et permettre à la voiture de passer. La famille quitte la villa sous un déluge de flashs. Certaines chaînes de télévision les suivent en direct sur l'autoroute en direction de l'aéroport de Faro où ils doivent embarquer à bord d'un vol d'Easyjet à destination d'East Midlands.

A leur arrivée à l'aéroport, ils ont droit à un traitement exceptionnel. Ils empruntent une porte dérobée. Ils s'installent au premier rang de l'appareil en compagnie de leurs enfants. Le deuxième rang est laissé vide pour préserver l'intimité de la famille. Leurs proches restés au Portugal règlent les derniers détails. Ils doivent notamment rendre la voiture louée par les McCann.

Kate demande à Susan Hubbard, la femme du curé anglican de Praia, de remercier tous ceux qui les ont aidés. "Je suis triste de n'avoir pu vous dire au revoir de vive voix, mais je reviendrai pour remercier tous ceux qui nous ont soutenu", écrit Kate dans un message qui est lu dans la petite église de Praia après leur départ. Kate et Gerry auraient souhaité se rendre à l'église la veille de leur départ avec les jumeaux, mais la présence de centaines de journalistes les en dissuade.

Après le décollage de l'avion, Justine McGuiness lit un communiqué à la presse. Les McCann assurent que ce retour en Grande-Bretagne n'est pas une fuite, mais qu'il a été décidé en accord avec le ministère public portugais. A son arrivée en Angleterre, Gerry étreint par l'émotion lit la même déclaration aux nombreux journalistes qui les attendent sur le tarmac de l'aéroport d'East Midlands. Il affirme qu'ils ne cesseront jamais de chercher leur fille. "Nous souhaitons que les jumeaux aient une vie normale autant que possible dans le pays où ils sont nés. Pour nous c'est très dur de rentrer sans Madeleine. Cela ne veut pas dire que nous avons cessé de la chercher. Nous ne pouvons laisser tomber notre fille tant que nous ne savons pas ce qui s'est passé. Nous devons continuer de tout faire pour la retrouver.

Kate et moi, souhaitons remercier une fois de plus, tous ceux qui nous ont soutenu ces derniers jours, ces dernières semaines et ces derniers mois. Nous aimerions aussi que notre vie privée soit respectée. Notre retour s'est fait avec l'aval des autorités portugaises et de la police. La loi portugaise nous empêche de parler de l'enquête. Malgré le fait d'avoir beaucoup à dire, nous ne pouvons le faire. Nous souhaitons juste dire que nous n'avons rien à voir avec la disparition de notre fille adorée Madeleine". Les McCann retrouvent ainsi leur maison de Rothley après l'avoir quitté il y a plus de quatre mois pour de simples vacances.

Les enquêteurs poursuivent leur travail. La priorité est de retrouver le corps de Maddie. La police pense que le cadavre de la fillette a été enterré dans le quartier de l'Ocean Club ou qu'il a été jeté à la mer. Les enquêteurs terminent leur rapport, une dizaine de volumes au total qu'ils remettent au Ministère public. Les McCann préparent quant à eux leur défense. Ils font appel au cabinet Kingsley Naley, célèbre pour avoir empêché l'extradition du général

Pinochet vers l'Espagne, une extradition réclamée par le juge espagnol Baltasar Garzon qui cherchait à le juger pour crimes contre l'humanité.

Le dossier de l'enquête bouclé

Les jours qui suivent le départ des McCann, tout semble les incriminer. Les médias britanniques rapportent que les traces de sang et de vestiges biologiques invisibles à l'oeil nu, découverts dans le coffre du véhicule utilisé par les McCann, correspondent "à 100%" au profil génétique de la petite Madeleine. Le directeur national de la PJ Alipio Ribeiro dément aussitôt ces informations lors d'une émission spéciale consacrée à l'affaire sur la chaîne portugaise de télévision publique RTP. "Aucun des résultats de ces examens ne permet de dire avec une telle précision mathématique que le sang appartient à x ou y", déclare-t-il. Il précise également qu'à ce stade de l'enquête, la détention provisoire du couple n'est pas envisagée. La thèse d'une mort accidentelle impliquant ses parents attend toujours d'être confirmée par des éléments matériels probants, tient-il à préciser.

La semaine qui suit la mise en examen, la justice portugaise se saisit de l'affaire de la disparition de la petite Britannique. Un communiqué précise que l'enquête peut conduire à de nouvelles mesures à l'encontre des parents. "L'enquête n'est pas terminée et de nouvelles procédures sont nécessaires à la suite desquelles d'éventuelles mesures de contrôle judiciaire seront étudiées", annonce le procureur général de la République après avoir reçu le rapport d'enquête de la police judiciaire.

Le rapport est alors transmis au parquet de Portimao, puis au juge d'instruction. Il comprend notamment les comptes-rendus de l'audition des parents de la fillette et les résultats d'analyse de traces de sang trouvées dans la voiture du couple. La justice se donne dix jours pour statuer sur le sort du couple. Un délai qui doit permettre au ministère public d'étudier l'éventuel recours aux mécanismes de coopération internationale. A ce stade, aucune mise en accusation formelle n'a été prononcée, et même si les enquêteurs privilégient l'hypothèse de la mort de Madeleine, l'absence de cadavre rend difficile la qualification du délit.

Journal intime de Kate saisi

La justice autorise la saisie du journal intime de Kate McCann pour le verser au dossier. La PJ dispose déjà de plusieurs photocopies, mais ne pouvait s'en servir comme élément de preuve sans l'autorisation du ministère public. La presse portugaise en publie des extraits dans lesquels Kate apparaît comme une femme épuisée par des enfants très énergiques.

Dans ce journal, elle se plaint fréquemment que ses enfants sont "hystériques" et parle de Madeleine comme d'une enfant débordant de vitalité. Une énergie qui l'épuise. Elle écrit que son époux ne l'aide pas dans les tâches familiales. Kate avait décidé de se lancer dans la rédaction d'un journal, qu'elle adresse à sa fille disparue, quelques jours après la disparition de la fillette. L'objectif était de décrire toutes les opérations et initiatives mises en œuvre pour la retrouver.

Courant septembre, le désormais célèbre porte-parole de la PJ, Olegario Sousa, cesse ses fonctions. Il explique officiellement que son travail ne se justifie plus. C'est désormais le cabinet de presse de la PJ qui occupera ce poste. Olegario se plaignait depuis quelque temps d'être limité dans son accès à l'information. Confronté à une pression médiatique sans précédent, le juge d'instruction en charge de l'affaire Maddie sollicite au Conseil de la Magistrature l'autorisation de s'exprimer publiquement sur l'affaire. Pour le juge, cette intervention est nécessaire compte tenu de l'ampleur médiatique prise par l'enquête criminelle. Le processus judiciaire en cours doit être expliqué au public. Des explications claires de la part des autorités permettraient de limiter les rumeurs les plus contradictoires sur l'enquête. Le conseil de la Magistrature refuse d'accéder à cette requête, estimant qu'à ce stade de la procédure, la justice n'est pas tenue d'informer le public.

Dans un communiqué, l'entité judiciaire rappelle que l'affaire Madeleine est toujours dans la phase de l'enquête, et qu'à ce stade, l'intervention du juge d'instruction vise à préserver les droits, les libertés et les garanties des personnes mises en cause, en autorisant ou non la réalisation d'investigations.

Les McCann, très bien entourés

De retour un Angleterre, les McCann recrutent un porte-parole de poids. Il s'agit de Clarence Mitchell, un ancien journaliste de la BBC, qui quitte son poste au service de communication du gouvernement britannique. Mitchell avait déjà assisté le couple au début de l'affaire. Il avait été dépêché au Portugal par le Foreign Office. C'est lui qui avait notamment organisé le périple européen du couple les semaines qui ont suivi la disparition.

Par ailleurs, les époux McCann décident de renforcer leur équipe de défense au Portugal en recrutant le bâtonnier de l'ordre des avocats. L'idée est que chacun des avocats se consacre exclusivement à la défense de l'un des époux. L'équipe des McCann est un de leurs points forts. Le couple a toujours su très bien s'entourer et bénéficier ainsi du soutien d'une armada de conseillers, avocats et porte-paroles.

Il y a eu Sherree Dodd, qui a exercé des fonctions de porte-parole. Ancienne journaliste, elle a travaillé ensuite pour le gouvernement britannique dans le secteur de la communication. Elle est proche des travaillistes.

Justine McGuiness lui a succédé. Elle a été recrutée par les McCann à travers une société spécialisée. Avant l'affaire Maddie, elle s'était illustrée pour avoir aidé une jeune britannique arrêtée en Inde pour possession de drogue. Condamnée à dix ans de prison, cette britannique a finalement été libérée. Candidate aux législatives du parti libéral démocrate, elle est battue de très peu de voix.

L'équipe des McCann avait également fait appel à Phill Hall, conseiller en communication. Cet ancien journaliste a notamment travaillé avec Heather Mills, ex-femme de Paul McCartney.

Tous ces spécialistes coûtent cher. L'opinion publique s'interroge pour savoir où les McCann vont puiser l'argent nécessaire pour financer tous ces services, mais le couple s'engage à ne pas puiser dans le Fonds Madeleine pour financer leur défense. Ils expliquent bénéficier notamment de la générosité de généreux donateurs, parmi lesquels le milliardaire Richard Branson, patron de Virgin, ou encore Brian Kennedy, patron d'une équipe de rugby en Angleterre.

Après le départ en Angleterre des McCann

Les enquêteurs portugais, persuadés à présent que la fillette est morte, redoublent d'efforts pour retrouver son corps. Mais ces recherches se révèlent une fois de plus infructueuses. La police évoque même la possibilité que le cadavre n'existe plus, qu'il ait été lancé à la mer ou qu'il ait été incinéré. La police judiciaire va jusqu'à interroger les crématoriums pour animaux de la région.

L'enquête s'intéressent également à un voyage des McCann le 3 août, soit trois mois exactement après la disparition de Maddie, à Huelva, une ville espagnole proche de la frontière. La police trouve étrange le nombre de kilomètres enregistrés au compteur de la voiture des McCann. Lorsqu'ils passent au peigne fin le voyage du couple, un trou dans leur emploi du temps attire leur attention. Une période de deux heures au cours de ce voyage les intéresse particulièrement. Ce jour-là était férié en Espagne. Qu'ont-ils fait ? Où sont-ils allés ? Qui ont-ils rencontré ? La police cherche à le déterminer. La possibilité que le couple ait pu transporter le cadavre vers le pays voisin, pour s'en débarrasser, est évoquée.

Le porte-parole des McCann ne tarde pas à réagir à ces informations véhiculées dans les médias. Le couple y est allé pour simplement poser des affiches de leur fille. Il déclare que les McCann n'étaient pas seuls lorsqu'ils se sont rendus à Huelva. Ils n'ont pas quitté Jon Corner, patron de l'agence de publicité qui orchestre la campagne médiatique pour retrouver Maddie. Ils étaient également accompagnés d'un journaliste reporter, chargé de recueillir des images pour mettre sur le site findmadeleine.com. Tous les deux ont voyagé avec le couple à bord de la Renault Scenic. Ils ont ouvert le coffre de la voiture à plusieurs reprises, devant des dizaines de personnes, car ils y transportaient le matériel de la campagne pour retrouver Maddie.

Nouveau signalement au Maroc

Fin septembre, un nouveau témoignage relance l'espoir de retrouver la fillette en vie. Une touriste espagnole affirme avoir aperçu la petite Maddie au Maroc. La différence avec d'autres signalements au Maroc, est que cette fois il existe une photo prise le 31 août. Sur le cliché relativement flou et de mauvaise qualité, on voit un enfant porté sur le dos d'une femme. L'image est remise notamment à Interpol qui l'examine à l'aide d'un logiciel de reconnaissance faciale. Entretemps, la photo est reprise dans de nombreux journaux. La ressemblance est frappante. Quelques jours plus tard, le verdict tombe. Encore une fausse piste. La petite fille blonde prise en photo au Maroc n'est pas Madeleine, mais la fille d'un cultivateur d'oliviers local, d'origine berbère.

Des reporters de l'Agence France Presse se rendent dans le village à flanc de coteau de Zinat, au nord du Maroc, et retrouvent la trace de l'enfant et de sa famille. La petite fille se nomme Bouchra Benaïssa. Elle est née le 24 octobre 2004. Les parents, Ahmed Ben Mohamed Benaïssa et Hafida Achkar, ont produit l'acte de naissance de leur fille et des papiers administratifs prouvant leurs identités.

A la suite de cet épisode, le porte-parole du couple fait état de la déception des McCann : "S'il est avéré que ce n'est pas Maddie, c'est une nouvelle décevante pour Kate et Gerry McCann. C'est pour cela qu'ils ne commentent aucun témoignage. J'appelle tout le monde à continuer les recherches et à oeuvrer pour le retour de Maddie en bonne santé au sein de sa famille".

Analyses des résidus biologiques de Maddie

La police a placé beaucoup d'espoir dans les derniers résultats des analyses des résidus biologiques et de mèches de cheveux retrouvés dans la voiture. Les enquêteurs espèrent qu'ils viendront confirmer leur thèse et qu'ils permettront notamment de déterminer si on avait administré ou pas des somnifères à la fillette ce soir-là.

Au fur et à mesure que l'enquête avance, les enquêteurs penchent de plus en plus pour un décès de la fillette à la suite d'une chute, soit dans les escaliers d'accès à l'appartement soit du canapé. "La police va devoir prouver que ça s'est passé ainsi et pour cela elle doit retrouver un corps", souligne Clarence Mitchell dans des déclarations à la presse.

Le rapport final du laboratoire de Birmingham doit être envoyé au ministère des Affaires étrangères portugais. Il doit arriver dans une enveloppe scellée par valise diplomatique. Il sera ensuite remis au ministère de la Justice qui le transmettra aux enquêteurs.

Le laboratoire de Birmingham utilise la technique "low copy number", qui permet d'identifier le profil génétique d'une personne à partir de petits échantillons comme de la salive, des cheveux, des empreintes ou autres fluides corporels. Cette technique a notamment été rendue populaire par des séries télévisées comme "Les Experts".

DISPARUE DEPUIS 5 MOIS

Limogeage du chef des enquêteurs

Début octobre, une autre information en apparence banale, qui passe quasiment inaperçue dans la presse, va précipiter la chute de l'équipe d'enquêteurs. Le quotidien anglais News of the world rapporte que le prince Charles d'Angleterre a reçu un e-mail dans lequel son auteur accuse une ancienne employée de l'Ocean Club d'avoir enlevé Maddie pour se venger de la direction du complexe hôtelier et dénigrer publiquement leur image.

L'information paraît sans intérêt car peu crédible. La police portugaise est tenue informée. Un journaliste du quotidien de référence Diario de Noticias appelle toutefois au téléphone l'inspecteur en chef Gonçalo Amaral pour lui demander une réaction à ce mail. Excédé, agacé par toutes les informations plus ou moins crédibles régulièrement publiées dans la presse, l'inspecteur lâche une phrase qui conduira à son limogeage. "La police britannique ne travaille que sur ce qui intéresse et convient au couple McCann", lance le responsable portugais, un homme fort et à la moustache grisonnante. "Cette piste est complètement écartée. Elle n'a aucune crédibilité aux yeux de la police portugaise". Et d'ajouter: "Ils ne cessent d'enquêter sur des informations suggérées par le couple oubliant que les McCann sont soupçonnés du meurtre de leur fille. Ce n'est pas un e-mail anonyme, dont nous pouvons très facilement trouver d'où il est parti, qui va nous distraire et nous éloigner de notre axe d'investigation".

Faux pas. La réaction de ses supérieurs ne va pas tarder. Le lendemain matin, le directeur national de la PJ Alipio Ribeiro, va découvrir ces déclarations dans la presse. Il tombe des nues. Gonçalo Amaral est aussitôt éloigné de l'affaire. Il est sanctionné pour avoir mis en cause publiquement l'impartialité de ses collègues britanniques. Le responsable de la PJ de Portimao, âgé de 48 ans et père de trois enfants, est prié de quitter ses fonctions le jour de son anniversaire. Il tente encore de se défendre arguant qu'il faisait en réalité référence aux détectives privés recrutés par les McCann, mais rien y fait, ça ne passe pas. D'aucuns expliquent que cette histoire n'est que la goutte d'eau qui a fait déborder le vase. D'autres raisons auraient également motivé cet éloignement. On lui attribuerait la responsabilité des fuites régulières sur l'affaire dans la presse.

Invité à réagir, le directeur national de la Police judiciaire portugaise fait valoir qu'il y a des limites à ne pas franchir et en profite pour faire la leçon publiquement aux autres inspecteurs. "Je comprends que les gens sont soumis à une grande pression et à une extrême fatigue. Il se peut qu'ils ne se maîtrisent plus et fassent des déclarations qui ne devraient pas avoir lieu. Mais, j'espère que ce type de réactions ne se répètera pas à l'avenir", prévient-il.

"Réserve, discrétion et pondération!", lance-t-il à l'équipe d'enquêteurs. Alipio Ribeiro menace de limogeage les inspecteurs qui seraient trop bavards avec la presse. Il reçoit le soutien du ministre de la Justice Antonio Costa: "C'est une décision qui relève du directeur national de la PJ, mais que j'approuve".

Sur le terrain, l'enquête continue d'être menée par la brigade d'enquête criminelle de Portimao, sous la direction du ministère public, avec six inspecteurs au total. Le départ de Gonçalo Amaral est plutôt bien accueilli en Grande-Bretagne. Il était devenu au fil des semaines la bête noire de la presse anglaise, qui l'accusait d'incompétence, de paresse, d'aimer les longs repas arrosés. Pour les McCann, le limogeage de Gonçalo Amaral est plutôt une bonne nouvelle. M. Amaral défendait l'implication des McCann dans la disparition de leur fille. Il se disait convaincu que "90% des crimes impliquant des mineurs sont commis par leur entourage proche".

Le porte-parole des McCann ne tarde pas à s'exprimer: "La famille souhaite que ce changement soit positif pour la suite de l'enquête. Il est dorénavant vraiment temps pour tous de faire cesser toutes ces absurdités et de relancer les recherches de Madeleine".

Quelques jours plus tard, le nom du successeur de Gonçalo Amaral est finalement connu. Paulo Rebelo, bras droit et homme de confiance du directeur national de la PJ, est choisi pour lui succéder et assumer cette mission délicate. Il devient le nouveau patron du service d'enquête criminelle de Portimao, service chargé d'enquêter sur la disparition de Maddie, son dossier le plus délicat.

Le nouvel homme fort de la PJ de Portimao a une longue expérience notamment dans la lutte contre le trafic de drogue. Il reprend l'enquête en main, tout en veillant à travailler dans la plus grande discrétion pour ne pas répéter les erreurs de son prédécesseur. De nouveaux résultats d'expertises en main, il retourne avec son équipe dans l'appartement 5-A de l'Ocean Club pour tenter de reconstituer et comprendre ce qui s'est passé la nuit du 3 mai. L'équipe reste environ cinq heures sur place. Malgré ce couac interne, la police maintient toujours l'hypothèse d'une mort accidentelle de Madeleine. En effet, d'autres résultats des expertises de "vestiges biologiques" recueillis dans la voiture permettent d'identifier l'ADN de Maddie. Pour autant, ils ne prouvent rien.

Le porte-parole des McCann monte au créneau: "Kate et Gerry n'ont rien à cacher. Tout ce qui ait pu avoir été retrouvé par la police portugaise peut être expliqué de manière innocente. Les soupçons à leur encontre sont absurdes". Moins catégorique quant à la responsabilité des McCann, la nouvelle équipe d'enquêteurs rappelle que toutes les hypothèses sont sur la table.

Invités dans le show d'Oprah

Le couple rompt le silence de ces trois derniers mois. Les McCann n'avaient pas parlé depuis leur mise en examen. A cette occasion, ils sont invités dans l'une des émissions les plus regardées au monde. Ils sont reçus dans le talk show prestigieux d'Oprah Winfrey, la célèbre présentatrice américaine, leader d'audiences aux Etats-Unis. Ils accordent également une interview à la télévision espagnole Antena 3 dans l'émission "360 graus" (360 degrés).

A l'occasion de cette émission espagnole ils font la promotion d'un nouveau numéro de téléphone mis en place dans le pays pour recueillir des informations sur Maddie. Le grand public est invité à apporter d'éventuels témoignages, informations en appelant le numéro mis en place par Método 3, l'agence de détectives à qui les McCann ont fait appel.

L'entretien est filmé chez le milliardaire Brian Kennedy, un important soutien des McCann. Il a lieu dans un salon majestueux au papier peint et aux rideaux rouges. Les McCann arrivent ensemble. Ils s'enfoncent dans un canapé classique et répondent aux questions du journaliste Roberto Arce.

Kate répond à la première question: "Je me sens triste, seule. La vie n'est pas gaie sans Madeleine, mais nous gardons espoir".

Les McCann, qui ne peuvent entrer dans les détails de l'enquête du fait de leur mise en examen, expliquent pourquoi ils sortent de leur silence. "Nous sommes persuadés que Maddie se trouve quelque part dans le monde. Nous voulons faire appel aux personnes qui se trouvent en Espagne, au Portugal et dans le nord de l'Afrique pour qu'ils nous aident, dit Kate. Malgré l'enquête, rien ne prouve que quelqu'un lui ait fait du mal".

Sur leur statut judiciaire Gerry répond: "Ce que nous savons, c'est que nous sommes innocents et que quelqu'un l'a enlevée. Je suis certain que nous serons blanchis. J'en suis sûr car nous n'avons rien fait. Je vous en prie, aidez-nous à retrouver Maddie. Aidez Madeleine. Si vous avez une information quelconque, ou des soupçons, aussi infimes soient-il, s'il vous plaît, appelez".

Le journaliste espagnol racontera à la suite de l'entretien comment il a été impressionné par l'organisation de la machine de communication du couple, prise en main par leur entourage qui contrôle tout jusque dans les moindres détails. Une structure bien huilée qui n'est pas sans rappeler l'organisation d'une campagne politique. "J'ai été surpris par l'organisation, la machine, le style campagne électoral avec des conseillers leur soufflant leurs moindres faits et gestes", note-il. "Kate a pleuré plusieurs fois, pendant l'entretien et à la fin. J'ai vu une femme tourmentée, physiquement abattue, très triste et émue, indique-t-il. Sa tristesse n'était pas fabriquée".

L'interview a dû être interrompue plusieurs fois pour que Kate puisse reprendre ses esprits. Antena 3 dévoile également un portrait robot du ravisseur présumé de la fillette à partir du témoignage de l'une des amies des McCann, réalisé par un spécialiste du FBI. Blouson marron, pantalon beige, cheveux bruns, on voit un homme de profile tenant dans ses bras un volume enveloppé dans un couverture.

Des enquêteurs privés s'emparent de l'enquête

Alors que l'enquête est dans une impasse, les McCann font appel à des détectives privés de renommée internationale aux méthodes parfois originales. Parmi eux, un détective sud-africain. Après avoir séjourné en juillet en Algarve pour tenter de dégager des pistes sur ce qui aurait pu arriver à Maddie, Daniel Kruger revient en octobre à Praia da Luz. Il bénéficie d'une certaine notoriété dans son pays pour avoir réussi à retrouver des cadavres d'enfants disparus. Il se targue d'avoir inventé une machine permettant de localiser des cadavres. En juillet, il avait estimé peu probable de retrouver la fillette en vie. Mais il revient à l'automne pour approfondir ses recherches. Il se fond dans la masse des touristes. Bermudas, tongs, cheveux hirsutes, il passe inaperçu.

Un autre détective sud-africain, Martin Van Wyk, accorde un entretien au quotidien portugais Correio da Manha. Il dit avoir été contacté, par e-mail, par la soeur de Gerry, Philomena McCann, mais qu'il enquête à titre personnel. Il livre ses conclusions aux quotidien : "Malheureusement, je pense que la fillette est morte et enterrée près d'ici, a-t-il indiqué. Je crois qu'elle est sortie seule la nuit en direction de la plage. Elle était allée chercher ses parents, mais quelqu'un l'a enlevée. Le lendemain, devant la pression médiatique, le ravisseur a pris peur et s'est débarrassé du corps".

Les McCann missionnent également une agence de détective espagnole : Metodo 3. Eux aussi ont une théorie. Maddie a dû être enlevée par un pédophile, emmenée en Espagne, puis conduite vers le Maroc. Selon l'agence de détectives, une quinzaine de pédophiles sont passés par le Portugal en mai. L'un d'entre eux pourrait en être le ravisseur présumé. La fillette peut se trouver dans les zones montagneuses marocaines. Les détectives affirment avoir reçu plusieurs témoignages dans ce sens. Des témoins disent l'avoir vu en compagnie d'une sexagénaire, qui pourrait être chargée de la cacher. Le directeur de l'agence, qui compte une quarantaine d'enquêteurs basée à Barcelone, Francisco Marco assure que dès que les enquêteurs disposeront d'éléments solides, ils les communiqueront à la police portugaise.

Dans le même temps, côté portugais, l'enquête se poursuit. Le nouvel inspecteur-chef Paulo Rebelo, passe en revu le travail qui a été effectué par son prédécesseur. Accompagné de sa nouvelle équipe, Rebelo retourne une nouvelle fois dans l'appartement de l'Ocean Club fin octobre. Il y reste près de trois heures, s'attarde à observer la fenêtre de la chambre où dormait Maddie et ses frères le soir de la disparition. Il soulève les volets, observe longuement le restaurant Tapas. A la sortie de l'appartement, l'équipe prend la direction de la plage. L'inspecteur vérifie dans les moindres détails le travail de l'équipe précédente.

DISPARUE DEPUIS 6 MOIS

Nouvel appel des parents

Maddie a disparu depuis six mois. Début novembre, Gerry reprend, à temps partiel, son poste de cardiologue à l'hôpital. Il avait demandé un congé pour se consacrer aux recherches de sa fille.

Kate lance un nouvel appel, comme le couple a l'habitude de le faire à toutes les dates anniversaire. "Six mois c'est trop long pour qu'une petite fille soit séparée de ses parents, dit Kate. Nous croyons que Maddie est quelque part et qu'elle va rentrer. Madeleine est une jolie fille qui mérite une vie heureuse et pleine d'amour. La meilleure place pour elle est de revenir au sein de sa famille".

Les avocats du couple se plaignent du travail des enquêteurs portugais et les accusent de ne pas s'intéresser aux pistes qui leur sont communiquées contraignant ainsi les McCann à financer eux-mêmes la vérification de ces informations qui leurs parviennent.

L'enquête piétine

La nouvelle équipe d'enquêteurs manque cruellement de nouveaux éléments. Les analyses de sang et les tests ADN dont ils disposent ne permettent pas de conclusions catégoriques. "Si le corps n'apparaît pas ou si nous n'avons pas une autre piste crédible, nous sommes loin des clés du mystère", confie un responsable des enquêteurs.

L'hypothèse de l'enlèvement est à nouveau sur la table au même titre que d'autres thèses. La police n'exclut plus non plus la possibilité que la fillette ait été tuée dans l'appartement par son ravisseur présumé.

Les enquêteurs obtiennent l'autorisation d'interroger les McCann en Grande-Bretagne. Une équipe portugaise se tient prête à se rendre en Angleterre. La police prépare une centaine de questions. Une commission rogatoire doit être remise au ministre de la Justice, qui la fera suivre aux responsables du ministère des Affaires étrangères portugais, qui l'adressera ensuite à leurs homologues britanniques.

Pendant ce temps, les McCann, aidés de leurs proches, organisent leur défense. Le couple fait réaliser une série de contre examens et analyses.

En attendant, une équipe d'enquêteurs portugais se rend en Grande-Bretagne pour s'entretenir avec des spécialistes du laboratoire de Birmingham chargés des analyses des résidus biologiques retrouvés dans l'appartement et la voiture des McCann. Ils doivent récupérer les dernières conclusions.

Et de conclure ensuite : "Ces résultats ne sont qu'une pièce du puzzle. Ils doivent ensuite être interprétés, placés dans leur contexte. Les résultats confirment les pistes mais n'apportent aucune certitude. Ils ne permettent pas de conclure à une accusation contre les McCann".

Un autre enquêteur d'ajouter: "Les preuves dont nous disposons jusqu'à présent sont loin de blanchir les McCann. Il y a de plus en plus d'indices allant dans le sens de leur implication, mais cela va être difficile à prouver. L'axe de l'enquête n'a pas changé. On continue de croire à l'implication du couple et de l'autre personne (Robert Murat). Nous tentons de le prouver".

A leur retour au Portugal, l'équipe d'enquêteurs portugais s'entretient avec le directeur de la PJ de Faro, Guilhermino Encarnaçao. Les résultats obtenus confortent les enquêteurs dans l'envie d'interroger une nouvelle fois les McCann. En l'absence de preuves scientifiques formelles, les enquêteurs misent sur les contradictions des témoignages.

Nouveau message des McCann à Noël

A la veille des fêtes de Noël, les McCann diffusent une nouvelle vidéo où l'on voit Maddie pendant les fêtes de noël de l'année précédente. On y voit une petite Maddie nerveuse, en train de déchirer le papier qui recouvre ses cadeaux. Elle découvre un sac à dos rose. Celui qu'elle emportera avec elle quelque mois plus tard au Portugal.

Le film est accompagné d'un message adressé à leur fille : "Madeleine, c'est maman et papa. Sache que nous t'aimons beaucoup. Sean et Amelie demandent de tes nouvelles tous les jours. Nous faisons tout ce que nous pouvons pour te retrouver". Puis, le couple s'adresse au grand public: "En cette période de l'année, alors que les familles se réunissent, nous vous supplions pour que vous nous aidiez à être auprès de Madeleine".

En cette fin d'année, un nouvel élément de l'enquête qui pourrait avoir de l'importance paraît dans la presse. La police est à la recherche d'un sac de tennis bleu appartenant à Gerry et qui a disparu en même temps que Maddie. Il pourrait avoir permis de transporter la fillette. Gerry aurait dit aux enquêteurs qu'il avait été volé.

Secret judiciaire levé

La période couverte par le secret de justice, arrive à son terme à la mi-janvier. Au Portugal, le code de procédure pénal stipule que le secret de l'instruction dure huit mois. Au terme de cette période, l'enquête est rendue publique si elle n'aboutit pas à une mise en accusation ou si l'affaire n'est pas classée. Ce délai peut être prolongé en cas de "complexité exceptionnelle" du dossier.

Dans ce cas une prolongation de trois mois peut être accordée par le juge. Le ministère public demande au juge en charge de l'enquête une prolongation de trois mois mettant en avant la "complexité" du dossier. Aucune mise en accusation formelle n'a été pour l'instant prononcée à l'encontre des McCann et du Britannique Robert Murat. Leurs avocats n'ont toujours pas pu avoir accès au dossier.

Fin janvier, le parquet annonce qu'il va devoir renvoyer à Londres, pour la deuxième fois, les commissions rogatoires émises dans le cadre de l'enquête et qui ont été rejetées par les Anglais, pour que les McCann répondent à de nouveaux interrogatoires.

DISPARUE DEPUIS 9 MOIS

La police fait marche arrière

Pour la première fois, depuis que les parents étaient dans la ligne de mire des enquêteurs, les enquêteurs semblent faire marche arrière. Début février, le directeur national de la Police judiciaire Alipio Ribeiro fait des déclarations au quotidien portugais Publico et à la radio Renascença, qui étonnent l'opinion publique portugaise mais qui confortent les McCann. M. Ribeiro reconnaît que la police a fait preuve d'une "certaine précipitation" lors de la mise en examen des McCann.

Ces déclarations montrent qu'il "n'y a aucune preuve contre Kate et Gerry, se réjouit aussitôt le porte-parole du couple. Kate et Gerry sont totalement innocents de toute implication dans la disparition de Madeleine et dorénavant, à la lumière des remarques de M. Ribeiro, nous exhortons les autorités judiciaires portugaises à agir de manière humaine et à lever le statut d'« arguido » le plus rapidement possible".

De manière tout à fait surprenante, un groupe de presse britannique passe un accord avec les McCann afin de publier des excuses publiques pour avoir insinué sans preuves que le couple était impliqué dans la disparition de leur fille. Le Daily Express et le Daily Star s'engagent en outre à verser une compensation de 550.000 livres au Fonds Madeleine. C'est une énorme victoire pour le couple car la démarche est très exceptionnelle en Grande-Bretagne. Ces excuses interviennent à la suite de plaintes des McCann, qui étaient prêts à aller jusqu'au procès si un arrangement à l'amiable n'avait pas eu lieu. Les avocats du couple précisent

153

qu'ils n'ont pas l'intention, pour le moment, d'intenter des actions en justice contre les médias portugais.

Quelques jours plus tard, l'Audi A4 de Sergei Malinka, l'informaticien russe entendu comme témoin dans les jours qui ont suivi la disparition de la fillette, est incendiée. A côté de la voiture, quelqu'un a écrit en rouge "fala" (parle). Des mouchards GPS ont également été retrouvés sous les voitures de Robert Murat et sa compagne Michaela, deux témoins clés de cette affaire. Méthodes d'intimidation et de pression? Beaucoup pensent qu'ils pourraient provenir de l'agence de détectives Metodo 3 qui enquête sur l'affaire depuis quelques mois. La police décide finalement de rendre les objets et surtout le matériel informatique saisis à Robert Murat et Serguei Malinka en mai 2007. Ils n'ont rien apporté de nouveau à l'enquête. Les experts en informatique de la PJ chargés d'analyser les disques durs des ordinateurs n'ont trouvé aucun contenu les liant à la disparition de Maddie.

Nouveaux témoignages, nouvelles vérifications

Des signalements de Maddie continuent d'avoir lieu dans plusieurs pays. Une étudiante néerlandaise affirme avoir vu la fillette en compagnie d'un homme, en blouson de cuir et aux cheveux bruns courts, sortant avec l'enfant du restaurant d'une aire de repos de Fabrègues, dans le sud de la France. Elle prévient les autorités. Les gendarmes se rendent sur place et demandent les images vidéo du système de surveillance. On y voit bien un enfant, mais le premier visionnage ne permet pas de l'identifier. On n'y voit pas non plus le véhicule à bord duquel elle voyageait. D'après les policiers, ces images ne montrent pas de "comportement anormal de l'adulte envers l'enfant". Par ailleurs, le comportement de l'enfant "ne laisse pas présumer une crainte de l'adulte". Les bandes vidéo ont toutefois été transmises à l'Institut de recherche criminelle de la gendarmerie national pour des analyses complémentaires. Mais une fois encore, il s'agissait d'une fausse alerte.

En mars, un sac, contenant des ossements, attaché par des cordes, est retrouvé dans le barrage d'Arade, à quelques kilomètres de Praia da Luz. A l'origine de cette trouvaille: un avocat originaire de l'île portugaise de madère. Marcos Aragao Correia est convaincu que le corps de la fillette a été jeté dans ce barrage. Il a alors décider d'entreprendre des recherches. Il se dit que s'il retrouve le corps de Maddie il bénéficiera alors d'une renommée mondiale. Pour cette initiative, il fait appel à des plongeurs pour fouiller le fonds du barrage. On y retrouve une chaussette présentée par l'avocat comme provenant d'Europe du nord et mettant ses hommes sur une piste, puis ce sac d'ossements. La police judiciaire est appelée sur place. Après vérification, il s'avère que les caractéristiques des os sont d'origine animale. Un chat, peut être, dit un enquêteur.

Affaire classée

Faute de nouveaux éléments, la police portugaise classe l'enquête en 2008, après 14 mois d'investigations.

Après avoir passé plusieurs mois à étudier le dossier, la police britannique a décidé d'ouvrir sa propre enquête en 2013. Les enquêteurs se sont rendus à plusieurs reprises au Portugal. Mais sans succès.

DISPARUE DEPUIS 10 ANS

Près de dix ans après la disparition de Maddie, le mystère reste entier. A l'occasion du dixième anniversaire de la disparition de la fillette, en mai 2017, les parents confiaient encore garder l'espoir de retrouver leur fille. "Ce n'est peut-être pas aussi rapide que nous le souhaiterions, mais de vrais progrès ont été réalisés", affirmait Kate McCann à cette occasion sur la BBC.

"Nous avons toujours l'espoir de retrouver Madeleine", a-t-elle répété. De son côté Gerry raconte avoir repris un semblant de vie normale ces dernières années et se dit soulagé de savoir que la police britannique avait lancé son enquête. Scotland Yard assure continuer à s'intéresser à des "pistes significatives", ajoutant qu'aucune preuve ne permettait d'établir avec certitude la mort de l'enfant.

***

L'affaire Maddie aura été non seulement l'une des affaires les plus médiatisées de ces dernières années mais également l'une des plus mystérieuses. Policiers portugais et britanniques, détectives privés et les meilleurs spécialistes au monde se sont intéressés à cette affaire. A ce jour, personne n'est parvenu à comprendre ce qui s'est passé le jeudi 3 mai en fin d'après-midi à l'Ocean Club de Praia da Luz, au sud du Portugal.

Deux thèses continuent de s'affronter. Un accident domestique que les parents auraient souhaité faire passer pour un enlèvement. C'est le scénario défendu par la première équipe d'enquêteurs portugais. Face à cela, il y a l'hypothèse d'un enlèvement par un pédophile. Il s'agit de la thèse défendue par les parents et explorée par les policiers anglais. Les deux comportent beaucoup de zones d'ombres et n'ont pas permis d'élucider l'affaire.

Découvrira-t-on la vérité un jour ?

Printed in Great Britain
by Amazon